Dig Two Graves

Craig Schaefer

Demimonde Books

Contents

Chapter One

I t all started with the book.

It had been so long ago that the Enemy sat down to pen the thing. His flickering photo-negative body snatched up a quill while occult bombardments pummeled the fields of corpse-flowers beyond his bunker walls of ossified bone. He didn't remember those moments so much as the feelings they instilled in him. Fury, revulsion, despair. Fear, though he'd never admit that to anyone. It was the first time he had ever experienced that emotion, and he decided it looked much better on his victims.

The humans had gotten clever. The best and brightest of three worlds had built a gateway between their dimensions, sharing knowledge and magic, spurred to action by the terror-mad warnings of a survivor from a dead planet. Normally the Enemy would have welcomed a real challenge, anything to distract him from the endless tedium of eternal life, but they'd caught him sleeping. They'd cut him off, cornered him on a backwater planet too pathetic to burn, and he could feel his powers buckling under their constant onslaught. Soon he'd fail, and fall. They'd have his body.

But they wouldn't have *him*.

He poured himself into the book. Soon it began writing itself, speaking in his own voice as stage directions cast the armies outside his bunker of bone like the heroes of a play. He invested a portion of his power into each profane chapter and sealed them with locks only he could open. Then he gave the finished book to Ms. Fleiss, his favorite thrall, and sent her through a one-way portal before marching out to meet his fate.

He was a long time gone after that. But just as he knew he would, he eventually made his way back to freedom. His captors had been dust and bones for centuries, their warnings lost to time, and no one remained to guard the prison gates. Fleiss was there, as he knew she would be, to place his cherished book—the missing pieces of himself and the key to regaining his full power—into his outstretched arms. All he had to do was pop the locks and drink it down.

Then he met Daniel Faust.

The insolent gutter-mage stood in his way again and again, thwarting his plans with a raw arrogance that left him trembling with fury. The Enemy usually considered himself above hatred. Hatred required you to care about the lives you destroyed, to feel something for them, about them, to feel anything at all. He was simply in charge of pest control and thought no more about the average human than the average human thought about a crushed ant.

But he thought about Faust. He thought about him all the time.

When the gunslinging magician had the audacity to break into the Enemy's own sanctum and lay hands on the book, Faust unwisely opened his mind and gave him a boon. He had two strong suspicions about the identity of the Paladin: Harmony Black, an FBI agent turned occult vigilante, and Ada Lovelace Canton, a college dropout and the leader of the revitalized Redemption Choir, a sect of demon-blooded warriors who stood in opposition to hell's plans. The book plucked their names from Faust's mind and inscribed them on the page, marking both women for death.

The Story So Far

D aniel Faust always knew he was going to hell. Still, he was surprised when it actually happened. On the night of his most successful heist, his traitorous brother Teddy—revealed to be the willing and eager pawn of the rakshasa queen Naavarasi—put a bullet in his heart and sent him plunging into a ravine, left for dead beside a backcountry road.

With the aid of his found family and beloved crew, Daniel clawed his way back to the land of the living. There were...complications. With her host mortally wounded, his body-jumping ally Emma was forced to lodge herself inside Daniel's temporarily empty skin. Daniel, meanwhile, was shunted into the husk of a brain-dead coma victim and wheeled out of a hospital under siege, as the forces of Naavarasi and the Enemy—the nemesis of all life and hope in the universe—assaulted the building.

They were saved by the last-second intervention of the Paladin, a resurrected cosmic entity and the Enemy's polar opposite and sworn foe. Only one problem: they still have no idea who the Paladin really is, and considering she's scheduled for a showdown to decide the fate of the entire planet, it's not a date she can afford to miss.

Daniel uncovered proof that Naavarasi had compromised the very machinery of hell, and that she'd been raising a cadre of sons to infiltrate institutions above and below with their shape-shifting mastery. Dan and his lover Caitlin managed to stop an assassination attempt on Cait's master, the mercurial Prince Sitri, and believed they'd dealt the deathblow to the rakshasa queen's schemes once and for all: with Naavarasi exposed as a saboteur and a traitor to hell's cause, her allies would have no choice but to cast her into the cold.

That was what they thought, at least, until word from Caitlin's sister reached them in the land of the living. Just as Caitlin is Prince Sitri's loyal hound, tasked with seeing to the security of his earthly assets on the West Coast, the demon known as Royce has long performed the same task in the neighboring Midwestern territory of Prince Malphas. Until now.

Royce is on the outs and Naavarasi, against all odds (and all logic and sanity), has been appointed in his stead. Not only is Malphas refusing to hand her over for punishment, he's protecting her at all costs. Prince Malphas has just triggered a political incident that could plunge hell into another brutal civil war, and no one—no one except him and Naavarasi—has any idea why.

Death is closing in. On one side, the self-proclaimed "mistress of illusions" and her homegrown army of shape-shifting zealots. On the other, a genocidal world-burning madman empowered by the magic of the first story ever told. And in the middle stands a Vegas hustler, a snake with a new skin and a few tricks up his sleeve.

Daniel has been a thug, a grifter, a gangster, and a wand for hire. He's never been much of a hero, but he's going to have to learn fast. This planet's expiration date is looming, and if the Paladin can't step up to the fight, Faust and his crew are going to have to take care of business on their own.

Just like the other dozen-odd characters of the First Story, the Enemy had no choice but to follow the beats of his own narrative. He could play at the idea of free will, but the simple fact was that he couldn't destroy this planet until he faced off with the latest incarnation of the Paladin. The Story demanded it. And he couldn't do that until he found her.

Then came the night he thought he could mop up every threat against him at once. Faust was on life support in a small backwater hospital, his flesh desperately clinging to life while his soul languished in hell.

When the dome of golden light washed over the hospital, igniting the cold and dark, a thrill gripped the Enemy's stone heart. His greatest foe was here, and that light was nothing less than the call to battle. He had to be cautious: it was no coincidence that Faust had just invaded his tower and stolen the Canton relics, magical trinkets designed to give the Paladin's next incarnation a fighting edge. He wondered if this was some elaborate ruse, if Faust had faked his injuries and chosen this place as their final battleground. If so, that flood of light had just ruined any chance of an ambush.

Faust's allies, a pack of ragged bikers, hopped on their machines and fled as the Enemy began carving his way through the golden dome. He cut a jagged hole, his power crackling and curling in the air like orchid petals and venomous roots. The Paladin's magic was stark, clean, clear and bold; his was seething and organic, ripe with acidic bile.

He ducked through the hole in the dome of light and rose to his full, flickering height on the other side, triumphant. Then he strode toward the hospital doors.

It was clear an evacuation was underway. A klaxon howled over the PA system and every door he passed was open, every bed empty, sheets tangled and fallen. Screams filled the air up ahead, growing louder as a few of the skeleton-crew staff, racing patients in wheelchairs up the hall and away from the threat, got a look at the stop-motion horror coming toward them. The Enemy was a scratchy inkblot scar in motion, a cheap special effect given horrible life. A man in a long white doctor's coat lost his nerve, got turned around in his panic, and barreled headlong toward the beast, the fight-or-flight response inspiring an act of desperate bravado. The Enemy never stopped advancing. He reached out one hand and effortlessly caught the doctor by the throat.

Skin to skin, the man was an open book, every second of his life laid bare. Time was a trolley on bloody tracks. The Enemy flicked through his darkest moments, his deepest miseries, with a special eye toward all the times when he could have died but fate spared him, preserving him for this very hour. *Infection, infection, boring...ah. There we go.*

"You were sixteen," the Enemy said. "Crashed your first car. Walked away with minimal scrapes. But what if..."

He flipped the trolley lever.

The bottom half of the doctor's body kept running, tearing away from his upper half with a sickening squelch, making it three more steps before it crashed to the white tile floor. Intestines rained down from the man's torso, splattering like a bowl of overcooked spaghetti. The Enemy tossed the doctor's mangled corpse aside and kept marching, relentless.

He turned the corner and froze.

Up ahead, a being of golden light flooded the corridor with hateful warmth. She was a Greek statue carved from molten gold, a woman in an armored breastplate and skirts, brandishing a broadsword that burned so hot the air shimmered around it like a desert mirage.

Finally. A worthy fight. The Enemy spread his arms and hands and fingers wide, stretching out with his power, filling the air with squirming worm-like tentacles that sniffed and drooled and bit. He advanced on the Paladin, anticipating her first attack, and...

She just *stood there.*

"Eh?" he said.

He lowered his arms. It hurt, coming this close to the light, but he could endure the searing ache behind his eyes long enough to investigate. Once he realized what he was looking at, the Enemy laughed. A belly laugh that shook him to his core. Then he reached one hand back and lashed out at the golden figure.

Her head ripped from her shoulders and went bouncing, rolling along the hospital tile. The figure collapsed and crashed like porcelain, golden shards shattering, then erupting into polygons and sparks before fading from sight until nothing remained but the Enemy.

It wasn't her. It was a projection. But not a ruse, not a trick, not a conscious puppet. In fact, there was a total lack of any sentient force driving this useless guardian, and he had a fairly good idea why.

The Paladin was here. Unquestionable. But she wasn't here to fight him for the fate of the planet.

She had no idea who she was.

He was looking at the wild manifestations of an uncontrolled and unknown power. Nothing but a self-defense reaction, as involuntary as your knee jerking under a reflex hammer. The real Paladin—if she knew who she was, if she had accepted it, if she had mastered herself and prepared for her inevitable duel—would never have been so sloppy.

To think he'd been worried about the Canton relics. *Let the Paladin have them,* he thought. *They won't even work for her.* This world's defender was sleepwalking through life, on a collision course with a battle she wasn't remotely prepared for and didn't even know she'd been charged to fight.

By the time he reached the other end of the hospital, where the last stragglers had evacuated through the ambulance bay, the golden dome had crumbled to nothing and the blessed darkness held sway, the world outside filled with cricket song and distant sirens. The Paladin had fled, along with Faust and his "family," but for once the Enemy didn't mind. The Paladin wouldn't get far, and once he tracked her down again, her sleeping powers would betray her, lighting up the night and marking her as vulnerable prey.

This was going to be *easy*.

Chapter Two

I was in Henderson, cruising along a quiet suburban street lined with palm trees and thinking about murdering my brother. This was how I spent most of my afternoons lately.

His house was up ahead. He lived in a two-level ranch with bone-white stucco and a pebble-bed front yard, ultra-modern with a little bit of Tex-Mex rustic charm. The silver pickup was gone from the driveway; that one was Teddy's. His wife's car, a Porsche Cayenne, sat parked out front. I glanced at the dashboard clock of my rented coupe, checked the time, and made a mental note.

His wife complicated things. So did his kid, a cherubic six-year-old who I'd met when Teddy had me over for a cookout. I had fond memories of that afternoon. Not long after that, Teddy ambushed me, put a bullet in my heart, and sent me straight to hell.

I got better.

Not all the way, considering I wasn't even wearing my own skin. My family came together to keep my wounded body alive and pull me out of the pit—well, they pulled, Caitlin pushed—but a string of near-fatal mishaps found our friend Emma ensconced in my skin and my own soul shunted into the husk of a brain-dead coma patient. My real body was in no shape to survive without life support anyway. As a skilled body-hopping demon, the kind we called a hijacker, Emma could heal it from within. In a few months, I was told, my body would be good as new and we could put my soul back where it belonged once Emma found a fresh host for herself.

What I had, for now, could best be described as a fixer-upper. Younger than my real body, this one had been physically fit once, but months spent motionless in a hospital bed left it with atrophied muscles and weakened limbs. Cait wasted no time finding a personal trainer to work with me, day in and day out, whipping me back into shape.

He was, to my shock, fully human, but after our first session together I was pretty sure the man was a demon. One of the more sadistic flavors. I hated every second of physical therapy, but the pain paid off. I moved from a walker to a cane to ambling on my own borrowed legs. After needing help just to get to the bathroom, I was back to curling weights—light ones, but still—and I was pretty sure I could throw a punch if I had to.

"It was the pickles that did it, really," I said into the phone.

Jennifer's genial drawl washed over the line. "Pickles? How d'ya figure that?"

"Caitlin got me a jar of those gourmet pickles I really like. Then she set them on my kitchen counter and refused to open them for me. Said I could have pickles when I got strong enough to do it myself."

"Diabolical."

"I've been staring at that jar for three weeks. Last night, I got it open. Best pickles I've had in my entire life."

"You out doin' your stalker routine?"

I flicked the turn signal, taking the long way around the block.

"It's not stalking, it's surveillance," I said. "I'm working out Teddy's schedule so I can catch him home alone when the time's right. So far he's keeping up appearances, going to his day job, acting like nothing happened."

Acting like he didn't turn on me, his only brother, and gun me down on a backcountry road. My grip tightened on the steering wheel.

"I watched him last night," I confessed. "Out in his yard with his wife and kid. I had my piece. Could have sniped him from the car window, done him right then and there."

"But you let him slide."

"I'm trying to figure out if his family is real. We still don't have any way of detecting a rakshasa when they change their shape and if those two are more of Naavarasi's brood, we have to be ready for a serious fight."

"Think they are?" Jennifer asked.

"No. I spent a whole afternoon with them once. If they were acting, it was the best acting job I've ever seen. And when the three of them are alone and don't think anyone is watching, they still play happy family. Then again, maybe that's what Naavarasi gave him for his treason. A comforting illusion."

Jennifer snorted. "Who the hell would sell their soul for a wife, a kid, and a house in the suburbs?"

I didn't have an answer for that. Not one I felt like giving a voice to. I was thinking more about the other possibility: that Teddy's wife and daughter were exactly who and what they looked like, blissfully unaware that the man of the house was a cannibal and a killer in league with one of the worst monsters I'd ever met.

They'd built a happy life in suburbia, and with one bullet, I was going to destroy it forever. Turn an innocent woman and her daughter into a widow and a grieving child.

Not a question of *if*, a question of *when*. This wasn't just about my revenge. If it were, then maybe, just maybe, I could let it all slide.

But Teddy was the cherished pet of Naavarasi, the rakshasa queen, and given that her plans were nothing less than apocalyptic—Cait and I had just foiled her assassination attempt on Prince Sitri, but we knew that wasn't the end of her game—he had to be stopped or he'd help her to sow suffering from here to hell and back again.

Enough surveillance for today, I decided. I had work to do and besides, riding past Teddy's place made my trigger finger itch. Best to move on, occupy myself with higher-minded things, before it demanded a scratch. My phone beeped and I glanced down at the screen, snug in the center console.

"Jen, let me call you back. I've got Pixie on the line."

Since my return from hell, the whole extended family had been out in force, chasing down leads and trying to get to the bottom of Naavarasi's schemes—and her mysterious promotion to the left hand of Prince Malphas. Pixie wasn't an occultist, but her hacking skills were close to magic in my book.

"I'm glad you're good at dealing with the weird shit," Pixie said after I answered the phone, "because I am out of my depth here. It's kinda baffling."

"Baffle away," I said, "I need a good mystery to distract me."

"I've been focused on Naavarasi's place in Denver. We know she's putting her kids in medical comas to bring them in and out of hell, and her restaurant is the safest place she can use for a staging ground."

I had set Pixie on that lead. We both agreed that Naavarasi was going to need hospital supplies, industrial chemicals, and equipment to make her plans a reality. Find the shipments, we'd find the place she was stashing her growing army of rakshasa warriors.

"I managed to pick up a paper trail for a string of shipments, marked as medical supplies, coming in from overseas and routed to her restaurant's doorstep."

I sat up a little straighter behind the wheel. "That's good!" I said.

"Wait for it. According to the tracking notices, the packages are coming from the distant country of Val Verde."

I furrowed my brow. It rang a bell, just a soft and distant one.

"Should I recognize that?"

"If you're into eighties action movies like I am," she said. "Val Verde doesn't exist. You ever see *Commando*?"

Now I got it. I put on my best Schwarzenegger impression—not a very good one—and said, "'You're a funny guy, Sully. I like you. That's why I'm going to kill you last.'"

"Are you—are you trying to do Arnold?" I could hear the wince in her voice. "Please don't, but yeah, that's the one. The guy who wrote it, Steve de Souza, uses 'Val Verde' any time he wants to set a story in a generic Latin American country, and over the years a lot of other writers have used it, too. It gets weirder. The boxes were shipped to Denver International Airport on an Oceanic Airlines flight."

That one I recognized right off the bat. "That's the plane from the show *Lost*. The one that crashes on the desert island."

"And a dozen others. It's basically become Hollywood shorthand over the years: if you want to show a plane in situations a real airline would never allow—like crashing or getting hijacked—just call it 'Oceanic Airlines' instead."

Interesting, sure, but it wasn't exactly the mystery I'd hoped for.

"What you're telling me is," I said, making sure I had it right, "whoever is supplying Naavarasi is muddying up the shipping record. They're being obnoxiously cute about it, but I'm not sure what the issue is. We do stuff like that all the time."

"But it's not fake."

Now I was confused. I rolled to a stop at the next light, windshield dark under the shade of a palm tree, and tapped the steering wheel.

"According to every computer at Denver International I could tap into, every shipping manifest, every log note," she said, "there *is* a country called Val Verde, there *is* an Oceanic Airlines, and they *are* shipping cargo through that airport. Then the trail just...stops. Disappears into electronic fuzz. But there's no sign of alterations, no forgeries, no signs of anyone monkeying with the records. No fake."

"But it has to be," I said. "The only other option is..."

"That Naavarasi is getting packages from a place that doesn't exist, shuttled on an airline that also doesn't exist."

"Good catch," I said.

"I'll keep digging," Pixie said. "I'm not gonna be able to sleep until I make it make sense."

Welcome to my world, I thought.

Chapter Three

The American was my dream deferred, hopefully not for much longer. I'd had this dream, for the longest time, of buying up a little slice of Vegas nightlife and making it my own. I'd been investing the profits from every dirty job into this place, a nightclub not far from the Strip and still under heavy construction, watching it grow from its skeletal foundations to an art-deco beacon. Inside, the furniture was still taped under thick plastic wrap, all done up in black vinyl and bright chrome, with neon piping along the empty dance floor in red, white, and sapphire blue.

Almost finished now, my time spent dead notwithstanding. Now the biggest holdup was my own original body as Emma worked to nurse it back to health. I was wearing a dead man's skin, and that was a rare advantage. I had shape-shifted, invisible just like Naavarasi and her children, and they wouldn't know it was me until I struck. Meanwhile, Emma, in my body, was pretending to be me and taking care of New Commission business while playing decoy.

Bottom line was, it was a matter of pride. I'd dreamed of opening the doors of this place for years. Now that it was close to becoming a reality, there was no way I'd stand anonymous on the sidelines and let Emma give an opening-night speech with my voice. I'd waited this

long; I could wait until I was back in my own skin and celebrate the
moment in style.

Caitlin met me at the door, dressed in cream-colored Prada with her
scarlet hair worn in a long French braid, and pulled me into her arms.
She squeezed, tight, then paused, holding me out at arm's length.

"It still feels odd," she said.

"Imagine it from my point of view," I told her. "My old body was a
quarter inch taller than this one. Wouldn't think that'd be a big deal,
but I keep noticing my sightline feels...off. Like the horizon isn't where
it should be."

"Hmm. Let me check."

She bent down, leaned in, and our lips met. I was lost for a moment,
floating, burning—then she broke the kiss with a smile.

"No," she said, "nothing wrong here. It will be nice to get you back
in your proper body, though. I accidentally pinched Emma's butt this
morning."

"How'd she react?"

"Well," Caitlin mused, "first she rolled her eyes back in her head.
Then she gasped and said, 'Do it harder, Mommy.'"

As I walked with her through the sleeping club, surrounded by the
ghosts of furniture under plastic tarps, I buried my face in my palm.

"I don't even talk like that."

Caitlin glanced to the ceiling, a sudden vision of innocence.

"Of course you don't, pet."

"You are keeping an eye on her, right?"

After the accidental body swap, Emma had made no bones about
her intention to get freaky. She hadn't worn a man's skin in over a
century and apparently missed some things. I had managed, with lots
of help from the rest of the family, to impress some basic rules upon

her: namely that I expected to get my body back in pristine factory condition, no extra miles on the odometer, and fully detailed.

"Oh, she's just teasing," Cait assured me as we walked through a swinging door, through the back rooms, and down a flight of bare concrete steps. "But on the Emma note, do prepare to enter the war zone."

I heard shouting up ahead, coming from beyond the glass wall of our new conference room. I'd built it as a place for the family to gather and scheme, considering our usual hangouts were the Tiger's Garden—open to magicians only, and no one else could even find the door—and Winter, a club that catered strictly to the hellbound set. Here, we could all meet up and scheme in comfort.

Or just yell at each other, apparently, as Melanie's tight voice drifted up the hall. "You're impossible, you know that? You're *impossible*."

As we passed the glass window looking in on the conference room, its long central table, and its high-backed executive chairs, I felt a strange twitch in my stomach. I still hadn't gotten used to the sight of Emma, in my body, standing like me, moving like me, talking with my voice. She rapped her knuckles on a manila folder, glaring at Melanie, my blue-haired teenage punk apprentice on the other side of the table.

"I'm not saying you're not allowed to date humans," Emma told her, "only that it's unseemly for a cambion your age to have no romantic interest in her own kind. Jax is a bright young man. He's quite handsome, very responsible—"

"You're trying to pawn me off on one of your creepy coworker's sons."

"I'm trying to prepare you for the future. Once you're done with college, you will be coming to work for Prince Sitri—"

Melanie laughed in shock, shaking her head. "Oh, that is *not* a conversation we're having right now. Dan? Cait? Help me, please?"

"Jax would be a very good and healthy romantic partner for you," Emma said.

Melanie put her hands on her hips, eyes sparking with a gambit.

"What if I'm into girls?" she said. "What if I'm not turning him down because he's a cambion, but because he's a guy? What then?"

Instead of showing the slightest surprise, Emma curled her lips—my lips, but it was definitely her smile—into a tight, eager curve, a lioness ready to pounce.

"*Are* you?" Emma asked.

The rage of teenage rebellion flickered, sputtering as Melanie realized the same thing I did: her mom had just outfoxed her, anticipating the argument before she even walked into the room.

Melanie's eyes glanced, nervous, to the folder under Emma's knuckles.

"If I say yes," Melanie replied slowly, "you're going to reveal that there's a second folder under that one, and it's exactly like the dossier on Jax but the second one is a girl, aren't you?"

"I don't know," Emma said, her smile glowing a notch brighter. "*Am* I?"

"Not to interrupt," Caitlin said, sweeping through the open doorway.

"Oh, no, we're definitely interrupting and changing the subject," I added. I pulled out a chair and dropped into it, kicking back. "I don't need to be in the middle of this."

"And yet," Emma said.

Caitlin took the chair beside me and reached for the conference phone at the heart of the desk. One side of the room, opposite the big glass window, was taken up by a video wall. The other two were done up with stark-white dry-erase boards, entire walls turned to canvases for taking notes in bright marker.

"I asked you here because there's a fresh problem in the mix," Caitlin said.

"A problem beyond the Enemy trying to burn the universe down," I said, "and beyond the psychotic rakshasa queen trying to plunge hell into a civil war. At the same time."

"And yet most likely related to one or both. I got a call from Royce. Hold on, let me get him on the line."

She set the phone on speaker and dialed, letting it ring. And ring. I tried not to fear the worst. Not that I was a fan of Royce's, far from it—the bastard had tried to orchestrate my final death, down in hell, and used an old buddy of mine to do it, blackmailing him into turning traitor. I wasn't going to forgive or forget that anytime soon.

But the fact remained, we were witnessing something that was, according to Caitlin, unprecedented in the annals of hell.

Naavarasi's sons had launched an assassination attempt on Caitlin's prince, Sitri, trying to make it look like an act of war. We stopped them in the act and exposed the plan, fully expecting, with the last of her bridges burned, Sitri's rival Malphas would hand the rakshasa queen over on a silver plate to avoid a fight breaking out.

Instead, he stuck his head in the sand, denied everything, and embraced the viper to his breast. Royce was Malphas's hound—Caitlin's equivalent in the court next door—and hounds served for life. Not this time. We had seen the announcement, smuggled out of hell, that Royce had been fired and now Naavarasi was the prince's earthly representative. A noble lady of hell, to be honored and obeyed.

In the face of a looming civil war, it was the most idiotic, rash decision Malphas could have made, and while I knew he hated Sitri with every fiber of his immortal soul, no one played games within games with the finesse of a demon prince. He had a reason. We just couldn't figure out what it was.

The phone clicked. I heard rasping breath, distant echoing clangs, the thrumming acoustics of a plane hangar.

"Can you talk?" Caitlin asked.

"For now," Royce whispered over the line. "I had to relocate."

"You're not at the safe house?"

"The safe house is gone," Royce said. "Two hours ago. They came in force, kicked in the doors. The next thing I knew a flash grenade was going off in my face. I had to run. I'm at—"

Caitlin was all business. She rested her slender, pale hands flat on the conference room table.

"Before you say anything else," she told him, "you're on the line with me, Emma—Prince Sitri's accountant—her daughter Melanie, and my consort Daniel."

"Is that what we're calling him now?" It sounded like Royce was trying to make a joke, but he was too desperate to find the humor in it.

"Daniel is a knight of hell, as appointed by Sitri himself. In other words, you're speaking directly to three senior officials of the Court of Jade Tears. Do you consent to continue with this conversation?"

I was taken off guard for a moment, but then I understood. The two courts were teetering on the brink of armed conflict. The last time a civil war came to hell, it led to centuries of endless blood and riot. Nobody wanted those bad old days back again—no one but Naavarasi and her band of merry killers—and right now, every move mattered. As Sitri's representative on earth, Caitlin was making sure every box was checked, every choice was documented and clear. History might question her, when all was said and done, but it wouldn't misunderstand her.

"I consent," Royce said.

"Now tell us your situation," Caitlin replied.

"I'm holed up in...Gary, of all places. Gary, Indiana. Word came down this morning, through a former friend who thought he'd get the jump on me. Prince Malphas didn't just fire and replace me. He's trying to get me killed."

Emma tilted her head, frowning. "I keep tabs on the Chainmen. Your name hasn't come up in any contracts."

"He's not going through official channels," Royce snapped. "He can't put out a bounty on me through the Chainmen because *I haven't broken any of hell's laws*. He simply announced that I'm an outcast. Outside of his protection, anyone's meat, and he won't retaliate against anyone who decides to take a shot at me. Well, surprise surprise, a century of enforcing the prince's will means there are a *lot* of people who hate me out there."

"Literally no one is surprised by that," I muttered.

"I tried reaching out to Nadine, hoping the Dead Roses could take me someplace safer than here, but..." He trailed off, suddenly cagey.

"That's like a steak throwing itself on the barbecue," I said.

"She's my friend," he shot back. "But...well, you're going to hear this eventually if you don't already know. Nadine is missing. Her people are losing their minds right now, trying to track her down."

"That wasn't us," Caitlin said.

Just the same, she shot a questioning look across the table at Emma. Emma shook her head and mouthed, "Definitely not us."

"I'm all out of options," Royce said, defeated. "So I have a favor to ask."

"Speak," Caitlin said.

"I'm asking for asylum," Royce said. "I am a political refugee, and I want to defect."

Chapter Four

The room fell silent.

"Say again," Caitlin told him.

On the other end of the line, Royce took a deep breath.

"I want to defect," he said, "to the Court of Jade Tears. I'm offering my service, my vow of loyalty, and all the information I've gathered on Prince Malphas over a century in his entourage. In return, I want Prince Sitri's personal guarantee of protection. Caitlin, you and I have known each other longer than...well. A bloody long time. You know I'm a goldmine of intelligence. It's all yours. All you have to do is save me from this nightmare."

Another silence now, a longer one. Caitlin's gaze was fixed, unblinking, on the conference phone. Her fingers curled, scarlet nails rapping the table as she made her choice.

"Your current hiding spot," she said. "Is it secure?"

"For now."

"Give us your exact location."

Once he did, she wrote it down.

"Help is on the way," she said. Then she tapped the disconnect button and hung up on him.

"Are we really going to do this?" Emma asked, her voice softer now.

"I haven't properly decided yet. I just told him that to calm him down."

"What happens if we bring him in?" I asked.

"Well," Caitlin reflected, "it's a dangerous act of provocation no matter how we spin it. Not nearly the same provocation as what Malphas is doing, harboring a known assassin, but it'll muddy the waters. Remember, what Malphas thinks doesn't really matter. What the *other* courts think will decide the course of events from here."

Made sense. From what I understood, the danger of infernal politics was never just two courts going to the mattresses. The problem was, the instant one of the fighters started to crumble, its neighbors would race in and carve it up like a Thanksgiving turkey. Then one of them would be bloodied from the fight, weaker now, and its neighbors would do the same to it. And again, and again, until the whole pit was embroiled in dog-eat-dog warfare, everyone fighting over the scraps of infernal civilization until nothing remained.

Exactly what Naavarasi wanted.

"That could be the gambit," I suggested. "Manipulate you into giving Royce asylum, make a big stink out of it, and hope the other courts decide to join this fight on his side instead of ours."

Emma raised a finger. "On the other hand, if this is a legitimate offer, Royce has a head full of secrets, and we could make good use of them. Especially now that his former prince's behavior has become...erratic."

"Can we trust him?" Melanie asked.

Emma shot her a look that could have curdled milk. Melanie caught it, arching one eyebrow.

"I mean, if this is all a trick, do we think he's in on it, or can we trust that Royce is being manipulated?" Melanie lifted her chin. "Scared people are easy to control, and if we can prove that Malphas is playing with him just to get at Sitri, he'll be twice as eager to work for us."

"That's...quite well-considered," Emma said.

"Thank you. Dan taught me that."

Now I was getting the look. There's something about catching an "I wish I could murder you" expression from someone wearing your own face. Not fun, not recommended. I put my fist to my mouth and cleared my throat.

"We can figure out what he knows once we have time to sit on him for a while," I said. "Do you have any place to stash him in the meantime? Somewhere off the radar."

"We do," Emma said. "We maintain a couple of emergency safe houses that are strictly off-book, even for our own people. Only Caitlin and I know the locations. Moving him to hell would be too risky until we know the whole situation—we can't have a disgraced hound being seen in the prince's domain—but we can make him disappear up here for a while."

Caitlin was deep in thought, her brow creased with worry. I knew why. Thanks to Naavarasi's head games, her homeland was teetering on the brink of civil war—a war the rakshasa queen was absolutely determined to spark—and Caitlin was expected to rise to the challenge. If she made the right choices, a string of perfect decisions despite a raft of contradictory and incomplete intel, she might be able to stop it. One wrong move, and the destruction of hell and the eternal deaths of countless souls would be on her shoulders.

There's no lonelier place in the world than the captain's chair.

I knew better than anyone how hard Caitlin worked. And I knew now, thanks to my sojourn in hell, how little respect she got for it. I'd been hoping to find a way to do my part, to help her out and ease her burdens. I still wasn't any kind of a cheerleader for Team Hell, don't get me wrong, but I'd go a long way to see my girlfriend smile.

"I'll go," I told her.

She swiveled in her chair, arching one sculpted eyebrow. "Pet?"

"I'll take care of it. If they're trying to both-sides this shit and make the Tears look bad, nothing would give them more ammo than catching footage of the prince's hound—or his accountant—making an illegal border crossing and snatching Royce. We need to handle this cool and quiet."

"You're not an outsider anymore," Emma pointed out. "You're one of Sitri's knights. Whether you take that seriously or not, you do hold rank in our court."

"Sure, but everybody knows he knighted me as a joke. I'm also widely known as a loose cannon who doesn't follow the rules. Ungovernable. I'm kind of a total asshole, really. Also, seeing as I'm not in my own body at the moment, they'd have to catch me *and* prove who I really am."

"Keep going," Emma said.

"Let my reputation work. If I can slip him out unseen, great. If I get caught, blame it all on me: I was trying to help and went off without asking permission first. I'm a big boy. I can take the heat."

Caitlin and Emma shared a long, thoughtful look.

"This could work," Caitlin said. "Time is of the essence, and I'm not offering Royce permanent asylum without talking to the prince first. Emma, if you prepare a place to keep him and verify security, I can travel to Carnival City and speak to Sitri in person, all while Daniel goes to retrieve our would-be defector. Three jobs, three sets of hands, and we get this done before the next sunrise."

"I'll go with Dan," Melanie said.

"You will not," her mother countered from the far side of the table. More concerned than angry now—I knew Emma well enough to recognize it, even when she was speaking with my voice. "This isn't some petty test or field exercise, darling. This is infernal politics. There are no higher stakes. It's not safe for you to get involved."

"If Naavarasi gets her way, nowhere is going to be safe for me or anyone else ever again," Melanie said. "Can't you see that? I'm here, Mom. I'm in the fight, whether you like it or not, and the more hands-on training I get, the more capable I'll be."

Suddenly, all three women were staring at me. Apparently I had been elected to cast the deciding vote. I started to show my open hands and demur; then I changed my mind. I didn't want to bring Melanie. Not because she couldn't handle it, but because of the same knee-jerk reaction I felt every single time she went into the field with me. The memory of Desi, my apprentice before her, bleeding out in my arms.

I had to get over that shit. Period. Melanie was a bright, thriving young woman with a serious talent for the occult—not to mention palmistry, card-sharping, and the art of the con, courtesy of Bentley and Corman's contributions to her underground education—and she'd proved herself more than capable. Then there was the in-escapable truth: with more than one apocalyptic disaster on the near horizon, simple odds told me that things were going to go very bad, very fast, for all of us.

Melanie was my apprentice. That meant she trusted me to get her ready for the storm. I had an *obligation* to do it.

"She should come with me," I said. "Look, I'm not going back there looking to scrap. The opposite: we're going to play it Bogart, slide in, slide out, and nobody will ever know we were there. The quieter we handle this, the more deniability we'll have once Malphas figures out Royce is gone."

"Besides," Melanie added, "weren't you just saying how you expect me to get a job with Sitri once I graduate? Well...isn't this exactly what you wanted?"

Emma pursed her lips and let out a sound of pure disgruntlement. Then she pushed back her chair, scooping up her manila folder—and the second one that had been neatly hidden under it. She brandished them as she rose.

"Fine. But you and I, young lady, are going to have a long conversation when you return home." She ruffled the folders. "And you're not getting out of it."

As she stalked out of the conference room, Melanie slumped back in her chair.

"I honestly would have volunteered for anything just to change the subject," she admitted.

"I'll remember that the next time I need my car washed," Caitlin said. She turned to me, reaching out, her hand caressing my forearm. Her thumb, velvet-soft, turned slow circles against my skin. "As for you...I need you to proceed with absolute caution. I can see a dozen possible traps ahead, all ready to spring, and there are probably more I haven't worked out yet. You're walking into a minefield."

"Just doing my part," I told her.

She pulled on my sleeve, hauling me forward in my chair and curling her arms around me in a bitterly tight embrace. Her fingers reached around the back of my head, stroking my hair as she put her lips to my ears.

"This isn't just for me. It's for my home. For everyone who stands to get hurt if that madwoman gets her way."

"I get it," I whispered back. "That's why I offered."

Her hand slid downward. Her fingers stroked around the back of my neck, suddenly squeezing in a firm marble grip.

"Good pet," she growled. "You don't know what this means to me. Rest assured that this is our best chance to toss a wrench into whatever Naavarasi is planning next. Go. Fetch. Take Royce into custody...and bring him to me. Unbound or in chains, as you see fit, but bring him back to me *alive*."

Chapter Five

N ormally I'd stick to the open roads for a job like this. I knew from experience that the infernal princes liked keeping sentries on airport duty: terminal exits were big choke points where it was easy to surveil hordes of people all day long, watching for known enemies and reporting anything fishy to the boss. On the other hand, a single car crossing state lines on any of a dozen possible roads was more of a needle in a massive haystack.

Time was the enemy. Royce had already been forced to flee from a safe house—a true case of false advertising if I'd ever seen one—and take shelter in the badlands. I had no idea how many people were gunning for his head, but I did know two things. One, Royce had been a hound long enough to make a metric ton of enemies. Two, Royce was kind of a dick.

Speed fought caution, and speed won. I had an edge: nobody east of Jade Tears territory knew that I was wearing another man's face. Emma made sure to put in public appearances so that any spies would catch "me" going about my daily routine, with nothing juicy to report. The body swap gave me a rare edge on the opposition, and I wanted to keep it that way.

I felt more naked than usual, though, as I got onto a Delta flight with Melanie at my side, two casual tourists on a trip to the American heartland. Airport security meant leaving the hardware at home. I had my omnipresent deck of cards, of course, but magicians who did *my* kind of card tricks were rare even in the wilds of Las Vegas. A card-slinging mage in Indiana would raise all kinds of questions that I didn't feel like answering.

"Got us covered," Melanie said as she slid into the tight airline seat beside me. She opened her sky-blue plastic purse and showed me her new deck of cards. Her very own.

Felt a little dusty on the plane, like I had something in my eye.

"Went with the Bee brand, huh?" I said.

Bicycle Red Dragon Backs had been my signature brand for years. The snap of a fresh card, the fan of a hand, the feel of perfect gloss against my fingertips...it was all a string of mnemonic triggers, invoking sense and muscle memory to tap into my power. Between her lessons from me, Bentley, and Corman—all three of us with strong opinions about the best brand of playing cards—I wasn't surprised she followed Bentley's path.

My cards bore rampant dragons, ready to fight. Melanie's were backed by a subtle waterfall of blue diamonds, matching the color of her hair, on a grid of ivory. A pattern designed to dazzle the eyes and snare a viewer's focus while the real trick slipped by unnoticed.

"I'd still be trying to learn the Oil and Water routine if Bentley hadn't loaned me his deck," she said. "No borders on the edges of these cards. Do you know how much easier that makes it to double- and triple-deal without getting caught?"

I stroked my chin sagely. "Mm, easy, yes. More powerful, no. Seductive and easy, the Bee brand card deck is. The path to the dark side, it is."

Melanie slumped back and reached for the halves of her seatbelt.

"No," she said. "If I can't quote Harry Potter, you can't quote that Star Wars boomer shit."

"Calls it boomer shit, she does, but knows that Yoda, I am."

"Please stop."

The plane roared up into a sunny desert sky, aimed east for hostile territory. We'd gone straight to the airport, not even stopping to pack for the trip. If everything went well, we'd be back by this time tomorrow. If it didn't, an overnight bag wouldn't help. The drink cart rolled up the aisle and we both got cans of Coke, though mine rode along with a tiny bottle of Bacardi. I sipped my drink from a plastic cup and gazed out the porthole at one shuddering wing, swallowed by a torrent of wispy, ragged clouds, while I went over the plan.

Melanie was a known quantity on the occult scene; she'd been seen with me in public, even made her first pilgrimage to the Bast Club, but she was fresh enough to stay under most people's radar. Nobody was on high alert watching for the teenage half-human daughter of Prince Sitri's accountant. If watchers at the airport did manage to flag her, I figured there was a pretty good chance they'd make a notation in their logbook and leave it at that.

Beyond that, the biggest risk would be the return home. Anyone stationed on airport duty would be watching for Royce. Going in by air and out by road felt like the safest play. Then again, that meant nearly thirty hours of sitting in a car with Royce. I figured I could shove him in the trunk as a last resort.

Melanie had been quiet for a while. I asked if she wanted to talk about it.

She raised her Coke, pausing in mid-sip. "About what?"

"Seemed like you and your mom were having some issues back there."

"Oh. That."

I nudged her gently with my elbow. "What's going on?"

"Nothing new," Melanie sighed. "She's just...trying to map out my entire life for me, as usual. Where I'm going to go, what I'm going to do, what choices I make—"

"Part of that is kind of a mom's job."

"Not like this! She's so insistent that I'm going to 'join the family business' after college. What if I don't want to? What if I have dreams of my own? I wish I could just be like, 'No, Mom, I want to go off to Broadway and be a star!'"

"Do you?" I asked.

Melanie grimaced. "No. It was just an example. But that's the problem. I don't...I don't know what I want to do after college. I don't even know what I want to major in. If I actually had a calling I felt passionate about, I could justify saying no."

I contemplated my cocktail with a smile.

"Melanie, let me tell you a powerful secret about being an adult. Not wanting to do something is all the justification you need. Like, last week Bentley and Corman had an extra ticket to the touring production of *Mamma Mia!* and asked if I wanted to go. I said no."

"Because...you had something else to do that night? Another commitment?"

"Nope. And it wasn't just because I think a jukebox musical based on the music of ABBA is literally a form of infernal torture, though I do. I just didn't want to. So I didn't. You don't have to justify not wanting to work for Prince Sitri. Not to your mom, not to anybody. It's your life and your choices."

Melanie curled her arms over her chest, shoulders shifting as she tried to get comfortable in the stiff-backed airline seat. The cabin rumbled softly, a lick of turbulence as we rose through mountain air.

"I just want a job where I can feel good about myself," she said, her voice softer now. "I want to do something that helps people. Something that makes their lives better, not worse."

When Melanie decided she wanted to learn magic, she asked me to teach her. Not for the first time, I felt like a royal piece of shit for saying yes. Being my student meant living in my world, down in the gutters and the filth. The same month I taught Melanie her first spell, I showed her how to pick a lock and how to fieldstrip a pistol. She was the last person I wanted anywhere near my gangster business. Yet here she was, neck-deep in it right next to me.

I told myself—and believed—that it was still the best thing for her future. Even without the double threats of Naavarasi and the Enemy, Melanie was a half-demon kid with a foot in two worlds. Given the chance, there were forces in both of those worlds that would use her, abuse her, and grind her up. If nothing else, I could give her a real chance of survival. I was teaching her how to work clean and fight dirty. When she blossomed into her own power and the wolves inevitably began to circle, she wouldn't be unarmed or unprepared.

Still, I tried to keep her away from the really nasty stuff. There was something pure-hearted about Melanie, an innocence I couldn't even remember losing. Damned if I'd steal hers. Looking out across my crew, my family of choice...she was the best of all of us.

If she got hurt going to rescue *Royce's* unworthy ass, I was going to have harsh words with some people. Myself, first and foremost.

We touched down at Midway Airport, on Chicago's South Side. I had Melanie walk fifteen feet ahead of me as we approached the point of no return, where you pass through airport security and back out into the civilian world. I wanted to see who was looking and who was making notes. She turned a couple of heads, one a fellow traveler, obviously not on the prince's payroll, and the other a man in a cheap suit sitting at an open bar. His gaze dropped and lingered on her body, but all he did after that was order another mai tai. He wasn't satanic, just sleazy.

Malphas's real watcher was perched on a chair over by the baggage claim. He was a younger guy with an artist's sketchpad on his lap, pretending to draw, but he gave each new arrival an eagle-sharp look and jotted notes on the page. Every now and then he'd grab his phone and snap a subtle photo before sending it off, presumably to his handler.

Melanie breezed right past him and he made a note but didn't give her a second glance. As I hoped, nobody was memorizing the face of the daughter of a prince's accountant. For the moment, we were safe. We wouldn't be so lucky if we brought Royce back this way, though: him, a watcher would recognize.

I met up with Melanie at the rental kiosk. Not long after that we were out in the lot under an oily sky, the air kissed by jet fuel and smoke, piling into a silver coupe and setting the GPS for Gary, Indiana. We'd be across the state border and closing in on Royce's location within the hour.

Assuming, of course, no one else found him first.

Chapter Six

The sun was starting to sink in a dirty tangerine sky as we rolled into Gary. I'd been here before. I'd also been to Detroit a few times, and I felt safer in Detroit. Gary started out as a booming steel mecca and when the steel work dried up, so did the money. The place wasn't a ghost town, far from it...but it had ghosts, from the shadows of graffiti-clad billboards to the sagging faces and broken windows of houses and factories left to rot in the hard Midwestern winters. We drove past open lots clogged with weeds and fallen fences, trash that drifted like tumbleweeds, and yard signs for political candidates who'd had their day in the sun half a decade ago.

We took a side street strewn with potholes, rumbling along the broken asphalt, trying to beat the sunset. My eyes were only human; the things gunning for Royce would, by and large, be natives of the night. And even if more hunters had tracked him down, I had to figure a few would be waiting for the relative safety of darkness before they made their move. I wanted to be in, out, and long gone before that happened.

Up ahead, I didn't like what I was seeing. A fence made of metal slabs, seven feet tall and corroded with rust, circled the compound of an old, abandoned steel mill. Cold, silent smokestacks towered over fallen sheds and the corpse of a red brick building, one wall entirely crumbled and exposing its moldy, ransacked guts to the elements. That, I expected from Royce's description of his hiding spot. The problem was out front.

"What do you see?" I asked. I did a drive-by, not slowing down, so she could get a good look at the entrance.

Melanie barely hesitated. "Van parked out front with Michigan plates. Not a rental, lots of road wear. There's chain and a broken padlock on the pavement, and the front gate's been shoved open a few feet, wide enough to walk right in."

I kept driving, intent on finding a spot to double back once we'd slipped out of sight.

"Dazzle me," I said.

"We've got company. There's no way Royce would have left a trail like that, even in a panic. At the very least he would have closed the gate after himself and tried to relock it on the other side. Also, knowing Royce, he wouldn't drive a van. More of an Aston Martin type."

"Good girl," I murmured. "Now tell me about the opposition."

That took her longer. She squinted out through the windshield, thoughtful, as I pulled over to the side of the road near the far back corner of the factory fence.

"Could be as few as one person, as many as...four or five? More if they really wanted to squeeze in. Depends on whether they're here to kidnap him or kill him on the spot."

"And how would we have handled this job if we got here first? Compare that to what you see."

Melanie blinked. Her eyes widened, just a little.

"We would have parked away from the gate, hidden the padlock and chain, closed the door and tried to make everything look untouched, just in case somebody came along while we were collecting Royce."

She snapped her fingers. "Either they're sloppy, they're in a big hurry and don't plan on sticking around long, or both."

I'd been told that teaching is one of the most rewarding jobs in the world. Sometimes, I could feel it.

"Hope for sloppy, but never bet on it," I told her. "Here's where you get out. Circle around, find a spot to hop the fence, and make a beeline for Royce."

She popped her seatbelt, opened the side door, then gave me a parting glance. "What are you going to do?"

"Run a distraction. We need to know how many guys are in there, what they're packing, and maybe—just maybe, if we're incredibly lucky—if they can be reasoned with. I've got a plan."

I didn't tell her it was a good plan, because I don't like lying to my family. As I let her out, then turned the coupe around and circled back toward the open gate, I felt more optimistic and upgraded it from "barely a plan" to "workable, with a strong chance of violence."

I left the engine running, hopping out long enough to jog to the gate, throw my shoulder against it, and force it open foot by straining, rusted foot. The old hinges squealed in protest, the gate dragging along the weeds and shattered pavement, but eventually it was wide enough to drive on through.

I got back behind the wheel and did just that, cruising right into the open compound. I even tapped my horn a couple of times, the tinny bleat echoing up to the teetering smokestacks, to make sure I had everyone's full attention. Then I killed the ignition, got out of the car, leaned back, and shoved my hands in my pockets.

I didn't have to wait long. A pair of familiar faces emerged from the ruins of the steel mill, trailing long sunset shadows as they approached me like twin gunslingers.

Mack and Zeke. I could have laughed. Almost. They were two of Malphas's most put-upon errand boys, mostly because they were made of equal parts bloodthirsty and stupid. Black-metal mavens who dressed like Mormons on a church mission and carried switchblades in their pockets, they were full-blooded humans but true believers in hell's cause. Or whatever they thought hell's cause was anyway. As far as I'd ever been able to tell, they took their album covers as Gospel, truly believed they were working for the Devil himself, and their bosses never bothered to clarify the situation.

Prince Sitri liked servants who could keep him entertained. Malphas liked 'em obedient and dumb. Normally that would put these two in the "too pathetically adorable to kill" category, except for two things. First, their willingness to shed blood in Lucifer's unholy name, preferably accompanied by a shredding guitar solo, wasn't an act: I knew they both had a body count, and they weren't shy about civilian casualties. Second, they weren't *that* dense. Royce was a powerhouse and they had the combined magical prowess of an Easy-Bake Oven. They had to know they were out of their league here.

Meaning either they had reinforcements on the way, or they weren't here alone. Somebody bigger and badder was pulling their strings.

"Afternoon," I said. "I'm here for the job interview."

Zeke, the skinny one, scrunched up his face. "What job interview?"

"You know. The job interview. I mean, c'mon, fellas, I drove all this way. Are you messing with me right now?"

I pretended to stifle a yawn, taking the chance to glance upward. My practiced gaze swept the stacks, the eaves of the half-collapsed central plant, the mounds of fallen rubble. I was hunting for sentries—or worse, a sniper—but all I caught was a stray bird taking flight into the fast-darkening sky.

I'd considered earlier that if a real monster figured out where Royce was, they might keep their distance and wait until nightfall to make a move, just to improve their odds. Wouldn't stop them from sending Mack and Zeke as expendable advance scouts, though. All the more reason to be long gone before that last golden sliver of sunlight sizzled down below the horizon. At least there wasn't a hint of recognition in their eyes: my new face was a perfect disguise, for the moment at least.

My deck sat snug in my breast pocket, my constant copilot. I considered calling to the cards with a snap of my fingers and dropping these two where they stood, but I held my ground instead. I didn't care that I was here repping Sitri's court. I cared that I was here repping Caitlin, carrying out a mission that could potentially be painted as an act of war, and if I screwed up, she'd be the one to suffer for it. I had to be careful, tactical about this, which meant violence was the last resort.

"You're in the wrong place," Mack said. "Get back in your car, reverse out of here, and don't come back."

My strategy was simple, simple enough that even calling it a "plan" felt a little ostentatious. I'd keep these idiots distracted long enough for Melanie to find Royce and pull him out of whatever rathole he was hiding in. Once they were clear she'd send up a sign and I'd make my graceful exit. If everything went right, they wouldn't even know they'd been hoodwinked.

Everything did not go right.

"You should listen to the man," Zeke said. The black plastic handle of a switchblade appeared in his curled fingers. He tapped the switch and a stainless-steel blade swung out, catching the dying light on its cold metal skin. He didn't brandish it, just held it casually at his side, but he took a hard step closer to me. He was maybe seven, eight feet away now.

A good knife fighter can cross an eight-foot gap and stab you a half dozen times in the space of a breath. Zeke did knife work for a living. I didn't like my odds.

I liked them even less a second later, as a low and throaty growl split the air. Mack and Zeke had a four-legged friend. A shaggy German shepherd, broad-shouldered and midnight black, prowled out to stand between them. I caught the crackle of wild magic, a faint glow in the dog's curious, intelligent eyes, and realized who I was dealing with.

Pinfeather.

We'd crossed paths in the bad old days, back when Caitlin and I were just getting to know each other and the Redemption Choir—the original flavor, before Ada Lovelace took over—was making trouble all over town. He was one of Malphas's spies and he posed as a harmless priest to lure me into a trap. A pretty good one, too, not that it helped him in the end. We spoiled his plans, Caitlin killed him for crossing her, and then, just to add insult to injury, his former master stuffed his soul in the body of a dog and put him on eternal guard duty as penance for his failure.

Royce was the former master in question.

"What a cute dog!" I said. "Does he bite?"

I felt dirty psychic claws scrabbling at my brain; Pinfeather was trying to soul-read me, probably wondering why this total stranger had a familiar scent. I threw up a mental wall while I kept my clueless smile on.

"Oh yeah," Mack said, slowly sidestepping to get around me. "He bites."

A second switchblade flicked open. I had Zeke and Pinfeather just ahead of me, Mack on my left side and still on the move, almost out of my line of sight. My deck of cards tingled against my breast pocket.

I knew I needed to draw: draw first, draw fast, and shut these three down before one of them made a move.

I stayed my hand. If there was any chance of talking my way out of this and keeping my cover intact, I had to take the risk. For Caitlin.

"You know, fellas," I said, easing toward my car door, "I think you might be right. This probably isn't the right address. I'll just, uh, slide on out of here and go on my merry way."

"Way too late for that," Mack said. Pinfeather let out a growl in agreement as his eyes blossomed in shades of yellow, like spills of dirty egg yolk.

"Our dog says you smell funny," Zeke added.

"Has he smelled himself lately?" I took another half step toward the car door. "I mean...dogs, am I right?"

"He says you smell like magic," Mack said. "And since you're not one of ours..."

Pinfeather showed his teeth. A rivulet of thick, syrupy drool dropped from the corner of his muzzle, spattering the broken asphalt.

I clapped my hands, sharp and loud. It was a petty trick to break their train of thought, and I hoped the sound would carry across the deserted steel mill. *Come on, Melanie. Could really use the all-clear signal right now. Where the hell is Royce hiding?*

"You got me," I said with a confident grin. "I'm from the home office. Prince Malphas sent me to test you guys, and I'm proud to say that you passed with flying colors."

The blade wavered in Zeke's hand. He gave the dog an uncertain look. Pinfeather responded with a hungry growl, slapping one thick paw against the pavement and stalking toward me.

"He doesn't believe you," Zeke said.

A new voice called out, off to my right, just above our heads.

"Would you believe we're from animal control?" Melanie asked.

She stood upon the burned-out husk of a capsized pickup truck, the rig abandoned to rot in a field of weeds. Her cambion blood was in full flush, her eyes a baleful yellow, dark veins blossoming across her face in the pattern of a butterfly's wings. Her outstretched fingers twitched as she held her left hand high. Three playing cards, three aces, spun and danced in the air around her fingertips.

"Put the mutt on a leash," she said, "or all three of you are going to the pound."

Chapter Seven

"Who the hell *are* you people?" Mack demanded. Zeke took a halting step back, staring up at Melanie as her cards danced across her outstretched fingers. The strain of commanding the spell made her entire body tremble, but she held on tight.

"Leaving," I said. "We're just leaving."

Melanie hopped down from the pickup's shell and scurried over, still harnessing the cards, ready to let them fly. We got into the car at the same time, slamming and locking the doors before I threw it into reverse. The trio watched us leave, eyes hard, aching for a fight and denied. The cards fell into Melanie's lap, one tumbling to the floor mat, as she slumped in her seat and closed her eyes.

"You okay?" I asked, watching the rearview and pulling out through the open gate.

"You make that trick look easy," she said.

"Lots and lots of practice. You'll get there. Let me guess: Royce wasn't even here."

She quirked a tired smile. "Who's your favorite apprentice?"

"It's a vast field of competitors, but one name does always rise to the top."

"Take a left, and follow the fence around to the back," she said.

Down in the long shadows and the tangled weeds, a lone figure huddled at the outer edge of the rusted metal fence. I pulled over just long enough for Melanie to hop into the back of our silver coupe, while Royce—looking haggard, his fancy clothes muddy and torn, bags under his eyes like he hadn't slept in a week—piled into the passenger side. I was already on the move, hitting the gas before he closed his door, and he gave me a confused stare.

"I don't know you," he said, suspicious now.

"Sure you do," I said. "I'm going out with your ex-girlfriend. But she likes me a lot more than she likes you."

He hesitated a moment, then leaned closer, squinting.

"*Faust?*"

"I find it weirdly disturbing that you figured it out that fast, considering how long ago you and Caitlin were an item," I said. "Are you just...not getting any, Royce? Century-long dry spell?"

He crossed his arms and pouted. "I'm busy. I don't get out of the office much."

"And it shows," Melanie chimed in from the back seat. She was relaxing now, recovering, and the mask of black veins on her face had almost faded away.

"Besides, I know you're training Emma's daughter—"

"'Emma's daughter' has a name and she's sitting right here," Melanie said.

"—and that you recently returned from an excursion to hell. It doesn't take a Sherlock Holmes display of deduction to connect these dots, old bean. Fortunately for you, I'm fairly certain those three back there are clueless. Whatever description they give Malphas won't help him much."

I really wanted to have a chat with Royce. About hell. Specifically about how he manipulated my old buddy Spengler into trying to have me whacked. I was on my best behavior, though, and that actually had to mean something for once. Ignoring him for the moment, I met Melanie's eyes in the rearview mirror.

"You did great back there, by the way."

"Thanks. Was the line okay?" she asked.

I lifted an eyebrow. "Line?"

"The animal-control thing. I was originally going to end it with 'or I'll have you all put to sleep,' but..."

"For you," I said, "that's pretty dark."

Melanie nodded, her mop of blue hair flopping. "Exactly, right? Then I thought I'd say, 'I'm going to take you down to pound-town,' but I suddenly couldn't remember if that was a fighting metaphor or a sex metaphor and I really didn't want to get that wrong."

"It depends on who you're having sex with, really."

Royce swiveled in his seat, head turning back and forth like he was watching a tennis match and didn't like either of the players.

"I mean, you always have some cool, confident quip up your sleeve," Melanie said.

I shook my head and flicked the turn signal, angling for a highway on-ramp.

"I only do that when I'm nervous," I told her. "Don't emulate my unhealthy coping mechanisms."

"Dear Lucifer," Royce said. "I just realized something."

I shot him a sidelong look.

"I used to think you were just unbelievably exasperating to deal with," he said. "But now I realize the true extent of it. Your very presence makes the people around you more annoying. It's contagious. You're a cosmic singularity of irritation."

"Damn right," I replied.

I curled my knuckles and reached back. Melanie leaned in and gave me a fist bump. Then I took out my phone and set it on the center console. I put a finger to my lips for silence. Caitlin picked up on the first ring and her voice filled the tiny coupe's cabin.

"Southern Tropics Import-Export," she said smoothly. "Caitlin Brody speaking."

"Hey, Cait, it's me. I just picked up our carryout order for dinner. Smells great."

Royce pursed his lips and curled his arms over his chest.

"Can't wait to eat," Caitlin replied. "But be careful driving back. I just heard about an accident. Take I-15 home, it'll be faster."

"Will do." I disconnected the call. "Shit."

"I'm assuming I'm dinner," Royce said.

"Never know who's listening in. That remark about I-15 was a code phrase. See, I *was* going to drive us back to Nevada. I figured if we went nonstop, the three of us trading off shifts, we could make it back reasonably quick. More importantly, safe."

Royce nodded, taking that in. "Malphas has watchers at every major airport."

"Unfortunately, that's exactly where we're headed. Something must have gone down and Caitlin needs you pronto, so we're flying home. Apparently it's worth the risk."

We cruised across the Illinois border, and then we worked fast. I dropped the rental car off at the Midway lot and we speed-marched through the terminal while I hunted for the earliest direct flight between here and home. Delta had one leaving in an hour and twenty minutes, longer than I wanted to stick around, but we'd make it work. Royce and Melanie kept watch, eyes on the sparse and tired commuter crowds, while I bought tickets.

"Main cabin?" Royce sniffed. "You couldn't even spring for the seat upgrade?"

"You're lucky I didn't stuff you in a suitcase," I told him. "Come on, I want to get through security. We'll be safer on the other side."

The suitcase plan almost looked better, once a TSA agent started giving me the hairy eyeball. Three people flying together, without a single piece of luggage between them, was red-flag territory. Fortunately Melanie had a big, cheerful, innocent smile and Royce had an impeccably posh British accent, so the staff sent us through the machines and waved us on by without another word.

On the far side of the scanners, we popped into a Hudson convenience store. It was a good way to check our tail and spot anyone suddenly veering off course or doubling back. We were either clean or the people watching us were better than Malphas's usual goon squad.

"The people on your trail," I murmured, easing up close to Royce and pitching my voice for his ears alone. "They the kind who would barge through a security gate and shoot up an airport?"

"Depends," he said.

"On?"

"On if they know I'm here or not."

"That," I said, "is incredibly unhelpful."

We were standing by the bookracks. I glanced over the lurid paperbacks, most of them romances, murder mysteries, or some flavor of techno-thriller, when a stray cover caught my eye. A blood moon hung over a sprawling neon cityscape.

The City at Midnight, read the Gothic cover font, by *Carolyn Saunders*.

"A new Carolyn book?" Melanie asked, easing up on my other side to take a look. "But she's..."

Dead. She didn't have to finish the sentence and I didn't want her to. My friend Carolyn was dead. I couldn't be too busted up about it: she was the latest incarnation of the Scribe, another endlessly looping soul trapped in the web of the First Story. As she assured me with her dying breath, she'd be back. Probably already was, a bright-eyed and rosy-cheeked baby learning how to take her first wobbly steps in some other parallel world.

I hoped she had good parents this time. I hoped they were treating her right. I wished I could find out, make sure. I flipped the book over and skimmed the back copy.

"Probably turned it in to the publisher before she died," I said.

A City Without Heroes Cries Out for Justice! read the tagline. Well, at least it wasn't another one of her "Donatello Faustus" epics. Thanks to her role as the Scribe she had a direct line into the cosmos, and she'd spent years writing thinly fictionalized accounts of my real-life exploits. A prison became a wizard's ice fortress, automatics became swords, and I was transformed into a cunning swashbuckler who stole from the rich to give to the poor (as opposed to "mostly just to myself") and had regular threesomes with vampire vixens. I glanced down, reading more of the blurb.

The Midnight Jury, the two-fisted man of mystery who swore to protect the mean streets of Noir York City, is missing—

I reached for my wallet. I bought the book. I spent the walk to the gate clutching my prize in a thin plastic bag, wanting to rip it open and start scouring it on the spot. But I had to stay disciplined, keep my head on a swivel and watch for threats, at least until we made it onto the plane.

Melanie gave me a curious look. "What's with you?"

"Message from beyond the grave," I told her. I knew that didn't clarify anything, but I was in the dark myself, fumbling for a light.

Once we boarded the jet—Royce grousing about the lack of first-class accommodations the entire time while we dutifully ignored him—I buckled in and opened the paperback.

As usual, Carolyn's work wasn't entirely accurate. The Midnight Jury wasn't a two-fisted man of mystery. *She* was a grizzled private eye who dressed up in a trench coat, fedora, and mask, slinging a pair of magic pistols.

Her name was Danielle Faust. I knew this because I had worn her skin for fifteen minutes.

When I infiltrated Northlight Tower, the Enemy's skyscraper lair, I made it all the way to the bastard's inner sanctum. His private penthouse office, where I found the book. *The* book, containing all the chapters of his bound power, waiting to be unleashed. All of his missing pieces. Naturally I tried to swipe it. The book had other ideas. It booted me into another place, another life, in a shadow-drenched nightmare city under the light of twin moons. My mind started to fracture under the strain and it took everything I had to claw my way back to reality. There wasn't time to try again, with the Enemy on his way. I had to abandon the book and run.

For the longest time, I assumed it had been a hallucination. A direct magical attack on my brain, snaring me in a waking dream. The city was called *Noir York*, for crying out loud, which felt like something I would have dreamed up as a kid after watching too many late-night Bogart flicks. The more time that passed, the less real it felt.

But here it was, in black-and-white. Places I'd been. People I'd talked to. Carolyn had written me a final message, one last gift, and I was holding it in my hands. All of her stories came from her visions. Visions of other dimensions, stark and concrete. Which meant the Enemy's book hadn't just put a whammy on me; it had literally shunted me into a parallel world.

I studied the murky outline of my own reflection. It was long past sunset now, and the darkness outside the brightly lit cabin turned the window at my side into a shadowy mirror.

"Why that one?" I murmured.

"Which one?" Melanie whispered, sitting next to me. Royce, on her other side, was either sleeping or pretending to.

I rapped my knuckles on the paperback.

"I don't know if she meant to do it or not—honestly, I could never figure out what Carolyn *meant* to do most of the time even before she died—but this book backs up what I saw at Northlight. It wasn't a hallucination. She saw it too, which means Noir York is a real place."

"Really dumb name, though."

"Dumb names happen. Just ask the folks who live near Gobbler's Knob." I stared down at the cover, feeling like a caveman with a clock. The pages held secrets, but I didn't know the right way to read them. "Here's my question: if the Enemy's book is powerful enough to launch someone into a parallel world, why that world in particular?"

"Random chance?" Melanie asked.

Maybe, but I didn't buy it. Nothing about that cursed tome was random. The Enemy had meticulously created it for himself, *from* himself, hiding his power behind locks only he could unseal. He didn't count on me and my crew coming along to make his life miserable, but then again, people rarely did.

That other world, that endless sprawling midnight city, was important to the Enemy. And considering his cosmic mandate was to burn the multiverse to ashes, one planet at a time, I didn't think *any* place was important to him. He wasn't a creature of sentiment. He was a creature of strategy and war.

Talk to me, Carolyn. I traced the bumpy raised font of the title with my fingertip. *Why is that world special to him? Why didn't he burn it like every other planet he's visited?*

What could a galaxy-destroying monster ever want to protect?

Chapter Eight

We touched down at McCarran without incident. As we walked through the concourse, Royce tugged my sleeve.

"Tell me something. Honest answer. Please."

He sounded more earnest than usual, so I decided to indulge him. "Shoot."

"What's the temperature like out here?"

"It's a desert. Hot and dry by day, cold at night."

He sighed. "Not what I meant. Your people. What I'm asking is, am I about to receive a warm and enthusiastic welcome, or do I get a black bag over my head and a hard interrogation first?"

I shrugged.

"If the shoe was on the other foot..." I trailed off. From the defeated look on his face, I didn't have to say another word.

"I really hate hard interrogations," he muttered.

"Want some gum?"

"No, I want—" He paused, reconsidering. "Do you *have* gum?"

I offered him a foil-wrapped stick of Juicy Fruit. He unwrapped it and popped it into his mouth, chewing anxiously.

Outside the terminal, out in the dark and the cold, a cargo van waited between a pair of electric light-puddles. The door rattled open as we walked past. Rough hands snatched Royce, dragging him off his feet and into the belly of the van. I heard zip ties ratcheting tight as the side door slammed shut again. The driver—a cambion I knew, one of Caitlin's errand boys—gave me a thumbs-up from behind the wheel.

"Should we be worried about him?" Melanie asked me as the van smoothly pulled away from the curb.

"There is no conceivable situation in which we should ever be worried about Royce."

She gave me a look.

"It's fine," I told her. "They'll probably just tune him up a little, until they're sure he's not some kind of double agent. Can't believe they didn't invite me to join in. Rude. Want me to drop you off at home?"

***

Home again, alone, I flicked on the lights and dead-bolted the door behind me. My place was a one-bedroom over a pool hall in East Las Vegas, freshly renovated and still smelling like new paint. Caitlin texted me; she was busy welcoming Royce to the fold—in other words, spinning his head around and pumping him for secrets—and she'd catch up with me tomorrow.

I had the evening to myself, a long list of questions, and a paperback novel.

Normally I didn't mix chemicals and magic. That was Jennifer's bag, and she was good at it. Still, I'd tried it a couple of times before when I needed some quick and dirty enlightenment, and I had a tiny stash left over from the last time Jen came over and we made magic mushroom pizzas.

I gathered pillar candles from my cluttered hallway closet. Royal purple, for intuition and vision. I laid them out upon the wood laminate floor of my kitchen, organizing them in the points of a hexagram. Around the candles I scattered loose stones—agates and citrines and polished chunks of jasper—to invoke the planetary powers of Mercury.

"Your sphere is communication," I murmured under my breath, tilting a small vial of oil against my fingertip. One by one, I marked the glass candleholders with Mercury's planetary sign. "And to your winds I do call."

I munched on shriveled black mushrooms while I ignited the candles with a cheap plastic lighter. The shrooms tasted like dirt and I felt green the second they hit my stomach, so I grabbed a can of ginger ale from the fridge. Then I killed the electric lights, sat down in my ring of candles, and read by their flickering orange glow.

There were two stories in my hands. I experienced them as my vision swam, catching the translucent ghosts of pages riffling past the paper ones, crystal type riding over black ink like a secret decoder in colored cellophane. The book was heavier in my hands now, the size of a college textbook, and then it was a television and then it was a movie screen and I tumbled in, swallowed by the pages.

Now I stood in a familiar and dusty house, a single lonely light burning in a back office, listening to the rhythmic clacking of a mechanical keyboard. I walked past an overflowing sink, empty fifths of Smirnoff and Bacardi competing for space on the dirty countertop, and looked out the back window.

This was Carolyn's old Midwestern farmhouse, but instead of a rippling cornfield, I gazed out over a metropolis. We were somewhere at least forty stories above the city streets, looming over art deco skyscrapers and spires of chrome. A zeppelin, with a spotlight in its belly sweeping across the teeming alleys far below, drifted in front of an ice-blue moon. Its companion, a waning crescent of brittle bone, hung just above it in the starless night sky.

I walked into the back room. Dream logic. I couldn't even be surprised to find Carolyn sitting there like always, grinding away at a new manuscript, a highball glass of straight vodka at her side.

"Carolyn?" I whispered.

She acknowledged me with a sideways nod but didn't take her eyes off the screen, didn't stop typing.

"Not the one you knew," she replied. "An echo, a memory. Everything the Scribe creates holds a bit of her essence between the pages."

"But you reached out to me. You wanted me to find that book."

"She didn't always know why she did things," the Carolyn-echo replied. "She often suspected she was an instrument in the hand of a higher power. Not the writer but the quill. So when the spirit took her, she told her little stories and trusted they'd find their way into the right hands and the right hearts."

"Tell me about Noir York," I said.

"Read the book. It's a true story. All of her books were true stories."

"Agree to disagree."

"She left you something in Springfield."

My brow furrowed.

"Springfield, Illinois?" I asked. "Why? I've never even been there."

"She left you something in Springfield," the Carolyn-thing said, repeating herself in the exact same tone and cadence. "When you get there...you'll know exactly where to look."

***

I was awake. Maybe. Half of the candles had gusted out despite the lack of any wind, turning the hexagram pattern into a chaotic, odd-angled and broken circle of shivering lights. I stood up and walked on clouds all the way to the bedroom, stripping off my clothes on the way.

I perceived my own mind on two distinct tracks at the same time. One was keyed in to the cosmic winds, following neon currents that wound through the air like trail markers, telling me where to go. The counterpart me sat back with a tub of popcorn and said *Oh yeah, he's high as balls right now.*

I pulled on a storm-gray silk sports coat, tailored and tapered slacks, and slipped into a pair of imported Italian leather shoes. I was halfway out the door before I realized I forgot to put a shirt on, my jacket thrown on over my bare chest, but I figured I could make the look work. A Lyft driver was waiting for me outside the pool hall and that was strange because I didn't remember ordering a Lyft, but I still got into the back seat and settled in for the drive.

There was a long line outside of Winter, as usual; not counting the heavy hitters on the Strip, it was the hottest nightclub in Vegas. And as usual I ignored the lineup, walking right over to the velvet ropes. The bouncer looked me up and down, seemingly unimpressed by my daring fashion choices tonight. Still, he was on hell's payroll and he'd been told that the guy with the new face was an old friend of upper management. A handful of partygoers groaned as he unclipped the rope and waved me through.

"Sorry, folks," he told them, "Magic Mike here is on the VIP list."

"I'm Dan," I said to the bouncer.

"Yeah. No shit. Dude, your pupils are like…" He sighed, shook his head, and held the door open for me.

Ivory snowflakes cascaded down an LED wall in time with the rhythmic, bone-jarring thump of the bass, the dance floor awash in laser light while an electronic dance album boomed down from a glass DJ booth, suspended overhead in a nest of dangling cables. You didn't have to sell your soul to get onto the VIP list here, but it helped; Winter was owned and operated by Prince Sitri's people. The premier place to see and be seen, but I wasn't here to meet anyone in particular. My body just wanted to dance.

Then, standing at the heart of the churning dance floor, lost in the crowd and the rhythm, I saw a vision. She was radiant, with long and wispy mermaid hair like spun gold, her eyes deep and baby blue. She wore a party dress, cut low and slit on the sides, and Barbie-pink heels to match.

She saw me and smiled, and her eyes became kaleidoscopes.

I watched them transform as she approached me, blue irises splitting apart, turning to a spray of fractals, whirling across the whites of her eyes. The fractals collided, sparking, spitting out fresh patterns and birthing themselves into new shapes.

"Dance with me," she said.

So we danced.

"I know you," I said, and my voice wasn't loud enough to rise above the music, but she heard me just fine. I saw the recognition in her eyes.

It happened in the city. Me—the *other* me, Danielle Faust—standing out on an amusement pier, facing off with her under the light of a towering Ferris wheel. She had hostages, and I needed to talk her down. It hadn't quite gone that way, though.

"Say my name," she said. I saw her lips move. Then I heard her voice in my head.

"Damsel."

"My real name," she said.

"I discovered something tonight," she had told me, under the Ferris wheel. *"I'm a psychopomp. That's a conductor. Not a choo-choo conductor, though."*

Other names had rattled through my mind like train cars. *Paladin. Enemy. Witch. Knight. Salesman. Thief.*

"You're the Psychopomp," I told her. "You're a character from the First Story. The conductor of souls."

The girl with kaleidoscope eyes gave me a smile.

"Be careful," she said, "if you meet me as Damsel again. That was an earlier incarnation of mine and I was very sick that time around. I won't remember this meeting because to her perspective, it hasn't happened yet. She may hurt you, and that would make now-me very unhappy."

"Why that world?" I asked. "What's the connection to the Enemy? Why is it special to him?"

"Your lover has a tiny joke," she replied. "What does your Caitlin say when she's asked how she feels about this planet?"

I knew that one by heart. I cracked a smile.

"She loves Earth," I said. "It's where she..."

My smile slowly vanished.

"It's where she keeps her stuff."

My dance partner inclined her head, whirling blue diamonds in her eyes.

"He went to Noir York," I said, "but he didn't burn it. He didn't burn it because he's *using* it."

More memories of my disjointed, chaotic jaunt came back to me. As my alter ego, I'd been out of town. I'd been hired to recover a unique book. A grimoire of great power.

The girl moved close to me, intimate as our bodies swayed. Her breath was a hot puff of strawberry-scented breeze against my earlobe.

"It's the same book," she whispered.

"There are two copies?"

She took my hand in hers.

"Three. Not copies. It's the *same book*," she repeated. Then she led me off the dance floor, winding past a cluster of small high-top tables. One of them had a martini glass sitting near the rim. She snatched it up in passing, right from under its owner's outstretched hand. He didn't notice at all.

She turned to face me, walking backward, sipping her stolen martini. It had a garnish, a scarlet plastic spear piercing a trio of fat, ripe olives. She plucked out the garnish and set the half-finished glass on another table.

"The Enemy is a master of dimensional manipulation," she said. "You've felt his power more than once. When he knew he was going to be trapped and laid plans for his eventual return to power, he wasn't about to trust the wellspring of his magic to a single book. Books can burn. Books can rot. The grimoire needed a way to protect itself against attack. And so he devised a cunning defense."

She held up the garnish and tapped the three impaled olives.

"It exists in three realities at the same time, sharing overlapping positions in interdimensional space."

"So if someone, say, pisses it off—like I did—it can shunt them into another world."

"More importantly," she said, "if it takes actual physical damage, it can retreat across the veil and heal itself in one of two other points in space-time. And then return, as if nothing ever happened. No single one of its manifestations can be permanently harmed by direct attack. It's impossible."

"So how do I get rid of this thing for good, before the Enemy manages to pop its locks open?"

"You begin by understanding the truth." She traced the olives with the tip of her finger. "The olives are not the book. The olives are an expression, the *idea* of the book. Even if you manage to gobble one up, an identical echo will take its place. The spear that impales all three is where the real power lies. You must break the spear."

"How do I do that?" I asked.

"You're more than halfway there," she said. "You know where two of the three iterations are hidden."

"Northlight Tower, here in my world," I said, "and somewhere in Noir York."

"All you need is a means of passage."

She leaned in one last time, showing sharp teeth as she smiled like the Cheshire cat.

"Find the third," she purred, "and light three matches."

***

My eyes snapped open to the sound of my alarm clock going off. It was 11:52 in the morning. I hadn't set my alarm for 11:52. I slapped it until it stopped chirping at me. I was lying on top of my bedspread, lengthwise, still in last night's clothes. The desert sun poked ice-pick fingers around the corners of my blinds, stabbing me in the eyes while my head throbbed. My mouth was dry as a fossil.

Last night came back to me like a patchwork quilt, disjointed memories and scrambled images, blurs of sound and light. And one promise, above everything else.

She left you something in Springfield.

My phone buzzed. It took me a second to find it, lost somewhere in the tangle of sheets.

"Hey, sugar," Jennifer said. "You busy?"

"I'm...what do you call a hangover from too many magic mush-rooms?"

"A great party you clearly didn't invite me to."

"Forget it," I groaned, pushing myself up. "No, I'm not busy. What's going on?"

"I'm a little concerned. Pixie's been working overtime trying to crack this weirdness with Naavarasi's mail."

"Yeah, she told me about that."

"Well," Jen said, "now she's not answerin' my phone calls or my texts, and that ain't like her. I was gonna cruise over to her apartment and do a welfare check. You wanna come with, just in case something's hinky?"

"Give me twenty minutes to take a shower first."

"I'll come pick you up," she said.

Chapter Nine

The first thing I saw, as we rolled into the parking lot of Pixie's apartment building, was what I didn't see. Pix's wheels were her pride and joy. She'd taken an old GMC van and rechristened it "the Wardriver" after filling it with an electronics and counter-electronics suite that would make an FBI agent drool. It was a rolling hacker base and a home away from home, and it wasn't here.

"Hundred reasons she might be on the road," I said, picking up on Jennifer's worry. "We should swing by St. Jude's. She volunteers over there all the time. If she's not there now, somebody probably knows where she is."

She looked dubious. I knew that feeling. I'd tried reaching out to Pixie too, after Jen told me she'd gone silent, and she hadn't replied to any of my texts. Considering we were her two best and most regular clients, she wasn't in the habit of ignoring either of us.

"I feel like taking a closer look first."

"Whatever you want to do," I told her. "I'll back your play."

Jennifer parked her trusty Prius at the back of the lot and we walked over, side by side. The place was a dump, a two-floor walk-up nestled along a dusty corridor of gas stations and tourist traps, with tacked-up bedsheets serving as window blinds. Before long I saw the first signs of Pixie's handiwork: up ahead, in the eaves overlooking the open first-floor walkway and a flight of bare concrete steps, the tiny gray orb of a wireless web-camera nestled in a glistening spiderweb. Another camera kept watch over the second-floor landing, peeking out from behind the dome of an overhead light.

At her door, halfway down the open walk with the sun streaming over a dirty white stone railing, we knocked. And waited. And knocked again. And waited some more. In the silence, I sent Pixie another text. She left it unread.

Jennifer looked from me to the door, then back again.

"I'm rusty," she said.

I took a knee and pulled out my eelskin lockpick case. As I set to work, I thought about my last few visits. The lock wouldn't be a problem. The other side might be.

"Once I get this open," I told Jennifer, "we'll have to move fast. She's got a Centurion Slimline alarm box, just to the right of the door. While I pop it open, I need you to run over to her kitchen nook and grab something I can strip wires with. Should be a cheap pair of scissors in her rummage drawer, left of the sink. We'll only have thirty seconds and we'll have to make 'em count."

I was focused on the pick, my tension rake slowly turning, hunting for the perfect angle. Out of the corner of my eye I saw Jennifer stare at me, crossing her arms.

"Do you have an elaborate plan for breaking into *everybody's* place?"

I paused, meeting her gaze. "Don't you?"

She thought about that, then shrugged.

"Fair."

The worry wasn't needed, as it turned out. The door swung open and instead of the expected shrill electronic chirps of an alarm box demanding a code, we were greeted with...nothing. Stark silence. I led the way into Pixie's cluttered hobbit hole of an apartment. Like some robotic castaway's treasures, electronic detritus littered every surface. Battered thrift-store furniture plastered in band stickers carried the husks of vintage computers, scooped-out monitors, and more teakettles than any one woman needed to own.

I cupped my hands to my mouth. "Pix? You here? It's us."

Nothing.

"That ain't right," Jennifer said, squeezing through the clutter and poking her head into the bedroom. "She wouldn't leave without setting that alarm. That is *not* somethin' she'd forget."

I wanted to disagree, because disagreeing meant Pixie was fine, but I couldn't argue with the facts. I made my way over to a folding card table by the window, where one of her many treasured computing rigs sat in a shaft of pale and dusty light.

"You ain't gonna crack her password," Jennifer called out, exploring the other side of the apartment. "When Pix protects something, it stays protected."

I couldn't argue with that either. I had a lot of larcenous skills, but out-hacking a hacker wasn't one of them. I focused on the stray papers on her desk. Crumpled receipts, empty junk-mail envelopes, she'd jot notes on anything that would hold ink and most of it was incomprehensible code mixed with a few math problems long enough to make my eyes water.

Except for one note, a torn scrap of loose-leaf paper. In her terse hand she'd written: *DEN - hotbed of conspiracy theories. Related? Ask Dan about power of collective belief.*

Then, under it, a single word. She'd circled it and underlined it twice.

Springfield.

I turned, hearing footsteps on the outer walk. The front door opened with a creak, and Pixie arched one eyebrow as she leaned in.

"Uh, guys?" she said. "Why the hell are you in my apartment?"

***

"All is forgiven," Pixie told us, "as long as you didn't break my front door."

We were back outside, out in the sun, crossing the weed-infested parking lot. She'd been off the grid, she told us. Clearing her head, trying to get some perspective on the impossible problem of Naavarasi's shipments. She looked just like she always did, wearing ripped jeans and a faded vintage Wrestlemania T-shirt, her arms covered in chaotic tattoos.

"I mostly watched a lot of vintage movies over at the Lariat," she said. "Five bucks and you can pretty much sit there all day in the dark. Good place to think. My phone was turned off the whole time. Just basic courtesy, you know? I didn't see any of your messages until I left."

"Get any insights?" I asked.

"The more I look into it, the more I think you were right. There's nothing super weird going on. Whoever Naavarasi's buying her supplies from, they're just getting cute with the paper trail. They're clever, too, better at covering their tracks than most, but I'll crack the code. Just give me a couple of days."

"I called the fam," Jennifer said, walking on her other side. "We're all gonna meet up at the American, have a sit-down and compare notes. Mama Margaux's gonna be late. She's dealing with her boyfriend, or her ex-boyfriend—"

"Antoine?" I said. "Same guy. I keep asking her to introduce us, but every time I do, they break up again."

"Sounds good. Can you give me a ride? Wardriver's in the shop." Pixie gestured to her usual parking spot, still empty.

"What happened?" I asked.

"Just wore out the brake pads. I can do most repairs on my own, but what I don't have are the tools. Anyway, I'm picking it up first thing in the morning, so try not to need it between now and then."

Caitlin met us over at the club. I caught her hip by the door and reeled her in for a kiss.

"How's the defector?" I asked.

Caitlin rolled her eyes. "The first words he spoke when the hood came off were 'Not in the face, please.' We're still questioning him, but I'm ninety percent certain of his honesty. Well, his honesty in this one isolated situation. He really has no idea why Malphas turned on him, or how Naavarasi suddenly became the apple of his prince's eye."

"So he's useless."

"I wouldn't say that," she purred, hooking her arm around mine as we walked through the empty, plastic-shrouded nightclub. "He has over a century of inside dirt on the operations of his old court. We'll be milking him for months."

I winced. "Can we...find some other way to word that?"

Ahead of us, Jennifer squeezed Pixie's arm.

"Worried me sick," Jen muttered. "Don't disappear on us like that again."

"I'll make it up to you," Pixie promised. "How about we go out for drinks later? On me."

Jennifer blinked. "Sure," she said.

"Never know," Pix said. "You might get lucky."

She hip-bumped Jen and gave her a flirty wink.

The bottom of my stomach dropped out, like nobody told me I was on a roller coaster until we went over the first hill, straight into a death dive. I looked to Caitlin. Her eyes were hard, sharp, fixed on Pixie's back. She gave a tiny, almost imperceptible nod.

Pixie didn't drink. Pixie was straight-edge. No booze, no drugs, no fun. Didn't mean she didn't go out with Jennifer and me on the regular, ordering sodas at the club while we tried to drink each other under the table, so I could let her first comment slide. Not the second one.

Pixie didn't flirt, either. She was asexual, a fact I uncovered back when Jen was smitten with her and I tried to play matchmaker. Jennifer took it gracefully and they'd been tight friends ever since, but that was as far as things went.

Apparently, someone forgot to tell Pixie that.

I clamped down hard on my suspicions and put on my best poker face as we walked downstairs, past the security door, into what would eventually be my new inner sanctum. Bentley and Corman were waiting in the conference room, giving us a wave from the other side of the glass wall. Melanie was sitting at Bentley's side, her attention rapt as he showed her the inner workings of a card trick.

"Hey, kiddo," Corman said, pulling me into a tight hug. He was still a big guy, especially standing next to Bentley, but I couldn't miss how he'd been looking...withered lately. His clothes were loose, almost too big on him now. My dads were getting older.

I tried not to stare at Pixie. I hoped like hell I was worried about nothing. I wanted to chance a warning, but I couldn't risk being overheard. Instead, as Pixie took a seat halfway down the table, and Jennifer and Caitlin casually flanked her, I decided to take the indirect approach. I scooped up a loose dry-erase marker and tossed it over to Melanie, who caught it in her cupped hands.

"You can take notes," I said, nodding at the whiteboard wall on the other side of the conference room—as far away from Pixie as I could move her.

"Me?" she asked, surprised.

"Just like you always do." I answered her, but I looked from Bentley to Corman as I did it, meeting each man's eyes in turn.

They didn't say a word. They didn't need to; the faintest tightness at the corner of Corman's mouth, the twitch of Bentley's nose, told me the score. Far from a regular event, I'd never asked her to do that before. The whiteboard walls were a standard feature of the room but we were running a criminal conspiracy here; we didn't take notes. Besides, even if we did, Melanie's handwriting was worse than mine. Now they knew I was sending a signal. About what, I couldn't say until I got them out of Pixie's earshot, but at least they'd be on their guard.

"Okay," I said, "let's get started. First up, in case anyone hasn't heard, we've got Royce in custody. Doesn't sound like he's going to be very useful."

"To the vast surprise of nobody," Jennifer said.

"Pixie's been working on tracing the shipments to Naavarasi's place in Denver. Pix, want to give a quick recap?"

While she spoke I stayed on my feet, slowly circling the table like a shark. I wanted it to look natural when I ended up behind her.

"Well," she said, "like I told you back at my place, it looks like whoever she's doing business with is going all-out to cover their trails. I'll be able to crack it, though. Just give me a few more days."

I thought about the scribbled note back on her desk, her reminder to ask me about the power of collective belief.

"And you don't think anything supernatural is going on?" I asked.

Pix shook her head. "Not in the slightest."

"What about Springfield?"

She froze, seizing up as her mental engine stalled. Just for a second, then she recovered like a pro.

"Dead end," she said. "I saw that name come up in connection with the shipments, but it wasn't anything, just a red herring."

"And the...power of collective belief?"

She narrowed her eyes. "Doesn't ring a bell."

I timed my follow-up carefully, holding it for the perfect moment: when my slow circuit around the room brought me to stand directly behind her.

"Got it from a note on Pixie's desk. You probably would have remembered...if you had written it."

She tried to jump up from her chair, but Caitlin and Jennifer were waiting for a sign and that was good enough. They grabbed her by the arms and roughly spun her around. Caitlin got her forearm against Pixie's throat, slamming her onto the conference table on her back and pinning her like a bug. Jennifer curled her fingers around the collar of Pixie's shirt and gave it a savage yank, ripping it at the neck and baring a bra strap and one smooth shoulder.

"She's got ink all over this shoulder," Jennifer hissed. "You only copied the tattoos on her arms. You half-assed the job, shitheel."

Pixie's eyes flashed tiger-orange. Vivid fur rippled along her arm, rising and fading in a flicker of color. She brought her knees up to her chest, tight, and lashed out her heels like pistons. They hit me in the chest with a bone-jolting crack and suddenly I was weightless, flying backward, hitting an empty chair and taking it down with me as I smashed into the carpet in a winded, dazed tangle of limbs.

The Pixie-thing backhanded Jennifer with one furry paw and grabbed Caitlin's neck with the other, eyes burning like jack-o'-lantern flames. One heave and she launched Caitlin through the conference room window, blasting her through to the other side in a shower of broken glass.

Chapter Ten

Caitlin hit the hall on the other side of the broken window like a rag doll, landing on her shoulder and rolling, trailed by a cascade of shattered glass that fell like glittering diamonds.

My cards were already riffling from their pack, leaping from my breast pocket into my outstretched hand as I pushed myself up from the floor. My chest burned like fire, one leg wobbly and threatening to buckle under my weight. The Pixie-thing—not Pixie at all now, as it grew, shedding its human form, pale skin melting into ripples of orange and black fur—loomed over Jennifer. The creature's clothes tore, seams popping under bulging animal muscle, bones crackling as its face stretched into a muzzle lined with drooling fangs.

I let a card fly. It winged through the conference room like a steel hornet, ripping across the rakshasa's shoulder and painting the whiteboard wall in a spatter of dark ichor. He spun around. One of Naavarasi's sons, no doubt of it now. He started to lumber toward me when Bentley flung out his hand, tossing a trail of white sand across the carpet in his path. The rakshasa suddenly wavered, confused as the air hardened between us. He turned and Corman was already there, slashing the air with his outstretched hand, throwing down a second jagged strip of enchanted sand.

"That won't hold for—" Bentley started to say. The rakshasa brought up both clenched paws and slammed them down. The occult shield crumpled like a wad of tinfoil. Before the creature could take another step, a second playing card—not mine—sliced across his cheek and drew an irritated yowl of pain. He spun on his heel, claws clicking as his baleful eyes focused on Melanie.

That was the distraction Jennifer needed. She ripped a razor blade across her forearm, her blood gushing. Then she captured the crimson flow on the whispered syllables of a spell and twisted it, braiding it like hair, calcifying it with the power of her will and turning the blood into a jagged, thorny spear that jutted from her wound. She rammed into the rakshasa from behind, impaling him through the kidney.

The spear broke in half as he twisted around and sent her reeling to the carpet with a brutal slap. Then he had all of a second to look up. With a feral roar, Caitlin launched herself through the broken window, hitting the rakshasa in a full-body tackle, momentum carrying them both onto the conference table, rolling over it, then hitting the floor on the other side with Caitlin on top. She rained punches onto his face, fangs snapping, gouts of black blood staining the carpet as he howled and struggled to squirm out from under her.

"Cait," I croaked, clutching my injured ribs, "we need him alive."

She tilted her head back, raising her blood-smeared cheeks to the overhead lights, and took a deep breath through gritted teeth as she fought to get her anger under control.

Then she nodded, once, and went surgical. She flipped the tiger-beast onto his belly and wrenched one arm behind his back. He screeched as she broke it at the elbow. Then she twisted the other one, breaking his wrist, shattered bone poking out through torn flesh and fur.

"Welcome to the rest of your existence," she growled in the creature's ear. "That pain you're feeling right now? I promise you: it only gets worse from here."

Corman helped me up, pulling me to my feet. I curled one arm over my chest, wincing.

"Find something to tie him up with," I said.

***

The nice thing about an active construction site was that there were plenty of odds and ends lying around, ready to be put to good use. Like a set of sturdy chains and some heavy-duty padlocks. We dragged the dazed rakshasa upstairs and wrestled him into a chair, trussed up like Houdini about to perform an escape routine. Our captive might have been a seasoned assassin, but he was no Houdini.

Jennifer got the first aid kit out from behind the bar and I held my shirt up while she taped my ribs.

"Nothin' broken," she said, poking at me while I winced, "but you're gonna have a beaut of a bruise."

"Lucky. Cait, you okay?"

She answered the question with a dour look as she strode past me, still picking bits of broken glass from her scarlet curls. Naavarasi's infiltrator had hurt her pride, not her body. Bad news for him. A physical injury, she might have been willing to forgive.

"Right," I said, pushing myself away from the bar and walking over to stand in front of our hostage. "Let's talk about how incredibly fucked you are. First question, and don't even think about lying: is Pixie still alive?"

The rakshasa's muzzle curled into a bloody, broken-fanged rictus.

"How would I know?" he growled.

Jennifer took a threatening step toward the chair. "Where is she? Where's Pix?"

"Does it upset you," he asked, "knowing how badly you failed her? A babe in the woods, no magic to speak of, no defense against our kind, and you walked her right into our claws. Her suffering is your fault."

"Speaking of suffering—" She reached for her razor blade and strode toward him. I got in between them, fast, and pitched my voice low.

"That's what he wants," I whispered. "You can't torture this guy for information. He's a zealot. Zealots don't break like normal people."

"Maybe I just wanna do it for my personal satisfaction," she fired back.

"He's trying to goad us into killing him. Death is the closest thing he has to an escape route, and he knows it. Don't take the bait."

Jennifer pursed her lips, dubious. "Got a better plan?"

"I might. Let me take a shot at him. If I fail, you and Caitlin can go third-degree on his ass all day and all night, but let me try first."

She relented. I stepped up to the plate.

Interrogation was an art form. What you gleaned from a stray word, a careless slip, a guilty glance, could tell you more than a full confession. Ideally, you should never ask a question you didn't already know the answer to. We didn't have that luxury today...but our prisoner didn't know that.

"Let's try this again," I told him. "You people jumped Pixie when you caught her investigating Naavarasi's paper trail. Naavarasi recognized her, knew she was part of the New Commission crew, and saw a golden opportunity to infiltrate."

"She died screaming for her mother," the tiger-spirit hissed. A fat slimy tongue lapped across his bloody chops. I bit back on a sudden surge of fear and shook my head.

"No, she didn't. She's still alive. You might be stupid enough to kill a perfectly good hostage, but your mother isn't. She'd keep Pix alive and safe until you came back from your mission. And you know why, right?"

I leaned closer, locking eyes with the tiger.

"Because you don't mean shit to her," I said. "And you were supposed to fail this mission. This all happened exactly the way Naavarasi planned it."

His flickering eyes narrowed to furious slits. "That's not true."

"I can prove it." I wasn't actually sure of that, but I sold the lie like I believed it in my heart of hearts. "Who briefed you and gave you your marching orders?"

"Mother did."

"And what did she tell you about Pixie and Jennifer?"

He shook his head, not following. "That...they used to be lovers, had a falling out, and were rebuilding their friendship."

I shared a look with Jennifer, who tilted her head.

"Lemme guess," Jen added. "She told you that you didn't need to waste time copying her shoulder tats because nobody would look."

"How...how did you know that?"

"What were your orders?" I asked, keeping him on the ropes before he could muster time to think and regroup. "Once you infiltrated the meeting and found out what we were up to, what was the next step?"

"R-return home," he said, "to the restaurant in Denver. I was told to travel there directly, no stops on the way."

"Sidebar!" I called out.

I gathered my family together in a circle, standing out of the chained creature's earshot.

"So what we have here is a sacrificial lamb," I murmured. "Naavarasi sent him out with faulty intel, on purpose."

"Best-case scenario, we don't notice and spill all of our plans," Bentley mused. "He goes home, reports in, and now Naavarasi knows everything that we know."

"Sure," Corman said, scowling back over his shoulder, "but what's the worst case? What does she get out of sending a clueless spy with a bad cover story? It's sloppy. She doesn't do sloppy."

I studied the angles like a billiards player lining up a shot. It wasn't hard to see the upside once I reminded myself to think like the self-proclaimed "mistress of illusions."

"Because it's a trap," I said. "Melanie?"

As always, she didn't disappoint me.

"We're supposed to figure it out," she said. "Naavarasi wanted us to realize we had an impostor, then follow him to her restaurant. Which means...she's not there and neither is Pixie. Probably a dozen rakshasa warriors waiting for us, or maybe just a really big bomb."

Caitlin nodded in agreement. "There's nothing we want in Denver. She wouldn't try to lure us there otherwise. This is all one big distraction to keep us chasing our tails while she does...whatever it is she's doing in Prince Malphas's court."

"Nothing we want at her restaurant," I said, "but I'm not ready to write off Denver just yet. Hold on, I want to try something."

I broke from the huddle and strode over to the chained-up rakshasa.

"Pixie is in Springfield."

A statement, not a question. He reacted with a sudden start, a flicker of guilty recognition in his burning eyes.

"Don't know what that is," he grunted.

"Really? Because back in the conference room you claimed it was a lead that didn't pan out. Not good at keeping your story straight, are you?"

"What's the difference? It's nothing. Meaningless."

That look of surprise when he found me and Jen at Pixie's apartment, I thought. *That was genuine. He didn't expect anyone to be there. So why go?*

Because he'd just finished abducting and copying her. He needed to scrub her apartment, find every last trace of intel she'd gathered, and make it all disappear. But we interrupted him, so he doesn't KNOW what Pix wrote down or what we might have learned from it.

"The thing about Pixie," I said, "is that she takes copious notes. And she'd been tracking your mama's shipping manifestos for weeks."

He was smart enough to give me nothing but sullen silence.

"We know all about Springfield," I told him. "You know, the Oceanic Airlines connection? Val Verde?"

"You're bluffing."

I was running on fumes, but Pixie's chicken scratch gave me one connection to lay on the table, if I could play it just right.

"I've already got my flight lined up. Nonstop, straight out of Denver International." I spread my open hands. "Come on, did you really think we wouldn't figure it out?"

Chains rattled as the rakshasa suddenly lunged at me, chair legs thumping, nearly toppling over before he caught himself. I stood calmly out of reach, and his body language gave me all the answers I needed. I stepped back and regrouped with the rest of the crew.

"Pix was laser-focused on those shipments," I said. "I'm betting she found something even bigger out there. Something at that airport that Naavarasi wants to keep hidden."

"Hence trying to steer us on a wild goose chase," Caitlin murmured, "and lure us into a trap in her old lair. If we die, she wins. If we survive but assume there was nothing of value to be found and go home empty-handed, she still wins."

"How very...*her*," Bentley said.

"Cait? Road trip?"

She gave me a grim nod. "With pleasure."

Melanie held up a hopeful hand and wriggled her fingers. I shared a glance with Caitlin, thought it over, then nodded my assent. More hands would make for lighter work.

"Recon and fact-finding only," I told her. "If shit gets weird or more of Naavarasi's kids show up, you're on the first flight back to Vegas."

"Deal," Melanie promised. I pretended to believe her.

"Seems to me," Corman said, "we've got a golden opportunity here."

I saw his angle. Our greatest weakness right now was the one Naavarasi concealed for over a year while she was playing out her long con: all of our methods and spells for detecting a rakshasa in disguise simply...didn't work. Every time we'd confidently pierced one of her disguises, it was because she wanted us to, building a sense of false security before yanking the rug out from under our feet.

She was raising an army of shape-shifting monsters, intent on invading both earth and hell alike, and we couldn't fight what we couldn't see.

"While we're gone," I said to Corman and Bentley, "go to work on this asshole. Figure out what makes him tick and find a way to pierce his disguises. We might not get another live specimen or another shot like this."

"I'll stay too," Jennifer said. "I've been wantin' to get my hands on some rak blood, to see what my magic can do with it."

She fixed the beast with a glare of cold, simmering fury. "Seems to me, he's got plenty to share."

Chapter Eleven

Another day, another flight, steel wings rippling in a jet-fuel mirage as they lifted us up to the azure sky.

"When this is all over," I said, nestled into my window seat, "I'm taking a vacation."

"Define 'this,'" Caitlin said, her fingertips trailing along my sleeve.

"I don't know. Multiple cosmos-spanning threats and the risk of an interdimensional apocalypse?"

"Live long enough, pet, and you learn to take these things in stride. My people already had one apocalypse."

I lifted my eyebrows, curious.

"The civil war, the years of blood and iron." Her lips became a pert bow. "Imagine the worst horrors of your world's 'Great War,' the trenches, the slaughter, the famine and disease, and then magnify it a hundredfold. We bombed ourselves into rubble and ruin. And yet the survivors clawed their way out. They rebuilt."

"That's...inspiring. I suppose."

She showed her pearly teeth. "I'm only saying that humans, with your limited life spans, have a misunderstanding of history. You often think that history is a rising line. That a civilization goes from primitive to sophisticated, from the caves to the high-rises. In reality it's more like a jagged and random path. Empires rise, empires fall and sometimes rise again, the humble rise to greatness and the great are forgotten, left in rubble like the statue of Ozymandias."

"Two vast and trunkless legs of stone in the desert," I said, recalling Shelley's poem.

"Look upon his works and despair, for his mighty deeds are long gone and no man alive remembers them." Caitlin quirked a smile. "But *people*...people remain. People survive. They find a way."

"While I agree with you in principle," I said, "I've been to one of the planets the Enemy burned. Nobody found a way out. He's a universe-class threat and we don't have the tools we need to fight him. Meanwhile, Naavarasi's running wild and shitting things up and we don't even know what her endgame is, only that she's trying to wreck both of our worlds. I don't need the distraction right now."

"She's very inconsiderate," Caitlin conceded.

"It'd be nice if our enemies lined up to fight one at a time is all I'm saying."

And now we were bound for Denver International, a little pocket of weirdness all its own. DEN had been a hotbed of rumors since the early nineties. Conspiracy theorists latched on to a dedication capstone bearing a Masonic compass and a mention of the "New World Airport Commission," with the promise that a time capsule under the monument wouldn't be unveiled until the year 2094. Inscriptions along the terminal walls were written in Navajo, with references to the periodic table of elements. A thirty-foot-tall sculpture of a cobalt-blue horse with glowing red eyes turned heads, and if that didn't seem odd enough, there was another runway where you could glide past a twenty-foot statue of Anubis, the Egyptian god of the dead. Then there were the literal gargoyles.

Depending on who you asked and what strata of the internet they hid under, Denver International was the source of a Satanic conspiracy, a landing strip for aliens, the place where wealthy elites would gather to celebrate the rise of the New World Order, or the front for an Illuminati science lab. Maybe all of those things at once. I was less than convinced. Most of the conspiracy theories swirling around DEN fell apart the second you applied some basic research skills. The rest I discounted because nobody in the occult underground wanted to claim the place. Malphas and his court had nothing to do with the airport's construction, and the rare times it had come up in conversation with Caitlin's colleagues, it was clear the infernal powers were clueless.

Of course, there were other powers. The Network was the closest thing I'd seen to a real-life Illuminati, and I wouldn't have put it past them to use an urban legend as cover, but they were more about subverting local cults and making their nests in isolated, dismal places like the old sanitation plant back in Vegas. The Network was a deadly and polished machine, but they were still career criminals at heart; a massive, hugely popular airport, sitting on federal property and filled with security cameras and armed guards, wasn't a very inviting hideout for most crooks.

At the end of the day, the question wasn't "Who would want to build a stronghold hidden inside of Denver International?" so much as "Who would want the hassle of *dealing* with a stronghold inside DEN?" My enemies were, with a few glaring exceptions, pragmatic people.

And yet here we were, sailing in over a dark-paved ribbon of runway, the plane shuddering on a rough wind as the landing gear touched down with a bone-jarring thump. As we walked through a crowded concourse, white walls on one side and glass on the other looking out over the tarmac, our first stop was obvious. We checked the parking garage. We were hunting for a needle in a haystack, but at least Pixie's van was a big needle.

We found it on the second level. The Wardriver sat caked in road dirt, the engine cold as ice. No damage, no signs of a fight. I popped the lock and checked inside. Predictably, when I pulled her sun visor down, a parking receipt fluttered free. I caught the cardboard ticket in my hand.

"Yesterday morning," I said. "She parked yesterday morning."

Meaning they'd had her for over twenty-four hours. Over a day, spent at Naavarasi's nonexistent mercy. My stomach clenched. I pushed my fears aside and quickly checked the back of the van. Again, nothing out of place.

"Something went down," I said, hopping out of the van, "but it didn't happen here."

"Naavarasi's people must have grabbed her once she got out of the van," Melanie said. She paused, squinting at the elevators up ahead. "Or she's still at the airport."

Pixie would have known the score. If she let the rakshasas drag her out of this airport, away from the bustle and the crowds, her odds of survival would drop like a rock. She would have raised hell first, done anything she could to draw attention even if it meant risking her life. The alternative was worse. And yet she'd just...vanished.

I led the way back into Terminal East, grappling with my own frustration, my helplessness. If there was a clue here, somewhere in this vast and sprawling airport, I had to find it. I just didn't know where to start looking. In the broad, towering gallery of baggage counters and ticket lines, I glanced at an arrival and departure board. I was looking for Oceanic Airlines. Of course I came up empty. No such thing.

A woman brushed past me. She was tall, with a mane of curly jet-black hair and long, pale arms, sheathed in a tight halter dress the color of freshly spilled blood. I smelled roses on the air.

Her? I thought. She was already past me, moving at a brisk clip, making her way through a dense crowd of travelers. I broke ahead, scurrying to catch up, intent on seeing her face.

I lost her at the edge of the pack. She was there, a retreating figure deep in the churning throng of people, and then she just...wasn't.

"Pet?" Caitlin said, jogging to catch up. "What did you see?"

"I thought it was..."

The Lady in Red.

"Nothing." I shook my head. "I made a mistake."

Then I glanced past Caitlin's shoulder, and my blood ran cold. The figure up ahead was anything but a mistake or a hallucination. He was real as me, a bland-faced figure in a bland gray houndstooth suit, with a face seemingly engineered to be as unremarkable as possible. He just slid off the eyes, designed to be forgotten.

I remembered him, though. I remembered because the last time we crossed paths, I put a bullet right between his eyes.

Mr. Smith was a fixer for the Network. He didn't seem to be a literal monster like some of their operatives or a world-class sorcerer. He just had this really irritating habit of coming back from the dead.

To be fair, that description could apply to me, too, but he made it look easy.

"Network ops on the scene," I murmured as Caitlin and Melanie followed my gaze. "You know the worst thing about airport travel? Can't bring our guns along."

"We don't need guns," Melanie said. "We've got a Caitlin."

"Okay, fair. But for this guy in particular, I want a gun."

They didn't need prompting. Melanie and Cait spread out, weaving through the crowds, a flanking maneuver as I stayed on Smith's tail. He was preoccupied. At first I thought he was engrossed in his phone, like most the people milling around the terminal, but the object half-concealed in his smooth-handed grip was made of transparent plastic.

The skin prickled along the back of my neck as he walked down a side hallway, past doors marked for airport employees and TSA only. Then he came to stand in front of a blank white wall at the hallway's end.

He raised the object in his hand. It was a flask, capped with a screw top and stamped with industrial lettering that I couldn't make out from here. I could see the contents just fine, though, sloshing up against the plastic with a mind of its own. The fluid glowed, a cool and luminous green that cast Smith's upraised face in unholy light.

Then he took a step forward, walked straight through the wall, and vanished.

I wasn't letting him get away. I broke into a charge, barreling in his wake, turning my shoulder as the wall loomed before me and praying I wasn't about to make a stupid and bone-breaking mistake. I felt a dizzying rush as I burst through the illusory wall, a wash of static like ants crawling over my body, and then I was on the other side with my eyes trying to adjust to a sudden gulf of darkness. We stood in a mechanical underbelly, a warren of tight tunnels lined with exposed pipes and valves, the metalworks rattling as some vast engine roared overhead.

Smith heard me coming. He wheeled around in the shadows and went for his hip, pulling a pocket-sized pistol as I closed the distance. I slapped his hand as he pulled the trigger. The bullet blew out a pipe, metal rupturing, white-hot steam hissing in a volcanic gout while my eardrums stung. We grappled for the weapon and I got him turned around, driving my heel into the back of his leg and forcing him to one knee before I ripped the steel free and flipped it around in my hand, pressing the muzzle to the back of his skull.

"Don't," he said.

Sudden footsteps burst to life behind me. The illusory wall baffled sound as well as sight: I didn't know Caitlin and Melanie were on my heels until they suddenly appeared on our side of the veil, blinking and disoriented.

"Look who I caught," I told them. "A walking dead man."

"Who *are* you?" he whispered. Then it registered. "Oh. You. You've lost some weight, Mr. Faust. And a decade of age. The new body looks good on you. The last we heard, you were dead and in hell. My employers should have known better than to assume that was the end of you. I told them it was a bad gamble to take you so lightly."

I snatched the thin plastic flask from his hand. One look at the stark black letters on the side and I knew where I'd seen this bubbling green goo before.

Ausar Biomedical, the stark print read. *Viridithol Lot ***93*, and then a production date too scratched up to read.

Viridithol was a miracle fertility drug, until it wasn't. When dozens of expectant mothers gave birth to mutated and deformed babies, the scandal brought the entire company crashing down. The truth was even worse: Ausar's scientists had found a gateway to the fallen Garden of Eden, and their miracle drug was made from the clippings of alien plants. I only knew about it because one of my oldest enemies, a corporate tycoon named Lauren Carmichael, thought she could use the drug—in tandem with a mass human sacrifice—to become a literal goddess.

I thought I was done with this shit. I thought the last samples of Ausar's doomed experiment had been rounded up and destroyed ages ago. Turned out I was wrong about a lot of things. The one thing I knew, for certain, was that Viridithol was literal, concentrated evil.

Cosmic cancer. I held the flask close to Smith's upturned face, keeping him on his knees.

"You know who I am, you know who my friends are, and you know what we're ready and willing to do to you." I loomed over him. "Seems like this place is soundproof. Which is good for us because it means nobody heard your gun go off. Bad for you because nobody will hear if it goes off again. You follow me?"

"Start talking," Caitlin told him.

Chapter Twelve

"You know that we had an...agreement with the Enemy," Smith said.

No shit. I remembered being tied to a chair at the edge of a cockroach-infested trash pit while Elmer Donaghy, the Network's golden boy, argued with Ms. Fleiss, the Enemy's...honestly, I wasn't sure what she was to him. His whipping girl, mostly. I tried to save her once. She didn't want to be saved. I didn't know how to deal with that and I was still figuring it out.

"He's obsessed with you," Smith said, "which worked out well for us, considering you've been a thorn in our side long before you even knew what the Network was. Your little spat with the Chicago Mafia, back in the day? We were backing Chicago. Damien Ecko, the necromancer? He was one of our assets, though he never knew it, even after he died."

I glanced at the luminous green flask.

"Going to tell me you were behind Lauren Carmichael, too?"

His shoulders sagged. "No. Actually, we didn't know about that affair until it was over and done. Embarrassing to admit. We would have helped you if we knew."

"Out of the goodness of your hearts?"

Mr. Smith sighed. "Will you forgive a cliché?"

"Depends."

"We're not so different, you and I," he said.

"That," I said, "is the one cliché I will never forgive."

"And yet I'm right. You command the Vegas mob—"

"*Second* chair," I said.

I could have taken the New Commission if I wanted to. After watching Jennifer get treated like the hired help by the boys from Chicago, when they bothered to acknowledge her at all, I decided she needed to be in charge. There was no shame in playing second fiddle to a world-class musician.

"You do exactly what we do," Smith said, "just on a...much smaller scale."

"*We* don't work for the Kings of Man," Caitlin said.

"No, of course not. You work for the powers of hell instead. That's much better."

Melanie came over to stand at my side. She stared down at the kneeling man, her eyes harder than I'd ever seen them. Black veins rippled and faded on her cheeks as she fought to keep her demonic blood under control.

"I was born this way," she told him. "Were you born to serve the Kings, or was it a choice you made?"

Smith curled his lips in a pale imitation of a smile.

"Actually, young lady, I was *created* to serve. Though I take your point. Let me turn that around and ask you something: have you considered how much happier you'd be on a planet ruled by the Network?"

Melanie pursed her lips and stared at him.

"The Kings feed on fear and misery," I said.

"And so do you," he replied. "Do you think you invented crime, my larcenous friend? The first thieves and killers in human history were on our payroll. A few of them are still around. You're no better than me."

Melanie shook her head. "If you people take over, nobody wins. Not even you."

"To the contrary." Smith chuckled, a low and rich sound. "The most favored servants of the Kings will live like...well. Royalty. After all, somebody has to guard the concentration camps."

The gun I took from him started to tremble in my hand. My fingertip stroked the trigger.

"As soon as I figure out how you keep coming back from the dead," I seethed, "we're going to make it permanent."

He shrugged like he didn't have a care in the world. "More enterprising souls than you have tried."

Caitlin crossed her arms. She'd been quiet, studying the man like an entomologist with a rare bug.

"Are you here on the Enemy's behalf," she asked, "or Naavarasi's?"

"Neither. We never had a relationship with that bestial...*thing*, and we cut ties with the Enemy. It was a relationship of pure convenience."

"I thought it was weird," I said. "The interdimensional Mafia hooking up with the ruiner of worlds? I mean, you're not stupid, I'll give you that much. You had to know he wouldn't spare you."

"We had no illusions. But like I said, he's obsessed with you. Made it easy for us to make a deal. When Elmer Donaghy captured you, we offered you up on a plate. Then you slipped away. We tried again, using your brother as bait, but..." He gave me a rueful smile. "We all know how that ended. Point being, the Enemy gave us what we wanted, so your continued survival was no longer our problem."

He glanced to the side, looking at Melanie.

"We stopped taking his phone calls after that. We, ah...what do you young people call it these days? We ghosted him."

The obvious question was what they wanted in exchange for my head. The obvious answer was in my other hand. I looked to the plastic vial of green, bubbling liquid, still bearing its stamp straight from the drug factory. Trying to fix their own mistakes, the brain trust at Ausar Biomedical had opened a doorway to the Enemy's prison. Then they conjured a pair of jailers, the smoke-faced men, but the cure was almost as bad as the disease.

"Eden," I said. "There's a portal straight to the Garden of Eden on this planet. The Enemy knows where it is. You wanted it for yourselves."

"And why shouldn't we? The Network was born in Eden. It belongs to us. Once he gave us the location of the conduit, we had no further use for the Enemy. We decided to let it play. Either you'd find the Paladin and manage to save this dying planet—at which point we'd step in and take control—or he'd burn it to ashes and we'd meet him on a more favorable battlefield sometime in the future. We are eternal, Mr. Faust. We can wait."

"We are also eternal," Caitlin said, staring daggers at him.

The corner of Mr. Smith's mouth dimpled.

"Ah, yes. Hundreds upon hundreds of parallel Earths, and this is the only one with a hell attached. You demons are...singular, really. Utterly alone in the cosmos. Even your creator abandoned you. It must be terribly lonely."

Caitlin's eyes flashed with fury.

"Lucifer," she spat, "will return to us."

"What tells you so? Faith?" He shook his head. "I'm a Network man. We don't deal in faith. We lay our bets with certainty. *My* gods are alive and well. I just talked to one this morning. Where is yours?"

Her left hand twitched at her side. Her fingernails began to stretch, turning black, sharp as a mortician's scalpel. I eased between them, giving her a tiny headshake. He was provoking her. Probably hoped she'd rip his throat out before he gave up any more intel, considering—as far as we knew—he'd be right back anyway.

I took in the tunnel around us. Steam still gushed from the ruptured pipe, washing the thick shadows in fog, the wet heat like Florida at high noon.

"Let's cut to the chase," I said. "Where are we, what's with the illusion-wall, and why are you walking around Denver International with a vial of Viridithol?"

"I don't know, I don't know, and that's the entire issue. We've commenced operations at the Eden conduit—"

"Doing what?" Melanie demanded.

"Join us and find out," Smith replied. "Barring that, you can go ahead and torture me for information if it makes you feel better, but I honestly don't know."

"Bullshit," I said. "You're the Network's top fixer. No chance you don't know what your bosses are up to."

He reached up and tapped his temple with a perfectly manicured fingernail.

"The information was removed from my brain before I was sent on this mission, in case I fell into enemy hands. Like...well, the exact situation we're in right now. Routine procedure. I know only what I need to know, nothing more and nothing less. I'm built for purpose, you see. My employers will restore my memories once I return to them."

"Optimistic," Caitlin said, "assuming you're getting out of here in one piece instead of several bloody chunks."

"Oh, I make no such assumptions. As I said, we don't bank on faith. You *want* to keep me alive."

"You're going to have to back that up," I told him, "because right now, I'm not feeling it."

He glanced from my gun to the vial in my other hand. "I don't have to teach you the basic principle of sympathetic magic, do I?"

He did not. "Like attracts like."

"Correct. Our Eden operation has suffered a major setback. The conduit's power is being...stolen. Siphoned. At first we thought it was the Enemy, some sort of petulant reprisal because he didn't get what he wanted out of our bargain. It isn't him."

I didn't have to ask how he knew. Caitlin offered up the answer first: "You have a spy in his organization."

"We've had several over the years actually." Smith's nose twitched in distaste. "He keeps *changing* them. Dealing with a madman who can rewrite a person's life with a touch of his hand is excruciatingly complicated, to say the least. It was easy enough to track the leak to this airport, but that's where the trail ran cold, so I was sent to investigate."

I held up the flask, feeling the burbling goo twitch against the warm, clammy plastic.

"You're using this as a compass."

"Like attracts like," he said. He nodded to the blank brick wall we'd all stumbled through. "Where we are at the moment, and who created that illusion, is as much a mystery to me as it is to you. I'm aware of Denver's reputation as a hotbed for conspiracy theories but, alas, this isn't one of our projects. All I know for certain is that this isn't a recent construction. There's no chance someone financed and engineered something like this at a major international airport without my employers noticing. Conclusion: it's been here for quite some time. Possibly from the early nineties, when the airport was originally built. That would have been the easiest time."

"Same people who made the portal to Eden?" I asked.

"Very possibly, though that's been around a lot longer. Centuries longer. I'm not normally inclined to editorialize before I know all the facts, but this place feels...grafted on. Something feels *parasitic* about it, and that rankles me." Smith raised his chin, looking me in the eye, and pushed his shoulders back. "I'm a Network man. We are the power behind every throne. We are the cold nugget of truth at the core of every paranoid delusion. We puppet the puppet masters."

"And you're so modest, too," Melanie muttered.

He ignored her and kept talking. "This wasn't the Enemy's work. Wasn't yours, either, clearly. You were our second most likely suspect, Mr. Faust. I hope you can take some pleasure in that."

"Little bit," I admitted. It was nice to be suspected. Meant they cared.

"It wasn't the work of the infernal powers, either. Prince Malphas didn't want this airport built in the first place."

Caitlin put her hands on her hips. "And you know that how, exactly?"

"Because when I started investigating, I found an interesting legal challenge dating back to 1988, opposing the annexation of Adams County. Do you know Royce, Malphas's hound?"

Former hound. Apparently the all-powerful puppet masters at the Network had some gaps in their intel. "We're familiar with him," I said.

"One of his civilian identities is the head of a prestigious law firm. His signature is on the opposition letter. Near as I can tell, there was no great scheme in play. Malphas had financial investments in the county, investments that Mr. Royce thought might be threatened by new construction. After that he tried to infiltrate the construction committee, presumably to embezzle funds from the federal investment. He failed, utterly. This wasn't hell's work."

I knew exactly who to blame. Pixie went missing on this very trail, and Naavarasi's claws were all over the place. That said, the facts didn't fit. The rakshasa queen was a dangerous powerhouse, I'd never deny that, but she wasn't a political operator, wasn't particularly rich, and she didn't have the juice to build a nest in the heart of an international airport.

Someone else built it, I thought. *Then she...found it? Took it for herself and put it to work?* I was playing straight poker, but I only had two cards in my hand. Not enough to win.

"I have a proposal," Mr. Smith told me. "Let's make a deal."

"A bargain with the Network?" Caitlin arched one sculpted eyebrow. "That never ends well."

"I disagree. It usually ends quite well for my employers. The simple truth is I have no leverage here, especially not with a literal gun to my head. You're free to murder me if you like. I cannot stop you, though we all know that I'll be back. Still, a painful inconvenience that I'd prefer to avoid. We have a common enemy here. And the enemy of my enemy..."

He trailed off, giving me an expectant look.

"You want to team up," I said.

"It's the most rational choice," Mr. Smith said. "I suggest a temporary truce. Peace. For the moment."

Chapter Thirteen

I told Smith to stay on his knees, and I kept his gun handy. I needed some advice. I stepped back with Caitlin and Melanie and lowered my voice.

"He's not wrong," I said.

Melanie blinked at me. "Are you serious? We can't trust him!"

"I didn't say anything about trust. But Naavarasi is running circles around us and she's got Pixie. We need all the help we can get, for her sake."

Caitlin nodded, grave. "Smith is motivated to cooperate. Bodily harm doesn't frighten him, but his masters do, and they ordered him to investigate the power leak. I don't know what they'll do if he returns empty-handed, but I'm fairly certain it will be *deeply* unpleasant. He's in over his head and he knows it."

"What if he stabs us in the back?" Melanie asked.

"I guarantee he'll try," I said, "but only once he gets what he needs. We'll just have to be faster on the draw."

I walked over and handed Smith the flask of Viridithol. The green goo cast a luminous glow against his perfectly smooth fingertips.

"I'm keeping your gun," I told him.

"I would expect nothing less."

"Let's be real clear on something," I said. "You need us. We don't need you. We can *use* you, but we don't *need* you. Contemplate that when you start feeling froggy. On your feet. You're taking the lead."

"Ah," he said, rising and stretching. "A canary in the coal mine."

I nodded up the tunnel. "You got it. Start walking."

The tunnel made no sense. In spots it went so narrow we had to squeeze through in single file, pressed in by naked and rust-spotted pipes on either side of the crumbling brick walls. Other stretches widened to the point you could drive a baggage cart right down the aisle. Yellow bulbs under wire cages offered puddles of light here and there, but there were no signs, no markers, nothing to even suggest what this place was meant for. As we made another right turn, the tunnel widening out and stretching into the darkness ahead, Melanie tugged my sleeve.

"This is impossible," she whispered.

"Highly improbable at least, I'll give you that. I've seen weirder."

"No," she said, "I mean this is literally impossible. Look."

She held out her hand, drawing an imaginary map with her fingertip along her palm.

"This is the direction we came in from. Then we turned right, about here, and another turn about fifty feet down the tunnel." She traced a jagged U-shape, showing me the problem. "We've been in this chunk of hallway *way* longer than we were on the first stretch, and headed in the opposite direction. Either I'm taking crazy pills or we should be standing in the ticket concourse right now."

On a hunch, I checked my phone. I expected no bars. What I got was one level beyond that.

"Anyone else have 'no carrier'?" I asked.

Everyone took out their phones. Even Mr. Smith, who carried a
bland late-model Android in an equally bland and gray herringbone
case.

"We appear to have left the building," he said.

There were voices up ahead. I raised a hand, taking point. I pressed
myself to the tunnel wall, getting low, and the others followed my lead.
Two voices, two men. I couldn't make out the words from here, but
the tone wasn't happy.

I didn't like the feel of the exposed pipe against my hand. It
throbbed under my fingertips, tracing the rush of water or maybe fuel,
but there was something disconcertingly rubbery about the rusted
steel. The pace of the flowing liquid came in steady, strident bursts,
like the beating of a heart.

"They're speaking Hindi," Smith breathed, right at my shoulder.

"Can you understand it?"

He squinted.

"One's grousing about being 'left behind,' some kind of guard duty
he didn't want. The other is..." Smith's slate-gray eyes turned curious.
"Afraid."

"Afraid of what?"

"This tunnel. Something happened here recently. Something that
scared him."

I checked the load in my borrowed gun. Four bullets in the mag.

"It's about to get a lot scarier," I said. "Cait?"

"Remove one," she said. "I'll try to keep the other one alive."

I had a target, and I had a weapon. Sometimes elaborate plans
weren't necessary. I strode openly up the tunnel, Caitlin at my side,
until the two men ahead stood framed in a bubble of harsh yellow
light.

I called out, "Excuse me, boys, we were just looking for Springfield, but we got a little lost. Help us out?"

They wore the jumpsuits and lanyards of baggage attendants, but one dropped into a crouch, throwing his rippling arms behind him and sprouting black iron claws as he hissed like a cat. I figured they weren't in the mood to play along. He fired at me like a cannonball, but I was already raising Smith's piece, locking him behind the iron sights.

My first bullet hit him in the shoulder, tearing through a mélange of flesh and orange fur as he transformed into his true form. He didn't even slow down. The second round blew out a lung and the third was a heart shot. He still plowed toward me, closing the distance with his claws out, determined to take me with him.

My last bullet went through his gut, but it didn't matter: he was already a dead man running. He lost his balance, hit the concrete tunnel floor, and rolled, crumpling five feet from where I stood. He took one last, desperate swipe at the air between us, then fell still.

The other rakshasa let out a blood-freezing roar as he threw himself at Caitlin, talons lashing for her upturned face. She caught him by the throat and scooped him off his feet. She was going to try to keep him alive, but that didn't mean he wasn't about to catch a beating. Squeezing his neck in a steel grip, she spun him around, slamming him against the tunnel wall to knock some sense into him.

The wall looked like sturdy, old brick. It fractured like an eggshell. The facade crumbled into a crater, half-swallowing the struggling rakshasa as he began to shriek. The world beyond the wall was a cyst of living, raw flesh and pulsating organs.

Then the cyst belched, and a torrent of shit-brown liquid splashed over the thrashing beast. The rakshasa screeched again, gray smoke rising from his melting fur, eyes shriveling and the flesh melting from his face as the acid ate him away.

Not eating, I realized, cold horror washing over me. It was *digesting* him.

"We have to go," I said. "Right now."

"What even is that?" Melanie breathed, her face stark and pale. "What is this place?"

One of the pipes on the wall groaned as it bent like rubber, stretching, the capped tip sniffing toward us like a blind dog.

"We're not inside a place," I said. "We're inside a living thing. *Run*."

The four of us barreled up the corridor as it came alive with sound. Shuddering, weeping noises from beyond the fake brick walls, the hammering of living pipes. I tossed the empty gun; it wasn't going to help, and I didn't need to be seen with it when we found our way back into the airport. If we found our way back.

Melanie cursed under her breath as we hit a dead end. A blank wall sealed off the far end of the tunnel.

"We're screwed," she said.

"Maybe not," I said. "Remember how we came in, in the first place? Illusionary wall. Those raks were guarding something."

"What if it's not an illusion? What if it's like..." Melanie gestured back toward the half-melted rakshasa. As I watched, his dangling shoes slurped into the fleshy cyst.

"Easy way to find out."

I grabbed Mr. Smith by the shirt collar, ran with him for a few feet, then shoved him straight at the wall. Momentum did the rest. He hit the bricks and then vanished, disappearing in a flash.

We were right behind him. I squinted at sudden bright light and a warm rush of air, my ears popping. Somehow we had emerged right back where we'd started. Smith rubbed his shoulder and gave me a baleful look.

"I suppose I should have anticipated that," he said, "but a warning would have been nice."

We walked together to the edge of the bright corridor, where it opened up onto the ticket concourse.

"If I warned you," I said, "you would have argued with me. Okay, so here's a mystery: why build a U-shaped tunnel—a tunnel that's literally alive—that spits you out exactly where you went in? What was the point of that? If it was just supposed to be a death trap, Naavarasi wouldn't have put her own boys on guard in there. And she would have lured us in, instead of trying to send us on a wild goose chase."

"Maybe not *exactly* where we went in," Caitlin mused. "Pet? Look around. What's wrong with this picture?"

Denver International was a ghost town. The churning crowds were gone, the commotion silenced. People with suitcases drifted by, here and there, looking like travelers out of time in vintage clothes. I'd never been in an airport this quiet; even Midway at midnight was louder.

"Excuse me—" Melanie said to one of the travelers. The woman, wearing an ensemble straight out of the sixties and carrying a Pan Am tote bag, drifted right past her like she couldn't see or hear Melanie at all. She tried again, planting herself firmly in one man's path. He stepped around her but otherwise didn't react, didn't even make eye contact.

Mr. Smith held up his vial of Viridithol. The glowing green liquid sloshed against the plastic, angled firmly in one direction even though he held it perfectly straight.

"Strongest reaction yet," he said. "We're close. I'll be honest, I have no idea what we're close *to*, but we're close."

I listened to the distant hum of cargo belts and the clacking of ticket machines.

"On your guard," I said, taking a slow look around the concourse. I caught a familiar whiff of disinfectant. "Don't trust anything you see, anything you hear. Don't trust anything you *smell*. This isn't right."

Smith gave me a sidelong glance. "The handiwork of the 'mistress of illusions?'"

I didn't think so, and that was what worried me.

Naavarasi was no slouch in the magic department—she fought Caitlin and me at the same time once and damn near won—but her greatest asset wasn't her raw strength, it was her mind. She was a Machiavellian monster who wove schemes inside of schemes, always playing to her personal strengths and neutralizing her enemies' advantages. That said, I'd never seen anything to suggest she had the power to create something on this scale—weaving a full-size illusory copy of a major airport out of whole cloth.

"I'm not sure it's an illusion, exactly," I said. "This isn't our Denver International. Doesn't mean it's not *a* Denver International."

"Meaning?" Melanie asked.

"Got a hunch." I glanced to the plastic vial and started walking in the direction of its lean, following the compass.

Go in one door, come out the other, flesh in the middle and suddenly you're standing in another world. I'd seen this before. In the basement of Club Winter, secured behind a steel door in a sub-sub-basement, was a misshapen creature with a hook-impaled foot in multiple worlds at once. Caitlin and her people used him to send messages to hell and back, but he had other tricks.

I remembered crawling into his open rib cage, sliding down a living, breathing throat, and coming out in the Low Liminal for a rendezvous with the Lady in Red. I had felt that same disorientation on the other side, the same ear-popping rush of air.

"Cait? I think someone's jacking infernal tech."

She saw it instantly. "The Conduit."

"The same, but not. Like two different cell phones, different cases, different looks and features, same basic concept. How long have your people known how to create those things?"

Caitlin frowned. "Longer than I've been alive, pet. That's pre-civil-war technology. Our civil war, not yours. I know a historian I can ask, but the answer may be lost to time."

Regardless, my hunch paid off. The Viridithol compass led us straight to a ticket counter in powder blue and white, one that hadn't existed before.

"No freakin' way," Melanie murmured.

Oceanic Airlines was in business, and a board behind the smiling attendant listed their outbound flights.

Every single one of them was going to Springfield.

Chapter Fourteen

"Thank you for choosing Oceanic Airlines," the perky attendant said, looking prim in a seventies-style uniform. "How can we help you today?"

"My friends and I need to get to Springfield," I told her. "Four tickets for the next flight out, please."

"Absolutely, sir! Let's see...we do have flight 815, leaving in just about an hour. Will that do?"

"Sounds great," I said. "By the way...what state is Springfield in?"

She froze in mid-keystroke and blinked at me.

"State, sir?"

"Yeah, you know...where is it, exactly?"

"Oh! The flight is one hour and thirty minutes in duration."

I shook my head. "Yeah, but in what direction?"

She blinked again. Something behind her eyes wasn't sparking the right way.

"It's one hour and thirty minutes away, sir. A very short flight."

Maybe figuring that was all I was going to get, Mr. Smith stepped up beside me. He laid a black credit card on the counter.

"Allow me," he said. "You're assisting with a Network operation. The least I can do is pay for passage."

Caitlin arched an eyebrow. "Excuse me?"

"Oh," Melanie said. "He does *not* understand the situation here. At all."

I agreed with her, but I still let him buy the tickets. I'm proud, not wasteful.

Our plane was a puddle jumper, a narrow-bodied jet with two seats on either side of the aisle. Still plenty of room to stretch out: the four of us were the only passengers. The plane itself was a dinosaur: no fancy seat-back television screens, no in-flight map or anything I could use to get my bearings. As I buckled up I made small talk with a flight attendant and he offered me the same vacant smile and uncomprehending stare I got at the ticket desk.

I was fumbling for a handhold, but the world seemed determined to keep me in the dark. Literally, as we boiled up into a murky, overcast sky, swallowed by dirty gray clouds that looked disconcertingly like engine smoke. The view outside the jet window was blotted out before I even got a bird's-eye look at the ground. Then we rose above the cloud cover, skimming across a blanket of stormy darkness from one edge of the horizon to the other.

Melanie was all over the cabin, moving from window to window, up and down the plane. She came back, dropped into the seat behind me, and lowered her voice.

"Somebody is really screwing with us," she said.

"At this point," I said, "we can call that a strong scientific theory."

"It's early afternoon. I figured I could spot the sun, and that would at least tell us which direction we're heading in."

"Good instinct," I said. "What'd you find out?"

She threw up her hands and dropped them onto her lap.

"Nothing. I can't see the sun from any of these windows."

"We could be going straight east or west," I said.

"I thought about that, but...look at the wing. Does that look right to you?"

Now that she mentioned it, it didn't. The jet's sweeping wing caught the sunlight on the curve of its steel, but not in a way that made any sense. There were multiple points of light, at multiple angles, and none of them seemed to line up with a sun either directly before or behind us.

It felt like we were in a movie studio. On a Hollywood soundstage, under a cluster of standing lights, waiting for an unseen director to roll the cameras on our next scene. Oceanic Airlines, the Val Verde connection...none of it was real, yet here we were, riding in a plane that didn't exist. As for our destination, "Springfield" was one of the most popular place names in the entire country; there were probably forty or fifty Springfields dotting the landscape from coast to coast.

It still fit the pattern. "Pop quiz," I said to the others. "When you hear the name 'Springfield,' what do you imagine?"

"Small town, middle of nowhere," Smith said.

"Americana," Caitlin offered up.

"*The Simpsons.*" Melanie shrugged. "Come on, someone had to say it."

Stereotypes, and stereotypes fueled perception. That felt meaning-ful in a way I couldn't pinpoint just yet. *Every state has a Springfield,* I thought, *and that means Springfield can be anywhere.*

The pilot, a disembodied voice on the intercom, announced we'd be touching down in twenty minutes. The jet shook as it descended through the storm clouds and finally gave us a view of the world from on high. We could have been just about anywhere. The land below was flat as a table, all farms and fields and lonely country roads, a snapshot of the American heartland.

Assuming that was still America, down there. Assuming we were even on an airplane.

Dial it back, I warned myself. *Naavarasi loves it when her enemies get paranoid because they start making mistakes in her favor.* I couldn't trust anything around me, but I was going to have to meet this place, this situation halfway, or I wouldn't be able to function at all.

We touched down on a lonely landing strip at a postage stamp called Springfield County Municipal Airport. A few hangars for private pilots lined the strip, along with a visitor center barely big enough for a fast-food restaurant. We had to wait, idling on the tarmac, while they wheeled a mobile staircase to the jet's door.

"Hey, Smith," I said, sotto voce. "Don't suppose your people have cracked the whole 'detecting a shape-changed rakshasa' problem, have you?"

"Someone in the Regional Threats department is working on it."

"Does this seem like a 'regional threat' to you?"

He let out a thin sigh. "I may have to propose bumping Naavarasi up a notch or two on the threat matrix. But, no. Our people have been fooled just as easily as yours."

I beckoned Caitlin and Melanie closer.

"Listen," I said. "This is beyond hostile territory. For all we know, everyone in this town belongs to Naavarasi. They don't know about my new face yet—"

"But they certainly know what I look like," Caitlin replied.

"Be ready for anything," I said. "When shit pops off, it's gonna pop off fast."

I had to eat my words after that. We stood outside the visitor center in strained silence, waiting for a bus to show up. And waiting. I glanced around, a warm breeze ruffling my hair, and took in the lay of the land. Springfield was apparently built in the bowl of a valley. Mountains rose up in the distance, any direction I looked, vast and disturbingly unnatural walls of stone penning the place in on all sides.

"That's another problem," Melanie said.

I nodded. "I didn't see any mountains from the air."

"There weren't any in sight," Caitlin said. "Flat, as far as the eye could see. And yet, now that we're on the ground...mountains."

A tinny, cheerful horn-beep turned our heads. A shuttle bus in forest green and white trundled up the access road, rolling to a stop in front of us.

"Hey there, friends," a chipper old man in a uniform shirt said, opening the door for us and poking his head out. "Need any help loading up—oh. No luggage?"

"It was kind of a last-minute thing," I said. "Bit of spontaneous tourism."

"Tourism? Here?" He chuckled and scratched the back of his head before waving us on board. "Well, if you like peace and quiet, suppose you could have picked a worse place to spend a weekend. The fishing's not bad, either."

"It's our first visit," Caitlin said. "Can you recommend a local hotel?"

He threw the bus into gear.

"A hotel? In Springfield? Ma'am, there's not a building taller than three stories in this entire town. We're not hotel people. Now, what we do have is one beaut of a bed-and-breakfast. Cozy, clean, very respectable."

"Sold," Caitlin said.

"I'll tell ya what: I'm only supposed to drive between the airport and the pickup spot near town hall, but I'll drop you off right at Mrs. Pickman's doorstep. It's barely a minute out of my way, no trouble at all."

Once I got a look at the town, it was hard to imagine any single spot in Springfield taking longer than a minute to reach. I thought I might be able to jog from end to end, if I really put my back into it. Heritage Street ran through the middle of town, a broad boulevard lined in sun-kissed oak trees and American flags. Faded posters with Norman Rockwell art advertised an upcoming Fall Harvest Festival, and a soda machine gathering dust outside a corner gas station only offered off-brands and blasts from the past. You couldn't find a Coke in Springfield, but apparently you could get a Tab or a Mr. Pibb.

I glanced at my phone, just to make sure we hadn't traveled in time, too. No luck. Our phones all insisted that they weren't connected to anything, that our carriers simply didn't exist.

The old man dropped us off halfway down Heritage. I tipped him a folded twenty, and he made it disappear into his shirt pocket with a smile.

"Just go on in," he said. "She'll take great care of you folks, I promise. Oh, and don't forget: when you're ready to head on home, the official shuttle pickup spot is just outside town hall. There's a bus stop and a sign, can't miss it. I make three runs a day, seven days a week."

Our destination was an old, stooping house of gray clapboard. A sign dangling above the front door just read "Bed and Breakfast" in an old-timey script font, surrounded by painted wreaths of green.

"Either that's a weird mistake," Melanie mused, gazing up at the sign, "or it's not a mistake and we should probably be worried."

"I don't see it," I said.

"You were never a Girl Scout," she said.

"Well...obviously."

Caitlin moved up to stand on my other side. "Look at the shape of the leaves, pet. It's poison ivy."

Chapter Fifteen

The toxic warning on the sign out front notwithstanding, the lobby of the bed-and-breakfast was cozy and warm, decorated with antique wooden rocking chairs, soft rugs over a freshly swept hardwood floor, and more lace doilies than I'd ever seen in one place.

"Hard candy dish on the desk, Hummel figurines on the shelves..." Melanie shook her head. "Looks like a grandmother exploded in here."

Mrs. Pickman was a wrinkled gnome of a woman with a smile that could light up any room. Draped in a long cardigan, she fumbled with her bifocals as she hobbled down the back stairs.

"Dear me, dear me! Guests!" She slipped behind the counter and leaned over an open ledger. "Oh my. Did you sweeties have a reservation? I'm so sorry, but I don't see you in my book."

"It was kind of a last-minute trip," I said. "Do you have any rooms available?"

She grinned and batted a wrinkled hand at me.

"Oh, dearie, does it look like customers are beating my door down, trying to get in? Of course I do, there's beds for everyone. I'll just need an hour or two to clean up and make it all nice for you." She glanced across our faces. "Two rooms?"

Melanie leaned close to me and whispered, "I am not sleeping in the same room as this creepy asshole. Probably wake up in a bathtub of ice with my kidney missing."

Mr. Smith eyed her, his voice bone-dry. "That doesn't make any sense. What could I possibly do with your kidney, here in the middle of nowhere? I wouldn't even have anywhere to put it."

"Three rooms," I said. "One for the gentleman, one for her, and one for my lady and I."

Her gaze dropped to my bare ring finger. Then to Caitlin's.

"A room with two beds," she said, more of a statement than a question.

Ah, small towns. Never change. "That'll be great."

"We're going to take a walk and explore a bit while you're getting our rooms ready," Caitlin said. "Are there any must-see local sights?"

Mrs. Pickman giggled. "'Must see'? In Springfield? Well, we've got a lovely park just outside town hall. Oh! And if you're feeling peckish at all, make sure to visit Shelly's Diner over on Frost Street. The cherry pie is fresh-made every day, and it's to die for. Make sure to tell her you're staying with me. She usually kicks my guests a little discount at the register. And of course I won't let you go hungry either. I serve supper at seven, on the dot, and breakfast is at nine in the morning."

"Much obliged," I said.

"Just...one thing before you go," she added.

Her smile faded. She shot a nervous look at the pebbled glass on the front door.

"You should be back here before sundown."

"Why's that?"

She glanced to one side and down. A lot of people did that when they lied.

"We've been having some electrical problems along Heritage Street. The streetlights tend to go out at odd intervals, and it's just not safe." Her smile came back but this time it was forced, riding on a humorless chuckle. "Besides, dear, this entire town rolls up the sidewalks at sunset. There's nothing out there that you need to be looking at."

***

"Okay," Melanie said as we gathered on the sidewalk outside the bed-and-breakfast, "that was really weird and ominous, right?"

"With sharp instincts like those," Mr. Smith replied, "you may have a great career as a magic detective ahead of you. You're even brighter than your teacher here."

I was about to say something, but Melanie cut me off with: "Networkbitchsayswhat?"

"What?" Smith replied. Then he frowned.

"Yeah," Melanie said. "You got jokes now? I got jokes too."

I patted Melanie on the shoulder. I'd seldom been prouder.

"Whatever the issue is with sunset around here," I said, "we'll figure it out tonight. I want to cover as much ground as we can while we've still got daylight. Obviously, don't show Pixie's picture around—that'd be a red flag to anyone working for Naavarasi—but see what you can figure out."

"I'll investigate the local businesses," Caitlin said. "Small towns do tend to have bars, which means nightlife, which means someone there can tell me what the real problem is."

Mr. Smith turned, tracing the horizon with his fingertip, dipping and rising along the walls of impenetrable and distant mountains.

"There is nothing reasonable about the topography of this place," he said. "I'll try to get the lay of the land and find a workable map."

I nodded. "Sounds good. Melanie, you're with me. Let's all meet up over at that diner Mrs. Pickman mentioned. Say, two hours from now?"

For once, Melanie didn't want to strike out on her own. I didn't blame her one bit.

One block up, we spotted a phone booth on the corner. I hadn't seen a pay phone in years.

"Tell me you know what that is, so I won't feel so old," I said.

She gave me her most finely curated eye roll. I shrugged and poked my head into the booth, hoping to get a look at the local yellow pages. No such luck: the chain that would normally hold a phone book dangled, torn ragged at one end. I had a strong suspicion that if we found any other booths in town, it'd be the same story. I looked up, started to say something, then froze.

"What?" Melanie said.

Teddy.

It was him, plain as day, half a block ahead of us. Dressed in a cheap suit with cheaper shoes, he lugged a heavy-looking duffel over one shoulder and trundled along the sidewalk like he owned the place.

"Stay here, stay out of sight," I told her.

"What are you going to do?"

"Get a little closer. He doesn't know I've got a new face yet."

I followed at a careful distance, putting my tradecraft to work. I kept obstacles like streetlight pillars and tree trunks between us as much as I could and ducked into alcoves to pretend to window-shop every time it looked like he might turn around. He didn't, not once, and that was a problem. We were in an impossible town in an impossible mountain valley, and my brother looked more at home here than he did back in Vegas.

He had home-field advantage. I took things careful and slow.

He turned up ahead, slipping down an alley between an antique shop and a video-rental store. I got close, ears perked in case he'd spotted the tail and was waiting right around the corner for me; I'd used that trick a few times myself. I heard the crunch of footsteps on loose gravel twenty feet ahead, so I took a deep breath and walked past the alley, casually giving a sidelong glance like an ordinary pedestrian might. If it didn't look hinky, I figured I'd double back and give chase.

It didn't look like anything. Teddy was gone.

Eyes high, checking for nasty surprises, I made my way down the alley. It ended in a blank wall and a couple of empty, battered trash cans. He had disappeared without a trace.

That wasn't part of his repertoire. At least it wasn't before now. In case I was being watched, I fumbled in my pocket, pretended to pull something out, and mimed tossing it into the trash can. Then I headed back up the street, where Melanie was waiting by the phone booth. I gave her a quick recap while we walked.

"He disappeared?" she said. "Wait, he can *do* that?"

What bothered me almost as much as the disappearance was the fact that he didn't need to do it. I was just another strange face on the street, no reason for him to run away from me—and considering I hadn't caught him glancing back once the whole time I was tailing him, I would have been impressed if he managed to notice me at all.

So why the disappearing act? We weren't going to find an answer on Main Street USA, so I started looking for an angle. I found one in the most obvious place.

"Let's go to the library," I said, nodding to the red-brick one-story building on the far side of the boulevard.

If you're a stranger in a strange land, the fastest way to fix that is a visit to the local library. Between newspapers, computers, and the reference section, most libraries—even a shoebox like this one—were a treasure trove of intel. More than hard facts, it was a way to find out what a community cared about. What made it tick.

My first hopes were dashed on the spot. The Springfield Library was warm and cozy, with '70s-era wood paneling and rust-red carpet under soft lights, air filled with the rich scent of old paper and well-loved books. A young librarian wearing cat-eye glasses gave us a silent, friendly nod from behind the circulation desk. I made a beeline for a pair of carrels on the other side of the room, each with a chunky desktop PC, and stalled out when I read the handwritten notes taped to the dead monitors.

Sorry, computer broken, repair guy is coming on Tuesday. -Staff

Coming on Tuesday. Next Tuesday, I was pretty sure. As in "always next Tuesday, never this Tuesday."

I had marginally better luck over by the periodicals. They carried one and only one paper: the *Springfield Tribune*, which, I discovered by flicking through a few issues, steadfastly avoided talking about anything outside the town's borders (or even admitting there *was* anything outside the town's borders). I couldn't find a single mention of what state we were in.

But I could see a pattern in the articles about stray dogs and fire-department renovations, a pattern showing what mattered to the locals. Headlines backed up our hostess's warning: the cops were officially telling people to get off the streets once the sun went down, due to the string of faulty lights on the main drag, and a curfew was in effect for anyone under eighteen.

The story was consistent, but it was also bullshit, especially once I caught the number of half-buried articles about people and pets vanishing without a trace. A cursory skim of the last two months' worth of newspapers resulted in four missing locals, which was a damn high ratio for a town this small. Bad wiring didn't cause that.

Melanie had wandered into the fiction stacks. I went looking for her, passing a display of grisly, lurid paperback novels by someone named Sutter Cane; a local author, I gathered. Melanie met me halfway up an aisle, brandishing a small stack of books, her expression pure confusion mixed with wonder.

"This place is..." She trailed off.

"Weird?"

"I think I need to use stronger language for this."

She held up the first book on her stack. The cover depicted a cosmic take on Botticelli's *The Birth of Venus*, with the goddess of love wearing a skin-tight space suit and brandishing a ray gun.

"*Venus on the Half-Shell*, by Kilgore Trout."

I tilted my head. "Should that mean something to me?"

"Kilgore Trout was the fictional alter ego of Kurt Vonnegut. Back in the sixties, in his novel *God Bless You, Mr. Rosewater*, Trout wrote this book."

Now it was ringing a bell. I wasn't sure she had anything to worry about.

"Didn't another sci-fi writer actually do it, as a joke?" I asked.

She nodded. "Philip José Farmer, in the seventies. That's what I'm saying."

She opened the book and turned it, showing me the title page *Copyright 1965, Kilgore Trout*.

"This isn't Farmer's parody," Melanie said. "This is the real thing. This is Kilgore Trout's book."

"But he's not..."

"My point exactly. And this. *The Philosophy of Time Travel*, by Roberta Sparrow?" She caught my blank expression as I looked at what seemed to be a dense college textbook. "It's from the movie *Donnie Darko*. Not real, but here it is anyway. Then there's the mother lode."

She led me around a corner. A row of fat hardcovers sat in a neat line, each spine painted like a Gothic landscape.

"The complete series of Misery Chastain romance novels, by Paul Sheldon."

I gave her a sidelong glance. "Didn't know you read romance novels."

She put her hands on her hips.

"I read a lot of things, but in this case, no. I read Stephen King. You know, *Misery*? Annie Wilkes? 'I'm your number one fan'?" She brandished an imaginary ax in her hands and gave it a chopping motion. "Paul Sheldon was the writer. These books don't exist. They *shouldn't* exist."

For the first time since we arrived in this madhouse, I knew exactly where to go. I was guided by voices, literally: the one in my head from my magic mushroom trip, telling me "*She left you something in Springfield.*"

Chapter Sixteen

I found my treasure buried, appropriately enough, on the bottom shelf. It was directly positioned underneath a tome of old pirate stories that bore a map and a scarlet *X* on the spine to mark the spot.

I had to smile. It was the sort of corny joke Carolyn would have loved. I tugged out the ratty, yellowed paperback below it, turning it to read the pulpy title, embossed over a blood-red sunset and a sprawling metropolis.

The City on Fire. The Midnight Jury, Book Two, by Carolyn Saunders.

The back cover, stark text over another dark cityscape, offered a grim synopsis: *With a gang war raging in the streets and the Argisene Grimoire's mad power running rampant, the streets of Noir York are burning. With his back to the wall, the Midnight Jury sends out a desperate call for allies. A new generation of heroes rises from the shadows...*

I opened it up, checked the copyright page, then showed it to Melanie.

"Copyright date...next year," I said.

Melanie blinked. "When it would have come out, if she hadn't died. So what does it mean?"

"No idea. No idea how she pulled this off, either, but she did."

I glanced up and down the narrow aisle. Then I slipped the paper-back under my shirt. Melanie's eyes went wide.

"You can't steal from a library!"

I stared at her. "Melanie? You...you know I'm literally a gangster, right?"

"So?"

"So...we...steal shit? A lot? You know, in addition to the drug dealing, the hijacking, the extortion—"

"That's different," she insisted. "It's a matter of principle. Stealing from a library is like stealing from a church."

I stared at her. She slowly lifted one eyebrow.

"In hindsight," she said, "that may have been a bad choice of analogies."

"Look, I get it. You don't rob libraries. But this isn't about principles: Carolyn *wanted* us to find this. It means something. And considering neither of us has a library card in this town, I don't see a better option on the table."

***

"Can't believe you stole from a library," Melanie muttered as we slid into a four-seater booth over at Shelly's Diner.

"Look at it this way. The book doesn't actually exist. Therefore I couldn't have stolen it."

"It's under your shirt," she said.

"Yeah, well, the copyright date says it doesn't come out until next year, ergo, you're gonna have to wait until then to be mad at me. That's just basic logic."

Her brain short-circuited quietly until the waitress came over. She was a bleached blonde who popped her gum, toting a pad and a well-chewed pen, and the name tag on her hot pink uniform read *Shelly*.

"New faces," she said, looking us over like she was memorizing every detail. "Don't see that very often."

"We're passing through," I said.

She took another look, me first, then my teenage companion, then back to me.

"You two...related or somethin'?"

Before I could reply, Melanie beamed proudly and curled her arm around mine, leaning in close.

"Can't you see the family resemblance? This is my father!" She turned to me. "Now, Dad, don't you have your reading glasses? You know you have a hard time with menus."

I forced a smile and patted the back of her hand. "Oh, I'll manage, sweetie."

Melanie turned back to the waitress. "You might have to speak up. Dad's a little hard of hearing. Getting on in years, you know?"

"That's fine," Shelly replied, a little louder. "We barely have much of a menu anyway. What we got is a heck of a line cook, though. Maybe you want a turkey sandwich? Pastrami on rye?"

"Mrs. Pickman says you make a mean cherry pie," I said.

She preened a little. "She's a sweetheart, but yeah, that's our claim to fame."

"Two slices. Actually, make it four. Our friends should be showing up any minute now. And a cup of coffee, black."

"Coke for me," Melanie said.

"Sorry, hon, ain't got that. We got Mr. Pibb, Fanta..."

"Anything that's bubbly and caffeinated."

"Can do," Shelly said, jotting a note on her pad and giving us a wink. She turned, hips swaying as she sauntered back to the serving counter.

I glanced at Melanie. "Your dad? Really?"

"You see the way she was looking at us? A grown man, traveling with a teenage girl in the middle of nowhere? She was about to report you for sex trafficking."

She wasn't wrong. Still. "You didn't have to lay it on that thick."

Melanie slapped my arm and put on the worst Italian accent I'd ever heard.

"Ayy, paisano! I'm just bustin' your balls, like we do in the Mafia. Gabagool, moozadell!"

"I can't take you anywhere."

"Says the book thief."

I had to say this much for my apprentice: she gave as good as she got.

Shelly's Diner was just like the rest of this town: frozen somewhere in time, back when phone calls were a nickel, coffee cost a quarter, and Chubby Checker was on the jukebox. We were catching stares from the regulars, but that didn't worry me much. I'd been in plenty of small towns—real ones, on real maps—and that was the behavior I expected from curious locals.

I was less thrilled with the new arrivals walking through the jingling front door. They were a pair of cops, townies in tan fatigues and Smokey Bear hats, one of them wearing his mirrored sunglasses indoors. The other made a point of looking us over, hands curling on his gun belt, before taking a booth with his partner. I studiously gazed out the window until he vanished from my peripheral vision.

The door jingled a second time, not long after that, and Caitlin strolled in. She didn't look happy. The two cops watched her like hawks as she came over and slid into the opposite bench of our booth.

"This town is deeply wrong," she said.

I tugged the paperback out from under my shirt and showed it to her. "We know. Library's full of books that don't exist, including this one. What'd you find?"

"A concerted effort to clear the streets after sundown. With one glaring exception, and it isn't a tavern, because there *are* no taverns in Springfield."

Out the plate-glass window, I saw Mr. Smith coming. He rarely showed more than a flicker of emotion, but his body language was tight as a drum. I made the book disappear again.

"Don't tell Smith about the book," I murmured as he pushed through the door. "That's for *us*, not for him."

He slid in beside Caitlin as Shelly came over with a tray. She set down four plates of cherry pie, fresh and still steaming from the oven. Caitlin glanced over at me, amused.

"You ordered for me, for once? Is this opposite day?"

I waited until Shelly took their drink orders—two coffees, his black, hers with cream and sugar—and walked out of earshot to reply.

"More like opposite town."

Smith stared at the plate like the wedge of pie might jump up and bite him.

"It's cherry," Melanie said, picking up her fork. "You eat it. Like so. Human beings call this 'chewing' and 'swallowing.'"

"Oh, please. I'm as human as you are," Smith said. He held up a finger, then pointed at me. "Wait. No. As human as he is."

"Agree to disagree," I said. "Find anything good out there?"

"Mainly that we're trapped. There's a road that leads out of town, in the opposite direction of the airport. I followed it. It led me on a lovely nature walk before dropping me off at the edge of Heritage Street, right where I started. The road *loops*."

"You know," I mused, "that would almost explain the airport. Not how it works or who built it, but the general idea."

Caitlin picked up my trail of thought. "The mountain valley. It's possible that air travel is the only way in or out. Would keep the place neatly contained."

"Lucky for you all, then," Mr. Smith said, "that I have a commercial pilot's license. Good incentive to keep me alive and on the team, yes?"

I gave him a hurt look. "You act like we've been sitting here plotting your murder."

"You haven't?"

"No, honestly. I figure that when I kill you again, it'll be more of a spur-of-the-moment, off-the-cuff kind of thing. You know, to keep it interesting."

I gave them a quick recap of our excursion, from spotting Teddy—and losing him in a blind alley—to the newspaper articles about the missing locals and their pets. I left out the part about finding Carolyn's secret gift.

Shelly came back with our drinks. Once she left again, Caitlin chimed in.

"Save for a single place, as far as I can gather, every business in town closes promptly by five. I hardly expected a bustling nightclub scene, but a small town without a roadhouse or a watering hole...that's a first for me. Mrs. Pickman wasn't exaggerating: Springfield literally closes at sundown."

"What's the exception?" I asked.

"A movie house, oddly enough. It's on a side street east of the town hall, one screen only, and they run exactly two showings a day: one lunchtime matinée, and a midnight movie. It's a vintage theater, too. Everything on the lineup is at least forty years old."

"Anything good?"

"Only if you like the oeuvre of Frank Capra." She shuddered. "Their selections are...repulsively wholesome. Again, with one exception. Tonight's midnight movie, featured for a one-evening engagement only, is *Night of the Living Dead*."

Melanie slouched low in the booth, twirling her fork in a puddle of deep red cherry sauce. Looked like she'd lost her appetite.

"None of this feels like a coincidence," she said.

I shot a quick look at the cops on the other side of the diner. Then kept turning, pretending I was hunting for the waitress, when I realized the one in mirror shades was staring right at us in stony silence.

"And yet," I said, "we're not up to our asses in rakshasa. Pixie's trail leads here, Naavarasi's boys were guarding the airport tunnel, I *saw* Teddy...and yet nobody's tried to jump us. Why not?"

"Suggests these are just ordinary humans," Mr. Smith suggested. "That said, their apparent disconnection from reality implies that they're under some form of strong enchantment."

"Not her style," I countered. "She didn't *enchant* my brother. She seduced him and lied to him and scrambled his brains with nothing but words and empty promises. That's what she does."

"Maybe she changed her style," he said.

I really hoped not.

Melanie leaned toward the window, craning her neck. "We've got maybe an hour before sunset."

"We should put it to good use and stock up on supplies while we can," I said. "We're all on the same page, right? We're not going to hide in our rooms after dark because we're afraid of faulty streetlights."

"I'm hoping this place turns out to be a little like home," Caitlin said.

"Hell?" Melanie asked.

"I meant Las Vegas, sweet. After dark, it becomes a *very* different town."

Chapter Seventeen

I wanted weapons for this. Preferably a sawed-off shotgun, or maybe my old Taurus Judge from back home. Something with real stopping power, just in case Naavarasi was arranging a welcoming party for us. All we had on hand was my deck of cards, though as Melanie reminded me, "We also have a Caitlin."

"More firepower makes for lighter work," I told her, leading the team up the main thoroughfare on a hunt for gear we could use. "Besides, I'm not gonna make Cait handle all the violence. That's just being a shitty boyfriend."

"There...are at least two police officers with service revolvers on hand," Mr. Smith said, nodding back toward the diner. "We could waylay them and deprive them of their equipment."

I stared at him, stopping dead in my tracks.

"Sure," I said. "Let's jump two cops. In a strange town, where we don't even know if the locals are human, where we don't know the score, where we don't know how many cops there are and we haven't even seen the local station house. Tell me, because I really want to know: how does the Network exist across a hundred worlds, when you people *suck* at doing crime?"

"Terror and overwhelming force," he replied.

"Yeah, well, we don't have either of those right now, so try to keep up. We're going to play this Vegas-style instead."

"Pointlessly loud, flashy, and full of braggadocio?"

"*Resourceful*," I said. "Come on, man. We built a major world city in the middle of a desert."

"One entire city in a desert," Smith said, utterly deadpan. "I must learn how you managed it. My employers have certainly never accomplished such a massive feat of engineering prowess."

I chose to ignore him. We found a sporting goods store, but beyond shelling out for a sturdy bag of golf clubs—I considered it, for a fleeting moment—they didn't have anything more dangerous than a wood-grained BB gun with a cowboy on the box.

"Better than nothing," Melanie said.

I disagreed and gently steered her away from the display.

Another block down was an antique store. We browsed through vintage porcelain, teacups, and flatware, but the closest thing to a viable weapon was an old silver-plated letter opener with a stylized eagle on the hilt. I picked it up and tested the blade against the pad of my thumb. It was duller than a piece of cardboard.

"Pet," Caitlin hissed.

I put the letter opener down and turned just in time to see her duck away from the shop's front window. Wasn't hard to see why, either.

"Go," she whispered. "He knows my face."

Teddy was back, strutting up the sidewalk, not a care in the world. Same cheap suit but something was different now: his duffel bag rode high on his shoulder, swinging merrily along and only sagging a bit in the back, like he'd lightened his load somewhere along the way. I slipped out of the store, leaving the others behind, and went after him.

He wasn't even bothering to check for a tail, and that bothered me. He probably wasn't worried about me, seeing as he thought I was still trapped in hell, but he had to be aware that by now, my entire crew and extended family knew he had shot me off that lonely bridge. Every gunslinger in the New Commission, not to mention anyone who wanted to be the New Commission's friend, was ready and willing to take my brother's head.

And he didn't care. Either he was supremely confident or supremely stupid, and my brother wasn't stupid. He was a victim of Naavarasi's brainwashing and, if anything, her influence had made him more paranoid, not less.

I wondered, not for the first time, if I could fix him. If I could get him away from Naavarasi and show him the truth—that I never abandoned him, that I always wanted to be a part of his life—maybe he'd open his eyes.

When I was a teenage runaway, probably right around the same time the rakshasa queen started grooming my brother, I fell in with a cult. I escaped, but it took running into the arms of Bentley and Corman to *free* me. They took me in, unraveled the barbed-wire strands of the lies I'd been tied up in, and helped me find myself for the first time in my life.

I wanted to do that for Teddy. I wanted to be that for him. If he came around, I could even forgive him for gunning me down, though my friends might take a little more convincing.

Of course that was a wish, not a goal, and nothing good ever came from getting those definitions twisted. My *goal* was to treat Teddy just like any of Naavarasi's other assets.

I was going to take him away from her. One way or another.

Teddy led me to the heart of town, where a roundabout in front of the town hall encircled a patina-encrusted bronze statue on a tall plinth. The statue depicted a proud soldier on a horse, leading a cavalry charge with his saber high, but the plaque on its base was so worn away I couldn't even tell what side of the Civil War he had fought on. Teddy's path curled around the statue, as if he was headed to the small park and playground on the far side of the roundabout.

I followed him around the plinth, only losing sight of him for a few seconds, then froze. He was gone again. This time, instead of disappearing from a blind alley, he'd turned into thin air right in the open.

I took a little time there, pretending to snap pictures on my otherwise useless phone, acting like a tourist just in case anyone was watching. Then I headed back empty-handed. I did spot a promising-looking liquor store on the other side of the street—a liquor store that closed promptly at five, that was a first for me—and contemplated gathering the materials for a Molotov or two. I tabled the notion for now; the local cops were giving us a pass so far and leaving us alone, compared to some of the small towns I deeply regretted passing through over the years, but walking around with rags jammed into bottles of high-proof alcohol was the sort of thing that drew the attention of the law.

Back at the antique shop, Caitlin greeted me with curious eyes.

"He pulled another Houdini on me," I grumbled.

"Interesting choice of words," Smith replied, drifting past. "I assumed you knew how all of Houdini's tricks worked."

"It's called a figure of speech."

"Sun's going down," Melanie said, nodding to the shop window. "We should probably pretend to wrap things up."

***

Back at the bed-and-breakfast, Mrs. Pickman treated us to dinner. She
didn't skimp; we gathered around her gingham-draped dining table
and she brought out a roast sautéed in plump cloves of garlic, a green
bean casserole, even a basket of buttery-soft dinner rolls. She apolo-
gized that the rolls were store-bought instead of made from scratch. I
really hoped she wasn't a villain in disguise because the woman was a
national treasure.

I took a bite of casserole, a French onion layer offering a perfect
crunchy crust to go with the taste of the rich, earthy beans. "Honestly,
this is great. You didn't have to go all out for us."

"Oh, poppycock," she said, batting a hand as she took a seat at the
table. "I love to cook and I'm usually alone, so I do this for all of my
guests. Wait until you see the breakfast spread."

She made small talk, asking us about our jobs and our travels. We
lied, mostly improvising on the spot, and she barely pushed at all. I saw
Smith's hesitance; he didn't take a bite of the food until I did, watching
to see if I keeled over on the spot.

In truth, I was coming around to his way of thinking, from back
at the diner. Even if I passed muster with my new body, and they
didn't recognize Smith or Melanie, any rakshasa who wanted to impress his queen—which was all of them—had Caitlin's face com-
mitted to memory. I strongly suspected these folks weren't disguised
shape-shifters, but instead they were just what they looked like: ordinary people, their minds fettered under some kind of mass enchantment. A spell weak enough to leave them their autonomy, but strong
enough to keep them from asking questions or realizing just how
much was wrong with their humble little town.

They were living dolls, playthings in a town-sized dollhouse, and I
didn't cotton to that.

I tested Mrs. Pickman a little, asking her about the state she'd been born in. She gave me the same blank-eyed, confused look we'd been getting since Denver International. Then I asked how she made the roast beef so tender and she instantly lit up, recounting the long story of her grandmother's family recipe and how it had been passed down for generations. She didn't even seem to remember what we'd just been talking about. If it was all an act—and I was still holding the possibility open—it was a damn good one.

We retired to our rooms on the second floor. Just not for long. We listened as our hostess hobbled into her bedroom at the end of the hall and shut the door behind her. Then a radio began to play, offering up the distant crackles, pops, and warbling laughter of an old Bob Hope show.

The four of us crept out, circled the carpeted landing, and made our way downstairs. I held my breath until I was sure she hadn't heard us. Then we rendezvoused on the sidewalk outside.

Springfield was different at night.

As promised, the illumination along the town's main strip was spotty at best. A few lights shone bright in the darkness, interspersed by dead streetlamps and others that flickered and buzzed, threatening to die at any moment. No one was on the street but us. No pedestrians, no cars, nothing. Just a long, ruler-straight boulevard, cloaked in shadows, adorned here and there with weak bubbles of pale white electric light.

Melanie cupped a hand to her ear. "Hear that?"

I shook my head. All I could hear was the electric buzz from a stray, tortured streetlamp.

"Where are the night birds?" she asked. "Where are the bugs? There aren't even any crickets."

I was certain I'd heard birdsong during the day, while we were out and about. *Everyone* in Springfield hid after sunset. Everyone but us.

"Stay close to me," I murmured.

We walked up the sidewalk, eyes sharp, watching in all directions. At least the four of us could cover each other's backs. I had no doubt that Smith might abandon us to die the second things got nasty, but I trusted his utilitarian philosophy: as long as he thought he could use us to get what he wanted, he'd keep the truce. I couldn't be offended by that, considering I felt the exact same way about him.

We walked to the heart of town, to the roundabout and the statue where I'd last seen, and lost, my brother's trail. A small park and a playground stood across the street, the lawn ruffling in a cold night wind, autumn leaves kicking and rolling across the grass.

I tugged Caitlin's sleeve and nodded. The park wasn't empty.

A little girl, maybe six or seven years old, sat alone on the swing set. She listlessly kicked her buckled shoes into the dirt, the chains of the swing rattling softly as she let it carry her forward and back, and she wore an archaic white dress adorned with puffy sleeves and powder-blue ribbons.

I held my hands up, gentle and open, as I approached her. I didn't want to scare the kid, and if she really was out here on her own, I wanted to get her home where she belonged. The "bad lighting" excuse was a cheap joke, but those disappearances I spotted in the local newspaper were real.

"Hey," I said, my voice soft. "Don't worry, you're not in any trouble. But you know there's a curfew for kids, right? You can't be out here after dark. It's not safe."

The little girl didn't answer me. She just dug her heels in harder, swinging faster now, clutching the chains as they squeaked. She locked eyes with me, staring, unblinking. I gestured for the others to stay back, then came closer. I stepped onto the wavering grass at the edge of the playground.

"Do you live around here?" I asked. "Do you want me to go and get somebody to help you? Your mom maybe, or your dad?"

"My mommy and daddy are dead," she replied in a monotone.

Then she leaped off the swing, landing in a graceful crouch, and stared up at me with her eyes burning. She pulled her lips back, showing yellow teeth and blackened gums.

"You're gonna die tonight, too," she promised. "You're gonna die screaming with all your insides on the outside, just like they did."

She twisted on the ball of her foot and ran, sprinting for the trees at the edge of the park. A peal of gleeful and childish laughter followed in her wake, until it suddenly vanished along with her silhouette in the dark. Cut off and gone, like she and her voice had been swallowed whole by the night.

Chapter Eighteen

"What," Melanie breathed, "the actual fuck."

"Language," Caitlin purred, staring into the shadows where the little girl had vanished.

"Look, I'm aware that the universe is filled with wonder and terror, but there are limits." Melanie turned to Mr. Smith. "Was that one of *your* weirdos?"

"I assure you, young lady, if the Network had field agents here, they wouldn't have needed to send me. Nor would I be quite as puzzled as I am right now."

Something stranger was coming our way. Rhythmic footsteps turned my head. On the other side of the roundabout, in a puddle of light under the only working streetlamp, a man was jogging in place. He wore a canary-yellow tennis shirt, running shorts, a hot pink headband, and a vintage Walkman radio clipped to his fanny pack. He pumped his arms, oblivious to anything but the music playing on his foam headphones.

Another figure loomed behind him, at the far edge of the circle of light. He stepped into view, towering a full head over the jogger, with a heavyweight boxer's body squeezed into a dull blue boilersuit. He wore a rounded latex mask emblazoned with the dead-eyed and carefree grin of a yellow smiley face. His curled and beefy hands, sheathed in heavy workman's gloves, cradled a pickax.

"Hey!" I shouted. "Behind you!"

The jogger spotted me, smiled and waved, still absorbed in his headphones.

Melanie ran out into the roundabout, cupping her hands to her mouth. "Behind you! *Turn around!*"

He seemed confused. Then he looked behind him, just as the man in the happy-face mask raised his weapon high. It came whistling down and impaled his right shoulder, sundering bone, blood spurting from the ragged wound like it was a crushed juice box. Then the man ripped it free and another gout of scarlet splashed over the killer's boiler-suit. The jogger crashed to his knees, choking and shaking, before he pitched to the sidewalk face-first.

"Also not one of ours," Mr. Smith said. "But if he's looking for a new job…"

A card leaped from my breast pocket. I spun it with a practiced twirl of my fingertips, aimed, and let it fly. It lanced across the roundabout, whining like a bullet, and carved into the killer's forehead right be-tween the blank circles of his mask's black eyes.

Smiley Face staggered back half a step, his body language more surprised than hurt. A thin trickle of purple goo, the color of poison berries, welled from the paper-thin cut in his mask. He reached up, plucked the playing card free, and crumpled it in his gloved fist. It burst into flame, a flash-paper eruption snuffed dead in a heartbeat. He opened his glove and let the ashes fall, littering the jogger's mutilated corpse.

Then his other hand came up, and the handle of the pickax slapped into his palm as he turned to face us.

Caitlin held up a warning hand, then began to stride toward him.

"Back," she said. "I've got this."

As she hit the roundabout she broke into a run, leaning into the speed, loping toward him like a wolf about to down a rabbit. Smiley Face stood still as a stone. He kept his feet planted and slowly raised the pick, rearing it back, ready to swing for the fences.

Caitlin waited until the last second. Smiley let the pickax fly, committing all of his muscle to the swing. The rusted, gore-streaked pick slashed the air over her head as she dropped low and fired a string of brutal punches, piledriver blows to his belly and chest. I had seen Caitlin hit a human that way, full force; what was left of his rib cage after the onslaught could barely fill a matchbox. Smiley Face just grunted, staggering again, but he stayed on his feet and he stayed in the fight.

He spun the pick handle, braced it, and thrust it forward, slamming the polished hickory into Caitlin's chin. She hissed, caught her balance, and lashed out with a snap-kick. For just a second, despite his lumbering gait and clumsy style, he was faster than her. The ax hit the pavement with a clatter and he caught her boot heel with both hands.

He twisted his hips, hauled her off her feet, and spun around while he twirled Caitlin like a toy. Then he let go. She sailed through the air and hit the plinth of the cavalry statue at the heart of the roundabout, colliding with a bone-rattling thud. She dropped to the grass at its base, face in the dirt and motionless.

"*Cait!*" I roared. I charged in and my cards leaped to my hands. I didn't have to command them. They knew what I wanted. They fired one after the other, a battery of razor-edged cannon fire to hold the juggernaut at bay—for a few seconds, at least—while I dropped to one knee and scooped Caitlin to her feet. She threw an arm around my shoulder and wiped her mouth with the other, spitting a wad of black blood into the grass. Smiley Face grabbed his pickax and kept coming, one slow, ungainly step after another, ignoring the half dozen cards that jutted from his boilersuit.

"I'm all right," Caitlin growled, leaning into me. One of her legs betrayed her, going soft, and she gritted her teeth as she limped away from the fight. "Just tore a muscle. Fifteen minutes of focus and quiet and I can fix it myself."

We weren't going to get fifteen minutes. We weren't going to get fifteen seconds. The behemoth on our trail was more of a machine than a man, fixated and programmed, coming for us in a relentless death march.

Melanie raced over and offered Caitlin her shoulder. We carried her between us, moving as fast as she could manage on her injured leg while Mr. Smith jogged just ahead.

"Not a rakshasa," Smith said. "Miss Brody? One of yours?"

Still wincing and catching her breath, Caitlin shook her head. "I don't smell any demonic blood in him. All I know is that I can't go another round with that thing until I heal my leg."

He was still on our trail. We were gaining ground, slowly, painfully, but Smiley Face strolled along as if he had all night and nothing better to do with it than to stalk and murder us all.

"The bed-and-breakfast," I said. "Everybody stays inside at night, right? And all the missing-person reports I saw in the town paper were about people who were out after dark, not a home invasion in the batch."

"He can't go inside," Melanie said. "Like a vampire without an invitation."

Smith grimaced and looked back over his shoulder, squinting at the slowly receding figure behind us.

"Vampires aren't real," he said. "I've walked upon over a hundred parallel worlds. Trust me: no vampires, no werewolves."

"I said *like* a vampire, jerk."

"Solid maybe on that," I said. "It's worth a try. If nothing else, we can barricade the door and it'll buy us time to figure out our next move."

I looked back and wished I hadn't.

The lights along Heritage Street flickered, erratic, a couple holding strong but dim while the others put on a disco light show. A good distance behind us now, Smiley Face passed through a puddle of lamplight, reached the edge, and the shadows swallowed him whole.

A second later he reappeared, still on our trail and passing through another pool of lamplight...twenty feet closer to us. As long as we were watching him, he lumbered along at a snail's pace. In the dark, out of sight, he moved like the wind.

He's drawing out the hunt, I thought. *With that kind of speed he could already be on top of us if he wanted to. Why the act? What's he getting out of this?*

I didn't have time to puzzle it out. Mrs. Pickman's place was up ahead, the windows dark, but someone else stood between us and home plate. It was Shelly from the diner, still wearing her pink waitress uniform, smiling contentedly up at the starry sky as she walked straight into danger.

"Hey, Shelly," I gasped, rushing up to her. "You gotta go, right now. Come with us. It's not safe out here."

For a second, she kept her eyes on the sky. I followed her gaze, on instinct, and paused.

The bony disk of a full moon hung directly above us, glowing cold and white in the belly of the night. I did a double take, but before I could even voice my question, Mr. Smith answered it for me.

"The moon was waxing, less than five minutes ago. Waxing gibbous, to be precise. And no, I have no explanation that doesn't break the laws of planetary physics."

"It's a beautiful night, isn't it?" Shelly asked, finally meeting my gaze with a placid smile.

"Listen," I said, "there's a killer after us. He just took a guy out over by town hall, right in front of us, and now he's headed this way. Come with us. We're going to take shelter at Mrs. Pickman's. We'll keep you safe."

Shelly chuckled, weirdly giddy.

"Keep me safe? Aw, sweetie, that's so thoughtful of you. It's fine, though. I can take care of myself."

I glanced back. Smiley Face loomed into sight, clutching his pickax in two eager gloved hands, maybe a block behind us now.

"Trust me," I told Shelly, "you can't."

She looked behind me and laughed.

"Oh, is that what you're worried about? It's fine, hon. There are far scarier things in Springfield after dark."

The waitress turned to me. Her eyes shifted, pupils dilating, the discs of her irises glowing silver in silent homage to the full moon above.

"Like me," she said.

Shelly tilted her head back. Her jaw snapped, then dangled, unhinging like a snake. Caitlin's hand squeezed tight around my shoulder as the top half of the waitress's face peeled upward, her eyes disappearing behind scrunched-up rolls of flesh, her face forcing itself onto her scalp as her skull cracked and deformed and her throat swelled up to twice its normal size.

She had new eyes now. Two of them, peering from the red ravaged tunnel of her throat, liquid silver and hungry.

"Uh," Melanie said, pulling Caitlin back with her. "Guys?"

A wet, glistening muzzle, rippling with matted black fur, began to shove itself up from Shelly's throat. It poked through her mouth and snarled, showing a second set of jagged teeth as Shelly's, squeezed to the breaking point, began to tear from her gums and rain down onto the sidewalk in spatters of scarlet. With a final *crack*, what was left of her skull shattered in a dozen pieces and she sloughed off her head like a cheap hoodie.

Her real head, poking from the torn neck of her human throat, was that of a feral gray wolf. Rivulets of drool dripped from her eager jaws as she let out a triumphant growl. She lifted her hands to the moon. They began to tear, ripping themselves open from the inside, razored claws pushing through the pads of her fingertips. Her human hands dangled, rent and bleeding and boneless, from her wrists.

Shelly dug her paws into her chest, yellow claws piercing through her uniform and the flesh beneath. Then she ripped herself wide open. Sloughing off her skin, shrugging off one shoulder to squirm a furry wet haunch free, then the other, a fat back paw stomping down onto the sidewalk.

Shelly's skin-suit squelched as it spattered on the pavement behind her. She raised her lupine muzzle to the bright bone moon and let out a world-shaking howl.

Chapter Nineteen

We ran, as best we could. Caitlin groaned as she put more pressure on her bad leg, forcing herself to keep up while Melanie and I helped her hobble across the street.

"No werewolves, huh?" Melanie snapped.

I wasn't sure if she was angrier at Smith or at me. I had told her the same thing, after all. Everyone in the occult underground knew, as an article of faith and certainty, that vampires and werewolves didn't exist. Werewolves in particular I felt pretty confident about.

Until now.

"Something you want to tell us?" I demanded, shooting a glare at Smith as we raced in search of something resembling safety.

"*Not ours,*" he said, and the panic in his voice actually made me believe him.

The werewolf legends of our world came, I was pretty sure, from tales of the King of Wolves. One of the Network's masters, and by extension, one of Mr. Smith's bosses. People blessed by the King got a little of the legendary razzle-dazzle: heightened strength, speed, and senses, turquoise eyes, and a hunger for human flesh just to round out the package. I'd met a couple of his "children" in my day, and both of them were dicks.

What they didn't do was transform. They didn't strip off their skin like a badly tailored suit and leave it in a steaming boneless heap on the sidewalk while they howled at the moon. The children of the King of Wolves also had their powers at all times, day or night, and as far as I knew they didn't care about the moon at all. This was a scene straight out of an old monster movie, not real life.

And yet here we were. Living it.

Shelly-wolf loped toward us, claws out and muzzle dripping with yellow drool, and I knew we weren't going to get away. Not with Caitlin's leg slowing us down, and I'd throw myself into that thing's mouth before I let it get Melanie and Cait. I was bracing myself, getting ready to do just that and buy them some time to escape, when Smiley Face burst from a patch of darkness, already swinging his pickax as he hurled himself at Shelly in the middle of the open street.

She caught his pick handle in her claws and punched him with her other paw, hammering his yellow mask again and again. He started to go limp and his fingers twitched, the rusty weapon tumbling from his grip. Shelly grabbed him by the neck and the crotch and hoisted him up in the air, high over her head, letting out another triumphant howl.

She threw him. The juggernaut went flying as if he was weightless, hitting the front window of the antique shop with a thunderous crash and a rain of falling glass. Then she went after him, running on all fours, eager to feast.

Smith ran ahead of us on the far side of the street, waving us on. "Up here! The sheriff station is just past the town hall. We can shelter there."

Solid idea. Cop shops were generally open twenty-four hours a day; even in a tiny town, there'd at least be one deputy around to answer phones and handle emergencies. Probably the most fortified place in Springfield, and our best chance at a safe haven to ride this out until sunrise. They'd have guns, too, but suddenly I wasn't so sure that'd help.

The last ten minutes played through my mind on a high-speed loop. I was searching for clues, something to make the impossible turn rational. Even for a magician the universe had boundaries and rules, and those rules were snapping like matchsticks all around us.

Then I saw it. There was a common theme here, a thread winding through the madness, invisibly holding it all in shape.

"Full moon," I panted, holding Caitlin's weight as we ran together. "It turned into a full moon because there *needed* to be a full moon, because that's when werewolves change their shape."

"The werewolves that don't exist," Melanie said, staring at me like I'd grown a second head.

"Exactly. Look, I've been paranoid about rakshasa because I know Naavarasi's got a connection to this place. Melanie, when you saw that little girl in the park, your first question was to ask if she was one of Smith's weirdos. Smith, you couldn't explain the guy in the smiley-face mask and the boilersuit, so you asked Cait if he was a demon."

"Point being?" Smith puffed, racing ahead of us.

"We're all behaving perfectly rationally. Trying to plug what we know into the observable facts. And normally that's the smart-money play, but think about it: Oceanic Airlines only exists in the world of fiction. This town, this...idea of a small town, only exists in fiction. The library is filled with books that were never written, the road loops back on itself, the valley is sealed off, and the people who live here don't even realize that they're trapped."

Helping Caitlin, jogging along on her opposite side, Melanie paled as she figured it out.

"Oh god. Don't say it."

"We're in a horror movie," I said.

Smith looked back at the receding wreckage of the antique-shop window. We could hear distant clangs, hammering, the sound of a china cabinet falling over and smashing three generations' worth of porcelain.

"At least one threat is out of our way," he said.

"Are you not listening?" I snapped. "That guy was a slasher. He'll be back."

"Slasher?" Smith echoed, not following.

"You know, like *Friday the 13th*? *Halloween*? Guy puts on a mask and hacks up a few dozen nubile teenagers?"

"I prefer the opera."

"Traditionally, slashers are invincible until they aren't. They might get knocked down a few times, even shot, but they always come back until the big finale when the Final Girl—usually the last survivor—puts him down for good. That's why he shrugged off Caitlin's punches like they were nothing. It wasn't time yet. Fucker's got plot immunity. He can't die until the script says so."

"So who's writing the script?" Melanie said, wide-eyed.

"No idea, but once I figure it out, we're gonna have a little story development conference. I've got *notes*."

A howl split the night at our backs. Shelly-wolf was on the street and hunting.

An oblong of electric light, up ahead, offered a faint hope of survival. The cop shop was open as expected, with a sheriff's badge emblazoned on the bulletproof window out front. It was a hut of white stone and pale rustic timbers with a flat roof that overhung the doorway and a string of concrete bollards out front to protect the facade. The bollards gave me an idea.

"This is important," I said. "Follow my lead in there. We're going to tell them that Caitlin got hit by a speeding driver, and we'll figure out our next move while they're taking her report. Do not mention Smiley Face or the werewolf."

"Why not?" Smith demanded.

Melanie knew the answer to that one: "Because in movies, small-town cops never believe anything the heroes say."

We shoved our way through the door and piled into the station house. I usually made a point of staying as far away from cops as possible, and I'd never seen a cop-shop this small before. Just a trio of desks squatting together in the middle of the room, some scattered wooden chairs, barely any security to speak of beyond a steel-plated door marked Employees Only in back. Two pots of coffee sat out on a credenza by the door, black for regular and orange for decaf, along with a mostly eaten box of donuts and some pamphlets on homeowner safety. A fake fern decorated one corner, its plastic leaves gathering dust.

The lights were on but nobody was home. Bulky old desk phones flashed softly in silence, half a dozen lines sitting on hold.

"Is this a police station or a real-estate office?" Smith muttered.

I turned and twisted the lock on the door. No idea if that would hold Shelly off for long, but it was better than nothing. Melanie and I eased Caitlin into the closest chair, where she took her injured leg in both hands and began to knead it, concentrating her power. I couldn't believe I was wishing for Vegas Metro to show up. At least they'd bring numbers. And shotguns. I cupped my hands to my mouth and called out.

"Hello? Anybody here? Our friend is hurt. We need some help."

Silence greeted us. This wasn't right. Even by small-town standards, there should have been someone working the phones and watching the shop.

A faint sound whined from behind the employees-only door, like the whir of a dentist's drill. My stomach went tight. I dropped my voice.

"Smith, cover the front and shout if you see anyone outside the window. Cait, just keep doing whatever you've gotta do to get mobile again. Melanie, watch my back but keep a safe distance. This could get nasty fast."

I gave the metal door an experimental tug. It was unlocked. It swung open, silent and smooth as butter on oiled hinges. That was when the smell hit me: the coppery stench of wet blood, freshly spilled. A lot of it.

Beyond the door was the town's jail, a narrow strip of bare concrete with a yellow painted line straight down the middle, three barred cells on either side. A dead cop, one of the men we'd seen at the diner earlier that day, lay sprawled in a broken heap on the floor. His throat had been ripped open, both of his arms snapped, his skin gone fish-belly pale.

I crouched down beside him, holding up a hand, warning Melanie to hang back. The metallic whining was louder now, coming from the cell just ahead and on the right, at the end of the cold concrete hall.

I pulled the cop's mirrored sunglasses down. His eyes were empty, ragged pits. Open wounds. I put the glasses back and then—keeping my attention on the noise ahead—reached down to the dead man's gun belt. His fat revolver was still in its rawhide holster, secured by a thick black snap.

Gritting my teeth, trying to be as quiet as I could, I tugged at the snap until it came free with a soft pop. Then I curled my hands around the walnut grip of his service weapon and drew it, the gun slithering free. I braced it in both hands in a tactical stance, muzzle pointed to the floor, and advanced up the corridor.

Chapter Twenty

T he first cell on my right was empty. The second was decorated in splashes of rust red from wall to wall. The corpse's torso, dressed in a gas station attendant's uniform, sat propped up on a thin cot. His arms and legs were elsewhere, scattered across the cell, one hand jutting up from the stainless-steel toilet bowl like it was reaching for help that never came. I didn't see his head and I didn't feel like looking for it.

One careful foot after the other, I eased my way closer to the last cell on the right and that whining, grating noise. The sound took on a new, higher pitch, mixed with a liquid, burbling noise like water trickling from a garden hose.

The second cop from the diner stood in the cell, the barred door between us hanging wide open, with his back to me. He was busy. He had the driver from the airport, the shuttle bus operator who took us into town, trussed up in a high-backed wooden chair with coils of scratchy rope. I thought the old man was dead until one of his bound feet twitched and he let out a faint groan, the sound almost swallowed by the shrill mechanical whine.

I took a step closer to get a better look, and the revolver felt five pounds heavier in my hand.

The driver's sleeves had been cut off at the shoulders. Two lengths of surgical plastic tubing ran from his bare forearms, poked into exposed slices of skin just above his veins. Blood ran down the transparent tubes like syrup, ruby raindrops pattering into a pair of plastic utility buckets. The whining sound had been the power drill in the cop's hand, as he ran a needle-thin bit into the old man's shoulder. He set the drill on the cell floor and threaded a third length of tubing into the open wound.

I raised the revolver and took aim.

"You know," I said, "normally I try to avoid killing cops, just because I don't need the hassle that comes with it. Doesn't mean I won't. Back away from the chair, keep your hands visible at all times, face the wall, and assume the position. I don't have to explain that to you, do I, officer?"

He whirled around. His eyes were pits of midnight and as he opened his mouth wide, letting out an ear-piercing screech, he flashed razor-sharp incisors at me.

My first round punched through his forehead. I gave him all six cylinders, round after round, and he staggered backward as I blew craters down the front of his uniform shirt. The last round tore through his belly, ripping out the small of his back, and dropped him in the corner of the cell.

"Dan?" Melanie asked, standing near the door at the end of the hall.

"Stay back," I said.

My gun was empty. He had one on his belt, and I wanted it, but I knew this wasn't over. As I considered my approach, the old man let out a faint, rasping wheeze, slumping against the ropes that bound him to the chair. His blood trickled down through the tubes, the third one spilling out onto the cold concrete around his shoes.

"It's okay," I told him. "Try not to move. I'll get you some help."

The old man opened his eyes. They fogged over from the inside, billowing black. He let out a guttural whine and peeled his lips back, his teeth growing, turning sharp and feral, as he struggled against his ropes with newfound strength. He bit at me, chomping the air, desperate to feed.

The cop sprang up like a jack-in-the-box and hurled himself at me. He flew, sailing through the air, a torpedo of flesh and hunger with his gnarled fingers grabbing for my neck. I threw the empty revolver to free my hands up, but I didn't have time for another move: he plowed into me, throwing me backward into the gray steel bars of the cell across the hall. The back of my head cracked against the cell door and I went down, seeing double, fighting through the breath-stealing pain. Dazed, I vaguely made out the creature standing over me, savoring the moment as he bared his fangs.

A playing card sizzled through the air like a heat mirage, slicing the side of the cop's neck. The wound dangled open, bloodless and pale, as he spun on his heel and hissed like a cat.

"Melanie," I croaked. "*Run.*"

Melanie's black veins traced butterfly wings on her face as she stood her ground and conjured another card.

"I've got this!" Melanie shouted. "I'll save you!"

And in one dizzying second I was in another time, another place, hearing the words that had haunted my nightmares for years.

"*I can do this, Dan. I can DO this.*"

It was the Armitel Equity heist. Should have been a simple in-and-out job: break into an office building, crack the safe of a crooked hedge fund manager, and make off with a cool hundred grand in bearer bonds. My first apprentice, Desi, came along just for the practice.

Then we found out the target had a sorcerer on his payroll, and an inside man had tipped him off. He knew we were coming and he was ready for us, conjuring a nightmare made of sand and teeth and crocodile scales.

I told Desi to run. She wanted to prove herself to me. Wanted to make me proud. And all I could do was watch while it ripped her apart. Her head bounced and rolled across the office lobby floor and stopped somewhere near my feet, her eyes still wide open, staring up at me.

Whoever built this madhouse made it run on horror-movie logic, but they didn't know a goddamn thing about *real* horror.

Now I watched the vampire cop fixate on Melanie. He bent a knee, launched himself, and took flight, yowling as he soared up the hallway. She tried again, firing another playing card that bounced off his shoulder, crumpled and useless. As I grabbed the cell bars and hauled myself to my feet, my head still throbbing and the world reeling around me, time lurched into slow motion, just like it had on that day.

I saw a flicker of realization on Melanie's face. Her best attack wasn't good enough to stop this thing, and now it was too late to run.

I think I screamed. I wasn't sure. I just knew I was on the move, fighting my sense of balance as my stomach lurched and the hallway stretched and slid, digging for every last bit of strength I could find. The vampire cop was on top of her, fangs out and intent on her throat, and she was pushing back against his chest with both hands. Her elbows were starting to buckle.

I hooked my arm around the cop's neck and hauled back for all I was worth, but it was like fighting a freight train. Caitlin leaped to her feet—then nearly fell again as her injured leg went out from under her, and she caught herself on the edge of a desk. Smith was standing at the far corner of the room, over by the fake plant, watching it all happen and doing nothing about it.

"Cait," I grunted, "*stake!*"

Caitlin flipped the chair she'd been sitting on, leaned on the desk for support as she drove her good heel into it, and snapped off a wooden leg. She scooped it up and sent it flying in an underhand throw.

I snatched it out of the air, flipped it in my grip so the jagged, splintery end was pointed straight down, and drove it into the cop's back. It tore through his uniform shirt, past his spine, straight into whatever he had left of a heart.

He exploded into a cloud of smoldering ash. The station house tasted like dirty cigarettes and looked like a crematorium as the vampire's remains billowed across the room, leaving nothing but empty, bullet-riddled clothes behind.

"Did he bite you?" I said, staring down at Melanie.

"N-no," she stammered, pale and shaking.

I pulled her to her feet, harder than I needed to. I clutched her arm and gave it a rough shake.

"You fucking listen to me right now," I said. "When I tell you to do something, *you fucking do it.* Do you understand?"

Melanie tried to pull her arm away. "Dan, you're—you're hurting me."

"*Do you understand me?*"

"Daniel," Caitlin said, her voice sharp. "You're frightening her."

I let go of her arm. I put my hand to the back of my head. I was going to have a hell of a bruise, but the skin wasn't broken. Still throbbed like someone had been beating on me with a baseball bat, and I needed to puke. Wasn't sure if that was from the head injury or the adrenaline.

"*I'm* frightening *her.* Christ."

A faint and feeble growl drifted from the cell at the end of the hallway. I walked over to the toppled chair and broke off another wooden leg.

"One second. Need to take care of something."

I put the old man out of his misery. Then I came back, crouched down, and plucked the revolver from the pile of empty clothes. Three rounds left in the cylinder. Better than nothing.

Mr. Smith was over by the window, watching the darkened street outside. Caitlin was deep in meditation, her hands pressed to her injured leg, her lips moving in some silent mantra as she knitted her torn muscle back together by sheer force of will. Melanie stood in the corner, arms crossed, staring at her feet. I felt deflated, my fear and my fury draining away in the aftermath of the fight.

"Hey," I told her. "I'm...I'm sorry. I shouldn't have yelled at you like that."

"I was just trying to help," she said in a small voice.

I reached toward her, and she flinched. My heart broke a little. I let my hand fall to my side.

"When you asked me to teach you," I said, "I dug my heels in. Hard. Wanted nothing to do with it. Not because I didn't think you were capable. I knew you were capable. But...you know you're not my first apprentice, right?"

She nodded, silent, her bottom lip trapped between her teeth.

"I took Desi on a job with me. It should have been a cakewalk. We got ambushed. I told her to stay back, but..." I leaned back against the wall and took a deep breath. "I think she was trying to impress me. Show how much she'd learned, you know? And she died. She died right in front of me and I couldn't do anything about it."

Melanie met my gaze. Understanding now.

"I need you to understand that being your teacher means I'm responsible for you. Not just for showing you how to do things, but knowing your limits and what you can handle. If I say you're not ready for something, it's not because I think you're weak or not good enough. It's because this shit is dangerous. Being a sorcerer is like juggling nitroglycerin. You can be the best juggler in the world, but one slip—just one—and you're dead. And I don't want you to get hurt. So I need you to trust me, okay?"

She opened her arms. I pulled her in, held her close with her head against my chest, feeling her tremble.

"Hey," I murmured, "look on the bright side. You are now, officially, one of the only magicians in the entire multiverse who can say they fought a real, actual, honest-to-God vampire. I mean, *don't* say it because nobody outside the family will ever believe you, but still. Take it as a point of pride."

She giggled at that. I rubbed her shoulder.

"You're coddling the girl," Mr. Smith said, standing a few feet behind me. "And a coddled child is a weak child. Not surprising. Is that how you lost your last apprentice, too?"

I froze.

"Give me one reason," I said.

"For?"

I didn't turn around. "You stood there like a goddamn statue when that monster attacked us. You didn't even try to help."

"I was gathering data," Smith said.

"You were useless. You've been useless since the start. So give me one reason, just one, why I shouldn't bash your fucking brains in. And you'd better make it good, because right now, I'm not inclined toward charity."

"I've already given you one," Smith said. "As far as we know, the only way out of here is by air. I'm the only pilot in this room. You can slay me if it pleases you, but, well...I'll revive, eventually, and you'll be trapped here forever."

Outside the station house, a wolf howl split the night.

"Of course," he added, "'forever' is a very optimistic word."

Chapter Twenty-One

I hated to admit it, but Smith was right. He was a treacherous, ice-hearted bastard who would leave us all to burn in a heartbeat, but he was also our ticket out of Springfield. I couldn't kill him. Worse, I had to protect him, and he knew it. I tabled my thoughts of revenge to focus on the task at hand.

Caitlin rose, taking experimental steps on her bum leg. She nodded, approving. "Good as new. So. Next steps?"

"We stay here until morning, obviously," Mr. Smith replied.

I shook my head. "Melanie, what did I teach you about walking into strange places?"

"The second you step into an unfamiliar room, find two exits and memorize them. Never stay in a room with only one."

"Why?"

Another hungry howl echoed down Heritage Street. Closer now.

"That's why," she said.

"Good girl." I turned to Smith and pointed at the window. "Bulletproof glass isn't going to keep that monster out, and if she decides to crash her way in, we'll be trapped with nowhere to run."

"I suggest we take the offensive," Caitlin said.

"You want to fight that thing?" Smith said, goggling at her.

"You're looking at it the wrong way," she replied. "We are *going* to fight her. Either she'll force the confrontation or we will. Our only choice is whether we take the initiative or we wait like sitting ducks and allow her to dictate the terms of engagement. In the former case, we have a fighting chance. In the latter, we die."

"In other words," I told Smith, "it's time to nut up or shut up."

Caitlin gave me a tired smile. "My precious love, eloquent as always."

"I try."

"Okay," Melanie said. "So...we're in a horror movie, and movie rules are in full effect. What do we know about werewolves?"

"They transform under the full moon," Smith ventured, "but as we've seen, the moon here isn't bound to any particular cosmic law."

I nodded. "It became a full moon because the plot needed it to be. And that's another reason we can't hole up here. 'Wait it out until dawn' is the first thing the heroes in a horror movie try, and it never ever works. Wouldn't have much of a story if it did."

"Silver bullets," Melanie said. "You need silver bullets to kill a werewolf."

I contemplated the gun in my hand. Three rounds, copper-jacketed, and they wouldn't even slow that monster down.

"No good," I said. "Even if we had silver, we don't have the tools to cast a bullet. Silver has a higher melting point than lead and it shrinks when it heats up, so you need a custom mold if you want to end up with anything that shoots on-target. This cop shop doesn't even have an armory, and I didn't see any gunsmiths on Heritage Street while we were hunting for gear."

Caitlin narrowed her eyes, thinking for a moment.

"But werewolf legends date back to medieval times, long before the invention of firearms. Originally, they could be killed just like any mortal creature. They were durable, and terrifyingly strong, but still vulnerable. Silver bullets were an invention of the cinema."

And like Melanie said, we were playing by movie rules. Springfield had trapped us in its twisted logic; we needed a silver bullet to take Shelly-wolf down, and there was no way to actually get our hands on one.

When I was faced with a rule I didn't like—which was all of them—I instantly started looking for a loophole. I snapped my fingers.

"Melanie. Why silver?"

"Well," she said, "I'm guessing...it's an alchemy thing? Silver is a lunar metal. Werewolves are tied to the moon, so they're subject to its power."

"Exactly. We don't need a bullet. The bullet is just a delivery mechanism. The magic is in the metal. If we can wound Shelly and get some silver into her body—preferably into her bloodstream—it should work just the same."

Smith looked dubious. "Do we *have* any silver?"

"No," I said, "but I know where we can get some. Cait, remember the antique store?"

"Of course, pet."

"They had a silver letter opener. I was thinking about buying it, but it was blunt and felt brittle so I left it behind. Wish I hadn't, but in my defense, I didn't have any reason to think we'd be fighting a werewolf tonight. You know. Seeing as they don't exist."

"Reasonable," she said.

"I wouldn't try stabbing her with it, it'd probably snap right in half, but if we can cut her open and *then* hit her with the silver—"

"Dead werewolf," Melanie said.

"She's out there," Smith said. "Right now. How are we going to get past her in the first place?"

I waved everyone over to the cluster of desks in the middle of the station house. Then I grabbed a pen from a coffee mug and ripped a piece of paper from a notepad, sketching out a quick, crude map of Heritage Street.

"Here's us," I said, drawing an X to mark the spot. Then another. "Here's the antique store. And over here, on the other side of the street, is a liquor store. Melanie, you remember how to cook up a Molotov cocktail?"

"Sure."

"Got your lockpick kit?"

She raised an eyebrow. "Come on. You'd kick my butt if I went anywhere without it."

"Indeed I would. Okay. So, this is the part of the plan you aren't going to like. We have to split up."

Caitlin blinked. "Pet? We're in a horror film, and you want...to split up. You shouldn't need me to tell you that's a terrible idea."

"Oh, I know it. It's worse than terrible. That said, I'll be taking all the risk. Cait, I want you and Smith to head straight for the antique shop. Grab the silver, along with anything that might pierce Shelly's hide. Melanie, you're going to the liquor store. Pick the lock—you can handle this, trust me—and put together a going-away present for Shelly. Two would be even better. I've never seen an animal that wasn't afraid of fire, and I don't think she'll be any different."

"And while we're doing that..." Caitlin said, a question in her eyes.

"I'm going to draw her attention," I said. "I'll make her chase me around the block a few times. Once you've got the stuff, meet up on Heritage and I'll funnel her straight toward you. Melanie, you'll hit her with a firebomb. That should soften her up. Once you do that, Cait can make the kill."

"You're going," Melanie said, "to let the werewolf chase you."

I walked over to the front door and squinted out through the glass, into the darkness beyond. The street was empty. Nothing moved. It felt like the calm before the storm.

"You'll be surprised to learn that I run really fast when I'm scared," I said. "Wait for me to clear a path, then move. We can do this if we work together. I believe in us."

I turned and looked over at Smith.

"When I say 'us' I'm talking about my girlfriend and my apprentice. Not you."

"I assumed," he said.

"That said, unless you want to be ripped into itty-bitty chunks and then eaten by a rabid wolf-monster, I suggest you pitch in."

I steeled myself and flipped the lock on the door.

"If I know my movies right, there's one last thing I have to do to absolutely guarantee that I'm the one who runs into trouble out there."

"Oh no," Melanie groaned. "Don't say it."

I nodded, sighed, and spoke the ritual words: "I'll be right back."

***

Silence greeted me on the boulevard. The town was asleep, windows dark, the full moon glowing in a canopy of glittering stars. Almost peaceful. Then I caught a faint rustling, snuffling sound, something slithery and wet. I followed it up the sidewalk.

Shelly, still in her wolf form, was hunched over the jogger that Smiley Face had axed earlier. She'd ripped his chest open and her snout was buried in his guts, like he was a bowl of human soup. A strand of raw intestine dangled from her claws.

"My apprentice says I'm handy with a quip in moments like this," I told her. "It's kind of a coping mechanism. Just between you and me, I'm beyond terrified right now and I can't think of a damn thing. Don't tell anyone, okay? I've got a reputation to uphold."

Shelly's silver eyes flicked toward me. She let out a slow, hungry growl as she rose up, her gore-drenched snout emerging from the dead man's stomach, peeling her muzzle back to show me her fangs.

"Wait, I've got this. How about...'Ma'am, I'm from animal control, and you're in violation of the leash law. I'm gonna have to take you to the pound." I winced. "Oh, goddamn it, that was Melanie's line. What is *wrong* with me tonight? I promise, I'm usually better at this."

Her growl rose an octave. She stood at her full height, a head taller than me and almost twice as wide.

"No, no, don't get up." I slowly backpedaled, keeping my eyes on her. "I'll see myself out."

Then I turned and ran. She reared her head back and howled at the moon, a cry of feral hunger and rage. Then she came after me.

***

The howl was Melanie's cue to go. She sprinted into the dark, light-footed and alone, her heart fluttering as she made a beeline for the liquor store. The front door was too exposed; they'd faced a slasher, a werewolf, and a vampire, all in the last hour, and she didn't need

Springfield conjuring up any more nightmares right now. She darted
down a tight alley and circled around back.

The lock on the delivery door was an off-the-shelf model, straight
from the local hardware store, the kind she'd practiced on a dozen
times before.

"Cheap and easy, just the way I like 'em," Melanie murmured under
her breath, crouching and sliding a tension rake into the lock. She
paused and tilted her head. "Wow. Dan's right. I really am picking up
his bad habits."

The door opened with a hollow *chunk* sound, and she slipped
inside.

Her cambion eyes didn't have much trouble with the dark. She
pressed her back to the door and pierced the shadows, taking a quick
look around. There wasn't much to see in the liquor store's back room.
Some standing shelves, a whole bunch of boxes—then the breath
caught in Melanie's throat.

A metal cabinet, shrouded in break-in-case-of-emergency glass,
hung on the far wall. She stood before it, gazing at the coiled water
hose inside...and the cherry-red blade of a fire-rescue ax.

"Oh, baby," she breathed. "Come to mama."

A minute later she pushed through the storeroom door and into
the deserted liquor shop, holding her new weapon in a two-hand grip.
She reluctantly set it on the checkout counter, next to a glass fishbowl
filled with cheap plastic lighters. She had to work fast. Casting an eye
to the big plate-glass window up front—nothing moving on the street,
for now at least—she scurried up and down the aisles on the hunt for
the perfect ingredients.

You couldn't use any old bottle of hooch to make a Molotov, she'd
learned. The higher the proof, the better the blaze. Most companies
these days shipped their most potent booze in bottles with little per-

forated metal caps over the nozzle for that exact reason; they wanted you to drink the stuff, not light up the town. But holdouts still existed, and she knew which labels to look for.

Melnaie slapped two bottles of Kentucky Bloom onto the check-out counter. The stuff smelled like paint thinner and probably tasted worse, but it'd get the job done. She snatched a purple plastic lighter from the fishbowl and gave it an experimental flick, just to make sure it worked. She nodded at the tiny, wavering flame and laid that down, too. Now she only needed a pair of wicks.

No time to be delicate. She grabbed her shirt at the shoulder and wrenched, hard, seams popping as she tore her sleeve off. Then the other. She sighed as she wound them into tight coils of ripped fabric.

"Really liked this top, too. Okay, two bespoke firebombs, seasoned to perfection. Let's just hope—"

She turned and froze in her tracks. She wasn't alone in the store.

Smiley Face stood at the far end of the middle aisle, watching her in stony silence. The black eyes of his yellow mask pierced right through her. For a moment, neither of them moved.

Then he raised his rusty and gore-streaked pick and slapped the haft against his gloved palm.

Chapter Twenty-Two

I wasn't going to make it.

To be fair, "outrun a werewolf" was never a good idea, but I didn't know how bad it was until Shelly dropped to all fours and barreled at me like a dog going after a juicy sausage. My lungs were on fire, every breath like inhaling lit gasoline, my arms and legs burning as my shoes pounded the pavement. I could hear her behind me, closing the gap with every galloping thud of her meaty paws.

Shelly had a body like a muscle car: hard, fast, and built to win on a straight road. I wondered how well she could handle curves. I veered left, angling for an alley between a pair of two-story apartment buildings. The ladder of a fire escape dangled just ahead, the lowest rung eight or nine feet above the asphalt. I'd only get one shot. I sprinted for it, jumped, caught the rung, and started hauling myself up hand over hand until I was high enough for my scrambling feet to find purchase.

I was halfway up the first set of metal stairs, the old fire escape rattling and jangling with every step, when Shelly followed me up. The scaffolding let out a screech of tortured metal, starting to lean under her sheer bulk, as she hooked her claws around the rungs and climbed. Her head tilted up toward me, eyes capturing the silver disk of the moon, her muzzle wide open and her tongue lolling.

I could feel the whole thing going; the fire escape had been built for humans, not four-hundred-pound wolf-monsters, and it began to slide as old support rods jolted free from the crumbling brick wall. I rounded the staircase, the rooftop just ahead of me. The scaffolding teetered, yawning now, only a thin and rusted pair of struts holding it to the side of the apartment building.

I put everything I had into one last push and jumped. I hit the lip of the rooftop just as the fire escape fell, crashing down in a thunder of twisted metal and billowing brick dust.

I rolled onto my back, gazing up at the starry sky, catching my breath while my heart danced a tango. I gave myself five seconds to rest, and that was being generous. Pushing myself up with a strained grunt, I looked over the ledge. Shelly was prone in the tangled wreckage, tangled up under a fallen set of stairs. Her muzzle twitched.

Did we...not need the silver? I wondered. Was Springfield cutting us a break?

Then she let out a furious growl, low and long, and rose from the wreckage. She shoved bits and pieces of broken metal off her pelt, wavering on her feet, and glared up at me. Let her, I figured; I was two stories up. As long as I could keep her here, holding her attention, it'd buy time for the others to get the job done. And at least for the moment, I was safe.

"Hey, girl. Hey, puppy." I waved at her. "You wanna eat this nice juicy arm, don't you? Sure you do. Jump for it, puppy. Come on, jump for it."

Shelly stood there for a moment, head tilted, an unnerving gleam of intelligence in her eyes.

Then she drove her claws into the brick wall, digging out chunks of old mortar to make handholds, and started to climb the side of the building.

***

Caitlin's cold gaze swept the dark interior of the antique store. It looked like a bull had rampaged through the shop, thanks to Shelly's brief bout with Smiley Face. Worse, the floorboards inside the doorway were a riot of broken glass around an empty body-shaped outline.

"On your guard," she murmured, leading the way with Smith close at her shoulder.

Smith glanced at the empty spot and clicked his tongue. "He really did get up and walk away."

"You doubted?"

"I don't believe in taking things on faith."

"Shame," Caitlin said, picking through the wreckage on a hunt for silver. "Faith can be a comforting thing."

"More like a lie you willingly tell yourself."

"More like a gamble based on what you understand to be true," she said. "Case in point: do I know that Daniel will survive this gambit? No. Do I have faith? Yes, because I've seen him slip out of a noose many times in the past. So I'm at ease, which is good, because if I was worried about him I wouldn't be able to focus on my own work right now."

A gleam caught her eye. She crouched down, shoving aside the splintered wreckage of a dresser drawer, and found the silver letter opener. She scooped it up, nodding to herself as she ran her finger along the blade, giving it experimental nudges.

Daniel was right; blunt and brittle, it was never meant to be a weapon and would probably snap right off against the werewolf's hide. They'd have to find another way to wound her first.

On the other side of the cluttered shop, Smith was studying her. "Why do you handicap yourself?"

"Meaning?"

"You're an incarnate demon. The most powerful of your kind. And yet you spend most of your time on a backwater Earth, surrounded by mortal humans. They're weak. Frail. They get old, they get sick, and they die."

Caitlin shrugged. "When the soul is eternal, mortality is just a state of matter. Alive, dead, as long as someone is damned I can keep them forever. And I like my world. I like humans."

"But you're *superior*. Wasn't that the entire point of creating your kind in the first place? Lucifer was trying to one-up the original design."

She hunted through the clutter, focused on finding a better weapon.

"We're faster and stronger," she said. "Those aren't measurements of character, or of value. Daniel cooks the most exquisite Italian cuisine—his garlic bread is to die for—and he gives masterful foot rubs. Did you know that?"

He squinted at her. "Why would I know that?"

"Because then you might understand a bit better. 'Superior' is an empty word because everyone, in my experience, is 'superior' at something. I'm often surprised and delighted at what my human friends can do. But you can't see the value of anything beyond conquest. Your gods are perpetually hungry, so hunger is all you know."

"The *universe* is hungry," he countered. "It's conquer or be conquered. That's cosmic law."

"Only because you want it that way."

She pulled open a broom closet behind the ravaged front counter. Mops and buckets spilled out, clattering across the floorboards.

"Honest question though," he said, "because my employers are continually baffled by hell's behavior."

Caitlin picked up a mop, twirled it in her hands, and nodded to herself, only half-listening to him.

"Find the most popular and cattiest mean girls in your local high school, throw them in a room together, and tell them to create a functional government," she said. "Oh, and they all have knives. There. Now you understand infernal politics."

"That much is obvious. What I mean is, you people gravitate to that one particular Earth, you're clearly fixated on it, so why haven't you conquered it yet? It's not a lack of ability or power, so what stays your hand?"

Caitlin rolled her eyes and let out a tolerant sigh. Then she drove her heel down on the mop, snapping the head off. She spun it around and tested the weight in her grip.

"We already conquered it. We take what we need, we get what we want. But that's the difference between you and me."

She turned. Her eyes glowed in the dark, molten sparks of copper swirling behind her irises.

"You play the game of conquest like a toddler bashing a xylophone with a mallet," Caitlin said. "We play it like a symphony of subtle notes."

"And success shows the superiority of the Network's approach."

Caitlin rummaged through a drawer behind the cash register and came up with a spool of packing tape. She flashed a smile.

"This will do nicely." She glanced over at Mr. Smith. "And if success is a measure of achieving one's goals, I think you may be wrong. I lead a challenging and fulfilling life, just as I desire. Do you?"

He glowered at her, silent for a moment. Then he waved a hand at the mop stick and the roll of tape. "What are you doing with that junk, anyway?"

Caitlin turned her gaze to the spray of glass shards on the floor by the entrance.

"Improvising," she said.

***

There was only one way off the rooftop. Right onto another one, across a gap and one story down, to the flat pebbled roof of the sporting goods store. I wasn't sure I could make the jump. Normally I would never risk it. But normally I didn't have a massive, flesh-hungry wolf-monster climbing the side of a building, intent on eating me alive.

It was a powerful motivator. I took a few steps back, judging the distance and how much speed I'd need to force out of my exhausted legs. Shelly's head crested the lip of the rooftop, eyes burning, flinging drool as she licked her chops in anticipation of her next meal.

I ran, jumped, and flew. The neighboring roof sailed up to meet me, too fast, my legs pinwheeling in the open air and my stomach lurching. I tucked my knees up and twisted my hips, hitting the roof with bone-jarring force on my shoulder and rolling, hissing through gritted teeth. My elbow nearly buckled as I pushed myself up again, no time to waste, reflexively rotating my shoulder to make sure nothing was broken as I staggered across the rooftop. No time to recover. That was a rough jump for me, but it'd be nothing for Shelly, and she'd be on top of me—literally—in just a few seconds. I slid down the forest-green vinyl awning of the sporting goods store, grabbed the edge, and lowered myself down, my legs dangling a few feet over the sidewalk below.

I let go and dropped, landing in a crouch, eyes on the empty street. I didn't see anyone. No idea where Melanie and Cait were, and I was about to flush a werewolf toward an ambush point with no ambush waiting. I didn't see any other options. I started to run, straight down the middle of Heritage Street.

A flicker of bright light caught my eye as I sprinted past the liquor store.

Then the plate-glass window erupted like a bomb, the night turning to high noon as a figure consumed in billowing flames silently staggered over the sill, stomping out into the street trailed by streamers of blue-hot fire. It was Smiley Face, still clutching his pick even as the inferno charred the handle black.

Melanie stood in the broken window behind him, a cheap plastic lighter in one hand, a second Molotov in the other.

Good girl, I thought. She had it handled. I kept running. Caitlin charged from the antique store, Mr. Smith on her heels, and she brandished the silver letter opener along with a weapon of her own: she'd fashioned a mop handle into a makeshift spear, fixing jagged shards of glass to the tip with packing tape. The broken glass was a razored nightmare, ready to make an unholy mess.

Smiley Face dropped to his knees. He never made a single sound as he burned, a living torch in the darkness. He pitched forward onto his face, motionless.

Shelly was coming, loping hard and fast, locked onto me like a heat-seeking missile. She didn't even turn as Melanie, hiding in the shadows of the broken liquor-store window, flicked her lighter and ignited the wick on her second Molotov. She reared her arm back and threw it as hard as she could, the bottle spinning and trailing sparks as it arced through the air.

The bottle hit the werewolf's back and broke, splashing her with a wave of burning liquor. She let out a keening screech as her fur caught fire, the blaze engulfing her in a heartbeat. She spun, wildly slapping herself with her paws.

Caitlin tossed me the letter opener. Then she gripped her makeshift spear in both hands, leveled it, and charged. The glass shards tore into the werewolf's belly and Caitlin kept going, using her leverage to push Shelly back, step by agonizing step. She swiped at Caitlin with her claws, yowling furiously, but the length of the spear kept her at bay. Pitting strength against strength, Caitlin slowly wrestled her toward the burning remains of Smiley Face, shoving her into the bonfire.

The werewolf's fur was sloughing off, baring blistered flesh and charred bone, as Caitlin pinned her down with the spear on top of the slasher's corpse, both of them burning together. I circled the fire and got ready.

"Now," I said, "pull her out!"

Caitlin wrenched the spear, heaving the half-dead monster out of the flames and onto her back. Her chest was a gaping cavity, ruined and smoldering. I brought the letter opener down with the last of my strength and plunged it straight into Shelly's beating heart.

She let out one last howl, a screech of raw, defiant fury, then fell still.

Melanie stepped over the broken windowsill, clutching a cherry-red rescue ax. The four of us regrouped on the open boulevard, the town still impossibly asleep and quiet. The only sound, now, was the crackling of open flames, washing over us with the mingled stench of burnt hair and blackened pork.

Caitlin studied her improvised spear. Half of the glass shards had snapped off, broken in the wolf-beast's belly, but what remained looked even sharper and nastier. She nodded her approval.

I had a cop's revolver tucked into my belt, with three bullets. Hardly an arsenal, but at least we had options.

I watched Mr. Smith give the dead werewolf an experimental nudge with his toe. Then he turned his attention to Smiley Face. The fire had nearly guttered out, leaving a charred, barely human corpse in a melted mask behind. He took a step closer.

"You don't want to do that," I told him. "Honestly, have you not seen *any* of these movies?"

"I've never encountered a creature like this," he said. "My employers will want a tissue sample, at least."

"Even I know why this is a bad idea," Melanie muttered as Smith stood over the slasher's body. He reached for the dead man's mask.

I could have intervened, but then I met my student's eyes and she gave me a wink. I nodded in response, biting back a proud smile. Then I crossed my arms and waited for the inevitable.

As Smith reached for the mask, Smiley Face suddenly sat bolt upright. He grasped his scorched pick in one hand, raising it high as his blackened glove shot toward Smith's throat.

Melanie brought her rescue ax slamming down, chopping into the slasher's skull and burying the ax-head in his brain. She put one foot on Smiley Face's shoulder and wrenched the ax free, pulling it loose with a wet, slurping *pop*, and the slasher collapsed like a broken puppet. Dead for real this time. For the moment, at least.

Melanie rested her ax on her shoulder and said, "Call me the Final Girl, bitch."

Chapter
Twenty-Three

We needed to get off the street, fast, and buy some breathing room. Springfield had thrown a masked killer, a werewolf, and a vampire at us, speed-running horror's greatest hits, and the night was far from over. I didn't want to see what else the town had up its sleeve, at least not before we came up with a strategy to fight back.

I picked the lock on the library door and ushered everyone inside. We kept the lights off, the blinds drawn, quiet as church mice as we infiltrated the stacks of impossible and never-written books. I thought about the paperback I'd swiped, the one that Carolyn never wrote in life; it had secrets for me, I was certain, things I needed to know, but I had to get time to read it first. This town seemed determined to keep us on the move, on the back foot and playing defense, like some invisible director gleefully stirring up the action every time the plot slowed down. So far, it was working. I was exhausted, running on fumes, with a sore shoulder and a pounding headache, and my companions didn't look much better.

Still, I had enough strength left to sucker punch Mr. Smith, throwing my fist into his gut and doubling him over. I brought him down with a shove, pinning him on the library carpet, and pressed the muzzle of the dead cop's gun up against the soft of his jaw.

"Hi," I said. "We're gonna have a talk now. What the fuck is going on in this town?"

"You know I have no idea," he wheezed. "If I did, I wouldn't *be* here."

Melanie and Caitlin loomed over both of us. Caitlin idly contemplated her broken-glass spear, while Melanie gripped her ax in both hands, ready to use it.

"Yeah, your fact-finding mission. Let's talk about that. So, you told us back at the airport that the Eden conduit is having...how did you describe it? Power issues? Like Naavarasi—at least I think we're all agreed that this is Naavarasi's work—is siphoning magic from the portal."

"And the trail led here. Yes. That's all I know."

"So the power that's being stolen from the Eden conduit is fueling an impossible town full of monsters, driven by movie logic." I leaned closer to him, our gazes locked. "So here's the million-dollar question: if that's the kind of magic Naavarasi is stealing, *what the fuck are you assholes doing to the conduit?*"

"I don't know," he said. "I told you already, they removed that information from my brain before I was dispatched. All I know is what I need to know."

"Yeah, well, see, I've been noodling that over. Assuming I believe you—and to be fair, I do, because your bosses are exactly the kind of psychos who practice impromptu mind wipes on their own people—you still have to know the essentials. You're aware of the conduit, you're aware of the power siphon, and they had to have left you enough details in that jigsaw-puzzle brain to diagnose and fix the problem. So dish: what are you lunatics up to?"

Smith glanced off to one side, lips pursed, silent as he calculated his response.

"Have you ever wondered, Mr. Faust, how the Enemy was able to rewrite months of your life, orchestrate your imprisonment, and pin the mantle of the Thief upon you when you're not even a member of the First Story?"

"Only on days ending with a 'y,'" I said.

In truth, I was so baffled by the mystery that I'd almost given up trying to figure it out. My real fear was it happening again. But for some reason, after I escaped prison and got the Thief's burden off my shoulders, the Enemy never tried to repeat the trick.

"So did we. Our brief alliance with the Enemy was intended exclusively to gain access to the conduit, as our sorcerers tracked significant cosmic flare-ups at the times when the Enemy was flexing his magical muscles."

"Significant?" Caitlin asked.

"Significant, like a sun going supernova and wiping out two heavily populated worlds in one of the parallel galaxies next door. Two of ours, as it happened. My employers were not pleased. May I sit up? This is highly uncomfortable."

I got off him and back on my feet. He stretched and winced, trapped between me, Caitlin, and Melanie. He was the only person in the room not brandishing a weapon, not to mention the only person in the room who didn't want him dead, and I was pretty sure he felt it.

"Then there was the Wisdom's Grave incident," he said. "One of our holy masters, the King of Rust, a *god*, murdered by a pair of characters from the First Story along with a handful of mortal allies." His gaze drifted from me to Caitlin and back again. "Of course, you know this. You were there. It's never happened before. Never, in all of history."

"Yeah, well," I said, "you need better taste in gods. Yours really suck."

He ignored me and kept talking. "When the Owl and her whore—"

"I think you mean 'the Witch and her Knight,'" Caitlin said, her voice pitched in a cold warning. "And they happen to be friends of ours, so watch your language."

"They injured us and they escaped us, vanishing into the multiverse together. Unforgivable. My employers decided that if they couldn't strike at them directly, we could try more radical methods of attack."

I blinked. "Oh, you unbelievable bastards."

"I don't get it," Melanie said.

I kept my gun trained on Smith, and I wanted to use it. If not for the fact that he had a pilot's license and we might need him to escape Springfield, I would have started with his kneecaps right then and there.

"What the Enemy did to me is tied to the Eden conduit somehow," I explained. "The Network wanted to know how the trick worked. Not because of me, I'm not that important."

"A refreshing and rare moment of humility on your part," Smith muttered.

"They're trying to screw with the Story itself," I told Melanie and Caitlin. "If they can learn how the Enemy moved the mantle of the Thief to someone else and rewrote someone's life from a distance, they can do it too."

"Such as," Caitlin mused, "eradicating the Witch and her Knight from the entire timeline. Or replacing them with different characters."

"Ones loyal to us," Smith said. "There is something...deeply satisfying about taking a hated enemy, wiping their mind clean, and turning them into a loyal lapdog."

He looked me in the eye, his lips curling into the thinnest ghost of a smile.

"You'll learn all about that, in time. All three of you will." He held up a finger. "But. As Robert Burns wrote, 'the best-laid schemes o' mice an' men gang aft agley.' We quickly ascertained two facts. First, as expected, the power of the First Story is intricately entwined with the Garden of Eden itself. We think that's where the Story was composed. Ground zero of the cosmic eruption, if you will. The Enemy isn't strong enough to alter the story with his own power, even at full strength. After all, if he could have, he would have done it centuries ago. Discovering the portal to Eden changed that. He was able to interface with the Story's energies directly. Playing it, like a talented amateur with a Stradivarius."

"What else did you learn?" Caitlin asked.

"That Eden may be one of, if not the, most dangerous, toxic, cancerous places in the entire multiverse."

I stared down at him. "And how many lives did figuring that out cost you?"

"They were mostly expendable. But doing any serious manipulation of the Story requires incredibly costly field expeditions. Worse, we discovered the same thing the Enemy did when he went after you: the First Story is...how do I put this? If the multiverse is a house of many rooms, the Story is a load-bearing wall. And if a load-bearing wall is demolished, so goes the entire house."

I thought about the "cosmic flare-ups" Smith had mentioned earlier. A sun going supernova, planets dying...

"It was because of me," I said. "All that destruction—it was a reaction to the Enemy screwing around with the fabric of the multiverse."

"Quite. In a sense, Mr. Faust...you are directly responsible for the deaths of over twelve billion people, all because you—nothing but a mortal magician, a thug, and a con artist—chose to stand in the Enemy's path. If you had known your place and stayed in your lane like the insect you are, none of it would have happened. I'm curious. Tell me, how does that make you feel?"

I couldn't feel anything. I couldn't let myself feel anything, not right now. That was for after the fight.

"And that's why he never tried it a second time," I reasoned. "When he pinned the Thief's curse on me and threw me in prison, he must have seen the consequences and realized how close he came to destroying everything. Including himself."

"But...isn't that his whole job?" Melanie asked.

Smith shook his head. "Not like that. Just like his compatriots, the Enemy is bound by unbreakable rules. He cannot destroy a world until he's battled the latest incarnation of the Paladin and won. He may *want* to, certainly. I'm sure that after all the trouble you people have caused him, he'd incinerate your Earth without a second thought if he could. Alas for him, he behaves the way he was written to behave. He cannot change any more than the proverbial leopard can change his spots. At any rate, once we realized the dangers, we called off the operation immediately. We're ambitious, not stupid. No amount of power is worth rolling the dice on destroying the entire multiverse. The Network plays a long game. We can wait."

"Hold on," I said. "So we're supposed to believe you canceled the project...but your bosses still picked up on a big power drain from the conduit and sent you to investigate? Why? Why would they even care?"

Mr. Smith took a deep breath. His shoulders sagged.

"We're clearly doing *something* with it," he said, "something different from the original plan, but that's the part they removed from my memory. If you'll forgive some speculation on my part, I think what we're witnessing in this town—the very existence *of* this town—is some sort of corruption of the First Story's power. Someone is harnessing it, shaping it to their own ends. I suppose you could call it...fan fiction."

The Canton relics. Now it made sense. When Teddy and Naavarasi ambushed me after the Northlight Tower heist and my brother put a bullet in my heart, I had just liberated the Enemy's entire collection of magical trinkets. Trinkets crafted by an old incarnation of the Paladin, with the intention of helping her later lives succeed in their eternal fight. I couldn't have guessed why they wanted them, especially considering the relics were stubborn little cusses and would only operate in the hands of true-blue good guys. I'd figured I was the target that day, and swiping my score before Teddy shot me was just a bit of added insult to injury.

"I got it twisted," I said. "It was never about me in the first place."

Caitlin frowned at me. "Pet?"

"Don't get me wrong, Naavarasi wanted me dead. Needed me dead and lost in hell, so she could try to frame me with that assassination attempt on Prince Sitri. But Naavarasi had decades to plan the hit on Sitri and she could have taken that shot any time she felt like it. No, she had two irons in the fire that day. That's why they hit me when they did. I was just a bonus. It wasn't about me. It was about the Canton relics. They're all infused with the Paladin's essence."

"Sympathetic magic," Melanie said, making the connection. "Like attracts like. She figured out a way to get a whole bunch of First Story artifacts together and use them like a magnet. Energy spills out of the Eden portal and it all pours in...right here."

I was curious about the "how," but what we really needed right now was a "why." Naavarasi was waging a vendetta against hell and earth alike, raising an army of shape-shifters to fight across two worlds, trying to kill Sitri while ingratiating herself with Prince Mal-phas, and screwing with my family—my family of choice *and* my flesh-and-blood brother—at the same time. Everything she did was focused, deliberate, a chess gambit planned out ten moves in advance.

So what the hell was Springfield *for*?

"Get up," I told Smith. "We can't stay here for long. If movie rules are still in effect, either we can stride out into danger, or the danger's going to come looking for us."

"Do you think we can make it back to the bed-and-breakfast?" Melanie asked.

I shook my head. "Got a better idea. Cait, what time is it?"

"Eight minutes to midnight," she said.

"Perfect. There's one, and only one place in this entire town that opens up after dark, and there's no chance that's a coincidence. You know, after everything we've gone through so far tonight, I think we've earned a break. Let's go to the movies."

Chapter Twenty-Four

The Tivoli was waiting for us. The one-screen movie house, an art-deco monolith adorned in chrome and brass, sat silent and dark, squatting at the end of a long, narrow street.

At the stroke of midnight, it came to life.

Rings of vintage bulbs circling the marquee ignited, strobing as they drew hot white lines around the stark black letters above the ticket booth:

Midnight Movie

Night of the Living Dead

2Nite Only

The four of us marched up the street, bloodied and bedraggled, side by side. We stopped in front of the theater. Caitlin planted the butt of her glass-shard spear against the pavement and gave me a sidelong glance.

"Penny for your thoughts, pet."

"The only place open at midnight, in a town where going out after dark gets you killed," I said. "Either we've been lured here, and this is some last-ditch attempt at a trap..."

"Or whoever built this place doesn't want anyone coming here," Melanie suggested. "Smiley, Shelly, the vampire cop...they were *protecting* it."

I gave it even odds, either way. Only way to find out if it was a trap was to spring it, and we weren't getting anything done standing outside in the dark. I waved the troops forward.

The ticket booth stood empty, to my complete lack of surprise. The lobby doors, appointed with quilted crimson padding, were unlocked and swung open at a touch.

The lobby was more scarlet and brass, with a hammered-tin ceiling and a small concession stand. Nobody was on duty, but fresh popcorn popped and leaped inside a glass case beside a rack of candy bars. I recognized some of the faded wrappers from my own childhood, a feeling of poisonous nostalgia; the only time Teddy and I ever got candy was when I boosted it from the corner store. The other brands were from before my time.

"I shouldn't have to tell you this," I said as we approached the door to the theater proper, "but be prepared for literally anything."

The theater was deserted. Light flickered from the projection booth above our heads to the silver screen straight ahead, looming over the final seats at the bottom of the sloping aisle. The rubber mats lining the aisles were sticky with spilled soda, pulling against my shoes as I led the way. The screen was a window into a world of black-and-white. Judith O'Dea was scrambling around a run-down farmhouse in the dark, having a nervous breakdown. Outside the window, a tall man in a funeral suit staggered toward her, his limbs flailing in a herky-jerky stumble.

The soundtrack was alarmed and bold and utterly cheesy all at the same time, the mood turned up to eleven with the kind of score you could only hear in a sixties sci-fi movie. It didn't ease my nerves any, especially when the movie was suddenly washed out by a squeal of static from the theater's PA system.

"You shouldn't have come here," my brother's voice said, echoing from all around us and nowhere at the same time.

Caitlin and I moved as one, standing back-to-back so we could catch a threat from any direction. I scanned the empty seats, my eyes adjusting to the flickering darkness.

"You shouldn't have shot me," I replied.

I knew I was throwing away my disguise. Calculated risk. We'd fought off everything Springfield had thrown at us, and if I was judging that tremor in my brother's voice correctly, he was nervous about it. We weren't supposed to be here. Weren't supposed to have made it this far. Frightened people made dumb mistakes; I wanted him good and scared.

"...Dan?" he said after a moment of shocked silence.

"My old body's in the repair shop," I said. "You know. Because you *shot me*, Teddy."

"You had it coming," he said, finding a little defensive bluster.

"Funny thing," I said. "There are people out there who could legitimately murder me and say I deserve it for what I did to 'em. Lots of people. But you...are not in that category."

He didn't respond. Melanie was prowling the aisles, peeking behind the rows of chairs, looking more angry than scared now. She plucked at a stray thread dangling from her ragged and torn shirtsleeve.

"Nice monsters, jerk. You owe me a new top."

I heard something, a muffled whisper over the speakers, and held up a hand for quiet. Caitlin gave me a curious look.

I couldn't make out the words, but the tone of a one-sided conversation—an increasingly tense one—was undeniable.

"He's on the phone," I whispered, hunting for the source of the broadcast. "The projection booth. He'd be able to watch us from up there."

"Calling Naavarasi?" Caitlin breathed.

"Probably asking for his marching orders. Which means she's not here. He's all alone."

I nodded to the flickering beam of light from the booth above us.

"Let's go get his ass."

"You know," Teddy said over the PA system, "this situation actually works out for me. I've been taking this place for a test drive, and there's one thing I haven't tried yet. Ready for your big break in show business?"

"I'm definitely about to break something," Caitlin growled.

I clapped my hands to my ears as the speakers erupted in a shrill metallic whine, agonizingly loud and high-pitched. The theater spun around me as the projector light became a manhole cover, then a window, then the mouth of a tunnel, roaring toward me, the white hot glow swallowing my senses whole.

***

"Get *off* me," Melanie shouted.

My senses all snapped back at once. I smelled fresh-cut grass, felt cool open air on my skin, an autumn breeze rippling through a graveyard.

The world had been completely drained of color. Everything was black and white and shades of gray.

Melanie was on her back in the mud, a pale man in a shabby, dirt-encrusted suit leaning in with his mouth yawning, trying to take a chunk out of her throat. She held him back with both hands, but it was a losing battle. I was already running, drawing my foot back, and I kicked him in the head like I was going for a field goal. He grunted and rolled off her. I grabbed Melanie's hand and hauled her to her feet.

"We have company," Mr. Smith said, pointing.

In one direction, an old farmhouse stood alone in a field by the cemetery. In the other, a disheveled foursome of men in ragged hospital gowns, the thin cotton stained with dark fluids, were staggering toward us with their arms outstretched. Things were moving too fast for my brain to catch up; we needed breathing room to figure this out.

"The farmhouse," I said. "Let's go!"

We sprinted for the front porch. As we neared, the door swung wide and a handsome young man, dark-skinned and determined, gave us a frantic wave.

"C'mon in, quick," he called out. "I was just about to board the door up! Everybody in!"

We piled into the living room—not much to see, just rustic clapboard and cheap antiques—and he slammed the door behind us. Our host was already on the move, hefting a table with its legs broken off, pressing it to the front door.

"Here," he told me, "hold this while I nail it in place. Oughta hold those things off for a little bit."

A pale and trembling woman sat on a sofa, staring into space. Melanie waved a hand in front of her face, then looked at me.

"Dan? What is happening here? And...why is the world in black-and-white? Is everyone else seeing this?"

"Yeah," I said, steadying the broken table. "I have some bad news for how the rest of this night's gonna go. This is Ben and that's Barbra. I'll tell you right now, Barbra's kind of useless, so don't expect much."

"They kept...grabbing at me and grabbing at me," Barbra whispered.

Ben's eyes went hard as he clutched a hammer and a nail. "How do you know my name, mister?"

"Long story, I'll tell you later. Right now we need to get this place fortified. Everyone, grab whatever you can. Anything we can use as a barricade: furniture, maybe pop some of the interior doors off their hinges. We've got company and they're here for dinner."

"How many did you see out there?" Ben asked.

"Five. For now."

He nodded. "Yeah, there were two before. Figure once they realize we're in here, they'll call their friends."

Melanie was on the other side of the living room, checking out a door by the sofa.

"Hey," she called out, "there's a cellar! We could hide down there."

"Swear to..." I took a deep breath. "Have you honestly never seen this movie?"

"What? No. This is boomer shit."

"Okay, well, bad things happen in the cellar, Melanie! Media literacy. It can save your life."

Ben looked between Caitlin and me. "Movie? I think your friend here is cracking up, lady."

"Oh, you don't know the half of it," she sighed.

We scoured the house, grabbing anything that wasn't nailed down and prying up half the things that were, hammering boards and scraps and covering the doors and windows as best we could. Even Smith rolled up his sleeves, though if he had any occult insights to share, he was keeping them close to the vest.

My brother had trapped us in a movie. Leaving aside the how for a minute, I marveled at the scale. A magical construct nestled inside a magical construct.

"They didn't build this," I murmured to Caitlin as we flipped the rustic kitchen table onto its back.

"Naavarasi and your brother?"

"I still think my theory holds. They're using the Canton artifacts to siphon power for…whatever she's got planned next, but not even the 'mistress of illusions' has this kind of skill. Besides, did you catch the way Teddy was talking back there?"

She nodded, grim, as she snapped a leg off the table.

"'Taking this place for a test drive,'" she quoted.

"Like a kid with a new toy. And I figured out what kept throwing me. We were expecting raks. She sent two of her kids to guard the tunnel at the airport, but we haven't seen a single one since. I think I know why."

I put the side of my foot against a table leg, grabbed it with both hands, and wrenched it from side to side until it began to wriggle loose. It broke free with a satisfying pop, two rusty nails jutting from the wood.

"They're using Springfield as their base of operations," I said, "but they don't *control* it. Not really. Doesn't matter if it's us or her own people: anyone on the streets after dark is begging for an unhappy ending. She won't risk sending her sons in here unless she has to."

"But she'll risk your brother," Caitlin said.

I tasted ashes in my mouth. She'd risk him without thinking twice. Use him until he was used up. If only I had a way to make him see that.

That problem would keep. We had a more pressing one. Namely, the fact that we'd been banished into an old movie I'd seen a dozen times.

A movie where everyone died in the end.

Chapter Twenty-Five

"Dan, Cait," Melanie called out, her voice quivering. "You should see this."

We ran up to the second floor of the farmhouse, past Barbra—sitting on the couch in a listless daze—and Ben and Mr. Smith hammering up another crude barricade. Melanie was in an empty bedroom overlooking the front of the house.

The walking dead had brought their friends.

White-sheeted figures staggered through the graveyard, lurching from tombstone to tombstone. Gnarled bodies with burn scars and mortal wounds, some stark naked and showing the autopsy scars over their flabby guts, stared up at us with dead, hungry eyes. There were at least twenty of them out there, and more shambling, mindless bodies among the trees in the distance.

After facing a slasher and a couple of classic movie monsters, at least this was a challenge I had some personal experience with. That didn't enthuse me. Zombies were real but thankfully rare; you needed to be a powerhouse like Damien Ecko or Herbert West to reanimate the dead. "Thankfully" because the damn things were terrifying. They were the ultimate pursuit predators: slow, clumsy, but relentless and untiring, and strong enough to rip you to pieces. Back when we were on Ecko's trail, I'd watched one of his walking corpses punch through a man's chest like it was made of tissue paper.

"Come down to the kitchen and help us with the barricades," I told Melanie, easing her away from the window. Some work would keep her distracted, if nothing else.

We were halfway up the hall when we heard the *thump*.

It echoed from just above our heads. Then another. The sound of heavy footsteps, pacing. Caitlin nodded toward the square of an attic-ladder hatch. I had the nail-studded table leg from downstairs. I gripped it, ready for my turn at bat, and locked eyes with her. She stepped back, gestured for silence, and pulled the dangling cord.

The hatch swung open. The attic ladder fell free, ratcheting down until it slammed against the hallway floor. A faint, reedy groan drifted down from above, along with the stench of rotting meat. A dead woman in a homespun country dress, her skin waxy and blistered, her eyes glassy-white, began to descend on bare and wobbly feet.

"Behind me," I told Melanie. I braced the table leg in my grip and pulled it back. If she got hold of me, I was a dead man. My only hope was to take her down first, and zombies could absorb an insane amount of punishment. Caitlin stood behind the ladder, ready to jump in.

A closet door in the room behind us groaned open on a squeaky hinge, and a second growl turned our heads. A walking corpse loomed in the doorway, a slack-jawed man with a gaping hole where one of his eyes had been chewed out of his skull. He reached out and latched on to Melanie before she could react, leaning in to take a bite out of her. I spun, brought up the table leg, and used it like a battering ram, slamming it straight into the dead man's face. He let go of Melanie, staggering back but still on his feet.

The dead woman grabbed me from behind, her arms circling mine and pinning me in a bear hug. I felt her hot breath on my neck as Caitlin yanked her hair back, turning her head a second before the zombie's teeth snapped shut. Caitlin gave her another tug and the dead woman's grip broke, sending me sprinting straight at the second zombie. I swung the table leg, cracking it across the side of his skull, and he went down like a sack of garbage.

I hit him again, and again, driving the table leg down like a sledge-hammer until his skull shattered and he painted the black-and-white floorboards in shades of wet gray jelly.

I turned just in time to see Caitlin wrestling with the dead woman. Cait grabbed her in a headlock and wrenched her neck until it snapped. Slowly, as tissue ripped and bones crackled, she twisted and pulled until the woman's head tore free from her shoulders. The de-capitated body hit the floor, motionless. Caitlin tossed the head aside, watching it roll down the hallway as we caught our breath.

I had to smile. I damn near laughed. Caitlin and Melanie both looked at me like I'd really gone crazy this time.

"Pet?" Caitlin asked.

"Movie rules," I said. I looked to the window, and the gathering herd outside. "We're playing by movie rules."

"Hello?" Melanie said. "Earth to Dan. Talk to us."

"They're *not our zombies*," I said. "In the real world, if you get surrounded by a herd of the walking dead, you've got zero chance of survival. But we're not in the real world. We're in *Night of the Living Dead*." I scurried to the top of the staircase. "Hey! Ben! You brawl with any of these things on the way over here?"

"Sure, mister," he called back. "They're cream puffs, one at a time. Problem is, they don't come one at a time."

I grinned wildly at Caitlin and Melanie. "Hell, in the original, a redneck militia is able to mop up most of the zombie problem by tomorrow morning. At least until Romero decided to make a sequel. Ordinary people can fight these things."

"And we aren't ordinary people," Caitlin said, eager sparks of copper dancing in her eyes.

"No. We're two magicians, an incarnate demon, and a Network op. We can handle this. We've got Ben, too. He's no slouch in a fight."

"And Barbra," Melanie pointed out.

I stared at her. "You *clearly* have not seen this film."

"What do you think?" Caitlin asked. "We're barricaded rather nicely at the moment. Should we stay put and try to outlast the inevitable siege?"

I had thought about that. Our odds were suddenly looking better. Not *good*, by any stretch of the imagination, but better. We might actually pull it off. Then I saw the lurking danger. There was a big unknown in this equation, and I didn't dare get it wrong.

"The zombies break into the farmhouse toward the very end of the movie," I said. "But that's the problem. We're *in* the movie. So what happens if we're still here when the closing credits roll?"

"Nothing good," Caitlin murmured. "But how do we escape when we don't know how Teddy delivered us here in the first place?"

Magical construct inside a magical construct, I thought.

I had an idea. If I was right, we might actually survive this. That said, the words "if" and "might" were doing a lot of heavy lifting.

"Okay," I said, "so this place is just like Springfield. It isn't real. I mean, it's real for all intents and purposes: injuries are real, pain is real, and we can die here..."

"But the world will bend to fit the rules of the story," Caitlin said. "Like the moon suddenly turning full so Shelly could change her shape."

"We're talking about a staggering amount of raw power, and the bigger you make a construct like this, the more fuel it's going to take. Exponentially, maybe. It has to be enclosed, a set, defined space. There have to be boundaries."

Melanie lit up. "Like the mountains all around Springfield! It looks like our world, but it's just a fake town in a fake valley with nothing outside."

"Exactly. Now, with the exception of a few cutaway shots, the entire movie takes place in and around this farmhouse. I'm willing to bet there's not much else out there. If we can get far enough away, we'll either hit a wall or a way out."

"What if we hit a wall?" Melanie asked.

"Then we click our heels together three times and say 'There's no place like home.'"

"I don't think that'll work," she said.

"Neither do I," I said, "so let's hope we don't hit a wall."

We went downstairs to rally the troops. Ben, Barbra, and Mr. Smith were huddled around the radio as a newscaster breathlessly relayed the facts: "*It appears that the freshly deceased are...rising from the dead and committing acts of mass murder—*"

I clicked off the radio. Ben jumped to his feet. "What's the idea, man?"

"The idea is, we're getting the hell out of here. Now. Ben, you drove here, right? But your truck's out of gas. It's parked over by the fuel pumps out in front."

"Yeah," he said, eyes narrow. "Thought I could refuel here, but the pumps are locked. You know a lot about me, mister. Don't think I like that very much."

"We can't stay here," I said, "and more of these ghouls are showing up by the minute. The longer we wait, the worse it's going to be. If we get you some fuel, can you drive us out of here?"

"No question about it," Ben said.

"Have you looked out the window lately?" Smith demanded. "There's a small army between us and the truck."

"Then we're going to get a workout," I said. "Here's the plan: we're going to load up on weapons, anything we can use to fend those things off. We'll make a beeline for the truck. Me and Cait will take point. Ben and Smith, you're covering our flanks. Melanie, your job is to pick the lock on that fuel pump. We'll hold the freaks off while you get it done."

Her eyes widened. "Me?"

I leaned closer to her and lowered my voice. "Cait doesn't know how to pick locks, and even if Smith can, I don't trust him not to screw it up. It's either got to be you or me, and I need to focus on the fight. Listen, this movie came out in 1968. If you can't pop some backwoods padlock that was built nearly sixty years ago..."

She held up her open hands. "Okay, point taken. Yeah, I can handle it. Long as you can keep 'em off me."

"Smith, the instant she gets the lock open, you grab the hose and start pumping gas. Run the fuel line for about ten seconds, no more than that. Ben, I need you behind the wheel and ready to gun it. We'll all pile in back and we'll get the hell out of here."

Ben shook his head. "Ten seconds' worth? Mister, my tank is dry. That's not gonna get us to Pittsburgh."

"Trust me, we're not going anywhere near that far. Now listen up, all of you. The only way to kill these zombies for good is direct cranial trauma. Shoot 'em in the head, brain 'em with a club, whatever it takes. Do not, under any circumstances, let one bite you. You get bit, you're dead. Eventually. Remaining life expectancy depends on the movie. Romero wiggled a little on that one."

"Who's 'Romero'?" Ben asked. "And hey, what about Barbra? We gotta take her, too."

I looked to the near-catatonic woman on the couch.

"If you absolutely must," I said.

I still had the vampire cop's gun tucked in my belt. Three bullets. Three head shots, against a horde, and only if I made each one count. Ben had scrounged up a rifle, a lever-action repeater with a handful of bullets. Melanie clutched her rescue ax, her hands squeezing the haft until her knuckles turned stark white. I passed out table-leg clubs to Caitlin and Mr. Smith, keeping the third for myself. I wasn't sure how many skulls I could smash before the stout rough-grained wood snapped in my hands, but I was damn sure going to make a good run of it.

"Seems to me," Ben said, crouching to peer out between a pair of boards over the nearest window, "most of these dudes are out in front. We should slip out the back and circle around. Means a longer run to the truck, but that way they won't all swarm us at once."

"Sounds like a plan. Ladies and gentlemen, I'm not going to sugarcoat it. My brother dropped us into a no-win scenario."

I triple-checked the revolver, made sure I could reach it in a heartbeat, and slapped the table-leg club against my open palm.

"That said," I added, "too bad for Teddy, but I don't believe in no-win scenarios. Let's desecrate some corpses."

Chapter
Twenty-Six

We gathered in the kitchen, taking up positions around the boarded-up back door. Melanie worked a claw hammer into another nail, wrenching it from a board we'd just put up, slowly tearing down the barricade.

The last plank fell free, clattering to the linoleum floor. She put her trembling fingers on the deadbolt latch and looked to me with a question in her eyes.

"Do it," I said.

She turned the latch and flung the door wide. We boiled out into the night, veering right, following the clapboard walls of the old farmhouse. Ben dragged Barbra along, wielding the rifle one-handed in the other. A bloody-mouthed ghoul in a hospital gown staggered from the shadows, limping with one arm outstretched. Ben waited until it got close, almost point-blank; then he brought up the rifle and fired. The dead man's head snapped back, skull erupting in a storm of gray goo and shattered chunks of bone, and he pitched face-first onto the lawn.

We can do this, I thought, for one fleeting moment of optimism.

Then a mournful, whistling howl went up, rustling through the trees, coming from every direction at once. They'd heard that. The horde was coming.

"All right, folks," I said. "This is it. Live or die, let's give 'em hell either way."

They came from the trees and the tombstones, the shambling dead marching like a ragged and starving army. On the other side stood Ben's truck and the fuel pumps, our only way out.

A dead man lurched at me, springing from the shadows of an outhouse. I whipped the revolver from my belt and dropped him with a bullet. Caitlin ran just ahead of me, swinging her stout table-leg club, flipping a corpse off its feet and then pulping its skull on the grass. Ben let go of Barbra long enough to work the lever action on his rifle, fire and repeat, his rounds punching through one ghoul's stomach and blowing out another one's kneecap, leaving it to crawl like a trench soldier through the blood-slick mud.

A zombie suddenly loomed in the corner of my eye. I turned, but Smith was faster on the draw, clocking it with his table leg and sending it staggering. I darted around another pair of walking corpses, dancing and ducking out of reach, snapping off another shot as one reached for Melanie. They had numbers, but we had speed and power on our side. As we cleared a path to the pumps and Melanie went to work, her trembling fingers nearly dropping her lockpicks, I thought we might actually pull this off.

Ben fired his last bullet. So did I, losing count in the action until I pulled the trigger on an advancing ghoul and my revolver snapped dry. Caitlin raced in before it could grab me and wrenched one grasping arm behind its back, breaking it like a twig. Then she hoisted the zombie up in the air and brought it slamming down onto her upraised knee, shattering its spine in a dozen places. She dropped it to the grass and left it writhing, already spinning to fight off a pair of dead men.

Ben wrestled Barbra into the passenger seat of the pickup truck. Then he brandished the empty rifle like a club, holding it by the muzzle and swinging wild, driving back the oncoming horde. Smith popped the truck's fuel cap, turning just in time to brain another dead woman with his table leg, driving her to her knees and then to the mud as the gore-spattered wood whistled down again and again.

"Got it!" Melanie shouted. The pump clicked and the lock released the fuel handle. I grabbed it and tossed it to Smith, who snatched it out of the air and slid the nozzle into the truck.

"Ben," I called out, beating down a burnt-faced ghoul a few feet from the pumps, "get ready to start the truck! We are *leaving*."

***

Naavarasi's voice on the phone was a deadly hiss. "You did *what?*"

Teddy scrambled from one side of the projection booth to the other. It was a tangled nightmare of valves and pipes and hoses and chugging machines, a schizophrenic steampunk nightmare, centered around the clattering, whirring projector. Through the tiny projectionist window he had a perfect view of the action, though his initial sense of triumph had spent the last few minutes quietly crumbling to ash. He flipped switches, spun valves, desperate to turn things around.

"I activated the theater relic," he said. "You wanted to test it! You told me so!"

"A reality-altering artifact, the powers of which we still haven't fully ascertained...and you fed our worst enemies to it."

"Isn't that sort of what you're supposed to do with your enemies? Kill them?" he countered. "This isn't exactly like putting Faust in a slow-moving death trap and then walking away..."

"Watch it," she snapped.

"I threw them into *Night of the Living Dead*. That movie has a one-hundred-percent kill rate."

"And how is that working out for you?" Naavarasi asked.

He peeked through the window and wished he hadn't. Up on the screen, Daniel and Caitlin were going to town on the restless dead, pulping skulls and ripping out throats, while the others worked to get the truck started. No mistakes like in the movie. No fire, no explosion, and they were treating the ghouls like piñatas made of flesh and bone.

"They're changing the script," he said.

"Teddy, we had a plan. You were supposed to convince them to *leave*."

"You mean go down there and face them myself? In person? My brother and his psycho friends all want to kill me."

Naavarasi let out a long-suffering sigh.

"He won't hurt you," she said. "We have his friend. As long as this 'Pixie' girl is in danger, he'll toe the line."

"You want me to risk my life on that?"

"Yes," she said. "Without hesitation. Because I know how Daniel thinks and I know you're not in any danger. A moot point now, I suppose. What are you going to do?"

Teddy gazed at a rack of film reels, each one labeled in black marker with a faded, spidery hand. An idea sparked. He harbored a tiny smile.

"My mistake was not going hard enough," he said. "We need a better class of zombies."

***

The hungry dead closed in from all sides. Cait and I did our best to hold them off, swinging our clubs to keep them at bay, dropping anyone who got too close to Smith as he pumped gas into the pickup. Ben covered the driver-side door, swinging his empty rifle like a bat, while Barbra sat, catatonic, in the passenger seat.

I brought the table leg down on a one-eyed ghoul's head and heard a pair of breathtaking cracks—one crack along the dead woman's skull and a longer, hairline one running along the wood of my makeshift weapon. It wouldn't last much longer and then I'd have nothing to fight with but my fists.

"That's it," Smith said, yanking out the gas nozzle and tossing it to the grass behind him. "Fire up the engine!"

A hundred feet away, off by the low stone fence ringing the cemetery, the earth erupted. Mud and clods of dirt blasted into the sky like a volcano as a trio of figures leaped from their restless graves.

They stood out from the black-and-white world around them, cast in vivid and glowing color.

Two of them, a man and a woman, looked like desiccated corpses dressed in eighties punk, all leather and denim and spikes. The third was nearly fleshless, big hungry eyes bulging from a skeletal face, his body dripping with what looked like black tar. His jaw distended, wriggling from side to side, as he pointed at us and groaned a single word.

"*Braaains!*"

Oh fuck, I thought.

They broke into a run. Not a slow shuffling gait, like the gray ghouls all around us, but a full-on sprint straight toward the truck. They knocked the other zombies out of the way like bowling pins. Ben stood there, paralyzed. *He's a character from a black-and-white movie*, I realized. *He's never even contemplated the concept of colors.*

Electric light shone on the horizon, beyond the tree line. A second of hope—maybe, somehow, the cavalry had come ahead of schedule—was shattered as a dozen misshapen, broken silhouettes charged from the light, another dozen or more on their heels, an army of the dead sprinting toward us in living color. I figured we had half a minute, maybe less, before they hit us like a tidal wave of biting jaws and hungry stomachs.

Ben found his mettle. He brandished his empty rifle and charged the tar zombie, meeting him halfway toward the truck. He swung and missed, the rifle glancing off the monster's shoulder. Black oil dripped from the creature's broken jaw as it fixed Ben with a manic grin.

"*Braaains!*" he roared, grabbing Ben's shoulders and yanking him close. His teeth clamped down on Ben's forehead, tearing skin, crunching *through* his skull like his bones were made of peanut brittle. Melanie ran in to help him, but I caught her by the arm, yanking her back.

"He's gone," I told her. "I need you behind the wheel. Get the truck started while we hold them off."

The passenger-side door ripped open, half a dozen hospital-gowned ghouls intent on a feast. They hauled Barbra out by the arms, dragging her into their pack and bringing her down, the air filled with frantic screams and the sounds of tearing flesh. One of the punk zombies ran at Melanie and I stepped into his path, my chair-leg club ramming into his belly to break his stride. He doubled over and I brought the club crashing down on the back of his head. The chair leg snapped right down the middle, leaving me with nothing but a jagged shard of wood and a prayer.

The pickup roared to life. It jolted forward a foot, then suddenly stopped.

"Something's wrong with it," Melanie shouted.

Nineteen sixty-eight, I realized. *Of course she can't drive it. It's a stick shift.*

Mr. Smith was a step ahead of me. He was being pressed hard, a quartet of black-and-white ghouls bracing him against the side of the pickup bed, and he swung wildly to drive them back and buy a little breathing room.

"Use the clutch!" he shouted back.

She leaned out from the driver-side door, eyes wide with panic. "*Which one is the clutch?*"

A denim-clad arm, musty and covered in bristles of yellow mold, clamped around my throat. Rotten breath washed across my cheek as the other punk zombie reeled me in for a bite. Then my face was suddenly wet, splashed in cold rancid blood, as Caitlin brained it with her club. She ripped it off me and I ran in to rescue Smith, driving the broken end of my weapon straight through a ghoul's eye.

The reinforcements were coming, screeching for brains as they raced across the graveyard. There were at least thirty of them now, howling in a mad chorus.

"I got it, I got it," Melanie called out as the truck's engine revved up a notch. "Everybody in!"

I piled into the bed of the pickup with Caitlin and Smith and pounded my fist against the window of the cab. Melanie gunned it and the truck lurched ahead, nearly knocking me off my feet. It rumbled over the uneven lawn, bouncing and jolting with every spin of the tires, kicking up sod and showering the ghouls in black dirt. She hit the old country road, swerving hard, as the horde ran fast on our heels. They were gaining ground.

"Melanie," I said, watching the front line of zombies closing in on the open bed of the truck, "drive *faster*."

For one heart-jolting moment the truck nearly stalled out, but she kept it under control and kicked it up to the next gear. One zombie, dressed in the torn and bloodied uniform of a paramedic, clamped his hand on the truck bed and started to climb in. Caitlin crushed his fingers with her club and sent him falling, rolling across the lawn, trampled by the rest of the pack as they stomped over him in their single-minded hunger.

Melanie angled the truck toward the light on the horizon. The pickup's engine whined, red-lining as she poured on the speed, wheels bouncing hard in the rough and throwing us around the bed. The horde somehow kept pace, still closing in, more hands latching on to the truck as we frantically battered them off. Then we hit the wall of light and—

Chapter Twenty-Seven

The pickup truck blasted through the movie screen and out into the real world. For a frozen, fleeting moment in time, we were airborne. Then the nose dove down hard and we crashed into the front row of theater seats, then the second, smashing through them like speed bumps. I felt like a sock in a dryer as I went tumbling, thrown from the pickup bed, tossed through the air and hitting the middle aisle of the cinema in a hard, bone-rattling roll.

I think I blacked out for a second. I was vaguely aware of my senses swimming back, blurry vision resolving into a picture of the truck with its hood crumpled and spewing radiator steam, windows shattered.

"Melanie," I croaked. "Cait."

"Here," Caitlin said, wincing as she shoved herself up from the pickup bed. Smith was just behind her, looking pale and shell-shocked but still breathing.

The driver-side door swung open on a twisted hinge. Melanie leaned out, exhausted and panting for breath, blood trickling from a cut on her forehead.

"I'm okay," she said, waving me back. "Just...just need a second."

The movie screen was a billowing disaster, four ragged and rippling corners around a giant gaping hole. The world, and us, was all back in color. All but the pickup, cast in black-and-white. The truck flickered, transient, a castaway from another world.

The projector died. The shimmering glow from the overhead booth faded, the sound of the clacking film reel slowing to a crawl, then falling quiet. Silence engulfed us. I helped Caitlin and Mr. Smith down from the truck bed, then checked on Melanie. Caitlin brandished a white handkerchief and pressed it to the cut, tilting Melanie's head back.

"Here," Caitlin said. "It's all right. Not deep. Head wounds just bleed a lot. Keep pressure on it."

A single handclap echoed through the theater. Then another, slow and sarcastic.

My brother was here.

He walked down the middle aisle, and he hadn't come unarmed. Besides the slim black nine-millimeter automatic on his belt, he wore Howard Canton's top hat and brandished Canton's wand, an ebony stick with a cap of yellowed ivory on either end.

"The difference between you and me," I said, "is that I can pull that style off. You just look like an asshole."

"A soon to be deceased one," Caitlin growled, standing at my left side while Melanie moved to my right.

"You know better than that," Teddy warned us. "We have your friend. Kill me and you'll never see her again."

He stood his ground ten feet away, keeping a careful distance. Not a safe distance, as the thrum of the cards in my breast pocket reminded me. I could end him, here and now, with a flick of my fingertips. After the ordeal we'd just survived, I wanted to do it. I wanted it like a man in the desert wants ice water.

But damn it all, he was right. We hadn't gotten to the bottom of what was going on in this nightmare town, and we had less than zero leads on finding Pixie. Teddy was our best hope, and he knew it.

"You were never supposed to come here," he said.

"You weren't supposed to shoot me," I said. "We all do things we shouldn't sometimes."

"You had it coming."

"Is that what Naavarasi told you?" I asked. "Or is that what you told yourself after, in the small hours of the night, while you were wide awake in your bed and wrestling with the guilt?"

Direct hit. His jaw went tight, his eyes flashing with hurt before he buried his real emotions under a mask of defiance.

"I hurt you, Teddy," I confessed.

He blinked at me. That wasn't what he expected to hear. But it was the truth, and I'd been needing to say it for a while now.

"You remember when we were kids?" I asked. "When we'd go to the convenience store and you'd cover while I boosted food for us to eat?"

My brother nodded, holding his silence.

"Mom was gone. Dad was crazy." I spread my open hands. "It was just you and me against the world, remember?"

"I remember," he said.

"Didn't I always take care of you? Didn't I protect you?"

His eyes narrowed. "You *stopped*."

"I never abandoned you," I said. "Whatever Naavarasi told you on that score is bullshit. I tried to kill Dad to stop him from beating us. And I fucked it up. Biggest regret of my life. I got shipped to juvie and you got stuck with the old man."

"He was twice as bad after that," Teddy said. "And he only had one son left to hurt."

"I made a mistake. If I could go back and do everything different, I would. But then...I got out, busted out, set off on my own, and tried to build something resembling a life."

"You never came to see me," he said. "You never checked up on me. Never helped me."

"And that was my second mistake. Dad was in the ground by then. You were free. I figured..."

He glared at me. "You figured what? That Teddy was fine? That Teddy could face the world all alone, still ripped open and bleeding?"

What I said next wasn't what I planned to say, the dozen times I'd rehearsed this confrontation in my head. I guess they were the words that needed to come out.

"I figured," I said, "that I was a toxic, worthless piece of shit and that you were better off without me."

He stared at me, silent now.

"However much you hate me, Teddy, you can't imagine how many years I've spent hating myself. I was dancing with demons and hijacking cigarette trucks while you were building a career and starting a family in the suburbs. I couldn't force myself back into your life. I knew I'd only taint it, ruin it, like I always ruined everything I touched. I couldn't do that to you. I figured you were better off without me."

"You figured—"

"Shut up," I told him. "I'm not finished talking. I was wrong, Teddy. I should have come back for you. If I'd had any idea that Naavarasi was grooming you, I would have moved earth and hell to stop her."

"She wasn't grooming me," he said, glowering. "I'm not a child anymore."

"Oh?" Caitlin asked. "And how old were you when Naavarasi began visiting your bedroom at night?"

He pursed his lips in a tight, quivering line. I clasped my hands in front of me.

"I'm sorry," I said. "I made the wrong call. I was wrong about you, and I was wrong about myself. See, it took me a long time to figure it out. Needed a lot of help from my friends. But...I'm not the man I thought I was. I'm better than that. I have a family of my own now, a family I love very much. They have my back, and I have theirs. That's how it's supposed to work."

Melanie's arm curled around mine, while Caitlin's warm fingers closed on my opposite shoulder.

"We can be family again too, Teddy. All you have to do is come home. Come home, and all is forgiven."

He fixed me with a suddenly furious glare, his lips twisting in a sneer.

"I don't need forgiveness for anything I've done," he seethed. "Especially not from you. Now listen up: you're going to head straight for the airport. You are going to leave. You are not going to come back to Springfield. Ever."

"And why would we do that?" Melanie asked.

"Well, let's see. You've experienced a few thrills and chills tonight, yeah? Classic monsters, a slasher, ghouls...but there's one subgenre of horror that we haven't really delved into yet."

Clutching Canton's wand in one hand, Teddy dug into his pocket and took out his cell phone with the other. He turned the screen toward us, a video connection opening up.

A camera focused tight on Pixie's face, some kind of metallic hammering, a clacking sound, running underneath the footage. Her head was bound in a contraption of leather straps, buckles, and stainless steel, with a pair of jagged metal plates pressed between her teeth. Her face was rapt, locked in an expression of absolute concentration and disciplined focus, while her eyes followed something just off-screen.

"How about a little torture porn?" Teddy asked.

I stomped toward him and Caitlin quickly stopped me, bracing a hand against my chest. Teddy jumped back, hitting me with a desperate, leering rictus.

"She's fine," he said, "for the moment. But that situation can change with the flick of a switch. Her continued survival is entirely up to you."

"We're not leaving without her," Caitlin said.

"Oh, but you are. Because we aren't going to hurt her. This wasn't a ruse to reel you in, don't you get that? It wasn't a snare or a trick. *You aren't supposed to be here.* Your girl Pixie came poking around and a couple of Naavarasi's sons grabbed her at the Denver airport. We didn't have time to adjust the plan, so we brought her to Springfield for safekeeping."

"We were supposed to go to Naavarasi's restaurant," I said. "That's where the trap was, right?"

"You never would have walked out of there alive," my brother replied. "It was a pretty good trap. Built it just for you. But spilled milk and all that. Let me bottom-line it: this entire Springfield situation has nothing to do with you. We have no reason to hurt Pixie, not unless you make us. If you stay, she dies. If you hurt me, she dies. If you do literally anything but head straight for the airport and take the next flight out of Springfield, she dies."

Chapter Twenty-Eight

We stood face-to-face with Teddy, locked in a standoff with Pixie's life in the balance.

"And if we do leave?" Caitlin asked him.

"We'll sit on her until our work is done. Then we'll give her back. Oh, don't get me wrong, you're going to pay a king's ransom, but between the Vegas mob and the Court of Jade Tears, I'm pretty sure you two can afford it."

Teddy was lying.

I'd like to say I had some brotherly sixth sense, but Teddy had become a stranger to me, twisted and corrupted by Naavarasi's endless mind games. I knew his mistress, though. And I knew Pixie.

Naavarasi scorned the trappings of human and infernal society, seeing them both as inferior to the rakshasa way. The idea of her ransoming Pixie was a joke; she had no interest in earthly money beyond its use as a resource, a means to achieving her world-shattering plans. Teddy was engaging in some classic projection: he knew that ransoming hostages for cash was something my family and I would do, so he figured I'd buy the story.

And I might have, if I hadn't racked up a lot of hard road and bad memories behind me from all the times I'd run up against his boss in the past. The idea of Naavarasi playing ransom games for money was like the Enemy robbing a bank. Sure, they *could* do it, but both of them were egotists who thought they were above getting their hands grubby.

Then there was Pixie. I'd worked with her enough times to know how she got when she was digging into a problem with both hands and a flashlight. Focused, determined, single-minded, and oblivious to the world.

Exactly how she looked on that video. She wasn't languishing in a cell, waiting for a rescue. She was *doing* something. And considering Naavarasi was presumably on the other side of the camera, she was doing it at her captors' command. We had already figured the reason for the lack of rakshasa in town: Springfield was a dangerous and seething beast that didn't discriminate when it came to targets. Anyone under its spell could become a victim at any moment.

You're here for a reason, I thought, staring into my brother's eyes. *Something you want, something you need, something worth the danger. But Naavarasi isn't going to risk her own life. And since you're here, trying to get us to leave town instead of standing at your mistress's side...*

Whatever Naavarasi is after, she's forcing Pixie to do it. And if we leave without her, we're never going to see her again.

I wasn't any closer to figuring out where they were keeping her, but Teddy's strategy had a fatal flaw. He was admitting that he couldn't really control the dark forces of Springfield. He'd just taken his best shot with the magic movie projector, and he missed. If he could stop us, he would have done it already. If he could keep us chasing our own tails until the town killed us all, he would try that too.

Meaning Pixie is close, I realized. *Within reach, because he's afraid that we're going to find her.*

In fact, I was willing to bet he was just scared enough to lead us straight to her. All he needed was the right push.

I breathed three words: "*Catch and release.*"

In the corner of my eye, dark veins began to spread across Melanie's cheeks, her cambion blood boiling. Caitlin's fingers tightened on my shoulder, telling me she got the message, before her hand slid down to her side and she slightly bent one knee, ready for action.

"You're a funny guy, Teddy," I said. "I like you. That's why I'm going to kill you last."

He did a double take, focused on my words instead of the growing danger.

"Are...are you quoting *Commando* at me?" he said. "That's an action movie. Wrong genre."

"Dan?" Melanie murmured.

"Go for the hat," I told her.

As one, we conjured our cards. A red dragon-back and a border-less blue Bee fired toward Teddy like twin hornets, blazing across the cinema. Melanie's knocked Canton's top hat off his head, sending it rolling down the aisle, while mine hit the ebony rod of the wand hard enough to smack it out of my brother's hand.

He backpedaled, eyes wide with sudden terror, and pulled his gun. Caitlin hauled me to the sticky floor as he opened fire, a pair of bullets blowing out a tombstone-shaped seat back and showering us in bits of jagged plastic and chair stuffing. I sprang back up, but he was already on the move, showing me his back before he vanished through the swinging door and out into the theater lobby.

I charged after him and hit the door with my shoulder, barreling through, reckless but dead set on following his trail to the bitter end and...

...I jolted to a stop.

The lobby was empty.

Caitlin and Melanie were right behind me, with Smith keeping a careful distance behind them, and we stood together in the empty, clean-swept foyer. Popcorn still burbled up in the glass case at the concession stand, the only sound left as the pounding of Teddy's footsteps vanished without a trace.

I cursed under my breath and doubled back. This wasn't happening. I stopped just shy of *wasn't possible*—I had seen too much of the universe to believe in those words—but what I was seeing didn't make any rational sense. This was the third time I'd followed Teddy, twice without him even knowing it, and the third time he'd vanished into thin air.

How was he pulling it off? Invisibility? Possible, but true invisibility was one of the first ideas nearly every budding magician looked into—and then abandoned because it was brutally hard and could shave years off your life. I couldn't pull that trick off, myself, and I didn't think Teddy had the juice. Teleportation? Definitely not. I had researched teleportation, back in my old and wild lone-wolf days. Even spent two months enchanting a device for short-range travel. Then I realized it had a seventy percent chance of literally turning me inside out. I had used it exactly once, to escape my burning apartment when the Redemption Choir was trying to smoke me out, and vowed to never do it again.

Even if Teddy didn't grasp the risks involved, if he was teleporting around willy-nilly I wouldn't have to lift a finger to stop him: the law of averages would have already torn him to shreds. So he wasn't turning invisible, and he wasn't using magic for an instant escape. What else?

Illusions, I thought as I scooped up Canton's wand from the floor where it had rolled to a stop against the back of a seat. *He's masking himself. That's more his speed—and Naavarasi's.*

Now I had a tool for that. Canton's wand had been designed by the former Paladin, capped with human ivory—one tip, the legend said, taken from the corpse of Harry Houdini himself—and empowered to strip illusions to the bone. A few seats down, Melanie grabbed the fallen top hat. She reached inside, and then kept reaching, until her arm was buried all the way up to the elbow as she scrunched up her face and felt around.

The hat was a pocket space, designed to conceal anything hidden inside it. And I mean anything. When I raided Northlight's vault, I managed to fit the entire Canton collection inside, stealing a small museum's worth of treasures in one fell swoop. From the shake of her head, we were too late: he'd already emptied it out.

"Hang on to it," I told Melanie. She put the hat on her head. I had to admit, it looked better on her.

I returned to the lobby, measuring my breaths, finding my focus and my footing. I was ready to get to work when a sudden, shrill jangle turned my head.

The pay phone in the lobby was ringing.

Wary, all eyes on me, I walked over and picked up the heavy black plastic receiver, putting it to my ear.

"Yeah?"

The voice on the other end was a guttural rasp choked with graveyard dirt: "Send. More. Magicians."

I hung up. Fucking zombies.

A few more deep breaths put me back in a focus state. The wand quivered in my hand, bucking a little as I raised it like a conductor's baton.

I know, you little shit. You're not happy. You were built by the Paladin, for the Paladin, and you don't like being touched by the bad guys. Deal with it. You're mine for the time being.

I whipped the wand downward, the same gesture I once used to tear away Damien Ecko's human disguise. Nothing happened.

I turned, faced another part of the lobby, and tried again.

Nothing.

"Maybe you should let me handle it," Mr. Smith suggested.

"I know what I'm doing."

He tilted his head. "Do you, though?"

One last try. Nothing. No feedback, not even a quiver of rippling magic, not a taste of latent energy in the air. No one had been doing spell-work in here.

"Maybe try out front?" Melanie suggested.

I looked to the outside doors on the far side of the room. No chance. I hadn't been on Teddy's heels, but I'd been close enough that if he had cut across the lobby and gone out the front, at the very least I would have caught the doors swinging shut. They had been closed up tight when I got there.

I had all the clues I needed. I knew it in my gut. I just had to put them together in an order that made sense. Walking through my memories, I recaptured the other times I'd lost him. Once in a blind alley. The second time, following him around the tall base of the Civil War statue outside the town hall. Now the movie theater lobby. No connection between the three locations.

Nothing but need. This town was lethal to one and all, and Teddy was alone. Naavarasi wouldn't have sent him out into the night without some way of getting around in relative safety, hiding him from the monsters and madmen that roamed the streets of Springfield after dark.

When I saw the answer, I almost laughed.

"I hate to say this," I told Mr. Smith, "but I think you just saved the day."

He arched an eyebrow. "I did?"

"Something you said to me earlier. I didn't think it through at the time, but...what's that old Sherlock Holmes line about eliminating the impossible?"

"Whatever's left has to be true," Melanie said.

"Follow me," I told them. "We're going back outside. We need to get to the town hall, and fast."

"Outside," Smith echoed. "Where the vampires and the werewolves are."

"Don't sell it short," I said with a smile. "They've got immortal serial killers, too. And probably a whole bunch of stuff we haven't even seen yet. And yet he's all alone out here and Teddy isn't worried about any of it. I just figured out why. Stay close because we've got to move fast."

Caitlin studied me, her eyes glittering. "What's the plan, pet?"

"Normally I'd never reveal another magician's tricks," I said, "out of general professional courtesy. That said, this is a pretty good one. Come on. I'll show you how it works."

Chapter Twenty-Nine

We stayed tight, we stayed low, and we moved with a purpose, darting from shadow to shadow, cover to cover along the lonely road back to the boulevard. I had maybe half a pack of enchanted cards left, Melanie still clutched her cherry-red rescue ax, and Mr. Smith had managed to hold on to his table-leg club—the oak wood cast in black-and-white, occasionally flickering with static, a relic from another place and time—but beyond that we were unarmed and sitting ducks. We had to get back off the street fast. I was rolling the dice on a hunch, and I hoped to hell I was right.

A distant, ragged scream split the night, suddenly cut short, silenced in mid-wail like someone had flipped a switch. Springfield had turned its attention elsewhere, the malevolent director of this film deciding to cut us a break for once.

At least that was what I thought, until the skin on the back of my neck started to prickle.

"Anyone else feel that?" I whispered.

"In my sinuses," Melanie said.

Caitlin licked her fingertip and held it up, feeling the cool night breeze.

"The wind shifted. Feels like a pressure front rolling in, but...not in a natural way."

As if anything in this hell town was natural. The road ahead of us looked clear, all the way to Heritage Street. I looked up to the eaves of the quiet houses lining the lane, alert for an attack from above. Nothing but dark windows behind tight shutters.

With a sinking feeling, I turned around and looked behind us.

Smiley Face was back.

He was a looming figure in the distance, about a block away, marching toward us with his rusty miner's pick tight in his gloved grip. His yellow mask was a charred and drooping ruin, held to his head with a makeshift web of leather straps and buckles, but other than that he showed no signs of his time in the fire. His blue boilersuit was pristine, his thick workman's gloves and boots dusty but unburnt. Even the haft of his pick, reduced to charcoal by the Molotov blaze, now looked weathered and old but still sturdy.

Lazy-ass continuity mistake, I realized. *This really is a slasher movie.*

We didn't have time for this. Right now, Teddy was making his way back to Naavarasi—and to Pixie. I didn't think they'd kill her, but that wasn't a chance I was willing to take. Besides, now they knew we were coming. The less time they had to get ready, the better.

"Dan?" Melanie asked, staring at the oncoming juggernaut.

I kept walking. Backward, eyes fixed on the distant killer as he shambled our way. We could easily outpace him, all the way to the town hall and the roundabout. Then again, I'd thought that the first time we crossed paths and he had a knack for popping up...

That was it.

I remembered how he gained on us, a slow and lumbering giant but blindingly fast in the dark, practically flying between the puddles of lamplight.

"Cait, Smith, eyes forward," I said, "you're going to guide us to the roundabout. Melanie, walk backward like me. Keep your eyes on Smiley and don't look away, not for a second. If we both watch him, odds are we won't blink at the same time."

Caitlin's hand closed on my forearm, guiding my footsteps up the sidewalk. I moved as fast as I dared, joining hands with Melanie to keep her steady. Speed-walking backward was a skill, and not one I'd ever had to learn.

"And...why are we doing this?" Melanie asked, staring back at the ungainly monster.

"Camp counselor is running from the killer," I said. "He's half a mile behind her, casually walking along. She breaks her heel and falls down. She picks herself up and...oh, here he is, jumping out from behind a tree and swinging his machete."

"I feel like you just described twenty different movies," she said.

"My point exactly. It's slasher-movie logic." I pointed back at Smiley Face. "He can be anywhere, but only when nobody's watching. As long as he's visible, he's slow as molasses. All we have to do, to stay ahead of him, is keep him in sight."

Melanie sighed, keeping pace with me. "Why couldn't Springfield have been built on romantic comedy rules instead? I could be having a meet-cute in a bookstore right now."

"You're too young," I told her. "First you have to move to the big city, get a job as an editor or a fashion designer, become jaded, give up on romance, and *then* get sent to a small town to learn the meaning of true love."

"Holy shit," Melanie said. "You watch rom-coms."

"Do not."

"He absolutely does," Caitlin stage-whispered.

"Lies and slander," I said.

"*Silver Linings Playbook* is his favorite," Caitlin added.

"Next monster we see," I said, "I'm throwing myself straight into its mouth."

There was no mistaking the change in Smiley Face's body language. He strained as he walked, like he was aching to burst into a run, but we had him pinned like a bug, forced to amble in a slow and unsteady gait. His hands flexed on the haft of his mining pick, clenching and unclenching.

Melanie caught it too. "What's going on with him?"

"I think he's pissed." I cupped my hands to my mouth and called out, "I get it, we're supposed to be running in terror. Don't like it when people don't follow the rules, do you, big guy? Hate to break it to you, but you're no Leatherface. You're not even..."

I trailed off, trying to think of the most pathetic villain I could.

"Kylo Ren?" Melanie suggested.

"In the ballpark," I said.

"The hyenas from *The Lion King*," Caitlin said.

"Hear that, dude?" I shouted. "You don't even rate henchman status."

Mr. Smith offered his own suggestion: "Humbert Humbert."

"Really?" I said. "*Lolita*? That's the first place your mind goes?"

"Is it not a horror story?"

"Got me there," I said.

On the inside, I wasn't a tenth as confident as I was on the outside. All I could feel was the hourglass running out, Pixie's life in greater peril with every passing second while an unstoppable killer dogged us from a block away, slow but relentless. And I had brought us all out here on nothing but a gamble. If I was wrong...

But I felt like we were all afraid together, and all pretending we weren't, together, and in that moment the Springfield dark seemed a tiny bit brighter.

Melanie had a good point. Why *couldn't* this place have been a rom-com? Sure, Springfield was mainlining energy straight from the Garden of Eden, the most dangerous place in the entire multiverse, but that didn't explain the whole story. Terror and death might have been an expected side effect, but not like this. There was no reason that primordial occult power from the dawn of humanity would take on the form of twentieth-century movie tropes.

Someone had deliberately shaped it this way. Which meant, in theory, it could be *re*shaped. We just had to get our hands on the controls.

We had built up a good lead. Smiley Face was falling behind, shackled by his own rules, growing smaller and smaller in the distance as he slowly plodded after us. Mixed blessing, I realized: as soon as he finally slipped out of sight, he could pop up right in front of us a second later.

That was one problem the movies hadn't prepared me for. There were a dozen ways to attract a slasher's attention. Booze, drugs, maybe a little premarital sex. Methods of making one go away, not so much.

"We're burning too much time here," I said. "Think we're going to have to rip the bandage off. Cait, can you see the roundabout up ahead?"

"Just barely."

"We're going to make a run for it. Everyone ready?"

"Ready," Smith said.

"The longer I stare at this guy, the freakier he gets," Melanie said, striding backward and trying not to blink. "So I'm actually okay with this plan."

"Say when," Caitlin told me.

The second we looked away from the killer he could—*would*—pop up right behind us. Unless I set the stage for a different scene.

"Cait," I said, keeping my gaze fixed on Smiley, "what's up ahead of us right now?"

"The roundabout and the cavalry statue are ahead. We have houses on the left side of the street, stores on the right, mostly one-story. Everything's locked up and dark."

"See any alleys, alcoves, any place where a person could hide and jump out at us?"

"Nothing that stands out," she said.

"Good. Okay, first we're going to migrate off the sidewalk and into the middle of the street."

Still walking backward, guided by Caitlin's steady hand, I stepped onto a strip of manicured grass and off the curb as we marched down the middle of the road.

"What's the plan here?" Smith asked.

"Rewriting the script. If we turn our backs, he'll be on us in seconds. Going to try to convince him to change tactics."

I cupped my hands to my mouth again, calling out to the dwindling figure.

"We can do this all night, asshole! We know your game. As long as we can see you, you'll never catch us. Truly pathetic showing. A genuine embarrassment to the slasher canon, my dude. You are bad and you should feel bad."

Smiley Face stopped in his tracks. He tilted his head to one side like a confused puppy.

Then he spun on his heel, stomping off behind a quiet, dark house, vanishing from sight.

Sucker, I thought.

"Run!" I shouted, wheeling around. The four of us broke into an all-out sprint, racing up the open street toward the middle of town.

"He could be anywhere now," Smith panted. "Isn't that what we *didn't* want?"

Movie slashers went after their victims in one of two ways: a relentless pursuit or a jump scare. We'd just nixed the former, so I reasoned he'd go for the latter tactic next, popping out from the shadows and swinging his pick for a sudden, brutal kill. Which was why I moved us to the middle of an empty street with plenty of open space around us. If he wanted to spring out and hit us with a murder surprise, he'd have to wait for an opportunity. We weren't going to hand him one that easily.

Town hall, the park, and the roundabout were just ahead, with the corroded bronze cavalry statue upon its tall plinth in the heart of the circular road.

"When we get to the roundabout," I said, feet pounding the pavement, "Caitlin, go left. Smith, flank right. We need to watch every side of the statue at all times so Smiley can't jump us."

"All right," Smith said, "but why are we doing this in the first place?"

"Back at the antique store, after Teddy disappeared on me for the second time, remember what you said to me?"

"No. Probably something suitably withering about your complete lack of discipline and reason."

"'Withering,'" Melanie gasped, running as hard as she could, one hand clamped to the brim of Canton's top hat to keep it from flying off her head. "Check out Thesaurus Jones over here."

"I said he pulled a Houdini. You said you were surprised that I didn't know all of Houdini's illusions."

"And?"

"I know most of them."

A second wind filled my sails as the statue loomed in front of us, an unknown soldier and his unknown horse leading the charge into danger. I was more focused on the plinth, a tall and angled base with a worn-away dedication plaque, a few feet wide and almost as tall, fixed by stout bolts to one side. I ran up and dropped to one knee in the wet grass, feeling along the corners of the raised plaque, heart pounding as I put my life-or-death hunch to the test.

"Teddy was on the streets by day, like us, but he took shelter at night," I said. "Springfield doesn't give hall passes. If you're out after dark, you're a victim."

"Which explains nothing," Mr. Smith said.

I showed my teeth, feral. "It explains everything. How is he disappearing? How can he travel all over town, alone and without Naavarasi protecting him, without getting killed? My mistake was overthinking it. The answer was right there the whole time. He did exactly what Harry Houdini would do."

I curled my fingers under the plaque and hauled back. It swung upward, silent, on a concealed and oiled hinge. It was a hatch, hiding a hollow shaft and the steel rungs of a ladder leading down below the streets.

"Houdini was a stage illusionist," I said. "Teddy isn't using magic to get around town. He's using *tricks*."

Chapter Thirty

"A secret passageway," Melanie murmured, staring at the open hatch and the ladder beyond, dropping down into darkness.

"Whole town's probably riddled with them." I tapped a fingertip against my temple. "Don't have to worry about the freaks on the streets if you go *under* the streets."

Smith put his hands on his hips and leaned closer to the hatch. An odd smell wafted up from below; it made me think of musky cologne and old books.

"Then why did we take the risk of coming all this way in the open?" he asked. "There has to be another trapdoor back at the theater, no?"

"And it could be literally anywhere in the lobby, whereas I remembered how Teddy lost me here. It was this exact spot, meaning the hatch had to be in the plinth or buried in the grass. Back at the cinema, we might still be searching for it. More importantly, we've got no idea what's waiting for us down there."

"Might be trapped," Caitlin mused.

"Exactly, and Teddy knew we were right behind him. Didn't feel like giving him a chance to spring an ambush. Right now, he only knows that we didn't follow him down."

"And he doesn't know that we know about the secret passages," Melanie said. "He thinks he's safe."

"That's the idea," I said.

Now we just had to put it to the test.

Caitlin stepped forward, holding up a hand. "I'm going down first. Watch my back."

"I should—" I started to say. Cait pressed her fingertip to my lips.

"I appreciate your willingness to protect me," she said, "always. But if something nasty is waiting at the bottom of that ladder, out of the four of us, I'm the most likely to survive it."

"You are built different," I conceded.

"Slightly," she said with a wink. She slid one slender leg into the hatch, then the other, grabbing the rungs and lowering herself down. I turned to Mr. Smith.

"You're next," I said.

He gave the hatch a dubious look. "We're just going to take a leap of faith, are we?"

"You could," I said, "but I'd suggest using the ladder and climbing down instead. Less likely to break something."

"Your utter lack of gravitas never fails to charm." He paused. "Oh, no, wait. I meant always fails to charm. Always."

"Let me put it another way: start climbing, or we're leaving you up here."

He started climbing down, reluctantly leaving the table-leg club behind so he could free up his hands. I took a long look around, studying the empty streets, the deserted park. The playground swings wobbled on their own, lifted by a cold night wind.

I felt the world shift.

It was stronger this time, or maybe I was just learning the ebb and flow of Springfield's dark melody. The air went still for a moment and then the wind returned, blowing in a completely new direction. The empty swings swayed from side to side instead of forward and back. Melanie glanced past my shoulder and froze, lips parted, face going pale. I didn't need her to tell me.

I turned to see Smiley Face marching toward us, lumbering with a purpose, less than half a block away. He gripped the haft of his miner's pick with both of his gloved hands.

"You're up," I told Melanie. "Get to safety."

"Dan—"

"Give me the ax."

This time she didn't argue. She tossed me the rescue ax. I caught it, twirled it around, and tested its weight against my palm, keeping my eyes on the killer. I heard Melanie scurrying behind me, making her way down the steel rungs.

I didn't have time to follow her, not with Smiley bearing down on me. He put on a sudden burst of speed, lunging in with his pick high, bringing it down in a whistling death arc. I juked to the left and swung my ax, but he was too quick. Wood cracked against wood as he blocked with his pick, the hafts of our weapons crashing together. Then he brought up his leg and fired his big boot out like a piston, hitting me square in the belly and driving the air from my lungs as I fell, landing hard on my back in the wet grass.

The rusty pickax head plunged toward my eyes. I rolled out of the way as the pick came down, burying itself in the sod, and dirt flew as he ripped it free. I was already up on my feet in a low crouch, hurling myself back into the fight. He braced his pick with both hands and fended me off, blocking like a staff fighter, taking a halting step backward. Then he turned his grip at the last second and the butt of the pick cracked against the side of my head, leaving me winded, stunned, white blurs flaring in my vision.

His rough workman's glove clamped around my throat, lifting me to my tiptoes, then off my feet entirely, my heels kicking in the air as I struggled for purchase. I wheezed for breath, fighting to stay conscious as the blood roared in my ears, the sound of my pulse pounding out on heavy metal drums.

"I don't qualify as a Final Girl," I rasped, "but some people do call me...the Guy."

With the last shreds of my strength I swung the rescue ax up, straight into Smiley's crotch. It ripped through his boiler suit and whatever he had underneath with a meaty *squish* and he let go of me, doubling over in silent agony.

He'd recover, but that was the opening I needed. I left the ax dangling between his legs and threw myself at the open hatch in the base of the statue, sliding through the narrow gap one leg at a time, taking hold of the old, wobbly steel rungs. I reached out and gave the plaque a shove, letting it fall back into place with a shuddering clang and sealing myself in darkness.

A moment later the metal ruptured, the miner's pick bursting through, piercing the air just to the left of my eye.

I dropped down, taking the rungs two at a time, hustling to safety—I hoped—under the streets of Springfield. A cold light waxed beneath my feet, the colors strange, rippling shades of orange and red that cast a colorful glow across the gray brick walls of the shaft. As I neared the bottom, I realized it came from a lamp dangling from an outstretched and rusty hook on the wall. There was something not quite real about it, like an oil painter's impression of a lamp, soft and deep, drawn with careful brushstrokes upon the skin of the world.

Caitlin, Melanie, and Mr. Smith waited at the bottom of the shaft. It opened up onto a short tunnel, more gray bricks cemented with bone-white mortar, the flagstones of a cemetery walk under our feet.

It smelled like old paper and musk down here, the air humid and clammy, and echoes carried the soft sounds of dripping water.

I held up a finger for silence and waited, looking up. Nothing.

"Nice to be right about something," I said. "Smiley knows we're down here."

"But he's not chasing us," Melanie said.

I looked to the shadows, waiting for my eyes to adjust to the oil lamp's light.

"Either the rules that run Springfield keep the monsters on the streets and stop them from venturing too far out-of-bounds," I reasoned, "or this place is warded to the gills. Either way, there are probably tunnels like this all over town. Teddy was never in any danger."

"We should change that," Caitlin purred.

"Oh, I've got some danger for his ass. Let's go." I turned to Melanie and Mr. Smith. "Watch where you step. There could be traps up ahead."

I was more concerned about a trap in our midst. There was something wrong with Mr. Smith. He'd been quieter than usual since we escaped the movie house, and while he was normally pale, it was hard to miss how the blood had leeched from his bland face, the little color he had fading to gray. He was moving slower, his reactions dulled, like some kind of cosmic lag was keeping him a second behind everyone else.

Then I realized why and fought the urge to bury my face in my palm.

"Smith," I said, "you unbelievable asshole."

He scrunched up his brow. "What did I do this time?"

"You know what you did. Or didn't do, more like. Show it to us."

All eyes on him now, he stepped back and put his shoulders to the monochrome wall.

"I have no idea what you're talking about," he said.

He was favoring his left arm, curling it at his side, his right hand compulsively massaging his wrist. I took one swift step and closed the distance between us, grabbed his arm, and yanked his sleeve back.

Halfway up his forearm, the meat of his arm had been ravaged by a ragged, flesh-tearing bite. Black tendrils wormed their way under his skin, spreading out in all directions, a slow and relentless infection. The area around the wound, about the size of a silver dollar, was as gray and lifeless as the brick wall at his back.

"Oh, nasty," Melanie breathed.

"I knew it," I said. "In every zombie movie, there's that one guy. The asshole who only looks out for himself and endangers the whole group with his selfish bullshit. And you know what always happens to him?"

"He gets bit," Caitlin said, glaring at Smith. "And hides it from everyone until it's too late, despite knowing the consequences."

"We don't know anything for certain," he argued.

Caitlin responded with nothing but a single raised eyebrow.

We'd already turned over an hourglass when Teddy escaped us at the movie theater. Pixie was here, somewhere, her life in the balance. Now we'd just flipped a second one, and the sand was for all of us. If Smith was right and the only way out of Springfield was by air—I didn't want to believe that, but I did—then we needed him to escape. Alive and un-zombified, since he was the only pilot around.

"How long do we have before he turns?" Melanie asked.

"Depends on the movie," I said. "Maybe a day, maybe hours. Let's stay on the safe side and figure 'hours,' meaning we need to get in there, grab Pixie, and get out."

"And your brother?" Smith asked.

"If we can figure out what he and Naavarasi are doing, great. If we can stop it, even better, but this is a rescue mission."

Smith let out a tiny chuckle. I gave him a look.

"Want to share with the rest of the class?"

"Oh, it's nothing," he said. "Just amused by your choice of words. 'Stop it' is a very reserved way of saying 'commit fratricide.'"

He didn't have to tell me that. The knowledge that this was going to end in one of two ways—with me dead, or Teddy dead—dogged my every footstep. I told myself it wasn't necessarily so. I still hoped, somehow, that I could find a way to reason with him. Maybe I could bring him around before it was too late.

Hubris, I knew. He'd been in the clutches of a master manipulator for years, and I had no idea how deep Naavarasi's claws went. A pep talk and a hug weren't going to change his heart. Still, I had to give it my best shot.

I'd been damned a dozen times over for the things I'd done. I knew that. Made my peace with it a long time ago. That said...sometimes I tried to do things that felt healthy for my soul.

Another lantern dangled from a wall hook, a ways up the narrow tunnel, casting more of that weirdly vivid oil-paint glow across the gray brick and ivory grout. We stepped through a curved archway and out onto a landing.

"Well," I said, frozen where I stood. "I was not expecting that."

Chapter
Thirty-One

T he trail ended at a semicircular outcropping of stone, a landing
with an old and worm-eaten wooden pillar on one end. There
wasn't a maze of pathways under the city streets. It was a maze of
canals. A rowboat, with oars as well as a small rear motor, was tied off
to the pier by a length of stout rope. Its hull gently rocked from side
to side, bumping against the stone outcropping. It wasn't floating on
water, though.

"Is that...oil?" Melanie asked.

I shook my head, crouching down at the platform's edge, taking
a closer look at the black, burbling broth. Vaulted tunnels stretched
out in two directions from here, flooded and lit by more dangling wall
lamps, their light cast across a sea of jet-black liquid. My ears buzzed
and my teeth itched, my body reacting to the concentrated magical
power like an allergic rash.

"It's Ink," I breathed.

Smith crossed his arms. "Impossible."

Ink, with a capital *I*. The Network's party drug had gone viral
nationwide, though according to Jennifer there wasn't much to its
chemical composition: it was an opiate mixed with a mild hallucino-

gen, all riding on a supernatural payload. The actual drug component was just there to get its users hooked; the real nastiness came once the Ink got its tentacles into your nervous system and the curse kicked in.

"Tell me again how you don't know anything about this place," I said to Smith, not looking back at him. "And make it convincing."

"The level of shock I'm in at the moment should be all the proof you need."

Now I did turn around.

"Your shocked face and your not-shocked face are exactly the same," I said.

"It's not my fault that you're immune to nuance."

Melanie crouched down beside me. Curious, she held an experimental hand out over the broth. The Ink reacted, rippling with tiny waves as miniature tendrils strained upward, sniffing the air, reaching to touch her. I gently pushed her arm up a few inches.

"Careful. You don't want any of that stuff on you."

"I know," she murmured, her expression a mélange of fear and fascination as she stared into the black. "I've seen what this crap can do, remember?"

I'd done my best to keep Ink out of Las Vegas. The New Commission's dealers all knew not to touch the stuff, a zero-tolerance policy, and I'd put a few out-of-town grifters in an early grave when they tried to sling it on our turf. Despite my efforts it was fast becoming a rave staple—ecstasy's even friendlier and bubblier cousin—and selling Ink was like printing money.

Not that the Network was driven by profits alone. The magical surprise in every dose had a corruptive, corrosive effect on the human will. Junkies became listless, open to the power of suggestion and hypnosis, utterly defenseless against occult manipulation. In other words, exactly the kind of customers the Network liked. I assumed there was a larger plan in play, that spreading Ink across the globe was just the setup to a bigger scam, but we hadn't figured their game out yet.

Smith leaned in, craning his neck to look up and down the vaulted tunnels. "Can't see how far they go, but even if we assume these canals are shallow, and that's the best-case scenario, the square footage on display here alone would require...enough Ink to fill an Olympic-sized swimming pool."

"So this isn't your main stash," I said.

"We don't have a 'main stash,'" he sniffed. "Ink is crafted in small batches, by hand, in artisanal laboratories."

"How hipster of you," Caitlin said.

"We've never brewed it in these quantities. There's no reason to. Even if we had a reason, our operations aren't scaled for it. Someone stole our formula."

I held on to the wooden pier and set one foot down in the belly of the rowboat. It wriggled a little on its rope tether, but it seemed seaworthy.

"All aboard," I said, sitting on the lead bench and reaching for the oars.

Smith stared at me. "You can't be serious."

"We can sail the sea of Ink, or we can go back topside and wait for an immortal maniac with a pickax to finish us off. It's really not a hard choice."

One by one they carefully climbed in, the four of us snug in the narrow wooden rowboat. I tilted one of the oars, experimentally dipping it as deep into the bubbling black soup as I dared. I couldn't feel the bottom.

"There is a motor," Smith pointed out.

"And we're not using it. Catch those echoes? Sound carries down here. They'll hear us coming from a mile away."

I rowed instead, dipping both oars and pushing us away from the platform after Caitlin untied the boat. We drifted free, sliding out over the oily broth, gliding down a long and curving tunnel. There were no hard angles down here, only smooth, bending walls and graceful turns, like we were sailing through the insides of a garden hose. Up ahead, another dangling lantern illuminated a branching path, the passage splitting in three directions.

The fastest way to beat most mazes was to pick a wall and cling to it. I stayed to the right, leaning into the oars and paddling us down another trackless, pointless tunnel, nothing to see but more mono-chrome bricks and more Ink.

Not pointless, I was starting to realize. As the passage curved like a bow and opened onto another three seemingly identical archways, I drew a map in my head.

"It's a fractal," I said.

Caitlin nodded; she saw it too. "A black snowflake."

Fractals were powerful things. Most magicians, myself included, still favored the old school—pentacles, hexagrams, concentric circles around blasphemous glyphs, that kind of deal—but a new school of thought was doing some remarkable work with geometry and math. Equations and algorithms had the power to name and bind. The Mandelbrot Set was a crucible.

This much Ink in one place was unprecedented, but we hadn't just discovered someone's drug stash: these tunnels formed one giant occult sigil and the Ink was the fuel, poured straight into its veins. A magical operation on a massive scale. If Springfield was a machine, some vast engine of fear calculated and tuned to squeeze every last drop of horror and pain from its brainwashed inhabitants, we were sailing through its operating system. The literal belly of the beast.

I could see the drug's soporific qualities at work. It might have explained why the locals were so locked into the Springfield mindset that they couldn't even contemplate what state they lived in or imagine the idea of leaving. Naavarasi was an illusionist and a hypnotist; a scam like this was right up her alley. I kept thinking about Ink's *other* properties.

"It was a side effect, wasn't it?" I pondered out loud. "You didn't expect Ink to work that way."

"I am," Smith said, "still not a mind reader, so you're going to need a bit more specificity."

"'The Owl lives,'" Caitlin said.

Right around the time Ink started seeping through the veins of the nation, that phrase showed up from New York to LA, spray-painted on store shutters and alley walls. It was a warning, to all of us, that the First Story had gone active on our planet. The Enemy, the Paladin, the Witch and her Knight, the Salesman, the Psychopomp, and more, all coming to life, here and now, ready to play their parts once again.

"Ink primes its users for more than psychic control," I said. "It opens them up to the Story. Ink junkies can feel it on a level that other people can't."

Smith crossed his arms over his chest, tight. He glanced off to one side and pretended to study the tunnel walls.

"We were...surprised, I'll admit," he said. "If you're looking for insights, I'm afraid I have none to share. Our limited investigations haven't exactly borne fruit. Yet."

"Likely not a coincidence, though," Caitlin mused. "Naavarasi is siphoning power from the Eden conduit, the home of the Story. Using a reagent that amplifies the connection is just basic magic."

Still didn't sit right with me.

"What's the price of this much Ink?" I asked Smith. "Production cost, not street value."

"Hard to calculate. We did design it to be cheap, so we could get it into as many hands—and veins—as possible. That said, a quantity on this scale...I don't even know where someone would acquire the raw materials. We certainly wouldn't be able to do it without importing stock from a parallel world. Probably multiple worlds."

"Humor me. Pretend a genie gave you three wishes."

"I'd use the first wish to kill you, slowly and horribly," Smith said, utterly deadpan. "I'd use my second wish to bring you back to life and my third to kill you a second time, in a new and altogether differently terrible way."

"Pretend you aren't a deranged creep, and you wished for a bottomless source of raw materials instead. Let's say you used the other two wishes for a brain and a heart. How much would it cost to produce this much Ink?"

Smith rubbed his chin, thoughtful.

"Millions of dollars, unquestionably. Tens of millions. But as I said, this isn't our work. Even if we had the materials, which we don't, we don't have the facilities for production on this scale."

I leaned into the oars, pushing our wobbly boat along the black canal, and looked back over my shoulder at Caitlin. "Naavarasi doesn't have that kind of money. She's a long way from broke, but a second mortgage on her restaurant isn't going to pay for a setup like this."

Melanie sat as close to me as she could, arms and legs tight. I didn't blame her. A Network operative once tried to lure me out by striking at her; he made sure that some kids at her school got a tainted batch of Ink right before a big house party.

I had seen photos of the aftermath. They still popped up in my nightmares. A dozen teenagers ended up dead, murdered by their friends or killed by their own hands, mutilating themselves in a psychotic fugue. Melanie was a smart kid, though: the second she realized something was up, she locked herself in the bathroom and survived the night, waiting out the carnage.

She was the only person unaffected, and I was never able to figure out why, though I figured her half-demon heritage offered her some protections that a mortal teenager wouldn't have. She knew what this stuff was capable of.

A faint buzzing sound echoed up the tunnel. I held up a hand for silence and stilled my oars, letting the boat drift quietly as I closed my eyes and focused.

It was a motor. Another boat, this one not operating in stealth mode, making its way through the sigil tunnels. As the sound grew louder, closer, I squeezed the oars like they were a pair of throats.

My brother was on that boat, and it was time for another family reunion. I was going to give Teddy one last chance to do the right thing. If he took it, I'd bring him home.

If he refused...I'd deal with it when the time came. A tiny spark of hope still flickered in my heart. Hell knows it should have gone out ages ago, probably right around the time he shot me, but I clung to it with every ounce of strength I had left.

He was still my brother. I wasn't giving up on him. Not yet.

Chapter
Thirty-Two

We followed the path around another fractal bend, a fresh petal of the black snowflake. Up ahead, the engine noise cut out, sputtered, and died. Silence, save for the gentle lapping of the inky broth against the monochrome walls, washed through the tunnels.

I heard faint voices. Up ahead the tunnels branched again, but this time was different: the left-hand path was wider, an open archway, and soft violet light shimmered across the sea of Ink. I braced one oar against the bricks, bringing the boat to a stop. Then Caitlin and I put our hands to the damp, clammy bricks and gently pushed ourselves along, sailing right up to the edge of the arch without making a sound.

We had found the heart of the labyrinth. The heart of Springfield.

Beyond the archway was an open lake, deep and wide enough that I couldn't make out the farthest walls of the chamber. A stone island rose from the Ink, tall and round like a drum, surrounded by a quintet of smaller islands, all bound together by swaying rope bridges. A long catwalk stretched from the central island to a landing where a boat, just like ours, was tied to a moldy wooden pier.

I recognized the shape of the structure intuitively. The five points orbiting the center, the bridges forming lines and connections. Melanie saw it, too.

"It's a pentagram," she whispered.

The violet light came from five gnarled wooden staves, one jutting upward from the heart of each orbiting island and topped with a fist-sized chunk of amethyst. The hearts of the crystals glowed, their inner fires casting the lake in the hues of an alien planet. From here I could make out a clutter around each staff, a pile of mismatched junk placed without any seeming rhyme or reason.

But there was a reason. Had to be. Because Naavarasi was here.

She stood upon the central island, tall and imperious, next to a dead spotlight with a rusty steel hull. Naavarasi had decided to get comfortable, apparently, and drop her human disguise. She was an olive-skinned woman in a jade sari that matched the poison-green paint on her sharp fingernails, but she had the head of a Bengal tiger, black stripes lining the orange fur along her muzzle, her feline eyes like burning citrines.

"Did he follow you?" she growled.

Teddy walked toward her, his head ducked a little, his shoulders tight. He had that duffel bag slung over his shoulder, the one I'd seen him walking around with by daylight.

"If he did, we would have heard the explosion," he replied. "I strung the pin of a hand grenade to the inside of the hatch."

Chalk up one point for my intuition. Half the reason for hiking all the way back to the statue was because I figured there was a solid risk of Teddy trapping the path behind him.

It was what I would have done.

"Come here," she commanded. My stomach twisted in knots as I watched her curl her fingers under his chin, stroking him like a trained dog.

Don't you fucking touch him like that, I thought. *You have no right.*

My cards thrummed against my breast pocket, wanting to fly. I stayed my hand and held my silence.

"And did you bring more fuel for the fire?" she asked.

He patted the duffel bag, then unzipped it and took something out. They were too far away to make out what he was showing her. A wallet, maybe?

"Courtesy of the NYPD, I've got Marie Reinhart's detective badge. And, thanks to an estate sale, a day planner that belonged to Ezra Ulysses Talon. I verified his handwriting. Still has a list of appointments from the day he died."

"Excellent," Naavarasi purred. "Put the badge on island two, and the planner...hmm, place that one on island four."

Caitlin's voice was a faint breath in my ear: "The Knight and the Salesman."

The Canton relics were just the tip of the iceberg. Naavarasi was snatching up anything she could scrounge, anything that had spent time in the hands of a character from the First Story. Artifacts and remnants, glowing in my second sight like scrap metal from Chernobyl, bathed in the background radiation of their original owners' lives.

"Of course," Naavarasi said, stopping Teddy in mid-stride, "it's a bit of an even trade, isn't it? Considering you lost Canton's top hat and wand."

"A temporary setback, Mistress."

"I've heard that before."

"Do you know the difference between me and my brother?" Teddy asked.

"I could barely begin to count them."

"Here's one: I've got my pilot's license and a Cessna Skyhawk. He doesn't. Right now Dan and his little friends are running around the streets, chasing their tails, probably getting jumped from every direction. Hell, they might already be dead."

"And if they survive until dawn?"

"My point exactly. Even if they outlast the night, they aren't getting out of Springfield alive. If this town doesn't eat them tonight, bones and all, it'll kill 'em tomorrow or the night after that. We'll get the hat and wand back. Probably end up picking it out of some werewolf's stool."

"Thank you," Naavarasi said, "for that lovely mental image."

"There's another consideration," Teddy added. "Our 'guest' isn't going to survive much longer. We'll need a new one. Might as well grab an intruder or two and toss them in the hot seat. Easier than going back to the real world for a replacement, right?"

Pixie. My jaw clenched.

"Have you checked on the prisoner?"

"Just came from there," Teddy said, gesturing back over his shoulder. "All systems are still in the green, but she's not looking so hot. You know you can only keep a human awake for so long. Messes with the brain."

"I am well aware of the frailties of your species," she said.

I had heard all I needed to. As much as I wanted to sail in like a pirate and start slitting throats, Pixie was down here somewhere, and her time was running out. Careful, quiet, I lowered the oars back into the sea of Ink and gently pushed. Our boat glided away from the open arch while Naavarasi's and Teddy's backs were turned, slipping past without a sound.

"Plan?" Caitlin breathed.

"We find Pixie and we get her to safety," I said. "Then we're coming back and burning this circus to the ground. I still don't know what Naavarasi is trying to accomplish here, but it ends now."

As we floated away from the arch, into another curving side passage, another petal of the massive glyph, Smith said a single word: "Interesting."

"I am also not a mind reader," I told him.

"Your choices of language. It's always her scheme, her plot, her goals."

I glanced back at him as I leaned into the oars. "And?"

"You don't hold your brother responsible? He's been her accomplice for years, no? He was the one who tried to murder us at the cinema. She wasn't even there."

"He's not her accomplice."

"What word would you use?" he asked.

I stared down the tunnel, the gray walls cast in the shifting oil-paint light of another dangling lamp.

"His head's all messed up," I said. "It's not Teddy's fault. She brainwashed him."

Smith answered with a dry chuckle. "Do you think that everyone who hates you must have been brainwashed, Mr. Faust? Dear me, there must be an awful lot of mind control going around."

I didn't answer him. Even if I'd wanted to, I didn't have anything to say. I kept on the oars and pushed our boat down the canal, still mapping the tunnels in my mind's eye, trying to make sense of it all.

The tunnel widened on the next straight, a narrow brick ledge offering a viable, if dangerous, footpath above the Ink. Midway down, another rounded outcropping and a wooden pier offered a place to dock, no other boats in sight.

"What do you think?" Caitlin murmured.

"Could be another ladder," I said. "Have to be exits and trapdoors all over town. Still...when Naavarasi asked Teddy if he checked on the hostage, I'm pretty sure this was the direction he nodded in. That ledge stretches in both directions, too. Might be a way to reach the middle island on foot. There has to be one somewhere."

"Has to be?" Smith asked. "How do you figure that?"

"Easy. When we were listening in back there, did you see the boat Teddy sailed in on?"

"Of course."

"Well," I said, "did you see any *other* boats? Naavarasi got there somehow, and last I checked, she can't fly."

Smith pursed his lips. I wasn't sure if he was more irritated at himself for not noticing or at me for pointing it out.

I brought us in for a landing and Caitlin tied the boat off at the pier. She grabbed Melanie's hand and hoisted her up while I clambered onto the dry stone with Smith right behind me.

A tunnel, like the one we came in through, led away from the canal. I expected we'd just find another ladder, and another secret path back to the streets above, but it was worth a quick look before we tried following the ledge.

"Eyes sharp," I said, taking the lead. "You heard my brother back there. He had at least one hand grenade and he's not shy about setting traps."

"I also heard the only way out is by air," Mr. Smith said.

"That you did."

"Which means I'm your only ticket home."

"That you are," I said. I looked him up and down. He was still pale, paler than usual at least. He was walking slower, lagging behind, like some part of his brain was getting confused about where to put his feet. "How are you feeling?"

"I'm not hungering for human flesh, if that's what you're asking."

Yet, I thought.

Rules were rules. He'd been bitten by a zombie. He was going to turn. No idea when, but every minute we spent in Springfield brought us one minute closer to being trapped here for the rest of our lives. "The rest of our lives" probably lasting two or three more nights, maybe a week if we were lucky.

The tunnel ended at a door. It was made of stout oak, rounded at the top, with a wrought-iron handle and a big chunky lock. I put my ear to the wood, hearing something on the other side. A steady, rhythmic mechanical clacking. It spurred a memory, bringing me back to my mushroom dream of Carolyn.

Someone was typing on the other side of the door.

The handle jiggled under my hand but wouldn't turn. Normally I'd take any chance to give Melanie more practice, but we didn't have time. I crouched down and fished out my lockpick case, finessing the lock with seasoned fingertips and feeling the tumbler pins roll one by one.

The lock clicked. The handle turned. The door yawned open.

"Pixie," I breathed.

Chapter Thirty-Three

The room beyond the door was a little bigger than a walk-in closet. No other way out, no hope, just a small folding table and a stiff wooden chair, a typewriter and a girl. The typewriter was a vintage avocado-green Selectric. The girl was in trouble.

Seated under the glow of a dangling lamp, Pixie typed away, a mountain of finished pages on her left and two open reams of blank paper on her right. The typewriter sounded off with a merry *ding* at the end of a line. She pulled the page out, threaded a fresh sheet of paper into the roller, and kept typing without missing a beat. The typewriter had no power cord, and even if it did, there weren't any wall sockets to plug it into. It worked, regardless.

Pixie was wearing the same cruel contraption Teddy had shown us on his phone: a head harness of chrome tubes and leather straps, pulled tight and fixed in place by a trio of dangling padlocks. The device lodged a metal plate between her lips, pressing down her tongue and silencing her voice.

She looked sick. Or maybe just exhausted to the bone, with heavy bags under her eyes and her shoulders slumped in defeat. She could barely keep herself sitting upright, but she kept typing anyway.

"Pix?" I asked.

She didn't look up at us. It seemed like she *couldn't*, as if her eyes were cursed, riveted to the page. She gave a tiny shake of her head.

I circled the table and read over her shoulder.

Faust circled the table and read over her shoulder, she had already typed, *hoping to glean some insight. He understood, at once, that this cursed device had exerted a strange hold over his friend. It reminded him, oddly enough, of his incursion into the Enemy's penthouse at Northlight Tower. The foul grimoire, the wellspring of the Enemy's power, had communicated with him much like this.*

At my side, Smith squinted at the page. "Is that true?"

"It's true," I said, "and Pixie doesn't know that, because I never gave her the details. I think she's working the keys, but the typewriter is doing most of the talking."

—but the typewriter is doing most of the talking, Pixie typed.

In truth, she wasn't sure where the machine ended and she began. They were one, had been one, for...how long? Minutes became hours became days of soul-deadening repetition, until there was nothing but the endless clacking, the toil and the fear. Her fingers were numb, her wrists aching like her bone marrow was filled with fire ants.

"Clever girl," I murmured. I turned to Caitlin. "She can't talk to us directly, so she's using the page. She's *narrating*."

Melanie edged closer to the table. "Pix? What happens if you stop typing? Can you tell us?"

She took a deep breath and showed us instead.

Her fingers stopped, lifting from the keys. A heartbeat later, a rhythmic clicking, like the relentless tick of a mechanical stopwatch, emitted from her head harness. The chrome arms began to ratchet back and the steel plate in her mouth—two plates, one against each set of teeth, started to spread. The harness forced her jaw open until tears welled in her eyes and she quickly put her fingertips back on the keys. The second she started to type, the machine reversed itself, easing up until her mouth closed tight and the ticking stopped.

That thing will rip her jaw right off, she typed.

"That thing will rip her jaw right off," Melanie said, circling Pixie and studying the device.

She couldn't speak, Pixie wrote. *Could barely think. Maybe that was a part of it. The typewriter was invading her, pushing out the parts that belonged to her and replacing them. All she wanted to do was sleep. Or die. She often thought that if she died, that would be all right. Sometimes it was the only thought she had left, the only one that was genuinely hers alone.*

"Not happening," I said.

Caitlin was leafing through the stack of finished pages.

"It's all here," she said. "Everything that's happened to us from the moment we landed at the airport. The werewolf, the vampire, being transported into a movie—she typed it all."

"You're confusing cause and effect," Mr. Smith said. "I believe we've found the source of Springfield's endless nightmares. Our course of action is clear."

"Is it?" I said, dubious.

He shrugged. "Kill the girl, save ourselves."

"That's how the Network plays," I said, "because you're a bunch of backstabbing dicks and you deserve each other. My crew doesn't work that way. We don't leave people behind."

Smith waved a hand at Pixie. "She's not exactly in a position to get up and walk away, now is she?"

Melanie was crouched behind her, studying the gears on the head harness.

"I think I might know how to disarm it," she said.

"How?" I asked.

"Because I've seen the movie your brother stole the idea from." She caught my blank expression. "Hello? It's a modified version of the reverse bear-trap from *Saw*."

"Haven't seen it," I said.

"Media literacy, Dan. It can save your life."

"You know I really hate it when you throw my own words back at me," I said.

Pixie captured every voice on the page like a court stenographer, but she wasn't transcribing: as she began the next line, she stayed one or two words *ahead* of Melanie's voice. Was the typewriter reflecting us or controlling us? A mirror or a leash?

"That's why I do it." Melanie gave one of the chrome cylinders along Pixie's cheeks a tentative poke. "This version isn't just mechanical, though. There's got to be a magical bond between the harness and the typewriter. She stops typing, the harness punishes her. Or kills her, if she doesn't get back to work."

"Every manager's dream," Mr. Smith said. "I'll have to look into the idea."

"We need to figure out how to snip the magical connection," Melanie said, "without setting off the trap in the process. Obviously we're only going to get one chance to do it right."

Pixie looked up. Her eyes—for a moment flaring with life, intense, awake—met mine before being dragged back to the page. Whatever she was typing, it was important. I went back to reading over her shoulder.

"We're nearly at critical mass," Teddy said, arranging a pile of mismatched odds and ends around an amethyst-tipped staff. "A couple more flights to reality and back, a few quickie relic hunts, and we'll be good to go."

"I don't intend to wait," Naavarasi said.

He shook his head, mute, not following.

She strode toward him, standing over him where he knelt, savoring her own power. Daniel was the one she wanted, the one she had always wanted, but Theodore was an adequate consolation prize. He was a loyal lapdog, willing to kill and die for his mistress. More pleasingly, the rakshasa queen knew that Teddy's corruption was a knife in his brother's heart. Of course, that wasn't even a sliver of the suffering she had planned for Daniel Faust.

When her work was done, Faust would crawl on his hands and knees and beg for the privilege of serving her. That, or face true damnation in a new hell. HER hell.

As I read the stark type, Caitlin's arm curled around my waist, pulling me close to her and holding tight. The typewriter wasn't wrong. My heart was a punching bag. I was sick and tired of being worked over, time and again, but being sick and tired of it didn't make the hurting stop.

Naavarasi put her hands on her hips and lifted her bestial muzzle to the ceiling of the lake chamber. Her tiger nose twitched, catching something in the muggy air. Something from Outside, not a part of her divine plan.

"'Divine plan'?" Melanie said. "Don't like the sound of that."

"I have too much experience to share your sense of optimism," said the rakshasa queen. "Your brother is damnably resourceful and so far he's survived everything Springfield has thrown at him."

"His back's against the wall," Teddy said.

"Which is, I have learned, the moment when he becomes the most dangerous. We can't trust that he won't find his way here and throw a spanner into the works."

"It's not like you're a one-man army," Melanie snorted. "We help."

I was annoyed on her behalf, and Caitlin's too. Disrespecting my family wasn't one of the top ten reasons why I was going to kill Naavarasi—she had given me way too many at this point—but it was still on the list.

Naavarasi's jade fingernails scraped along the rusty hull of the dead spotlight, Pixie typed. *She stared into the depths of its darkened lens like a fortune teller searching for the future in a crystal ball.*

"Begin the preparations," she commanded. "We're doing it tonight."

"Mistress—"

"Do not question me, Theodore. I am in absolute control here. And once our work is done, I hope your brother does make his way down to us. I don't think he's going to like what he sees. Neither will his infernal w hore."

"Well," Caitlin said, arch. "At least I got a mention in the story."

I was paralyzed, rooted to the flagstones under my feet. Whatever Naavarasi was about to do, we had to stop her. And we had to save Pixie. She was sagging, fading, she'd been awake and typing for days and I didn't know how much longer she could hold out.

"Hey," Melanie said. "Go. You and Caitlin go. I've got this."

"Melanie—"

She put a hand on my shoulder and looked me in the eye.

"You don't want me punching above my weight class. I get it, okay? But this isn't like...fighting a vampire. It's a machine with a magical trigger and a few hardware-store padlocks. I can handle it. You taught me how."

It wasn't a question of knowledge. Of course she could handle it. In theory. But if she made one wrong move, one slip...she'd have to watch as Pixie's face was torn apart. It would haunt her for the rest of her life. Other people had been destroyed by less.

I had two kinds of blood on my hands. The blood I shed by choice and the blood that spilled when I made the bad call, acted too late, decisions that ended in disaster despite my best intentions. It was the second kind that kept me awake at night. I didn't want Melanie to have to carry that kind of weight.

Caitlin leaned close and whispered in my ear. She knew what I was thinking. She always did.

"The world is full of dangers, pet. And yet we must still push our fledglings from the nest. If you ever want her to spread her wings and fly, you have to accept that she can handle the burdens of freedom."

I gave Melanie one long, last look, then nodded.

"Okay," I said. "We're going to find Naavarasi and shut this whole operation down. Cut Pixie loose and take her to the boat. We'll meet up with you once we're done. If things turn sideways, run back to the ladder and go topside. We'll find our own way out."

"Just one thing," Melanie added, casting a flicker-fast glance at Mr. Smith. "I need two pairs of hands for this."

I didn't like that. Then again, Melanie didn't want to be left alone with Smith any more than I wanted to leave her alone with him. She wouldn't ask if she didn't really need the help. I took him by the sleeve and tugged him just outside the open door, cornering him before I pitched my voice low.

"I know you think the best way to stop the typewriter is to let Pixie die," I said. "Now, I'm not going to threaten you because we both know that's pointless. We need you to fly us out of here. There isn't a bluff in my arsenal that would convince you otherwise."

"Correct on all points," Smith said.

"So let me remind you of a few salient points. Number one, getting her out safe and sound will have the exact same effect as letting her die. So if you suddenly feel the urge to, say, let your fingers slip and cause a little accident while you're helping Melanie, keep in mind that it's a waste of your time. Number two, we have no idea what we're going to be up against between here and the airport. The more people on our side, the stronger we'll be. Number three...I'll owe you one."

The first two points pelted off his utterly bland expression. The third piqued his interest.

"You will, will you?"

"Don't go getting greedy," I said. "Let's just say I have a sense of honor when it comes to these things."

"We have an operation that can excise that part of your brain. It's quite elementary, really. Would you like the number of the clinic?"

"Have I called you a deranged creep in the last ten minutes or so?" I asked.

"I believe you did, actually."

"Okay, then I don't need to say it again." I turned to Melanie. "Smith's going to help you out while me and Cait take care of business. Don't turn your back on him."

"Obviously," she said. "And, hey. Dan."

I paused, meeting her gaze.

"Thanks," she said.

She didn't need to elaborate. Thanks for trusting her, I guessed. Thanks for letting her stick her neck out and put her heart on the line. Pixie's survival was in her hands now. One way or another, this night would stay with her for a long, long time.

"Besides," she added, "I've got something to prove."

"You don't have to prove a thing to me," I said.

Melanie laughed. "Not to you. I think your brother built this thing."

She laced her fingers and cracked her knuckles.

"I'm gonna prove that I'm a better magician than he is. When you see him, do me a favor? Tell him that a teenager just kicked his ass."

I promised to relay the message.

Chapter
Thirty-Four

C anton's wand didn't like me. None of the Canton relics did, at least the ones I'd had the chance to study. They were weapons forged for a cosmic war, a grand operatic battle between the forces of good and evil.

That wasn't my scene. I was not built for theological debates and when it came down to it, I was a pretty easy-going guy. The way I saw it, there were two kinds of people: folks in the life—magicians, criminals, gangsters like me—and civilians. If you were a civilian, you had nothing to fear from me, though I might give your insurance policy a workout. If you were in the life, you were fair game. And so was I, and so was everyone else who made the conscious choice to walk on the shady side of the street. It was what we all signed up for.

My code was simple. Fuck with my family, my cash flow, or my planet, you were going down. Hands off what was mine, and you'd be just fine. It might not have been the most elaborate moral framework and maybe my sense of ethics was a tiny bit stunted, but it worked for me.

It didn't work for Canton's relics at all. Each of the dead magician's trinkets was imbued with some of the Paladin's primal essence, a gift intended to help her future reincarnations, and they played by old-school rules: there was good and evil, black and white, and if you were standing anywhere in the gray you might as well be dancing a tango with Darth Vader.

It didn't matter that I was searching for the new Paladin and actively bringing the fight to the Enemy's doorstep. I was still one of the bad guys, and the relics didn't even want me touching them, let alone putting them to work. Which was a damn shame because when I thought about the heists I could pull with those things...

Come to think of it, that probably wasn't helping.

Canton's wand bucked against my curled fingers as I led the way along a three-foot-wide ledge, the stone walkway riding along the tunnel's bend over a canal of burbling Ink, with Caitlin just behind me.

I get it, I thought at the wand. *You don't like me. That's fair, most days I don't like myself either. But Naavarasi should be capital-E Evil by your standards, and we're on our way to fuck her up, so maybe cut me a little slack? Besides, you were built to banish illusions and she's the self-proclaimed "Mistress of Illusions," so...*

The wand bucked harder, fighting me. I held it up to my face.

"Oh," I said out loud. "Are you *scared*? Too afraid to go up against the big bad rakshasa queen? Is that it?"

I started clucking, making chicken sounds at it. Caitlin put a hand on my shoulder.

"Pet?" she said. "Why are you bullying an inanimate object?"

I let my arm drop to my side. The wand gave one last petulant wiggle; then it calmed down and went still.

"Because Howard Canton was a dick," I muttered.

"Considering our leading Paladin candidates are still Harmony Black and Ada Lovelace..." she said, her voice trailing off.

"The Paladin: savior of the multiverse, absolutely no fun at parties."

I was glib because I needed to be. I had too much fear in my chest, swirling like a tornado of rocks in the pit of my stomach, for anything else. I was afraid Melanie would slip, Pixie would die, and my apprentice would spend the rest of her life with a friend's blood on her hands. I was afraid Naavarasi was about to kill us all or worse: the last time Cait and I had fought her, she nearly kicked both of our asses and I knew we hadn't seen the bottom of her bag of tricks. I was afraid that even if we won this battle—*when we win*, I tried to tell myself—we'd end up stranded in Springfield with no way home.

I was afraid my brother was lost to me, forever, and there was no bringing him back.

The only cure for that kind of fear was to walk right into the storm, start throwing punches, and fight through to the other side. *Nothing to it but to do it*, I thought, putting one foot in front of the other. As we walked the curving ledge, the air grew thick. Muggier at first, the humidity of a Florida swamp, ripe with the smell of old paper and faded leather. Then I caught little sparks in the air, motes of light flaring like fireflies, shining in my second sight. Wild magic. Stray magic. Naavarasi's stockpile of relics was leaking like a nuclear reactor built on the cheap.

"There," Caitlin said.

Up ahead, looming from the darkness, the ledge ended in a swaying rope bridge just like the ones that joined the islands of stone. It stretched over the canal and through an open archway wide enough to drive a truck through. We'd found our way back to the heart of the black snowflake. We'd found our way back to Naavarasi and Teddy, and they didn't know we were coming.

"Do we have a plan?" she murmured.

"I'm working on it. But considering everything Naavarasi's put us through...how do you feel about some extreme, shocking violence accompanied by a truly gratuitous amount of bloodshed?"

She was still behind me, but I heard the smile in her voice. "Those are a few of my favorite things."

I tilted my chin up, pushed my shoulders back, put on my game face, and tried to ignore the relentless pounding of my heart.

"Let's go," I said.

* * *

While Mr. Smith stood in the corner, looking shakier and less focused by the minute as the zombie-bite infection spread through his darkening veins, Melanie went to work. She studied Pixie's head harness from every angle, testing the buckles and locks with her fingertips while she probed it with her mind. When she let her vision slip out of focus, she made out crimson strands, like ragged and fraying lengths of thread, tying the harness to both the typewriter itself and to each of Pixie's fingers while they worked the clacking keys.

The threads didn't extend to the three padlocks that fastened the death machine to Pixie's face. One dangled against each of her cheeks and the third, a larger lock, rested against the back of her scalp.

"Can't be that easy," she said to herself, deep in thought. She couldn't just...pop the padlocks and take it off her. Could she? *They grabbed Pixie when she came snooping around,* Melanie thought. *It wasn't planned, and they weren't expecting trouble. Spur of the moment. The locks keep her from taking it off by herself, and the magic threads are there to set off the device if she stops typing. That's all they really needed to do.*

But there was always the chance of a fail-safe. The crimson threads pulsed with information, magical communication coursing up and down the lines like binary code.

"Pix, listen," she said. "I think I can get you out of this, but...I've got to try something risky. There's a chance—not a big one, I don't think, but a chance—that I'll set the trap off by accident. Do you want me to wait for Dan to come back and let him handle it?"

Her answer spilled out on the page, stark black type on crisp white paper.

She wasn't going to make it, Pixie typed.

She was dying. No food, no water, no sleep for two days and every leaden key-press sapped what little strength she had left. She struggled to think through the exhaustion and the pain. She wanted to live, God, she wanted to live, but death was an escape of its own and maybe it wouldn't be that bad.

But she trusted Melanie. Daniel Faust had dragged Pixie into this insane world of magic and monsters, but he was also her guide in the wilderness, a protector and a friend. If Dan said that Melanie could save her, Pixie believed it. She believed in Melanie. She could do it.

Melanie swallowed, hard, and took out her lockpick case.

"Thanks for the pep talk," she said. "Okay. We're doing this."

She lifted one of the small padlocks, the one resting against Pixie's left cheekbone. It was an off-the-shelf Master Lock. Kid stuff.

"Dan taught me how to open one of these with a hammer," she said, sliding a slender tension rake into the keyhole. "We will not be doing that today. Obviously."

"If picking that lock triggers the device," Mr. Smith pointed out, "you'll never get the other two open in time. She's good as dead. And she's going to die badly. I mean, having your jaw ripped off? Terrible way to go. She'll probably linger for a few minutes, maybe even longer as she bleeds out. The agony will be inconceivable."

"Daniel isn't here."

He peered at her, not following. "And?"

She adjusted the top hat on her head, a piece of Canton's legacy, and gave it a firm pat.

"Meaning, right here and now, filling his shoes is my job." Melanie locked eyes with him, glaring. "So shut your mouth and learn your place, zombie bait."

Smith blinked, surprised, and held up his open, perfectly smooth hands.

"Touchy," he said.

"I realize you don't know what it's like to have a friend's life in your hands, because you don't *have* any friends, but I'm under a little bit of stress at the moment."

She focused on the padlock, her bottom lip trapped between her teeth.

"I've spent a lot of time and energy trying to be a nice person," she muttered. "And I'll tell you one thing: I'm real fucking done with *nice*."

Her pick found the final pin in the lock. This was it. The moment of truth. She held her breath and made her move.

The padlock popped open. The crimson threads of magic shimmered in her second sight, taut like the strings of a violin, but they didn't sense the intrusion. Pixie kept typing, her fingers moving slower, her shoulders slumped and her head starting to bow as exhaustion overtook her.

One lock down, two to go, and time was running out.

Chapter
Thirty-Five

Teddy and Naavarasi stood upon the central platform, the hub of the five round stone islands, joined by rope bridges in a pentagram formation that rose from the lake of Ink. The black tar burbled and lapped against the stone. Tendrils and pseudopods rose up from the broth, straining to reach the piles of relics that lay carefully arranged around each amethyst-tipped staff. There were more than sparks in the air now; I caught fully formed glyphs in the corners of my vision, sigils charged with power that shimmered and broke in the muggy air.

There was no point in stealth. They were going to see us coming along the bridge, rough wooden planks jolting and swaying under our footsteps, so I announced our arrival instead.

"Shut it off, shut it all off," I called out. "You people are in criminal violation of the Environmental Protection Act."

Naavarasi said something under her breath, her tiger jowls contorting in sudden fury and her feline eyes burning. I didn't speak Hindi, but I knew a curse word when I heard one. Teddy just glowered, turning to face me and Caitlin as he edged closer to his mistress.

"What?" I said, stepping off the bridge and onto the island of stone. Caitlin moved to stand at my side. "Nothing? You don't like *Ghostbusters*?"

"That's not even a horror movie," Teddy snapped.

"You don't remember, do you?" I asked him.

His lips parted. He didn't answer me. There was something in his eyes, something under all the suspicion and hate, but it felt like he was fighting to force it down.

"We watched it when we were kids," I said. "You were scared of the library ghost."

"That never happened," he said, his voice barely a whisper.

"Sure it did. You remember. I can tell." I pointed to my own eyes. "And you remember what happened after that. I checked under both our beds, and the closet, to make sure she wasn't hiding in there. Every night for a week. I made you a promise, Teddy. What did I say? That when things got scary, I'd always be there to protect you."

His eyes hardened as Naavarasi put her hand on his shoulder. Her jade-painted nails dug into his button-down shirt, possessive.

"You *lied*," he hissed. "You abandoned me. When I needed you most, you weren't there."

"But I was," Naavarasi added. "And now my darling Theodore isn't afraid of anything or anyone."

I shook my head and smiled. "Still trying to make me jealous, huh? Seriously, you're what, a thousand years old? You should have grown out of your high school drama phase by now."

She wrinkled her orange-furred snout. "As if I would ever care about your feelings."

"Ah, but you do," Caitlin purred. "You see, we just came from a visit with our friend Pixie. You know, that marvelous typewriter tells quite the tale. And it doesn't skimp on the inner monologues."

I looked to Teddy. "Do you know what she calls you? Her consolation prize."

"Bull," he said.

"Hey, don't take my word for it." I nodded back over my shoulder. "Go and look. Read for yourself. It's right there in black-and-white."

"Don't listen to him," Naavarasi warned. "He's trying to divide us."

"Not like you're really together, is it?" Caitlin asked. She glanced over at Teddy. "You're not Mr. Right, dear. You're just Mr. Right Now."

Before he could respond, Naavarasi pulled him close and whispered something sharp into his ear. Teddy nodded, reluctant, and she let go of him. He stepped sideways, keeping us in his sight, moving toward the rusted and dead spotlight at the heart of the island.

His mistress stood alone, with the head of a Bengal tiger and the body of a dancer, sinuous and lithe as she spread her feet and squared her stance. We all knew there was only one way this would end—in blood and pain—and the queen of the rakshasa was ready to throw down.

So were Cait and I, but we couldn't get the party started just yet. We needed answers.

"Okay," I said. "Go for it. Monologue."

Naavarasi blinked. "Excuse me?"

"Springfield. This whole town runs on horror-movie logic, right?"

"It does."

"So," I said, wriggling my open hand at her. "It's the third act. We're the heroes of the story and you're the villains."

"Like hell we are," Teddy snapped.

"You've been unmasked," I said. "Figuratively. Which means, according to tradition, now's your chance to tell us all about your nefarious master plan. You know, before we die."

Caitlin leaned close and whispered in my ear. "Isn't that more of a superhero movie thing?"

"I'm working with what I've got," I whispered back.

Naavarasi tapped her orange-furred muzzle with a sharp fingernail, contemplative.

"I suppose I would enjoy an audience for my moment of triumph," she decided. "Considering how long the two of you have been thorns in my side, I'll savor your despair like a fine wine."

And you still want me, I thought. *You can't say it in front of Teddy, but you don't want me in despair, not really. You want me to be impressed.*

She spread her hands wide, taking in the stone islands and the lake of Ink around us.

"You see before you the trappings of a grand ritual. The first and only of its kind, in all of history. And I am its architect."

"I know you're siphoning power from the gateway to Eden," I said. "I have to admit, that's pretty slick."

Caitlin joined in, catching my vibe. "And collecting all of those First Story relics? Must have taken you years. I don't think I'd have the patience, or the discipline."

"Of course you wouldn't," Naavarasi said. She turned back to me, her tone softening. "But it's not about the energy we take. This is a two-way conduit. We're going to create a power surge and send it right back up the line, all the way to the Garden of Eden. A surge carrying my words, my spell, my *will*."

She put her hands on her hips and showed us her teeth in a hungry feline smile.

"I'm going to rewrite the First Story."

Caitlin's jaw dropped. My blood ran cold and it took me a second to find my voice again.

"Look," I said, shaking my head. "You don't want to screw with that. At all. Do you know what happened when the Enemy tried messing with the Story?"

"Of course I do. Why do you think I ingratiated myself into the Enemy's organization and spent so many degrading, thankless months playing the toady for that...creature? I wanted to know how everything worked."

"Do you know why he never tried it a second time?" Caitlin asked.

"Because he's a slave of his dead author and ruled by his nature. If he wasn't written to do something, he can't do it, period."

"Because," I said, recalling Mr. Smith's words, "if the multiverse is one giant house, the First Story is a load-bearing wall. You start messing with it and the whole place could come crashing down. All of it. Every world that is or ever was. That's why the Enemy never repeated the experiment. He realized how close he came to causing a cosmic disaster and it scared the crap out of him."

"Contemplate that," Caitlin added. "The greatest threat to the survival of life itself, a creature who literally exists to burn world after world, thought that tampering with the Story was too great a risk to take. He saw his own annihilation in the cards."

"He's a coward and a fool. I am not. I am fully in control and I will not fail. You'll see, once I ascend."

"Ascend?" I asked. "Wait. What exactly do you think the Story is going to do for you?"

"Isn't it obvious?" Naavarasi chuckled, relishing the moment. "I'm writing myself into the narrative."

I stared at her.

"Caitlin? Make a note."

"Of?" she asked.

"Today," I said, "I heard the dumbest goddamn plan. Just the most empty-brained nonsense imaginable, and I want to remember this moment because I'm not sure anyone will ever be able to top it."

Naavarasi's eyes narrowed to slits. "You object?"

"To you *cursing* yourself?" I asked. "Hell, if it wasn't a threat to the stability of, you know, *all of existence*, I'd pat you on the back, wish you luck, and stand aside. Besides the Enemy, have you ever actually met any of the Story's characters? I have. They aren't happy people. Before they figured out how to slip the loop, the Witch and her Knight were brutally murdered, oh...maybe a few hundred thousand times? Or, hey, I saw my brother brought you some stuff from Ezra Talon's office. Know how he died? Someone chopped his hands off, ripped out his tongue, and left him to choke on his own blood. I wasn't there. I know because that's how the Salesman always dies. And will always die. For eternity. Why would you want to do that to yourself?"

Naavarasi shook her head and sighed.

"Oh, Daniel. I expected better from you. Where's that roguish cunning I so very much enjoy? The First Story is a moral lesson for human imbeciles. The suffering is baked into the plot by design. But not my design."

Naavarasi raised one open hand high, her fingertips trailing stardust. She wove an illusion from dust and Ink, drawing upon the air, crafting a sky of constellations. I recognized faces that I knew, characters from the Story, a pantheon of pain. And a new one, at the center: hers.

"I will become the Mother of Tigers," she purred, "and I will write my own terms. There will be no lessons to learn. No sins to be punished. No untimely deaths or curses hanging over my head. All of the advantages of being bound to the fabric of the cosmos itself, and none of the downsides."

I wanted to ask "*What advantages?*" but Caitlin was a step ahead of me. Copper motes swirled in her eyes as she studied the queen.

"You...aren't actually immortal," Caitlin said.

Naavarasi looked glum. "My dirty secret. My kind live long, and we live well, but we do age and we do die. I have woven strategies upon plans inside of plans, my perfect symphony of revenge, and I've been raising an army of sons to carry out my design, but...I can hide my wrinkles, but I can't hide the truth. I only have so many years left. It might not be enough to see my crusade through to the end. I need more *life*."

"And if you join the Story," I said, "the second you kick it, you'll come right back as a newborn baby."

"Again, and again, and again," she replied. "Without my memories, of course, and on a random world somewhere in the cosmos, but those are fixable problems."

I nodded, seeing it. "When the Enemy escaped his prison, Miss Fleiss found him and nursed him back to health."

"As my sons will do for me. And I've already recorded several hundred hours of my personal notes and histories, to bring my next incarnation up to speed." She showed me her fangs. "I will be eternal. I will outlive the stars. And you will *never* be rid of me. Even death will offer no hope of escape, once I harrow hell to its very foundations. Your souls will be my toys, my playthings to break as I please. Forever."

I glanced sidelong at Caitlin. "I'll give her this: honestly, solid monologue."

"A for effort," she said.

I looked back to Naavarasi. "Can't let you get away with this, so...I think this is the part where we fight."

The rakshasa snickered. I didn't like the sound of that. Too confident by far.

"Oh, I don't think so," she said. "Haven't you caught on? You said it yourself: you're the protagonists of this story. And if this had been any other genre, that might have been enough to guarantee victory. But we're making a horror film here. The kind where the monsters win and the heroes die in the final act. You walked into my lair, put yourself in my hands, and laid your own necks on the chopping block. Now reap the rewards of your actions. *Theodore!*"

I saw my mistake a split second after it was too late to do anything about it. Teddy had looked shaken, earlier, and I'd assumed Naavarasi sent him away from her to free up room for our inevitable brawl. He had mostly been quiet since then and I hoped against hope that he was having some deep thoughts about his loyalties. I should have known better.

She was positioning him for the fight. He lashed out with his heel and kicked the rusted hull of the spotlight. It swung on its hinged base, dropping the dead, blackened lens toward us.

With a single twisted word from Naavarasi's tongue, the spotlight ignited. The harsh white light washed out the world and swallowed us whole.

Chapter Thirty-Six

*T**hey suddenly stood upon a new plain of stone, perched above a vast ocean of Ink and beneath a boiling open sky,* Pixie typed, her bleary eyes slipping in and out of focus as her exhausted fingers forced themselves to work. *There were behemoths in the depths, vast leviathans, and while Faust knew this was some grand illusion, the terror that clenched his gut in a cold fist was all too real.*

"Hold on," Melanie breathed, popping the second padlock on Pixie's harness. "We're coming. Just two more minutes."

She touched the third and final padlock, resting against the back of Pixie's head, and hesitated. If there were any kind of a fail-safe, a trap that would spring the device when someone tried to tamper with it, it would have to be here.

Otherwise someone could just...take it off her. Like I'm doing. The million-dollar question is, did Teddy think of that or not? She studied the crimson strands of magic that bound the harness—and Pixie's twitching, trembling fingertips—to the Selectric's keyboard.

"Okay, Pix," she said. "I know you're not a magician so you can't see 'em, but you've got...strings on you. I'm going to cut them off. I don't think it'll hurt or anything, but brace yourself because I don't know exactly what's going to happen after that. Hopefully nothing."

"What has hope done for you lately?" Mr. Smith asked her.

"More than you have," Melanie shot back.

She gathered her focus. Hardest thing she'd ever done, with her heart galloping a mile a minute and her thoughts racing in all directions, but she had to try.

Her thoughts became a blade. The blade was in her hand. She shaped it, lengthened and sharpened it. Then she raised it high, like an executioner's ax, and brought it sweeping down.

The crimson threads snapped, broken and burned, withering to ash. The harness began to click. Pixie's eyes went wide with terror as the plates in her mouth slowly began to separate, forcing her jaw open.

"Help me!" Melanie said, grabbing the padlock at the back of the harness. Smith raced over and held the lock steady while she dug her picks into the keyhole. The device was slow but relentless, ratcheting wider by the second. Pixie let out a helpless choking sound. Then she started slapping the heel of her hand against the chair, struggling to stay still.

Hair-thin lines of blood welled at the corners of her mouth as her skin was stretched to the breaking point. Her bones would be next.

Come on come on come on, Melanie thought, nearly fumbling the tension rake. One tumbler, two and—

The padlock popped open. Melanie ripped it from the hasp and Mr. Smith pulled the device free, hurling it across the room. The ticking sound became the chime of an alarm going off and suddenly it snapped wide open, locking like an inverted bear trap in midair before it hit the brick wall and clattered to the floor.

Pixie sagged in her chair, her shoulders tight and her head bowed, one hand rubbing her jaw. She shook like a leaf in a storm.

"Hey, hey, it's all right," Melanie told her, gently wrapping her in her arms.

Pixie answered with a choked sob. It was all she could manage, too exhausted for anything else.

"You're safe now. You're safe. We're going to take you home." Melanie looked over at Smith. "Take her other arm. Let's get her onto the boat."

They eased her to her feet. *She feels so...light*, Melanie thought. Like her ordeal had hollowed her out inside. But she was going to live.

I promised I'd take her home, she realized. *And now I have to keep that promise.*

***

Something cracked across the back of my skull and I staggered, almost going down as one of my knees buckled, one leg already aching and my spine on fire. Naavarasi was hitting us on all sides. Her image floated in the sky, larger than a god, cackling with feline glee as tigers and misshapen beasts swarmed all around us. I swung Canton's wand, blasting a spectral wraith to ragged scraps that melted into puddles of paint. Two more took its place.

"Pet!" Caitlin shouted, grabbing my wrist. She yanked me to one side, hauling me off-balance just as an orange-furred beast with two heads and mouths lined with shark teeth charged from behind. She threw herself onto the monster's back, grabbed one head, and wrenched it to the side, breaking its neck. Its tail snapped like a bullwhip, lashing across her shoulder, cutting through clothing and tearing her flesh.

I'd thought we were going to be playing the same game as the last time we dueled: picking out the real Naavarasi from a horde of illusions. But the game had changed. Here, in the hellscape of her enchanted spotlight, at the heart of the power surge, her phantoms could kill.

We couldn't tell what was real, what wasn't, and the lake of Ink had supercharged Naavarasi's natural powers. Canton's wand couldn't keep up. Neither could we. I still had some fight left in me, but there was no denying the truth.

We were going to lose.

***

They laid Pixie down in the boat. Her eyes drifted shut, sleep conquering her.

"She's going to need emergency medical attention," Mr. Smith said. "The dehydration alone could kill her, not to mention the possibility of permanent nerve damage in her hands—"

"I *know*," Melanie seethed, hitting him with a glare so intense that he took half a step back.

She had been afraid, but she didn't have room for fear now. It had all been squeezed out of her, replaced by boiling rage. She had spent a lifetime bottling up her anger, locking it away, but the dam had finally burst and there was no fixing it.

"Ever since I was a little kid," she said, her voice dangerously soft, "people have told me how I'm supposed to feel, what I'm supposed to be. 'Oh, you're half-demon, you need to be working for the princes and hell's agenda.' The fact that I don't *want* to doesn't seem to matter."

"There are...other opportunities," Smith said, his voice cautious.

She leaned closer to him, gritting her teeth.

"And you. You and your Network buddies are even worse than the demons. Then you've got people like Naavarasi. You know what you all have in common?" She inched closer, nearly sending him off the edge of the landing. "You *take*. You take, and you take, and you eat, and you eat, and you don't care who gets hurt. Fuck, that's being too charitable. You get off on hurting people who can't fight back, because deep down inside, you know that you're pathetic and weak, and inflicting pain makes you feel strong. The world is only a bad place because people like you *make* it bad. And *I have had enough!*"

"W-what are you going to do?" he asked, a stutter in his voice.

Melanie looked back up the tunnel, to the open door and the avocado-green Selectric.

"Magic," she said. "Watch Pixie. Anything happens to her...you know, I'm not even going to threaten you. Use your imagination."

She walked back into the cell and stood before the typewriter, her fingers curling at her sides. The relic had dominated Pixie's mind, turning her into a conduit for Springfield's power. But Pixie wasn't a magician, and Melanie wasn't strapped into a torture device designed to make her comply.

She ripped the half-finished page from the platen, crumpled it up, and tossed it into the corner. Then she threaded a new one.

"Time to change the story," she breathed.

"I couldn't agree more."

Melanie spun, hearing a strange but familiar voice. Carolyn Saunders, in the flesh—and a garish Christmas sweater and mom jeans—leaned against the wall with her arms crossed.

"Carolyn? But...you're..."

"Dead as a doornail, kid. Ah, but this..." She sauntered over, trailing her wrinkled fingers along the Selectric's case. "This brings back memories. It was my first typewriter. Bought it from a pawnshop with my paper-route money. Wanna know the funny thing? I never wrote a single book on it. Honest. I didn't become a pro until years later, after I upgraded to a first-generation Mac. I guess when it comes to the magic stuff, the things you've got an emotional tie to are what matter most."

"You're the Scribe," Melanie said. "Characters from the First Story don't go to any afterlife and they can't be ghosts, so...hold on. You're not Carolyn at all, are you?"

She flashed a smile, the crow's-feet at the corners of her eyes crinkling.

"I'm an echo. Nah, I'm sure the real Scribe already reincarnated somewhere. A bright-eyed, rosy-cheeked, empty-headed baby with a hard life ahead of her and no idea what she really is. Not until the war finds her and drags her in, so she can live this shit all over again."

Melanie considered Naavarasi's stockpiles, all the relics she'd gathered in one place.

"Things the characters are connected to, sentimental objects, things they felt emotional about in life...they carry part of their essence."

"And then some. Of course, I wasn't thrilled when tiger-mama made me the Energizer battery at the heart of her giant death machine. Come on, vampires and werewolves? If I was still alive, I'd say 'kill me.' If I had a soul, I'd say writing that shit physically hurt it. I couldn't stand up to Naavarasi's power, but I found a few tiny ways to make an end run around the rules."

Melanie thought back to the library. *The City on Fire*. You wrote that for us to find."

"You've still got it, right? Better hang on to it, because...well, number one, that's my last novel for this lifetime, so it means a lot to me on a personal level. As much as anything can mean to me on a personal level, seeing as I'm just the lingering psychic residue of a dead woman. Anyway, I've been doing some digging. There's dirt in that book that Daniel is going to need and there's only one copy in all of existence. No reprints."

"Won't matter if we die here."

"Well," the echo of Carolyn told her, "I guess you'd better do something about that, huh?"

Melanie nodded to the typewriter. "May I?"

Carolyn began to fade from sight, her body turning translucent as she slipped away. She gestured to the relic with a dry chuckle.

"By all means. Hey, you know my formula for a slam-bang climax?"

Melanie shook her head.

"Go big or go home, kid. Go big or go home."

And then she was gone. Alone, Melanie scooped up the typewriter. The antique was a bulky monster, achingly heavy especially once she cradled it in one arm, but her newfound rage gave her newfound strength. She began to walk, following the ledge where Daniel and Caitlin had gone before her. She held the Selectric in one arm and placed the fingers of her other hand on the keys, staring at the blank and pristine page.

It wasn't over, she typed with one fumbling hand.

Battered and bruised, but still unbroken, Daniel and Caitlin stood side by side and hand in hand, facing Naavarasi's twisted hordes. The odds seemed insurmountable, but they still had each other. Today they would die on their feet, not on their knees.

She paused, thinking, then pecked out the next line letter by letter.

And then they heard the horns.

Chapter
Thirty-Seven

I was dead on my feet. Battered, bruised, and dirty, my shirtsleeve torn, my forehead stinging and wet as blood trickled into one eye. I smeared it away with the back of my hand. Caitlin was breathing heavy, running on fumes, her pale skin marred with half a dozen jagged cuts. The world was a battlefield and I'd lost track of how many of Naavarasi's creations we'd sliced down and ripped apart, leaving the stone platform drenched in scarlet gore.

It wasn't enough.

Still gleefully watching us from above, a disembodied and spectral tiger head in the sky, the rakshasa queen gave us a moment to breathe. It wasn't mercy. She just wanted to twist the knife and make sure we knew how hopeless this all was. Her forces pulled back, surrounding us on all sides. It was a grotesque gallery of nightmares: tiger-men with four muscular arms ending in scythe-claws, six-legged beasts sprouting tumors and whipping tentacles, and she replenished the fallen with nothing but a whim. We were trapped in her spotlight's hallucinatory mindscape, pinned at the nexus of Naavarasi's power.

My hand found Caitlin's. She squeezed tight.

"Not how I wanted to go out," I said. "Still, I'll take the sheer level of overkill as a sign of respect."

Caitlin nodded. "She's taking us seriously. So. Death or glory?"

The problem with a death-or-glory charge is that fifty percent of the time you don't get glory. I wasn't ready to die just yet. I'd been thinking, as much as I could think in the swirling and endless chaos, and hunting for a way out of here.

Out was a misnomer in the first place, I was pretty sure. The world had washed away and transformed into a black ocean when Teddy hit us with the spotlight. We might have been shunted into another pocket realm, a construct in a construct like back at the movie theater, but I didn't buy it. Everything here was a figment of Naavarasi's cruel imagination, as her massive and disembodied head leered down at us from above, like we were pieces on a game board.

Concentrated hypnosis attack, I thought. Our bodies were still standing on the island, right where we were before, transfixed by the light while she fought us on the mental plane. If I could figure a way to snap us out of it, we could even the odds in a heartbeat. She just wasn't giving us a chance.

Then we heard the horns.

Cait and I weren't the only confused ones. Naavarasi's creatures craned their boneless necks and answered the blaring brass horns with guttural howls. Either she was graduating to some new kind of mind game or...

Or that's not her, I thought.

A vast and curving bridge of weathered, mossy stone materialized at the edge of the battlefield, soaring over the ocean of Ink. And in the distance, the thunder of hoofbeats roiled under a mighty shout: "*Sons of Rohan, sons of Gondor, this day we fight!*"

"What," I breathed, "the actual fuck?"

From the way her face contorted in the sky above us, her snout twitching, Naavarasi was thinking the same thing.

Caitlin smiled.

"Pet," she murmured, "I think your dear apprentice just changed the genre."

The cavalry was here. Literally, as the first wave of horsemen boiled over the bridge in a storm of thrusting spears and shining shields. They wore a mishmash of armor from every fantasy potboiler I'd ever seen or read. Saracens rode alongside Roman centurions, while Egyptian chariots and scimitar-slashing elves in gilded plate bore down on the misshapen horde.

"For Camelot! For Narnia!" their commander bellowed. "For Westeros and Wakanda we ride!"

"*Wakanda?*" I silently mouthed. Caitlin gave me a nudge with her elbow.

"She's on a roll," Cait said.

The battle lines clashed in a storm of steel. The cavalry rolled through the monstrous army, cutting down Naavarasi's creatures left and right while horses died, chopped at the knees and throwing their riders, a tidal wave of death. I didn't have a moment to lose. Finally blessed with a second's peace, I took measured breaths and found my focus, stretching my magical senses and hunting for a way out.

We hadn't been forgotten. A mutant tiger with overgrown teeth and paws built for mutilation pounded toward us at full speed. Cait moved to take the hit, bracing herself—and then a man in black swooped in, a cape billowing behind him as he swung on a chandelier rope. There was no chandelier, and the rope didn't seem to be attached to anything, but that didn't stop him from leaping free, landing on the tiger's back, and driving a pair of wavy-bladed daggers into its neck. It dropped, skidding along the blood-soaked stone, and he leaped off it just in time to offer Caitlin a courtly bow, all in one smooth motion.

He looked exactly like me, but with a domino mask over his eyes and a curly handlebar mustache.

"Fear not, good lady," he proclaimed, "for no mere monster can match the blinding blade-play of Donatello Faustus!"

"Kill me now," I muttered.

Caitlin's eyes glittered. "Charmed."

"Of course," he said, sly, "I cannot guarantee your safety, my sweet damsel. For I am well-known as...the thief of hearts."

With that he drew her into an embrace, sweeping her off her feet and dipping her low in his arms, and planted a long, smoldering kiss on her lips.

"*Hey!*" I snapped.

He pulled her up and let go, both of them breathless. Then he turned to me and offered up a salute.

"And now I must return to the battle, for there is plunder to be taken and women to be wooed!"

He grabbed the dangling rope—which still wasn't attached to any- thing—ran and leaped, swinging back into the fray. I cupped my hands to my mouth and shouted after him.

"That mustache makes you look like a hipster barista, you dick!"

I stared at Caitlin. She wore a tiny smile and a blush on her pale cheeks. She looked back at me and shrugged.

"He is...technically you," she said.

"I would *never* wear a cape. Or that mustache."

Naavarasi looked like she was in as much disarray as her forces. She glared down at the board, control slipping from her grasp. I felt her confusion, her rising anger, washing over my face like the heat from an open furnace door. I followed it with my mind, tracing it to the source.

There. Now I could see it. Just beyond her ghostly face in the sky, a pale silver sun cast a corona of light. Canton's wand trembled in my tired grip.

Don't do it for me, I thought at the wand. *If we die here, the Canton relics are lost forever. Do it for the new Paladin, whoever they are. I need to deliver, and I can't do it without your help.*

Cold power, like ice in my veins, spread along my arm. I raised the wand high, focused on the distant corona. The cap of bone flared, trailing glowing embers. We became one, focus and force combined, as I whipped the wand downward.

The sun exploded in a rain of glass.

***

We snapped back to reality, standing side by side before the smoking, broken, and burned-out hull of the spotlight. The warring armies were gone. It was only me, Cait, Naavarasi, and Teddy, and from the looks on their faces they knew the odds had just gone full tilt.

"Amateur mistake," Caitlin said, fluffing her fire-red curls with a toss of her fingers. "If you give us a spotlight, you'd best know that we're going to shine."

Teddy's nerve broke. He threw back one side of his jacket and went for a holstered gun, grabbing his piece and aiming at Caitlin. I only had a few cards left, barely enough for a hand of poker, but I let one fly. It carved across his trigger finger, drawing a strangled cry as it sliced him to the bone. He dropped the pistol, clutching his bleeding hand and looking to Naavarasi for help.

She was distracted, turning to the rope bridge as the sound of uneven, mechanical clacking drifted out over the lake of Ink. Melanie walked along the swaying planks, the avocado-green Selectric cradled in her arm, typing with her free hand. Her brow was tight, eyes focused as she fought to hold her concentration.

"Pet," Caitlin said, her copper eyes fixed on Naavarasi.

"Yeah, babe?"

"Let's finish this."

We spread out. She focused on Teddy, closing in on him like a mountain lion spotting a tasty rabbit, while I brandished Canton's wand and prepared myself to take Naavarasi head-on.

The wand tingled. Then it throbbed against my palm, my skin sizzling like it was gloved in static electricity. Canton's wand had never done that before.

The static sensation rose all around us, swirling like a dust devil. From the looks on their faces, Naavarasi and my brother were feeling it too. The relic piles, scattered across the islands of stone, began to shudder as the amethyst crystal staves glowed with inner light.

"Mistress?" Teddy asked, his voice on the edge of panic.

"That's not me," Naavarasi snapped. Her baleful orange eyes focused on Melanie. "Kill her! Kill her *now!*"

Teddy dropped to one knee, reaching for his fallen pistol with his good hand. Caitlin brought her heel down on his fingers, bones crackling as he screeched.

I was watching Melanie.

There are moments when the world changes. So often, they start as tiny things. A butterfly flaps its wings, and a storm brews on the other side of the globe. A duke is assassinated in Austria, and the entire planet spirals into war. Everything in life is a consequence, the reaction to countless choices made by countless numbers of people. When those consequences loom large enough, we call them "history."

Watching history unfurl is an awe-inspiring and terrible thing. And we had a seat at ground zero.

Melanie was glowing. Consumed by the typewriter's magic, struggling to master it, she didn't even seem to realize. With every step closer along the swaying rope bridge, she took on a cast of shining gold. The relics around us thrummed and danced as the concentrated power of the First Story, straight out of Eden, fired down the line and washed over the underground lake. The reservoir of Ink became molten gold and it sang, stretching tendrils into the air like upraised arms, a wordless hymn that resonated in the pit of my stomach. Melanie's halo of light turned to metal, a suit of polished and gilded armor forged for her and her alone.

The Paladin had arrived.

"Wanna see a trick?" she asked, meeting Naavarasi's gaze. "I can destroy your whole plan with just two tiny magic words. I don't even have to say them out loud."

Naavarasi's tiger eyes went wide with panic as she realized what Melanie meant. "*No!*" she screamed.

Melanie put her fingers to the typewriter keys and tapped them out.

THE END.

Chapter Thirty-Eight

The typewriter let out a mechanical *ding*. Then I nearly fell, the ground lurching out from under me and going sideways. The underground chamber shook, rocked by the sound of distant falling stones, and a blanket of dust rained down from the vaulted ceiling.

The world flashed around us, layers of reality warring for control. The Ink strobed from gold to black, Melanie's armor vanished, the glow a dying candle-flicker, and the ground shook as the walls trembled and began to show long, jagged cracks. Naavarasi grabbed Teddy by the scruff of the neck and ran, dragging him toward their moored motorboat. I didn't have time to chase them, with fist-sized chunks of brick pelting down from above; I ran at Caitlin, shoving her out of the way as a cinderblock hit the floor beside her and burst into rubble. The air swirled with choking brick dust, whipped into a blinding storm.

The whine of two engines filled the air as Naavarasi untied their boat and fired up the onboard motor. A second boat was coming in hot, with Pixie slumped unconscious against the prow and Mr. Smith working the rudder.

"Melanie," I called out, "let's go!"

She had her top hat off and was grunting, straining to wedge the Selectric inside. The brim bulged but she finally won, the bulky typewriter vanishing into the hat's dimensional pocket with a pop of compressed air. Smith brought the boat up along the edge of the island and Caitlin grabbed hold of the side while he idled the engine.

"The other relics," Melanie gasped.

I grabbed her arm and tugged her along. "Not worth dying for, c'mon!"

As we clambered onto the boat, Smith looked baffled. "What did you people *do*?"

"Finished the movie," Melanie told him.

And if the movie was done, so was Springfield.

Smith gunned the engine. Our boat soared down the canals, veering hard with every twist and turn, skipping along the turbulent waves of Ink while rubble rained down at our backs like cannonballs. The whole underground was shaking itself apart. We made it back to the landing. Caitlin scooped Pixie up, carrying her over one shoulder like a firefighter as we sprinted along the shuddering tunnel and climbed up the rungs of the towering shaft to reach the surface.

I pushed myself through the hatch in the base of the statue, hit the wet grass, and rolled out of the way. I squinted up at white, fluffy clouds in a turquoise sky. It was morning. The town was waking up, blinds opening and streetlights winking out along the boulevard as locals emerged to walk their dogs and collect the morning paper.

But the ground was still quaking, the grass feeling like a hammering fist against my back, and I didn't think it was going to stop. I got on my feet and helped Caitlin with Pixie, gently pulling her through the hatch.

All the while, my mind was racing a mile a second. I could almost make myself believe that the gold, the glow, the shining armor, had all been some fever-dream side effect of the wild magic in play.

But I knew better than that.

How many times had I said it? Melanie was the best of all of us. I just didn't understand, until now, how right I was.

That subject would keep. We needed to get out of town while there was still a town to escape. We'd never make it to the airport on foot. We needed wheels, fast. I remembered our arrival and the old driver's words: *"Oh, and don't forget: when you're ready to head on home, the official shuttle pickup spot is just outside town hall. There's a bus stop and a sign, can't miss it."*

The old man was dead, staked and dusted back at the police station, but his shuttle bus was right where he said it would be: a little ways up the street, parked and abandoned at the curb.

I led the charge and jumped into the driver's seat. While Cait and Melanie laid Pixie down on a long vinyl bench, checking her vitals, I tore off the rough plastic panel under the steering wheel and exposed the guts underneath. I stripped red and orange wires with my penknife, moving with practiced haste, and they sparked as the copper ends touched. The engine revved to life.

"Just so you all know," I called out, pulling the crank to close the shuttle's doors, "the last time I drove a bus I was trying to break out of prison, and it didn't go so great."

Mr. Smith tilted his head. "But you didn't crash, right?"

I stomped the gas pedal. The bus lurched ahead, squealing, leaning hard as I spun the wheel at the roundabout.

"But...you didn't crash, right?" he asked again.

We were two blocks down Heritage Street when a louder, burlier engine roared out along a side street. A metallic purple Lotus Esprit blasted out of an alley, tires screaming as it pulled a hard left turn, launching down the road just ahead of us.

"Naavarasi," I said. And Teddy.

"Like rats from a sinking ship," Caitlin hissed.

We'd never catch them, not in a shuttle bus. As the Lotus burned rubber, the gap between us growing wider by the second, we had other problems. The bus shook with a meaty thud as something landed hard on the roof. Then we heard the rhythmic thumping of heavy boots.

"Tell me that isn't what I think it is," I said.

Then the roof above my head ruptured, the head of a miner's pickax thrusting through the cheap, thin metal, the rusty tip of the pick stopping a quarter of an inch above my scalp.

I clutched the wheel tighter as the road bucked under us, the earthquakes growing in intensity by the minute. The sky ran with smears of gray paint, a roiling storm overtaking the clear blue sky, coating the small town in unnatural darkness as lightning crackled in the murky clouds. Then, with an electric *crack* I could feel in my bones, a lance of raw power streaked down from the sky and hit the roof of the bed-and-breakfast.

The building exploded into a whirlwind of paper. Crisp white pages covered in stark black type washed across the street in a flood and I hit the windshield wipers, trying to brush them away as they clung to the glass and blocked my view of the road.

Smiley's rusty pick slid from the ruptured hole. Then it came down again and gouged another crater in the roof, nearly hitting Caitlin as she jumped back a step.

Up ahead a man was walking his dog, cheerfully oblivious to the chaos all around him. He turned and gave the bus a friendly wave. Then he erupted. He was a paper man walking a paper dog, their bodies made of a manuscript, and the wind took them both and billowed and blasted them along the sidewalk.

The earth opened. Up ahead, a jagged crack split the street in half, rapidly spreading to cut off our escape. I looked in the rearview, watching Smiley's pick. I held my breath, waiting for him to pull it back out again and raise it high for another blow.

Then I spun the wheel and stomped the brakes at the same time. The bus veered off to the left, narrowly missing the chasm in the road. Off-balance and without any leverage, Smiley slipped and fell, rolling along the roof. I watched him plunge off the side, hitting the asphalt on his melted mask, tumbling in our dust as I got the bus back under control and leaned heavy on the gas.

"See you in the sequel, asshole."

Springfield was dying. Lightning rained down, burning crimson like the slash of an editor's pen. The library detonated in a tornado of paper; then the steeple of the town church went up, a congregation transformed into words on a raging storm. The road jolted again and I gripped the wheel, engine screeching as I pushed it into the red. Naavarasi's Lotus was a speck in the distance now, but we didn't have much farther to go.

"Give me an update," I called out. "How's Pix?"

"It's not good," Melanie said. "We've got to get her to a hospital. I know first aid, but she needs real professionals."

"Smith? You hungry for human flesh yet?"

Slumped alone in a bench seat, he gave me a tired glare. He was gray as stone now, bloodless and glistening with clammy sweat, and the edges of black veins pulsed from under his shirt collar as the zombie-bite infection ravaged his body.

"Actually," he said, "I've been reconsidering our deal."

I did not have time for this.

"Cait," I said, "I can't take my eyes off the road, so would you please beat the living shit out of this man? Don't hurt his hands. He'll need 'em to fly us out of here."

"Gladly," she said.

Smith snorted. "As if I fear pain. I'm the Network's fixer. I've experienced flavors of torment you can't imagine."

"Oh," Caitlin said, "you should really give me more credit than that. I've been told that I'm very creative."

He fixed his haggard, bloodshot eyes on Melanie.

"You," he said, his tone an accusation, "are the Paladin. How long have you known?"

The look on her face, captured in the rearview mirror, told the whole story. She didn't. She was just as shocked as the rest of us, clinging to shreds of denial like a tattered cloak in a blizzard.

"Well," Smith said, "no matter. The nice thing about my...unique condition is that death is a temporary inconvenience. I'll expire here, but I'll live on once again, safe at home, with a more-than-ample report to file. My superiors will be very pleased at the news that I abandoned the thorns in our side, along with the Paladin herself, in a collapsing pocket dimension. Sorry, my dear child. No saving-the-world antics for you. Your world belongs to *us*."

Caitlin loomed over him. She parted her lips, showing him a maw of shark teeth.

"Ah," Caitlin said. "But you have to die first. Isn't that right? I haven't figured out how you keep coming back from the dead, but it seems you can't get a new body until you've relinquished the old."

"What of it?" he said, his eyebrows knitting in suspicion.

"I have no intention of allowing you to die," she said.

He barked out a tired laugh, pulling back a sleeve to show her the twisted black venom coursing, like ropy worms, through his bulging veins.

"Did you lose the plot? I'm infected. I'll admit to not being much of a horror-film aficionado, but I'm fairly certain there's no cure."

Caitlin's smile grew wider.

"Indeed," she purred. "You're going to become a zombie. A feral, cannibalistic, nearly mindless shell of the man you used to be. And I...am *not* going to slay you."

She eased behind his seat and placed both of her hands on his shoulders. Kneading, deadly intimate, as she leaned close and put her lips to his ear.

"I'm going to take your arm," she said, "and twist it, and twist it, until it tears from your body. Then I'm going to rip off your other arm. And both of your legs. I'll cauterize the stumps with fire, to keep you from bleeding out, and reduce you to nothing but a torso with a head and a broken spine. Then I'm going to take a power drill and bolt a wire muzzle over your mouth, driving screw after stainless-steel screw into your skull, to keep you from biting anyone. And then I'll take that same drill and bolt a pair of long canvas straps to your bones. Do you know why I'm going to do that, Mr. Smith?"

He froze, lips parted but silent, his eyes wide. He gave a tiny shake of his head.

"Because I'm going to wear your dismembered torso like a backpack," Caitlin told him. "I'm going to take you everywhere. My pet zombie. I'll call you Stumps. And I will never, ever, *ever* allow you the mercy of death. Can you imagine it? That's what your eternity looks like."

Smith swallowed, hard.

"Maybe...I was rash in my change of heart," he said.

"Maybe you were. Would you like to revise your earlier statement?"

"Swear you'll let me go," he said, "and I'll fly you out of here."

She patted him on the head. "Was that so hard?"

She walked up to stand beside the driver's seat, looking pleased. I took my eyes off the shuddering road just long enough to give her a sidelong glance.

"Damn, Cait."

"Darling, to get the respect you deserve, sometimes you have to remind people of who you are." Her fingers traced the curve of my shoulder. "And sometimes you have to remind them *what* you are."

We burned down the road, the maelstrom at our back, the airport dead ahead.

Chapter Thirty-Nine

The clouds over the municipal airport roiled like black smoke, hot winds whipping across the grass and the narrow strip of runway. Half of the aluminum hangars lining the strip hung open, their doors wide and their bellies empty. I rolled straight down the runway, head craned, hunting for our escape route.

Catching the sight of vanilla wings and a nose streaked in blue, I slammed on the brakes. The shuttle squealed and lurched off the tarmac, tires spinning in the wet grass and spraying clods of dirt before it jolted to a dead stop.

A six-seater plane sat alone in its hangar, engine cold and windows dark. Smith and I ran up on it while Cait and Melanie eased Pixie to her feet, gently carrying her off the bus.

"What do you think?" I asked Smith. "Can you get us out of here?"

"If it's fueled, I can fly it. I'll need help getting the engine started and some time to run down the preflight checklist."

Thunder boomed like a cannon as the storm front washed in. Cherry-neon lightning flashed on the horizon.

"Bad news about your checklist," I said.

He still went along with the plan but grumbled the whole time as we got Pixie on board and laid her out in the back.

"This is shockingly dangerous and irresponsible," he said, taking the pilot's seat and flicking switches along the cockpit console.

"That's the name of my garage band," I said, grabbing the copilot's chair.

The propeller spun to life, and we rolled out of the hangar. Smith worked the pedals, turning out onto the runway and angling our nose toward freedom. We weren't alone. Another smaller plane, a khaki-painted Cessna Skyhawk, was bouncing along the tarmac just ahead of us and pouring on speed.

"It's them," I said. I turned to Smith. "I've never said this before and never thought I would ever need to, but...follow that plane."

Teddy's Skyhawk lifted off, rising hard and fast and aiming for the storm. We were right behind him. The force of lift pushed me back in my seat, stealing my breath as Smith pulled hard on the yoke and we went airborne.

The storm tossed us like a child's toy. The airframe made a tin-can rattle and the wings shook, my stomach plunging as we suddenly dropped hard, slammed into an air current, and lurched back up again while Smith gritted his teeth and clung to the shuddering yoke. The Skyhawk was dead ahead, angling its wings toward a distant sliver of light in the heart of the billowing black.

Emergency lights strobed amber all along the cockpit console. A buzzing alarm rang out, flooding the cabin with its harsh and dissonant whine.

"We're not going to make it!" Smith pulled one trembling hand back on the throttle as he milked the engine for every last bit of power it could muster.

"Steady," I said, eyes fixed on the growing crack in the storm. It shone like liquid silver, the light from a different and distant sun. "Hold it together, just one more minute—"

A second klaxon stridently rang out over the first. A dial on the panel flashed blood-red above the glowing words, *Fuel Tank 2 Disabled*.

"*Steady*," I said.

The Skyhawk vanished through the sliver in the storm. We were right behind it. The silver rip was edged in white crystal, fractals of magic blossoming like wildflowers at the intersection of worlds.

We flew through the tear in reality and out the other side.

***

The storm was gone. So was the world we came from.

We were sailing over an open desert, sand and empty country roads below, a pristine blue sky above and mountains rising in the distance. The plane still shook and smoke spat from the propeller, washing the cockpit window in soot. One wing trailed a shower of sparks as an electrical fire flared in the wiring. Smith leaned over, flipping rocker switches and checking his instrument panel.

"We have to land, right now," he said. He clicked another switch and I heard the steady hum of the landing gear swinging open. "Everyone buckle up and brace. This is going to be unpleasant."

I watched Teddy's Skyhawk peel away, fading into the distance as he and Naavarasi made their escape, but I wasn't stupid enough to argue Smith's point. One way or another, this plane was going down.

The nose dipped and bounced as he tried to steady the wings, angling us toward a long strip of open dirt road. We plunged down fast and hard and he pulled back on the yoke at the last second, smoothing our arc as the landing gear slammed against the ground. We lurched, rising hard into the air again and then right back down, the stomach-churning dive of a roller coaster gone out of control. The hull rattled, engines screeching as he fought to slow our speed.

One more brief, dizzying thrust into the air, one more bone-rattling landing, and the plane stayed stuck to the dirt road. We bounced, jolting in our seats as Smith reined the machine in, finally bringing us to a crawl, and then a shuddering stop.

The engines died with a fading whine and a string of dry clicks. The screaming alarms went silent, cut with the power, and the cockpit console went dark.

I didn't do anything for a moment. I just breathed. I was grateful to be alive, and breathing had never felt so good.

Caitlin was in the seat right behind the pilot's chair. She leaned forward.

"You have hell's gratitude for your cooperation, Mr. Smith."

His eyes narrowed, uncertain. "Well, I'm just happy we were able to—"

She hooked one arm around his throat, squeezed hard, and yanked his head to the side. His neck broke with the sound of a snapping broomstick. Smith sank in his chair and slumped to one side, glassy-eyed and dead.

I blinked at her. "I was going to do that, you know."

Caitlin sniffed and checked her nails. "You killed him last time. It was my turn."

Fair.

She stayed behind a minute, to separate Smith's head from his body and make sure he didn't get back up again. My Italian loafers dropped down into the dust of a desert road. I lifted my face to the sun. It was a dry heat, clean and real. At my side, Melanie pulled out her phone, lighting up when she saw that she finally had cell service again. Then she pulled up Google Maps and her face dropped.

"We're in New Mexico. Somewhere outside of...frickin' *Albuquerque*?"

"Stay here and keep an eye on Pix. I'm going to go flag down a ride. Or jack one, whatever." I paused. "I'll be right back."

Melanie's head shot up from her phone, eyes wide. "*Dan!*"

"What?" I said, walking backward with a wave. "If I really do come right back, it'll prove we're not in a horror movie anymore. That's called multitasking."

***

I stole a car. People didn't really pick up hitchhikers anymore.

We raced Pixie to the closest ER, where they loaded her onto a crash cart and ran her into the first open triage room. I paced in the parking lot and thought about how badly I needed a stiff drink, until Melanie came out to deliver the prognosis.

"They think she's going to pull through. They've got her in a bed, she's stable, and she's on an IV drip to get some fluids in her system. She was so dehydrated..." She chewed on her bottom lip. "I don't even want to go there. She's going to be okay."

"What about her hands?" I asked.

She shook her head. "Way too soon to say anything. Once she's out of the woods, we'll know more."

"You want to...talk about the other thing?"

Melanie met my eyes. She looked lost.

"I really don't. Can we go home? Please?"

I didn't blame her. Besides, we couldn't stick around and watch over Pixie's recovery, no matter how badly I wanted to. Teddy and Naavarasi were on the move. Caitlin called for some backup from the home office: until we were able to come back for her, Pixie would have armed men watching her hospital room door around the clock. I made sure she'd have the best room, the best care, the best of everything, all on my dime. It didn't feel like nearly enough.

The Vegas Strip greeted us like a long-lost friend, wrapping us up in the familiar like a warm, soft blanket. At the American, my half-finished dream of a nightclub, our friends had some good news.

"Y'all look like you been beat to hell and back," Jennifer drawled, eyeing me and Caitlin as we walked in.

"We weren't anywhere nearly as nice as hell," Caitlin replied.

"Hey, kiddo," Corman said, pulling me into a bear hug. "Guess what?"

"Tell me something good," I said.

Bentley was right behind him, brandishing a smoked-glass vial with an eyedropper built into the cap.

"Oh," Bentley said, "I think you'll be pleased. We've been running experiments on our unwilling guest, and I believe they've borne fruit. Come. Let me show you."

They had the rakshasa we caught all trussed up in the supply room, shackled to a chair with more chains and padlocks than an escape artist. He was back in his human disguise, still imitating Pixie's form. I bit back a surge of anger as we watched the captive rak through a window in the swinging door.

"A rakshasa wearing a human shape," Bentley said. "Untraceable, undetectable, indistinguishable from the real thing unless they slip up."

"That is the crux of the problem," Caitlin said.

Bentley handed me the vial. "Try these, son. One drop in each eye."
The eyedropper came out, filled with scarlet elixir.

"Is this...blood?" I asked.

"That's the base ingredient," Jennifer said. "Then we worked a little mojo on it and tossed in a heaping handful of secret herbs and spices. Between my blood magic and your dads' alchemy, I think we cooked up a nice recipe. Give it a shot."

I tilted my head back, looking to the ceiling, and winced as an ice-cold drop splashed into each of my eyes. I blinked, the world looking wavy and coated in a cherry glaze before it snapped back to normal.

Almost normal. I looked through the window in the door. The rakshasa had changed. No. He hadn't, but my perception had. Now I saw two figures in the chair, overlapping one another in space like a pair of filmstrips laid on top of one another. I saw the fake Pixie. And I saw the rakshasa beneath the skin, a man-tiger woven out of shadows and teeth.

"Sweet, huh?" Jennifer said. "Each dose lasts about an hour."

I didn't have words. This was a game changer. Naavarasi's greatest weapon was her—and her children's—power to hide in plain sight. We'd just ripped that weapon out of her hands. And she had no idea.

"How much can we brew up?" Caitlin asked, her eyes glittering with fascination.

"We drained this one as dry as we dared without killin' him. What we've got is good for a few solid batches. We can tap him for more blood once he recovers. Of course, that means keeping a live rakshasa around, and that's a risk all its own. Don't gotta tell you how wily these critters are."

I watched him, intent. Even now he was squirming with precision and purpose, trying to strategically inch his way out of his bonds.

One shoulder burbled and compressed like a sponge as he squeezed his body into a more flexible shape.

"Let him go," I said.

All eyes were on me. I nodded to myself, the plan firming up in my mind's eye.

"To be more specific," I added, "we're going to pull out of here, hide and watch from a safe distance, and let him 'escape.' The way he's working at it, I don't think we'll have to wait long."

"And then we follow him," Caitlin said, catching on.

"All the way home."

Chapter Forty

The rakshasa wriggled free of his bonds and slipped out through the conveniently unguarded club, as planned. Still wearing Pixie's face, he headed for the Strip. Halfway there, he ducked into a Buffalo Wild Wings.

He came out as a tourist, a frat boy with a vaguely obscene T-shirt and a blond quiff that poked up like a rooster comb. I would have lost him right then and there, if not for the eyedrops keeping his shadowy tiger form, wreathed in a seething scarlet aura, front and center in my altered vision.

The next stop was the Metropolitan, where he crossed the casino floor, got lost in a pack of gamblers, and came out the other side as a burly, bald pit boss in a suit. Then he dipped into a bathroom stall and emerged as a scraggly, disheveled man with two days of stubble on his cheeks, doubled back over his own tracks, and blended with the crowds along the boulevard.

"I'll give her this," I said over the phone as I lingered half a block behind my quarry, "Naavarasi teaches her kids good tradecraft. They could be a lot sloppier and still get away with it."

"On your guard, love," Caitlin purred in my ear.

I gave a play-by-play as I followed the rak. We had people on foot, others stationed in cars, a small but tight dragnet ready to snap shut at my command. He walked the Strip, turning toward another casino a few doors down from the last one. Instead of going inside, though, he joined the taxi line with the other tourists.

He was rolling off in the back seat just as Caitlin's snow-white Audi Quattro squealed up to the curb. I jumped into the passenger seat and she started driving before I got the door closed.

***

I crouched by a folding card table in a motel that rented rooms by the hour, silhouetted in a sliver of dusty light from the edge of a paper window blind. The room smelled of stale cigarettes, the shower was caked in mildew, and I wouldn't have touched the bed without getting a full battery of shots first, but we weren't here to crash.

Caitlin was at the other window, holding the dome of a parabolic microphone. Wires ran to a reel-to-reel tape recorder on the card table, its gears slowly churning with the sound of faint, distant static. One of Caitlin's people, a yellow-eyed cambion from the home office, wore bulky ear-can headphones and transcribed every word onto a yellow legal pad as we listened in on the room across the courtyard.

Our target had gone in there an hour ago. Soon his buddies joined him, two carloads of Naavarasi's sons pulling into the lot out front. I watched them from the window, their glowing shadow-forms overlapping in space with a mismatched gallery of ordinary civilian faces, everyday clothes.

They were speaking Hindi, which was why Cait brought a translator. The cambion's brow was furrowed, his lips pursed as he scribbled on the legal pad, occasionally offering commentary.

"Oh, he's mad," the half-blood chuckled. "He doesn't understand how you realized he wasn't the real Pixie."

I glanced over at Jennifer and Caitlin. "That's called 'cognitive dissonance.' He *knows* Naavarasi gave him bad intel. He has to know that."

"But he can't admit that his tiger-mama set him up," Jennifer said. "So what do ya think? We got eight raks in a room and they don't know we're comin'. I could call up some of my Calles boys real quick. Chuck a Molotov through the window, flush 'em out, gun down anyone who doesn't burn?"

The idea appealed to me. Strongly, after everything we'd just been through. Pixie was in the hospital thanks to Naavarasi, and we didn't know if she'd bounce back or if she'd be coping with the damage for the rest of her life. Naavarasi had hurt my people. I wanted to hurt her right back.

But then she'd ask questions. She'd want to know who found and killed a pack of her sons, and it wasn't like there was a long list of suspects in Vegas. Eventually she'd realize that we must have cracked the code and pierced their disguises.

"No." I shook my head. "We're going to let them go. It's too good of a card to waste. When you've got an ace up your sleeve, you don't whip it out to win a five-dollar pot."

"You wait for somebody to go all-in," Jennifer said, following me. "Then you take 'em to the cleaners."

The translator raised his pen. "Excuse me? Who is 'Theodore'? That somebody important?"

I whipped around, eyes sharp. "What are they saying?"

"Hold on, they're all talking at once..." He paused, head tilted. "Okay. So, Naavarasi's pulling out of Las Vegas. This Theodore guy thinks you and Miss Brody are probably dead, but he doesn't want to take any chances—"

"Look at that, he *can* be taught," Caitlin said.

"—and Naavarasi agrees. One of the raks is on the phone with the guy right now. I can't hear his side of the conversation but...okay. Hold on. They're splitting up. The gang's supposed to pick up his wife at her office, their kid at daycare, and bring the whole happy family to McCarran so they can take the next flight to Denver. Sounds like Theodore's giving them a cover story to convince the wife and kid to cooperate. They think he's on a business trip."

"They're not rakshasa," Caitlin said.

I'd been wondering about that ever since Teddy showed his true colors. He had the perfect family, an adoring wife and a bright-eyed, precocious little girl, and questions kept me awake at night. Were they plants, shape-changers playing a role to give my brother a believable family-man disguise? Or had he actually made a human connection with someone, a relationship that genuinely meant something to him?

Now I knew. Teddy was capable of love. He just didn't have any for me. His family was real.

And now I had to decide what to do about that.

"Wait," the translator said. "Okay, now I get it. They were all shouting at once. Here's the gist of it: this Theodore guy is supposed to go straight to the airport, no questions, no excuses. He's insisting on going home to grab something important first. He won't budge, so the raks are playing rock-paper-scissors to decide who has to go on escort duty."

I was already halfway to the door. I grabbed my jacket.

"Pet?" Caitlin asked.

"I need to get there before he does," I said. "Going to have a word with my brother."

***

A long black sedan pulled up to the driveway of Teddy's perfect house, in his perfect suburb, as the sun began to dip in the sky and draw long shadows down the quiet, manicured streets. Standing in the corner of a second-floor window, I tilted my head back and refreshed my eyedrops. Now, blinking away the tears, I saw how the driver and one of the passengers had sprouted red and rippling heat-mirage auras.

The other passenger was Teddy. He made his escorts wait in the car as he hustled up the walk all alone, shooting anxious looks over his shoulder while he unlocked the front door and let himself in.

I heard him racing around downstairs, grabbing things, opening drawers and rummaging. He was about to abandon his home; I imagined he was deciding what he needed, what he couldn't bear to leave behind. I waited to make my move.

I wasn't sure, at first, why I waited. No. That wasn't true. I waited because I was going to give Teddy one last chance to do the right thing. I was afraid of what was going to happen if he said no.

But the only way to handle fear was to face it. I listened to the tromping of his feet on the stairs, coming up, and ducked to one side as he headed into his daughter's bedroom.

He was digging in a brightly painted toy box, crouched beside a vibrant floral bedspread, when I leaned against the open doorway and cleared my throat.

"I told you I'd kill you last," I said. "No lie."

He turned and froze, eyes wide like a deer in a semi's headlights. He gave a furtive look over my shoulder, to the room up the hall where I'd been hiding.

"Oh," I said, "are you thinking about bum-rushing me, racing for the office, and grabbing that gun you keep duct-taped under your desk?"

I wriggled the janky .32, holding it in an easy grip at my side.

"Got it right here."

He showed me his hands. "I'm unarmed."

"Yeah. I know."

"If I scream—"

"If you scream, you die. Oh, and I've got half a dozen shooters covering this house. Your rakshasa buddies won't even make it up the driveway before they permanently shape-change into chunks of Swiss cheese." I was curious, so I nodded at the toy box. "What's so important, anyway?"

He sheepishly held up a doll. Some kind of Barbie, I think, battered and well-loved.

"My little girl," he said. "She's scared of flying. I thought...it'd make it easier if she had her doll."

I slumped against the doorframe and puffed out a sigh.

"Christ, Teddy. What am I going to do with you?"

"I assume you're here to kill me."

"You know what they say about assumptions." I shook my head. "I'm done. You know? I've tried to apologize. You won't accept it. I told you the truth. You won't believe it. But please, get this through your fucking skull once and for all: I don't want to hurt you. Tell me something. Your wife. She doesn't know about any of this, does she?"

He bowed his head, mute, eyes dropping like the shame was weighing him down.

"I bet Naavarasi has all kinds of good reasons, though. Every time you feel the guilt of lying to the people who love you most, she tells you why it's really good for your wife and kid to live in the dark. And you believe her, for a while."

"You don't know anything about her," he snapped.

"She groomed you, Teddy."

He gritted his teeth, face reddening. "That never happened."

"How old were you when she started visiting your bedroom at night? Had to have been right after I got sent to juvie, right?"

He didn't answer me.

"It's not your fault," I said. "She's not your lover, Teddy. You're her victim. You always were. And you didn't do anything to deserve that."

"You don't understand. You could never understand what we have together."

"Don't I? Maybe you don't, either."

He narrowed his eyes, a question in his look.

"She ordered you to go straight to the airport," I said. "But here you are, risking your life for a doll. For the longest time I wondered if your family was just a front, a mask you could throw away when you were finished hiding. But they're the real thing, aren't they? You love them."

His answer was soft, tremulous.

"More than anything."

"Let me tell you what's going to happen. There's a reckoning coming. After what she just pulled, my entire crew is preparing to go scorched earth on Naavarasi's ass. And on that day, I'm going to kill her. And I'm going to kill anyone and everyone who stands with her. No hesitation, no exceptions, no mercy. But you don't have to die with her. You can make a choice, right here, right now, and pick a better future."

He stared at the doll in his hand.

"Meet your family at the airport," I told him, "and go anywhere but Denver. Anywhere. Get as far away as you can and start a new life. You deserve a new life, Teddy. Your wife and daughter deserve a new life."

"After everything," he said, his voice barely a whisper, "you're going to let me go? Just like that?"

"Just like that," I said. "I thought I could get you to join me. I understand now that's not going to happen. You're not ready to forgive me and maybe you never will. Maybe I don't deserve to be forgiven. But this isn't about me, and it isn't about you. It's about that woman and that little girl. They're innocent, Teddy. Don't drag them any deeper into this nightmare. Take your family and go. You don't have to fight in this war."

His shoulders sagged. He swallowed, hard, and gave me a tiny nod.

"Okay," he said.

"Okay," I said. "Have a good life, brother. I wish things had been different, but...this is what we've got. Maybe, someday, years from now, we can try to start over. If you want to. But right now, I just want you gone."

I tossed the .32 to the carpet between us and turned my back on him.

For a second, just a second, I thought everything was going to be okay.

Then he lunged for the gun, snatched it up, aimed at my back, and pulled the trigger.

The gun went *click*. I turned around. He kept squeezing the trigger—*click, click, click*—as his face fell and he realized I'd given him an unloaded pistol.

My own weapon of choice was a sleek nine-millimeter. I pulled it from the holster under my jacket and took out the narrow storm-gray tube of a sound suppressor, threading it onto the barrel.

"I've had movies on the brain." My tone was casual, conversational, while I tried to pretend my heart wasn't breaking. "You know what I hate? Those scenes where the hero takes the high road and rejects violence, but then he's forced to kill the bad guy in self-defense five seconds later. Always felt cowardly to me, you know? Like the director knows we all want to see the villain die, but he also wants the protagonist to be morally righteous and keep his hands clean, so we get this wishy-washy ending where the good guy has his cake and eats it too. Anyway, I took the bullets out of your gun."

Teddy's lips parted. He froze like that, staring up at me with a useless hunk of metal in his trembling hand, nothing left to say.

"I swear to you," I said, "if you had let it go, if you hadn't reached for that weapon, I would have let you live. But you just showed me exactly why I can't risk it. Every day you're above ground, you're a threat to me and mine."

I aimed straight for his heart.

"I thought I could fix you. Heal you. But whatever's broken in that head of yours doesn't want to be healed. Just understand this: you didn't make me kill you, Teddy. I earned that weight on my soul. It's mine, not yours."

I shot my brother dead.

Then I went home.

Chapter
Forty-One

It was midnight and I was down at the zoo. Well, down at the edge of the Monaco's casino floor, sitting at a glossy black high-top for two and drinking my fourth Jack and Coke of the night, but that was close enough. I watched the dice roll and the money flow, bathing in the endless chimes of the slot machines, a chaotic symphony of light and noise. Usually, it made me happy.

It was always going to end this way, I told myself for the thousandth time, replaying the afternoon in my head until I could smell the gunsmoke. Maybe so. Didn't change the fact that I'd destroyed three lives today, not one. Teddy's wife and daughter would never know the truth, would never—could never—understand the dark forces that had risen up from the underground and taken the life of a man who meant everything to them.

I had done that. Every tear they shed, every bit of heartache, was on me. The fact that it had to be done to keep even more people from dying didn't change a thing. It wasn't fair. I wished I could fix it all with a wave of a wand, but that was a kind of magic I'd never learned.

The best I could do for them, in the end, was pull some post-mortem strings. When they finally realized he wasn't coming out,

Teddy's rakshasa escorts went in, found the body, and panicked. They took off, probably pissing their pants trying to figure out how they were going to explain it to Mama Tiger.

Not long after, an anonymous call brought EMS to the scene. The first responders were on the New Commission payroll, and so was the cop with them. Once they took the body, a cleaning crew scoured the place from top to bottom and bleached the violence away. A friendly coroner—a degenerate gambler who was trapped under a mountain of debt thanks to one of my private poker games, desperate for a way out—was keeping my brother's corpse on lockdown, strictly viewable only from the shoulders up, until it was ready to be cremated.

The official report would say that Theodore Faust died of cardiac arrest, due to a previously undiagnosed heart condition. Just one of those terrible things that happened every day. A mundane tragedy. In a month or so I'd have a Commission operative "reveal" that Teddy had a string of secret investments, the proceeds of which now belonged to his widow and daughter. It'd be enough money to put the kid through college, at least.

Best I could do.

"Room for one more?" asked a soft voice at my side.

Melanie. She was looking lonely, adrift, holding a glass of something fizzy on ice. I waved her over.

"Always," I said. "Whatcha drinking?"

"Coke," she said, sitting down at the small table. We were side by side, gazing out over the crowds, the lights, the madness. Together but alone.

"Leave your fake ID at home?"

"Figured you'd bust me for it."

I almost said, "*If you can save the world, you can have a drink*," but I tripped on the words. She caught the look in my eye and gave me a humorless smile.

"I know, right? It's like that old line: why can you join the army at eighteen, get sent to fight and kill and maybe die, but you can't legally drink until you're twenty-one? It's obscene when you think about it."

She swirled her straw in the glass, tilting her head back and gazing up at the casino lights.

"But I haven't just been drafted. I'm the whole damn army."

"You're not doing this alone," I said.

"Aren't I? I'm the Paladin. I have to fight the Enemy. It's what I was born to do. Literally, it's the reason I exist. And if he wins, this entire planet...this *entire planet* is going to die. I just found out that I'm responsible for the safety of *every single person on Earth*. And you know what's worse? I've been doing it since the dawn of time. And as far as we know...I lose, Dan. I lose a lot."

"You win a lot, too."

She stared at her glass and shook her head.

"I don't know how I'm supposed to function now. I...how the fuck do I go to school, or think about the future, or a career? I don't have a future anymore."

"You do, though," I said. "The way I understand it, once you two have your duel, that's the end of the Story this time around. If the Enemy falls, sure, he'll reincarnate, but rules are rules: once you run his ass out of town, he *can't* come back to this world, ever again. You'll have the rest of your life to live however you want."

I thought I was offering her hope. From the look on her face, I might as well have backhanded her.

"You don't get it," she said.

"Help me to understand, then."

Melanie stared out across the swirling crowds of tourists and gamblers, gathering her thoughts.

"These people...they don't know what the world is really like, not like we do. They don't know what happens when you die. All they can have is faith." She bit her bottom lip. "I never needed faith. I'm half-demon. I've known, since I was old enough to understand what I really was, that this life is just one part of an endless existence. Sure, I'd die someday, and then I'd just go to hell and keep doing whatever I was doing. A change of address, that's all. And that's something I *knew*, not something I *believed*. You see the difference?"

"Sure," I said.

"And now I find out—whoops!—that shit doesn't even matter because I'm not even a real person."

"Hey," I said.

"I'm a character in a story, Dan. I wasn't born. This body was, but me? I was written. I can't change my future. I've got to fight the Enemy, and if I mess up, eight billion people are going to die. And if I win, great, I get a few decades of peace."

She took a shuddering breath, tears welling in her eyes.

"And then," she said, "I get to reincarnate on another world, with all of my memories wiped, and go through this all over again. And fight all over again. And live or die, that's my eternity. I don't get to be with my family in the afterlife. I don't get an afterlife at all."

Her jaw trembled. I reached out a tentative hand, touching her arm. She let me.

"I'm going to lose my friends," she said. "I'm going to lose you. I'm going to lose...I'm going to lose my *mom*. And I know we fight all the time but..."

The dam broke. I opened my arms and held her while her shoulders shook, my shirt wet as she buried her face against my chest.

"I don't want to lose my mom," she whispered. "I don't want to lose myself. But someday I'll be a different person, on a different world, and I won't even remember any of this just like I don't remember all the times it happened before. I'm...I'm *nothing*."

"Melanie," I said, "listen to me. The Story is a trap, but it's not a perfect one. I know two people who slipped the loop. If there's any way to get you out of this, I swear to you—"

She pulled back, suddenly fierce, and shook her head. She wiped the back of her hand across her eyes and took a sniffling breath.

"Don't you dare," she said.

"Mel?"

"First of all, we just dealt with someone trying to screw with the Story. You heard what Mr. Smith said: it's a load-bearing wall. One wrong move and everything comes crashing down. You're not going to take a risk like that. Not for me."

"The problem with those assholes," I said, "is that all they've got is a hammer so they think everything's a nail. Brute force is too dangerous, sure. So we'll try finesse instead."

"And what then? Let's say you whip out some magical solution that frees me from the curse. So? Doesn't change the fact that the Enemy isn't going to quit. And if there's no Paladin to oppose him, he can't lose. He'll burn world after world after world, until there's nothing left, because that's the only thing he *can* do. How am I supposed to live the rest of my life knowing that I could have stopped him but I walked away instead?"

She fixed me with a wet-eyed stare, grave now. Resolved, or resigned. The last stage of grief was always acceptance.

"This isn't fair. And it sucks. But that doesn't change what I have to do. This is my responsibility. I didn't ask for it, but it's mine."

Spoken like a Paladin, I thought. I held up a finger, then walked over to the bar. I came back with a pair of Jack and Cokes riding on cocktail napkins. I sat one down next to my empties, the other in front of her.

"You're old enough to save the world, you're old enough to drink."

She gave me a wan smile and raised her glass in salute.

"To...this unfair bullshit."

"To this unfair bullshit," I said and clinked my glass against hers.

We watched the human zoo. A moment later, thoughtful, Melanie spoke up again.

"I haven't told her yet."

"Your mom?"

She nodded.

"I don't even know where to start," she said.

"You can start by telling her she's going to have you around for a long time to come. Because you're not going to lose this fight."

Melanie raised an eyebrow. "Come on. I'm a fledgling magician with four good moves, and three of them are literally just card tricks. He can rewrite a person's entire life with a touch of his hand. How am I going to beat a monster like that?"

"I've crossed paths with the Enemy a couple of times now," I said, "and one thing really stuck with me. He's old-fashioned. It's part of how he's written. He's the archetypal Big Bad, the final boss, the villain in the fairy tale."

"And?" she said.

"He's been locked away for a long, long time. Worlds change. He still thinks he's going to get some kind of high-noon showdown, with him in black and you in shining armor, face-to-face and toe-to-toe." I sipped my drink and snorted. "*Fuck* that noise. Fate cast you as the hero of this story, but you've got a whole family of certified bad guys backing you up. We are going to lie, cheat, and steal for every advantage we can get. While you go high, we'll go low. And when high noon finally comes, we're going to gang up on that asshole, curb-stomp him, and kick him in the balls until he gives up his lunch money. He's going to wish he never *heard* of our planet."

A faint smile trembled on her lips.

"You almost make it sound like we can pull this off," she said.

"I don't play to lose," I said.

The Canton artifacts, save for two, were gone now. Lost in the cataclysm of Springfield, drawn to wherever a collapsed pocket world goes when it all falls down. Still, the previous Paladin's work hadn't gone without bearing some fruit.

I took out the wand, ebony capped in bone, and held it out to her.

"I think this belongs to you," I said.

She swallowed, nodded to herself, and took it in her slender hand.

"I think it does," she said.

Chapter Forty-Two

I took a day for myself, at home. I had some reading to do.

We hadn't just rescued Canton's top hat and wand—and Carolyn's old typewriter—from the ruins of Springfield. I still had Carolyn's last gift, the lurid paperback we found in the library. I kept the book on my left, a notepad on my right, and I read between every line.

The next night, I called a family meeting.

We weren't all going to fit in the new conference room at the American. This was an all-hands-on-deck situation, and then some. Caitlin and Bentley were sweeping up the nightclub proper, pulling back plastic sheets and unveiling the pristine new tables and chairs, while Corman lined up a row of bottles, fresh from the liquor store, along the chrome-hulled bar.

Call it a soft opening, I thought.

We still had to wait for everyone to show up, but I had something important to do first. I tugged Emma's sleeve—I still couldn't get used to her wearing my body, my face—and pulled her aside.

I took her down to the conference room, just the two of us. I talked, and she listened. Then I went back upstairs and found Melanie.

"Somebody needs you," I told her.

I watched from outside, through the broken conference-room window, as Emma jumped to her feet. She pulled Melanie into her arms, both of them clinging tight.

They were going to be okay, I decided. They were going to be okay because I was going to *make* it okay. I had no idea how, not yet, but that was my problem to solve.

What I had was a target. And tonight I was gathering my troops for war.

People filtered in over the next hour, gathering up in the club, pouring drinks and grabbing snacks from a grocery-store game-day spread. Mama Margaux, draped in a white dress and headscarf, held a daiquiri glass in one hand and hugged me with the other.

"Mama! You patch things up with Antoine?"

Behind her, Bentley made a frantic slashing motion across his throat. I had made a terrible mistake.

"That man," Margaux seethed, "is dead to me. He's no damn good and I will *tell* you why—"

"Reno in the house!" called out an old, familiar voice.

I hadn't seen Nicky Agnelli in a dog's age, not since he was pinned with a federal rap and had to flee his Vegas throne. The half-demon gangster was dressed in sleek Armani—he *almost* looked as sharp as I did—eyes veiled behind his steel aviator sunglasses and flashing a perfect pearly grin. He had a girl on each arm, identical blond bombshells in slinky black dresses.

"What's wrong with this nightclub?" Juliette asked. "Where's the music? Why are there poor people here? I don't go out to look at poor people."

"Like, do they *even* have bottle service?" her sister Justine sniffed.

I clasped hands with Nicky and he reeled me in, slapping my back.

"Goddamn, Dan. You're a sight for sore eyes. I'm gonna be honest, I liked your old face better."

"I'm working on getting it back. Emma says another month or so should do the trick. How's Reno treating you?"

"Eh, it ain't Vegas, but I get my beak wet. I do like this little sister-city-cooperation thing our groups have going here. That said, from the tone of your message, I'm guessing tonight ain't about a big score, is it?"

"To the contrary," I said. "I think you're going to want in on this."

"Dan," Juliette said. "If you have a new body, does that make you a virgin?"

"I..." I blinked. "No."

"We were just thinking," Justine added, "seeing as you're terrible in bed, this could be a chance for you to start over."

I buried my face in my palm. "We. Never. Slept. Together. That happened in one of Carolyn's books, not real life."

"No," Juliette said, "I'm pretty sure we had a threesome. And you were nowhere near as sexy as Donatello Faustus."

Desperate, I looked around the room and spotted Royce playing the wallflower, sullenly nursing a martini.

"Hey, girls," I said, "Royce is here. You should go say hi."

They both lit up like kids on Christmas morning.

"He's a *poor* now," Justine gasped. "He's destitute and homeless and Prince Malphas totally wants him dead."

"Let's go make fun of him!" Juliette chirped. They rushed over, hand in hand.

A delighted squeal at the door turned my head. Reno was here, and Chicago had arrived.

"Darlings," Freddie called out, the elegant fire-haired fashionista clad in designer couture. A row of shopping bags from posh Gold

Coast boutiques dangled along one of her arms. "I've brought presents for one and all. Well, for the people I know. The rest of you are just friends I haven't met yet, so come over and shower me with alcohol and affection."

At her side, her friend Halima—a mousy, spectacled woman in a headscarf—wriggled her fingers in a sheepish greeting. Halima was a museum conservator by day, a mystic by night, and probably the only force keeping Freddie on anything resembling an even keel.

I couldn't say as much for the man on her other side, pale and fastidious in a lab coat and a turtleneck sweater. He gazed around the half-finished nightclub and gave a sniff of derision.

"Just so we're clear," said Herbert West, "I am here under protest."

"You're here," Freddie murmured, leaning sideways, "because if you don't play nice, I'm literally going to eat you."

"I'm glad you came," I said, trading hugs with Freddie and Halima. "Even you, West."

"*Dr.* West," he said. "And yes, it has been impressed upon me that your need is a dire one. I am not immune to pleas for compassion, even coming from..."

He trailed off, eyes narrow as he studied my new face.

"Go ahead and say it, Doc."

"An *Italian*," he breathed.

I rolled my eyes. "I'm a seventh- or eighth-generation American."

"And yet," he said. "And yet."

He pointed two fingers at his eyes in an *I'm watching you* gesture, then drifted over to the bar.

I had sent my recruitment call far and wide, to old friends, old allies, even a couple of old enemies who had more reasons to fear the coming apocalypse than they did to hate me. Maybe half the guest list had turned up. I had hoped for more, but it was time to get this show on the road. I'd bring any latecomers up to speed when they showed.

As I called for attention, though, and the crowd gathered around me, we had one more arrival to greet.

"Pixie," I said.

She stood in the doorway, watching, silent. She had a little life back in her freckled cheeks and heavy braces on her wrists.

"I didn't get my invitation to this party," she said.

"Hon, you should be resting," I said. "You need time to recover. After everything you just went through..."

She crossed the room and stood toe-to-toe with me, staring hard into my eyes.

"I *need* this," she whispered.

I believed her. I gestured to a nearby table.

"Grab a seat, then," I said.

I produced two visual aids, tossing them onto the table. Two books: *The City at Midnight* and *The City on Fire*. Carolyn's final gifts.

"You've probably heard the rumors," I said, "so here are the facts, straight up. My apprentice is the new Paladin."

Freddie waved her hand in the air. "Where is that poor sweetie? I brought her a gift."

"Downstairs, sorting some things out with her mom. She'll be up later. Bottom line is, she's got a dance date with the Enemy. If she wins, our world is free and clear and his ass is *banned*. No getting past the velvet ropes, no bribing the bouncer, he's obligated to fuck off forever and find another planet to bother. If she loses, everyone dies. *Everyone.* Including, obviously, everybody in this room. So I'd better not hear a single one of you ask for a reason to help her out. If you need a better motive than survival, I don't know what to tell you."

I looked out across the gallery of nodding faces. Even Justine and Juliette were on board, at least for the moment. Everyone in the room knew what the Enemy was capable of. We'd only get one shot to make things right.

"As powerful as he is," I said, "the Enemy's not at his full strength. Most of his power is trapped in a book and once he pops the rest of the locks on that thing—locks that he crafted in the first place—there'll be no stopping him. We can't let that happen."

Mama Margaux raised her hand. "Seems to me, that means we should just do what we do best. Do we know where he keeps it?"

"That's the tricky part. It's been interdimensionally forked, for its own protection. I had a whole metaphor with three olives and a cocktail spear, but I forgot the olives, so...long story short, the Enemy's book exists in three different parallel worlds, simultaneously. That's why it can't be hurt: burn it in one world, it'll just retreat, heal itself on another, then sprout a fresh copy right where you left the ashes. It's also sentient, at least on some level. The last time I tried to snatch a copy, it shunted me into another world as a self-defense mechanism."

"So we can't touch it, we can't swipe it, and we can't destroy it," Nicky said. "But that's exactly what we gotta do if we want to cut this asshole off at the kneecaps. So...how?"

"By doing something the Enemy never planned for," I said. "We know that one copy is kept in the penthouse of Northlight Tower, his stronghold."

"What if he moved it?" Pixie asked.

I shook my head. "Possible but not likely. The Enemy's greatest weakness is that he's a slave to the way he was written. He's incapable of change, and he's both arrogant and overconfident. Hiding the book, in his mind, would feel like a show of weakness. He's not afraid of an assault on Northlight because he can't imagine his own defeat.

Not by lowly mortals like us. Also, he knows that I tried to snatch the book and nearly lost my mind in the process. He won't expect me to come back for seconds."

"That's one copy managed," Freddie said, tossing back a swig of gin. "We have a line on its siblings, darling?"

"Carolyn had visions. We all know this. She saw things—sometimes us, sometimes echoes from the worlds next door, all part of the Scribe's curse. I don't know if she had any idea what was coming when she died, but she knew that what she dreamed was important enough to write down." I rapped my knuckles on the two paperbacks. "She left us something in Springfield. She left us a *map*."

I took a step back and spread my hands wide.

"Ladies and gentlemen," I said, "I propose that we work together and pull off the greatest heist in history. We're going to steal the Enemy's book. More specifically, we're going to steal all three incarnations of the book, on three different parallel worlds. And we're going to do it all at the exact same time."

***

Everyone was in. All in, all the way to the bitter end.

The gathering broke into pockets of discussion, debate, while Bentley and Margaux argued finer points of dimensional magic and Nicky and Royce argued over tactics and firepower. We'd be hashing this out all night, but that was fine by me. My crew was together, tight, and ready to brawl our way to doomsday if we had to.

Caitlin took me aside. She was hesitant, that gentle look she got when she had to say something that would hurt me.

"I thought you might want to know," she said, "for your own peace of mind."

I knew what she was going to say, but I had to hear it. "Tell me."

"My sister's men reported back through the infernal conduit. Teddy's soul was captured in hell's antechamber. They took him without incident, before Naavarasi's people could rescue him. He's being held under the strictest security my prince has to offer."

I nodded. They locked him up and threw away the key. It had to be done. Still.

"Hey," I said. "I don't want him...you know. Tortured or anything."

"He murdered you," Caitlin said, dour.

"I got better."

"He *hurt* you, pet. Is that a crime you've ever known me to forgive?"

"I'm not asking you to forgive him," I said.

My brother and I were born from the same roots, raised under the same roof, with a dead mother and a violent alcoholic madman for a father. I fell in with Bentley and Corman. They raised me and taught me how to be a man. Teddy fell in with Naavarasi, and she taught him how to be a monster.

Our lives diverged the night I tried to kill our father, botched the job, and got sent up the river. What if he had been the one with the knife? What if he got all the opportunities, the nurturing, the love that I had, and I was left with nothing but an abusive guardian and an apex predator whispering sweet lies in my ear every night? Were we different men because of something innate, something inside us, or did our paths diverge because of the influences that shaped us?

I'm no philosopher. I only knew one thing for sure.

"He risked his life for a doll," I said. "He knew. He knew someone would be gunning for him—if not me, our people, looking for payback—and he did it anyway. He did it because he didn't want his little girl to be afraid of flying."

Caitlin stared into my eyes, holding her silence. One of her hands closed gently over mine.

"There's good in him, Cait. I know there is. Doesn't change the fact that he had to die. Or that you need to keep him locked up tight in hell. Maybe forever, if he can't change his heart. I just...I think that's punishment enough."

She took that in. Then she gave me a slight nod, relenting.

"I'll see that he's kept in comfort," she said.

"Thank you."

That was all we had to say, for the moment, so we leaned against each other and listened. Debate swirled around us as the greatest criminal minds I knew argued about how to achieve the impossible. Hashing out the plan was going to take a little while.

That was fine. We'd get there. First we'd undercut the Enemy and do everything we could to prepare Melanie for the fight of a lifetime. Next up: Naavarasi.

They'd both made the same fatal error, I realized. The Enemy and the tiger queen had declared a vendetta against humanity and the infernal courts alike.

Their greatest weakness was simple: they could afford to lose. The Enemy could find another world to plague, and Naavarasi could take her sons and travel the cosmos. But our eyes were wide open and every soul in this room knew the score. If we lost this fight, it meant the end of everything. If there was a better motivation to win, I couldn't imagine it.

Our worst nightmares wanted a war. Fine. My army was ready to scrap and we aimed to come out on top. I planned to deliver a message, clear and simple. A message to the Enemy, to Naavarasi, to the Network, and to any other monstrous freaks eyeing our world like a lunch buffet: *If you want to keep your fingers, hands off our fucking planet.*

Face defeat? With this much at stake?

Not a chance in hell.

Afterword

A friend and I have had a running joke for years: she asks what the new book is about, at which point we both do our best (worst) impressions of Vin Diesel from the *Fast and Furious* movies and proclaim, *"It's about family!"*

It really is about family, though. The kind you're born with but mostly the kind you build for yourself, the folks who protect your heart and trust you to protect theirs, the ones who will be there when the going gets hard and the world gets weird.

This may come as a shock, I know, but things are about to get *very* weird around Las Vegas.

As always I give thanks to the team who pulled me across the finish line: Kira Rubenthaler brought her editing chops to the game, shaping up my words into something resembling a book, and James T. Egan tackled the cover design. And as always, thanks to you for reading! I can't do what I do without you, so you're an essential part of the crew.

Time for me to get to work on Dan's next adventure. Be safe, live well, and remember: if a zombie bites you, *tell somebody*. It's an important rule.

Also by

Want more of this stuff? You have my eternal gratitude. Here are a few
jumping-on points:

The main spinoff to the Faust series begins with Harmony Black (and
a later volume, Right to the Kill, serves as a soft series reboot.)

Meanwhile, if you want a closer look at the bizarre world of Noir York
(before Dan heads back there), Any Minor World features a pair of
unlikely heroes drawn across the dimensional divide.

And if you're in the mood for a change of scenery, Ghosts of Gotham
kicks off the Sisterhood of New Amsterdam books, delving into a New
York landscape haunted by Greek gods and monsters. I like it. You
might like it too.

Made in the USA
Las Vegas, NV
11 July 2024

92183935R00194